América del Norte

América del Norte

NICOLÁS MEDINA MORA

SOHO

Published by Soho Press, Inc.
227 W 17th Street
New York, NY 10011
www.sohopress.com

Library of Congress Cataloging-in-Publication Data

Names: Mora, Nicolás Medina, author.
Title: América del Norte / Nicolás Medina Mora.
Description: New York, NY: Soho, 2024. | Includes bibliographical references. | Text chiefly in English; some text in Spanish.
Identifiers: LCCN 2023053985

ISBN 978-1-64129-680-9
eISBN 978-1-64129-565-9

Subjects: LCGFT: Political fiction. | Novels.
Classification: LCC PR9200.9.M67 A83 2024 | DDC 823/.92—dc23/
eng/20231206
LC record available at https://lccn.loc.gov/2023053985

Interior design by Janine Agro

Printed in the United States of America

10 9 8 7 6 5 4 3 2 1

EU Responsible Person (for authorities only)
eucomply OÜ
Pärnu mnt 139b-14
11317 Tallinn, Estonia
hello@eucompliancepartner.com
www.eucompliancepartner.com

For my mother

It is not enough . . . to look at the exploited classes. You also have to look at the exploiting classes.

—Louis Althusser

Events travel through time and grow faint in the distance until they seem to become past, but there are certain regions of the spirit where all that has come to pass remains present. What happened continues to happen. It lives on: a luminous ghost fluttering in the vastness of the night. This is why a watcher of the skies who stood on a particular star and pointed his most powerful telescope toward our world would see, at this very hour, Hernán Cortés and his soldiers gazing over the Valley of Anáhuac for the first time.

—Alfonso Reyes

. . . because America has swallowed the entire world . . . this is why I am writing in English (and not you writing in Spanish) . . .

—Heriberto Yépez

América del Norte

All the characters in this novel—especially the real ones—are imaginary.

Dramatis
Personae

YOUR CORRESPONDENT

- Sebastián Arteaga y Salazar: Mexican reporter. Student at the Iowa Nonfiction Writing Program. Insufferable pedant.

THE NEOBAROQUE ARTISTS

- Lee Williams: American musicologist. Sebastián's partner.

- Esteban de Mier. Mexican filmmaker. Sebastián's friend from high school.

- The Bear: Mexican painter. Sebastián's friend from high school.

- Daniel Landero: Colombian ballet dancer. Lee's former partner.

THE AUSTRO-HUNGARIANS

- Luciano Fernando Arteaga y Salazar: Mexican translator. Sebastián's ancestor.

- Alberto Arteaga y Salazar: Mexican politician. Sebastián's father.

- Laura Arteaga y Salazar: Mexican anthropologist. Sebastián's mother.

- Inés Arteaga y Salazar: Mexican entrepreneur. Sebastián's younger sister.

- Álvaro Arteaga y Salazar: Mexican college student. Sebastián's younger brother.

- Luisa Arteaga y Salazar: Mexican gardener. Alberto's mother.

- Raúl Arteaga y Salazar: Mexican lawyer. Alberto's father.
- Arnaut Bosch Sr.: Mexican-Catalan heir. Sebastián's godfather.
- Arnaut Bosch Jr.: Mexican-Catalan drifter. Sebastián's childhood friend.
- Urbino Graue: Mexican oncologist. Raúl's lifelong friend. Laura's physician.
- Fernando de las Casas: Mexican friar. Laura's confessor.

THE IOWANS

- Mayeli Revueltas: Chicanx student at the Iowa Nonfiction Writing Program. Sebastián's classmate.
- The Decanonizer: American student at the Iowa Nonfiction Writing Program. Sebastián's classmate.
- The Pseudo-Anthropologist: American student at the Iowa Nonfiction Writing Program. Sebastián's classmate.
- The Delightful Kid from Michigan: American student at the Iowa Nonfiction Writing Program. Sebastián's classmate.
- Charlotte "Charlie" Nguyen: Vietnamese-American student at the Iowa Writers' Workshop. Sebastián's friend.
- Constant "Connie" Amadea Adler: American student at the Iowa Writers' Workshop. Sebastián's astrologer.
- Irina Januta: American professor at the Iowa Nonfiction Writing Program. Sebastián's teacher.
- François Denys Bartholomée Bouvard: French Professor at the University of Iowa. Chair of the English Department. Sebastián's supervisor.

- Billy Mosley: American undergraduate at the University of Iowa. Sebastián's student.
- Zoraya Fields: American undergraduate at the University of Iowa. Sebastián's student.

THE NEW YORKERS

- The Shakesperean: American actress. Sebastián's former partner.
- Aviva Benhabib: Mexican reporter. Sebastián's friend from college.
- Claire Lawrence: American reporter. Aviva's maid of honor. Sebastián's friend from college.
- Carlos de la Torre-Wells: Dominican-American manager at a little magazine. Alanna's partner. Sebastián's friend from Brooklyn.
- Alanna Goodwater: American editor at a small press. Carlos's partner. Sebastián's friend from Brooklyn.
- The Revomissionary: American Zapatista. Sebastián's college classmate.

THE MEXICANS

- Martina Toledo: Zapotec nurse.
- Edwin Mendoza: Poblano grocer.
- Jane Preciado: Guanajuatense hotel worker.
- The Minor Deities: Chilango waiters at El Centenario.
- The Man with the Broken Camera: Chilango photographer. Regular at El Centenario.

THE COPS

- Moisés Sandoval: Mexican Federal Police. Sebastián's bodyguard in 2016.

- Pedro Campeador: Mexican Federal Police. Sebastián's bodyguard in 2017.

- Darwin Castellanos: Mexican Federal Police. Sebastián's bodyguard in 2006–2009. Ludwig's brother.

- Ludwig Castellanos: Mexican Federal Police. Sebastián's bodyguard in 2006–2009. Darwin's brother.

- Emiliano Catrín: Mexican-American memoirist. Former Border Patrolman. Alumnus of the Iowa Nonfiction Writing Program.

THE MUSICIANS

- Jean-Philippe Rameau: French composer, eighteenth century.

- Chavela Vargas: Costa Rican–Mexican chanteuse, twentieth century.

- The Troubadour: Mexican busker, twentieth century. Regular at El Centenario.

- Alan "El Contra-punk-to" Espinosa: Mexican cumbia arranger and synthesizer virtuoso, twenty-first century.

THE WRITERS

- Nezahualcóyotl: Mexica poet-king, fifteenth century.

- Hernán Cortés: Spanish novelist, sixteenth century.

- Christopher Marlowe: English playwright, sixteenth century.

- Carlos de Sigüenza y Góngora: Mexican polymath, seventeenth century.

- Sor Juana Inés de la Cruz: Mexican poet, seventeenth century.

- Georg Wilhelm Friedrich Hegel: German philosopher, nineteenth century.

- Friedrich Nietzsche: Stateless writer of Zoroastrian fan fiction, nineteenth century.

- José Juan Tablada: Mexican poet, twentieth century.

- Ezra Pound: American poet, twentieth century.

- Walter Benjamin: Stateless traveling magician, twentieth century.

- George Orwell: British essayist, twentieth century.

- Alfonso Reyes: Mexican essayist, twentieth century.

- José Gorostiza: Mexican poet, twentieth century.

- Carlos Pellicer: Mexican poet, twentieth century. López Obrador's teacher.

- Antonieta Rivas Mercado: Mexican belletrist, twentieth century. Vasconcelos's lover.

- Alejo Carpentier: Cuban novelist, twentieth century.

- Juan Rulfo: North American novelist, twentieth century.

- Gabriel García Márquez: Colombian nonfiction writer, twentieth century.

- Roberto Bolaño: Chilean poet, twentieth century.

- Andrea de Olivares: Mexican poet, twenty-first century.

THE MESSIAHS

- Maximilian von Habsburg: Austrian emperor of Mexico.

- Nazario Moreno: Mexican cartel leader and memoirist.

- José Vasconcelos: Mexican politician and memoirist. Pellicer's teacher. Rivas Mercado's lover.

- Andrés Manuel López Obrador: Mexican politician. Pellicer's student.

THE UNACCOMPANIED MINORS

- The Boy with Spiked Hair: Kaqchikel parkour artist. The Girl Who Did Not Speak's brother.

- The Girl Who Did Not Speak: Kaqchikel teenager, about whom we know almost nothing. The Boy with Spiked Hair's sister.

THE LORD-IN-BONDAGE

- Moctezuma Xocoyotzin: Great speaker of Tenochtitlan.

Prologue

Mexico City

September 1847

*In which the outcome of this tale
is revealed from the start.*

Entre las naciones como entre los amantes

Like the Spaniards before them, the Americans landed in Veracruz and marched west, away from the malarial fevers of the Tierra Caliente and up the jagged slopes of the Sierra Madre, past taciturn agaves and stern oyameles and the blinding snowcaps of half-asleep volcanoes, until they reached the high valley where the air was thin and clear and the white light of the autumn sun fell vertical and merciless on the ill-defended capital, casting angular shadows on the barricades where the remnants of an army of barefoot conscripts whiled away their final moments, dulling terror with liquor and gambling, gathering stones to throw when their obsolete muskets ran out of ammunition, not so much resolved as resigned to die in a futile stand against an enemy destined to rule the continent.

The truth, however, is that none of it was fated. At the start of the nineteenth century, conflict between Mexico and America was likely but not inevitable. The war that transformed the United States from an uneasy federation of small Atlantic republics into a global empire was but one of infinite possible outcomes: trusting coexistence grounded on commerce, friendship born from shared commitments to self-determination, even a gradual blurring of the lines that in due time could have brought about the death of two nation-states founded on genocide and slavery—and given birth to a North American Commune.

But history is the transmutation of contingency into necessity, and what need not happen did. In the cool hours before dawn on September 12, 1847, the artillerymen of the United States Army trained their howitzers on the last significant fortification between them and Mexico City: Chapultepec Castle, a stone complex atop a steep hill, built as a manor, that now housed a military academy. Sixteen-inch rounds began falling on walls adorned with ornate masonry but offering scant cover. The thousand men of the garrison—among them cadets as young as thirteen—had no choice but to stand under fire for twelve hours, watching shrapnel tear and shred their friends.

The following day, hundreds of US marines charged up the hill, taking cover behind *venerable cypresses decorated with long hanging moss, dear alike to Cortés and Moctezuma.* When they reached the parapet, they leaned siege ladders against the walls and began to climb in a swarm. At first the marines died in scores, their bodies tumbling on their brothers and dragging them to their deaths. But they were many and their adversaries were few. By midmorning the defenders had been overrun.

In the years after the battle-dust settled, the Mexican republic would try to make sense of the humiliation it had suffered. The future had looked so promising just decades earlier, when New Spain broke free from its hemophiliac metropole to become one of the largest countries in the world: a vast realm, rich in silver and in people, that stretched from the forests of Oregon to the jungles of Darién. Now, however, Mexico City had been conquered a second time. How to look in the mirror? What to tell the young?

The factual record offered no answers. And so the nation's patriotic scribes reached for myth, or rather for epic: a form where the beauty of heroism is enough to redeem defeat. The scribblers set out to find Hectors for their North American Troy—and found them in the cadets of Chapultepec. Over the course of countless retellings, the memory of the child-soldiers underwent a process not unlike the one Freud describes in *The Interpretation of Dreams.* Truths too painful to contemplate became half-truths, which in turn became wish-fulfilling fantasies, which were then passed off as truths.

The logic of literature replaced that of history. Nonfiction became fiction. Soon the central story Mexicans told about the war was the tale of a handful of boys who'd fought to the end, long after all hope was lost, retreating to the highest tower rather than surrendering with their older comrades. When the Marines reached the platform, the last surviving cadet tore the Mexican flag from its pole, wrapped it around his adolescent body, and leaped off the cliff.

The dreamwork allowed Mexicans to convince themselves that the Americans had defeated them not because they were worthier but merely because they were stronger. But to believe one's fantasies is the definition of madness. And so perhaps it would behoove us to counter the epic of the Heroic Children with another tale—one taken from history rather than from dreams. A few weeks before the cadets of Chapultepec committed ritual suicide, a very different young Mexican arrived in Washington for a secret audience with the secretary of state, James Buchanan, who would later become president. His mission was simple if not easy: negotiate an informal agreement that would protect the interests of the Mexican aristocracy.

The secret agent, don Luciano Fernando Arteaga y Salazar, was the scion of an old family from Durango, a horse-breeding clan whose founder had received his hacienda in recognition of his services to Cortés. He'd been sent to England at a young age to receive a proper education, then travelled the continent armed with letters of recommendation that introduced him to the best minds of the age. By the time he returned to Mexico, he'd become something rarer and more dangerous than a cosmopolite: a translator.

When it became obvious that the war was lost, the notables of

Mexico City summoned Arteaga y Salazar to a private meeting at the country estate of the archbishop's illegitimate son. They explained that, while patriotic honor demanded that they continue to publicly support the war effort, their responsibility as unacknowledged stewards of the nation compelled them to look at things unsentimentally. The countless revolutions and counterrevolutions that had kept the country on fire ever since independence suggested that the people of Mexico were simply incapable of pursuing their own best interests. Reunion with Spain was not only impossible but also undesirable—the notables remembered the condescension with which their peninsular cousins had treated them. But the American invasion, perfidious as it was, offered an unexpected opportunity. And so Arteaga y Salazar assumed a false name and sailed from Campeche to Philadelphia, where he made contact with American agents.

On that day in September, however, almost nobody in Mexico City knew of the young translator and his secret mission. After the fall of Chapultepec, the surviving Mexican forces fought on throughout the day, putting up fierce resistance near San Cosme. But then, at nightfall, the Americans fired artillery shells on the crowded city center. The Mexican commander-in-chief, don Antonio López de Santa Anna, that one-legged Simón Bolívar impersonator, gathered the dregs of his army and quietly abandoned the capital, declaring that he hoped to spare its inhabitants a week of house-to-house butchery followed by nights of looting and rape. It was only much later that the people of Mexico learned that Santa Anna's retreat had nothing to do with protecting the innocent—and everything to do with the agreement Arteaga y Salazar had brokered in Washington.

At dawn on September 14, the Americans marched into Mexico City. Terrified of ambushes, they advanced in perfect silence, surprised to encounter no resistance. As rumors spread, crowds gathered on rooftops to watch the ghostly procession of the conquerors. Once his troops had secured the central plaza, the Zócalo, General Winfield Scott, known to favor fuss and feathers, dressed in parade uniform and mounted a handsome white horse, hoping to cut a fine stamp on his entrada. He rode onto the square, where he supervised the raising of the Stars and Stripes and reviewed his triumphant ranks as they broke into a spontaneous rendition of "Yankee Doodle."

The corpulent general took possession of the National Palace and climbed to the balcony to address his troops and the people they'd conquered. He'd just begun a pompous speech when a group of women who'd gathered in the plaza interrupted him with heckles: "¡Cállate, puerco!" Then a shot went off from some high window, wounding a US officer in the leg. The Americans turned their cannon on the crowd and opened fire with grapeshot munitions.

When news of the victory reached Washington, the American republic debated just how much land to annex. Some rallied behind the cry of ALL OF MEXICO, arguing with the governor of Virginia that SLAVERY SHOULD POUR ITSELF ABROAD WITHOUT RESTRAINT AND FIND NO LIMIT BUT THE SOUTHERN OCEAN. But in the end the rulers of the newborn empire decided to keep only the northern half of the country they'd defeated. The reasons, in the words of one Senator Calhoun, Democrat of South Carolina, were straightforward:

> To incorporate Mexico would be the very first instance of the kind of incorporating an Indian race; for more than half of the Mexicans are Indians . . . I protest against such a union as that! Ours, sir, is the Government of a white race. The great misfortunes of Spanish America are to be traced to the fatal error of placing these colored races on an equality with the white race.

The dream of a united North America was forever lost. The two nations were never joined, neither in marriage nor by conquest, and instead remained divided by a line—so thin as to be invisible, so stark as to be impassable—that cut not just across the land, but also through the heart. It should come as no surprise that love between their children became impossible.

Part I

Mexico City

May 2016

In which Your Correspondent returns to his hometown to apply for an American visa, tours his father's new house, chats about political theory with his bodyguard, has uncomfortable encounters with old friends, gets lost on the way to La Condesa, attends horrible parties, ponders the Second Mexican Empire and the tragic fate of his godfather, visits his grandmother, reads Alfonso Reyes, and in general feels out of place.

"¿Vives del otro lado?" said the elderly officer at the Mexico City airport.

"That's correct."

"How long are you staying?"

"Couple weeks."

"Seeing family?"

"No—I mean, yes. That too. But I'm here to apply for a new American visa."

The officer raised an eyebrow. "Of course," he muttered. "Why else would you come back?" He stamped my passport and handed it to me. "Bienvenido, paisano," he went on, using the Mexican government's official term of endearment for citizens living in the United States.

Se vende: Casa Porfiriana

My father's new house stood on the edge of downtown. The neighborhood had become fashionable again only in recent years, but it was developed in the late nineteenth century, when the owners of a successful circus decided to get into real estate. Emboldened by the improbable prestige of their most famous performer—an English clown who earned the esteem of General Porfirio Díaz, the dictator who ruled for thirty years before the outbreak of the Mexican Revolution—the impresarios bought a large tract of land on what was then the city's outskirts. They commissioned a group of well-regarded architects to build elegant houses designed to appeal to the city's elite. Betraying their colonial anxieties, they christened the development after a fashionable European city: Colonia Roma.

Much of the neighborhood was built before 1910, when the uprising against the dictatorship tempered the high-end real estate market. My father's new house, however, dated from 1917, the year when the victorious rebels promulgated a new constitution. The date helped explain the house's reactionary architecture. Unlike most buildings in La Roma, which took their cues from the town houses of London or the grandes maisons of Paris, my father's house evoked a Spanish colonial palazzo. It was built for a man who made a fortune speculating on rubber, the kind of guy who gets a kick out of pretending he is an hacendado paying his respects to the viceroy before returning to his acreage in Durango. Every detail, from the tile pattern on the courtyard floor to the molding on the edges of the balconies, seemed designed to incite nostalgia for New Spain.

When I toured the house for the first time, I saw a familiar volume on one of the shelves—a stuffy anthology of English-language poetry someone had given me when I was sixteen. I realized the shelf held the books I'd left in the house where I grew up, far away from La Roma, at the western edge of Mexico City. That neighborhood was called El Contadero, because it used to be a small town where farmers counted their livestock on the way to the city markets. Oyamel forests surrounded the houses. Early in the morning, heading to school, I saw old men driving mule-drawn wagons piled high with firewood. The air smelled like tree sap and wet dirt. In the weeks before the feast of the Virgin of Guadalupe, white and blue garlands appeared over the avenues, almost forming a canopy.

I last saw El Contadero in the summer of 2009, before I left for college in the United States. A few months later my father's political fortunes took a turn for the worse, and he and the rest of my family left for a diplomatic post in London. I received an email from my mother: *We've sold the house in El Contadero, but don't worry, we put your books in storage.* Sitting in a filthy dorm room in New Haven, I was surprised to discover that, for all my determination to leave the past behind, I was devastated by the thought that the tree sap, the wet dirt, the garlands, the oyameles, the mule wagons, and the patch of sunlight that fell on my bedroom floor between ten in the morning and noon were lost forever.

"Everything all right?" my father said.

I realized I'd been standing in the middle of the living room for several minutes, staring at the furniture in silence. "Yes. The house is beautiful."

"Thanks. It was a bargain."

Café gratis con su desayuno

By then most of the people who'd once wanted to kill me were dead or in prison. Besides, my father was now a Supreme Court justice, a far safer job than his earlier position as attorney general. Still, the government insisted on assigning me bodyguards as a matter of protocol. The new guy was called Moisés; he was a midranking officer of the Federal Police. I bought him breakfast and discovered he was going to night school for a graduate degree in political theory. I asked who his favorite thinker was. He answered without hesitation: Gramsci.

Over café con leche, he told me about his previous assignment: guarding a senator in a northern state. Once, he said, his team had escorted the principal to a party at a hacienda deep in the desert. On the way back, a group of uniformed men stopped their convoy at what looked like a military checkpoint. It quickly became apparent the men were not government soldiers. The car with the principal sped off, but Moisés and his partner were unable to get away. Dozens of armed men surrounded them. His partner wanted to hand over their weapons, but Moisés knew better.

"If you surrender, they'll just torture you for information and dump your body somewhere in the sierra. And if they don't find your body, you're presumed missing, and your wife doesn't get her widow's pension. So it's always better to go down right away. That way you can take a few fuckers with you."

One of the men walked to Moisés's side of the car and tried to open the door. Moisés kicked it as hard as he could, hitting the narco in the face. "¡Ya te cargó la chingada, hijo de tu puta madre!" Moisés yelled, his gun to the man's head.

The narco laughed. A large man in a military uniform appeared behind him and pointed a revolver at Moisés. "Do you know who we are, oficial? We're the Zetas. But who are you? Intelligence? Judicial investigations?"

Moisés pulled out his ID with his free hand and waved it at the man. "I'm a bodyguard!"

"Who's your principal?"

"Your whore of a mother."

The fat man laughed again. "Ah caray oficial, ¿sí estás bien pinche loco, verdad? I'll tell you what. If you put down your gun, I'll do the same."

"No fucking way."

There was a moment of silence. Then, to Moisés's surprise, the man lowered his revolver. "You can go. But tell your principal not to come back here without permission."

Moisés asked if he could have another coffee. I blinked in disbelief and asked why he thought the Zetas had let him go.

"No clue. Maybe they wanted to send a message to the senator? We never told him, of course—he woke up back home with a headache and no idea what had happened. Anyway, I'm happy to be here now. I'd much rather talk about Gramsci and drink café con leche than shout at fat narcos. Police work's a bitch."

Mejorar la raza

The word *criollo* comes to Spanish from the Portuguese *crioulo*, the substantive form of the verb *criar*: to breed or to educate. In current Spanish usage the term can refer to a horse whose phenotype suggests a good pedigree, but whose ancestry cannot be certified. In the caste system that organized life in colonial Mexico, it designated the descendants of Spaniards born in the Americas.

The word used to carry an aftertaste of dust and mold, but around the time I went back to the capital to apply for a new visa, I began finding it in contemporary contexts. An article in the left-wing newspaper of Mexico City criticized the Mexican delegation to the Bogotá Book Fair for inviting only creole writers. An acquaintance studying in the United States wrote an essay apologizing for his "creole privilege." A stranger on Twitter dug up nine generations of my family tree to show we were descendants of Agustín de Iturbide—the first and only sovereign of the First Mexican Empire, an incompetent megalomaniac who ruled for less than a year immediately after independence—a fact the stranger took, not unfairly, as evidence that an "inbred creole mafia" ran the country.

All of which raised a question: Were the creoles white? By skin tone and social position, certainly. In the eyes of the WASPs I met in college, however, all Mexicans, even those of unmixed European ancestry, were metaphysically brown. The proposition was absurd, but so was race-thinking in general: in America a single drop of non-European blood meant one would never be truly white; in Mexico every additional drop of European blood made one progressively whiter. Hence the awful phrase one still heard at creole family gatherings when some great-aunt learned a cousin was marrying a blonde: vas a mejorar la raza. You're going to improve the race. You're going to better the stock. You're going to breed fine horses.

El alimentador de zumbido

Two weeks before I flew to Mexico City, I asked my editor to join me for a cigarette downstairs.

"What's up?" he said, eyes on his phone. "News is breaking, so make it quick."

"I got into the writing program at Iowa."

By then I'd lived in the United States for seven years. I emigrated at eighteen, in theory to go to college at Yale, in practice to get away from the indolence and paranoia of the Mexican ruling class. After I graduated, I scrambled to find a job that would sponsor me for a visa, and to my relief I was hired as a police reporter at a New York website that was pivoting from cheeky quizzes to serious journalism. I soon found a large group of friends who worked for little magazines, fell in love with a Shakespearean actress, and moved into her apartment in Crown Heights.

For a while I was happy in the knowledge that I didn't have to be a writer, that I could be a scribbler who read Charles Reznikoff on the way to the NYPD's monthly press conferences. But then I grew restless. I watched with jealousy as my friends graduated from interns to staffers and began publishing their first books. Meanwhile I spent my days composing copy rather than prose. One night, after an exhausting day at the newsroom, I looked up the application requirements for the Iowa Nonfiction Writing Program, and decided to take my chances. A few months later the department chair called to let me know I'd been admitted. I was elated—but did I really want to leave New York? My friends? My girlfriend?

I didn't. But I did want to be a writer.

"Congratulations!" my editor said. "Where do you want to go for your goodbye drinks? Old Town is closed for repairs, but I'm sure they'll be open two weeks from now."

"The program doesn't start until August, so hopefully by then . . ."

"Sebas, we aren't waiting until August to have your goodbye drinks. You just gave your two-week notice."

"Wait—what?"

I'd hoped to keep my job until the week before the start of the program, mostly because I wanted time to say goodbye to my friends and my girlfriend, but also because the procedure to change my immigration status from guest worker to international student would take at least a couple of months.

"The bosses don't like keeping people around once they know they're leaving."

"But what about my visa? If you fire me . . ."

"Nobody's firing you, Sebas. You quit."

And indeed I had, I thought as I recounted the conversation to Moisés while he drove me to the family tailor to get a new suit made.

"See, that's the problem," he said. "You don't want to be just a writer. You want to be an American writer."

Contingencia ambiental

The rainy season came late that year, the exhaust of millions of cars lingering in the atmosphere. The air tasted metallic—burned the eyes, stung the throat. Mornings were filled with rituals: Vaseline for the lips, small doses of antihistamines, a saltwater nasal spray. The government issued frequent advisories against outdoor exercise: jogging for an hour in Mexico City, a concerned voice repeated on the radio, harmed your lungs as much as a pack of cigarettes. That claim seemed dubious to me, but the absence of rain implied the absence of clouds, which meant it was ninety degrees in the shade. This presented two choices: close the windows and stew in sweat or open them and drown in mucus. Either way, you suffocated in moisture.

Se ofrecen: tutorías para el GRE y el GMAT

It'd been two days since my sister, Inés, the artist, locked herself in her bedroom. My father asked me to summon her to breakfast. I suspected he didn't dare to do it himself. I knocked—no answer. I put my ear to the door and whispered, in the most cheerful tone I could muster, that her food was getting cold.

"If I eat," she said, "I'm pretty sure I'd throw up."

She'd been like this since she returned from Portland a few months earlier. The mail room at her college had lost her application for a work permit, which meant she missed a crucial immigration deadline, which meant that, sixty days after graduation, she was on a plane to Mexico City with all her worldly possessions and no exit strategy. That shouldn't have been a terrible fate, but she hadn't lived in the country since she was fifteen, when our family moved to Britain.

I used to think she'd been lucky for leaving so soon. She was spared the cruelties that Mexican private schools reserve for intelligent women: either an ostracism verging on torture, or an anxious popularity bought at the cost of an eating disorder and the constant performance of idiocy. She was aware, of course. For her undergraduate thesis she'd made an installation in which a set of bulletproof glass panes hung from the ceiling, suggesting the ghost of an SUV like the one our bodyguards used to drive. On each of the windows, she etched the contours of British pastoral paintings: rolling hills, peaceful steeples, a country house overlooking a moor. She called the work *Both/Neither*, but it was clear which term she found more welcoming.

"Can I come in?"

"Sure."

I found her pale and sickly, her thick duvet lifted halfway up her neck, her face all but buried in the folds of a black-and-white bathrobe that had whimsical panda ears sewn onto the oversize hood.

"It's going to be okay. We're going to get you out of here. Have you thought about going to art school in the US? That would get you a visa . . ."

"I'm already working on an application for an MBA."

"Since when are you interested in business?"

"I figured it'd be my best bet. You know, for a company to sponsor me."

Guía Roji

On my third day in the capital, I walked out of my father's house to visit Esteban, one of two friends from Mexico with whom I'd stayed in close contact. He lived nearby, about fifteen minutes by foot, but I had to look up the route on Google Maps. I didn't know that part of town well—I didn't know it at all. Before I left for college, I wasn't allowed to walk in the street. Bodyguards drove me everywhere, even the few blocks to my godfather's house.

I waved Moisés away and said I would prefer to go on my own, but I harbored the secret hope he'd refuse. That way I'd at least be able to say I tried. To my surprise, he waved back and returned to the armored car and his photocopied Walter Benjamin.

I headed down the avenue, took a left onto a one-way street, and began counting the blocks to the boulevard that separates La Roma from La Condesa. One, two, three, ten, twelve. Could I have missed it? I walked for ten, twenty, thirty minutes before I was forced to admit I was lost. I took out my phone to look at Google Maps again but my American telecom company didn't provide service in Mexico. By the time I showed up at Esteban's place, he'd waited for more than an hour.

"Finally!" he said when he opened the door. "I was starting to worry the cartel had gotten to you."

He led me into the apartment and took me to the darkroom he'd set up in the bath, covering the windows with black paper. Dozens of prints hung from a clothesline, dripping chemicals over the shower tiles.

"Are you doing still photography now?"

"Nah. These are for the documentary."

He took a print from the line, pulled a red-tinted flashlight from his pocket, and shined it on the photograph. It was hard to make out the details, but I could tell the image showed a ditch in a field.

"Irrigation works?"

"No, my boy. Mass grave."

Later that night, as I tried to fall asleep in the polluted heat of that awful rainless season, I thought of a story a friend had told me about a situationist architect from Istanbul. She wandered the hills of the city, carefully noting each turn she took, and then made immense maps, the size of walls, marking her routes with different colors of thread. At significant points, wherever the lines intersected, she pinned photographs, newspaper clippings, note cards scribbled with street signs, graffiti, and overheard conversations.

The next morning I walked to the stationary store on the corner, a tiny establishment that catered to elementary school students. I asked the clerk for a map of the city, the biggest she could find. She disappeared into the back of the shop and rummaged for several minutes before coming back empty-handed.

"I'm sorry. Can't you use your phone?"

Mexicano, contempla aquí tu historia

On a cragged hill, three miles west of the cathedral, at the end of a winding road flanked by diseased elms and flowering cacti, high above Reforma Boulevard's corporate skyscrapers and incongruous palm trees, directly over the fault line that will one day swallow the city's million street dogs and twenty million souls— there stands the castle. The site has a long history, stretching back to pre-Columbian times, when it served as a ceremonial retreat for the rulers of Tenochtitlan. Since then it has been known as Chapultepec, the hill of the grasshoppers. But for three short years, between 1864 and 1867, the palace at the highest point in Mexico City had a different name: Miravalle.

The name is ridiculous, something out of a bad Byron poem. The couple that came up with it were afflicted with the sort of temperament that retains late into adulthood an affection for adolescent romanticism. They came from a world enamored with storm and stress, where a novel about a lovesick young man's decision to take his own life could trigger a suicide epidemic among university students. They possessed the kind of wealth and status that results in an overdevelopment of the imagination. Before they took possession of Chapultepec, they had Miramare—a hideous palace just outside Trieste, perched on a cliff overlooking the Adriatic, that evoked a second-tier novelist's idea of a medieval ruin.

In that other castle, on October 2, 1863, a delegation of Mexican aristocrats arrived for an audience with the couple: Maximilian von Habsburg, the younger brother of the emperor of Austria, and his wife, Charlotte of Belgium. They'd come to make the pair an offer worthy of Coleridge's opium dreams: to become the first emperor and empress of a restored Mexican monarchy. The people of Mexico, the aristocrats explained, were tired of their ill-fated experiment in democracy. The House of Habsburg no longer ruled over the diminished Spanish Empire, but the first European rulers of Mexico had been the couple's ancestors. Maximilian and Charlotte were the legitimate sovereigns of Mexico by divine right.

This was not the first time that Maximilian and Charlotte had thought of Mexico. For years a network of exiled criollos had haunted the capitals of Europe, looking for a suitable royal who could redeem their troubled nation. Consummate conspirators and flatterers, they had grown close to Napoleon III's wife, using her influence to make sure news of their plans reached Vienna and Miramare.

At first the archduke and archduchess hesitated. Mexico was far away, not so much a place as an idea. But then they grew restless. They went on long trips aboard their yacht, the *Phantasie*; they attended royal funerals and baptisms; they advised their relatives on minor matters of state. All the while the idea of Mexico remained in their minds, growing more defined as their daydreams filled the blanks. They began to imagine what it would feel like to be the protagonists of their own epic rather than tertiary characters in the empire's soap opera.

By 1863, when Napoleon III occupied Mexico and his criollo supporters offered the crown to Maximilian, the couple was ready to accept. They renounced their European titles, packed hundreds of trunks full of paintings and silver, and set sail for Anáhuac. Along the way they changed names, becoming Maximiliano and Carlota of Mexico.

Like the Americans before them, the couple arrived in Veracruz on May 28, 1864. The Mexican aristocrats had promised them crowds waving white handkerchiefs, but when Maximiliano and Carlota disembarked, the harbor was empty. The country they had agreed to rule was in the throes of civil war—a conflict between rich and poor, liberals and conservatives. Veracruz was nominally controlled by the aristocrats and their French allies, but most of its people supported the Republican government of Benito Juárez, an Indigenous Zapotec who was elected to the presidency in 1861 on a platform that included redistributing the wealth of the Church and abolishing the legal privileges of the landowning minority. Struggling to keep their composure, the emperor and empress boarded a train for Mexico City, where at least there was a parade.

I tried to imagine the scene as I wandered the castle, long since converted into a museum. I walked through endless corridors; past cellars, kitchens, libraries, dining rooms, sitting rooms, drawing rooms, music rooms, servants' quarters; across gardens in the English, French, and Mexican styles; through ballrooms hung with the portraits of bishops and viceroys. I tried to imagine what it was like to play a part in that make-believe imperial court while knowing it was only a matter of time before a growing army of furious peasants entered the city and climbed the hill and began to batter the gates of the castle, which you foolishly and at great expense had transformed into an architectural version of your yacht.

The conservatives were few but commanded many pious campesinos, for whom Juárez, a foe to the Church, was an enemy. The problem was that Maximiliano didn't prove enough of a

Habsburg for his Mexican supporters. In his formative years, the future emperor had nothing to do but read philosophy and fantasize about becoming a wiser ruler than his brother. I pictured him wandering the halls of the Hofburg, muttering fragments of Hegel, daydreaming about ruling over a perfect state in which the Geist would at last unleash its potential. From the moment he landed in Veracruz, the emperor set out to enact liberal reforms indistinguishable from Juárez's. The aristocrats thought they had imported a reactionary traditionalist but found themselves prostrated before an enlightened despot.

After two years of brutal fighting from the deserts of Chihuahua to the port of Acapulco, the tide turned against Maximiliano. The French had been able to intervene in Mexico only because the American Civil War had left the United States incapable of enforcing the Monroe Doctrine. But now the Union had defeated the Southern rebels. The government in Washington, hostile to monarchists and European meddlers, informed Paris that it would not tolerate a continued French presence in Mexico and, to make sure the message got across, sent fifty thousand troops to the border. Besides, Napoleon III had pressing concerns closer to home: he had embarked on a war of colonial conquest in North Africa, committed to defending the pope against Garibaldi, and watched with growing anxiety as Bismarck's designs for a unified Germany expanded to include Alsace.

Deserted by the French, the aristocrats abandoned their emperor. On May 15, 1867, Juárez's forces captured Maximiliano. After a cursory trial, the sovereign was found guilty of capital offenses against the republic and condemned to death. If the museum's romantic captions are to be believed, the emperor proved an honorable man by accepting his fate and calmly walking to the firing squad. He is said to have given his last few pieces of gold to his executioners and asked they shoot him in the heart rather than the head so he might have an open-casket funeral for the benefit of his beloved mother.

Maximiliano died but the Habsburgs never left. Ever since the Second French Intervention, Mexico's rulers have all shared an Austro-Hungarian temperament: a vulnerability to zealous passions, a predisposition to the fevers of ambition, a weakness for fantasy, an inability to see that the only hope for the country lies in their destruction.

Ante todo, claridad en la prosa

The sun of Mexico City used to be a cliché like the bright lights of New York. The capital, I read in book after book, was once bathed in the most glorious sunlight on earth—one that didn't just illuminate, but enlightened. Alfonso Reyes put it best when he compared the Mexican highland to the southern rainforests:

> Our portion of the earth, the Valley of Anáhuac, is better and more salutiferous than the equatorial regions, at least for those who seek alertness of will and clarity of mind . . . Here the air is a luminous ether through which objects seem to step forward, as if drawn individually.

I considered this equation of sunlight and thought as I read a battered anthology of Reyes's essays on the roof of my father's house. By then the city had ten times as many residents as it did in 1917, when "Visión de Anáhuac" was published. Five million cars crowded the streets. There were factories and garbage fires. The sun was pale and sickly—a terminal patient hiding behind the curtain of a shared hospital room. Anáhuac was no longer la región más transparente del aire.

I headed inside. Who could think under that light?

"So you plan to stay in the States forever?"

Esteban and I were walking through a park in La Condesa. It was high noon. The sun fell hard over the dust and yellowing grass. There wasn't a molecule of moisture in the air.

"I guess?" I said. "Been there for so long I kinda feel like my life is over there."

Esteban sat down at a bench, looked around to make sure there were no cops in sight, and lit a cigarette. He offered me the pack. I declined with a wave.

"You quit?"

"There's kids around."

"You can't be serious."

"What?"

"Have you converted to Protestantism? Given up gluten? Sworn allegiance to the Stars and Stripes?"

"Whatever. Poison the preschoolers."

"I know you hated it here in high school. But now everything is different. Your dad isn't in the news. You wouldn't have to see your old classmates. And the whole writing thing? You could do that here—and in Spanish, no less!"

"I know, right? Writing in the language of the oppressor. How unpatriotic."

"If it was just the language, I wouldn't care. But once upon a time you wanted to write novels—big, weird, ambitious Latin American novels. And now, after a few years in the North, you've been reduced to wanting to write for *New York*, the *New Yorker*, the *New York Times*, and the *New York Review of Books*."

"You forgot the *Paris Review*."

"The name is false advertising." He got up from the bench and stretched his arms. "I'm thirsty. Aren't you?"

"After that struggle session? You bet."

"Let's head to El Centenario. I owe you a drink."

We walked in silence until we reached the edge of the park, with its nineteenth-century signs asking citizens to keep an eye on their children and their dogs.

"This is where that scene in *The Savage Detectives* takes place, isn't it?" Esteban said. "When Ulises Lima finally meets Octavio Paz and they have nothing to say to each other."

"Don't they meet at Parque Hundido?"

"Could be. In any case, there's a reason he named the character Ulises. Everyone ends up coming back."

El amor a la distancia

"Sebastián, please come downstairs?" my father called. "We're going to Skype with Mamá and Álvaro."

I got up from my makeshift bed in the TV lounge and walked to the living room, where my father and sister were waiting, his laptop open on the coffee table.

"She'll be glad to see us all together," my father said as he dialed.

After a few seconds, my younger brother appeared on the screen, looking older than he was.

"Hello!" my father said. "How's Álvaro the Great? Taking care of our Washington outpost, yes?"

"Fine."

"Where's Mamá?"

"She's not feeling well. The anti-nausea pills don't work with the new chemo. We should let her rest."

"Of course. But tell me, how's school? And soccer?"

"School's fine. Soccer's fine."

My father's smile faded. "Glad to hear."

"I've got homework—okay if we talk another time?"

"Absolutely. I miss you, kiddo."

"Yeah, we miss you guys!" my sister said.

"We miss you too," my brother said. "Talk to you later." He hung up the call and disappeared from the screen.

"Not the most talkative kid," my father said.

"Can you blame him?" my sister said. "He's too young to care for her alone."

"He's not taking care of her alone! We're all taking care of her together."

. . . y agarraste por tu cuenta la parranda

My father insisted on throwing a party in my honor. He asked the staff to line the roof garden with narrow tables crowded with votive candles, ordered catering from a hip taqueria, invited my high school friends, and bought several cases of mezcal.

The guests arrived at sundown. They asked what had become of me. I tried to explain. I failed.

And so I drank. They drank. My father drank.

Music blasted from hidden speakers. I tried to lower the volume but the others laughed and turned it back up. Before long everyone was dancing. Only I remained seated, clutching my glass in embarrassment.

Then, to my relief, the Bear, my painter-friend, walked onto the terrace. "Sebas!" he said. "It's been so long! To what do we owe the honor of your presence? You need to visit my studio—there's so many things . . ."

Before he could finish, a kid I hadn't seen in a decade all but tackled me with a hug. "Bellboy!" he yelled in my ear, the awful nickname I'd had in middle school striking me like a slap on the face. "Why the fuck haven't you called? Have you *forgotten me*?"

I pried his hands off me and headed to the bathroom and splashed water on my face. When I came back, my father had gone to bed and the music had grown louder. A friend asked me to dance. I declined.

"¡Ven!" she said. "Chance hasta te doy un beso."

I spun around a few times, took a theatrical bow, and fled.

At three in the morning, Arnaut, my best friend from childhood, staggered up to me. "C'mon, Sebas!" he slurred. "Why so sad? This is your party!"

He reached for my neck and tried to kiss my mouth, and as I turned away I remembered chasing rabbits and riding horses and hiding from stray dogs in the acres of forest and prairie that surrounded his house at the foot of the mountains of Mexico City; remembered playing guitar by a campfire and watching Westerns dubbed into Spanish; remembered his father, my godfather, the handsome heir who'd grown less handsome and less of a millionaire with each year and with each drink, until one day he died of liver failure in his office near the edge of the land he was about to lose to loan sharks, in the arms of my oldest friend, who once again tried to kiss my mouth.

"No," I said, gently pushing him away.

He stumbled to the dance floor, cornered one of his brothers, and tried to kiss him. His brother punched him in the face. With Moisés's help, I dragged Arnaut downstairs. I called a taxi for my friend, who could barely stand but insisted that walking home would do him good.

And then, deep under the earth, immense rocks shifted.

The seismic alarm began to blare. According to our grade school drills, we had about thirty seconds before the ground began to shake. People poured onto the street from houses and bars. Their faces had the fatalistic calm that comes from growing up in a valley surrounded by active volcanoes. The alarm quieted, the silence was heavy with expectation. Then, after half a minute, nothing.

"So much drama for no reason!" a man yelled as he filed back into the cantina across the street.

The car arrived and I persuaded Arnaut to get in. Upstairs the party had carried on uninterrupted. The music was louder than ever.

"It's just too much," said the friend who'd asked me to dance, tears running down her face.

"What's too much?"

"Everything. Everything's too much."

Que viva Cristo Rey

A still from a YouTube video: five teenagers wearing dark suits sit in a row of formal chairs, flanked by two uniformed servants. Improbably, the boy on the far left holds a live jaguar on his lap.

The boys are seniors at the Cumbres Institute, a Catholic school associated with the quasi-fascist Legionaries of Christ. The video is an ad for their graduation fête, the conceit being that the boys are holding auditions for their dates. One after another, slender models dance before the teenagers. The little emperors reject each one with a thumbs-down reminiscent of imperial Rome. The film mercifully omits the logical conclusion of such Neronian scenes: the boys' jaguar devouring the spurned models. Instead, the viewer is treated to a montage of women chasing the boys around Mexico City, begging for a chance to wash their pubescent feet.

The whole thing is baroque and grotesque, the sort of cultural document that future historians will cite as evidence that early twenty-first-century Mexico was on the verge of a violent convulsion. And yet, every time I watch the video, I can't help noticing that the boys are running away from the women. They look at them in disgust, preferring instead the company of their classmates. The video suggests another tape: a porno in which five Catholic boys succumb to long-repressed desires and spend their graduation night fucking one another under the watchful eyes of their pet jaguar.

But, of course, the Cumbres boys will never make that other film. In Mexico, not even the oligarchs are happy.

Un catalán en Austria-Hungría

When he died, my godfather (although in truth he wasn't godly or my father—he wasn't even my godfather, not in the eyes of the Church—but he was my best friend's father, and, for a time, while my father was busy pursuing his ambitions, he became something of a father to me, in part because he was so different from my real father: tall and handsome, with a full beard and flowing locks, care-free, concerned with living well rather than with making a good living—a predilection that was possible because he had inherited a not-insignificant fortune from his father, the founder of a liquor-import company who'd immigrated to Anáhuac as a child, after *his* father had fled Majorca in the last days of the Spanish Republic—a life that he pursued, unencumbered by an old Mexican name, in a comfortable house that he'd built on a large plot of land at the western edge of Mexico City, in a rustic style—wood on the ceilings, Talavera on the floor—that teetered on the edge of bad taste: besides the main house, with its wood-fired hearth and four fireplaces, there were several outbuildings, a heated pool encased in a greenhouse, stables for six horses, a chicken coop that housed a colony of rabbits, an office of uncertain purpose, and a tree house where Arnaut and his siblings and I spent afternoons pretending to be American pioneers, a rather un-Mexican game that we'd picked up watching old Westerns with my godfather in the inaugural event of weekend-long sleepovers, in which a small crowd of Austro-Hungarian children flocked to his estate to learn the basics of what he called, without an ounce of irony, the country life—how to ride a horse, pitch a tent, build a fire, shoot a gun—but which every time, without exception, devolved into forty-eight hours of barbarism: we cooked over a campfire fed by wood we'd chopped with a *real axe*, in a kind of glorious irresponsibility that was rare for those of us who came from households where life transpired under crucifixes and where the idea of spending a morning catching rabbits was unthinkably undignified; and, in retrospect, I can see that my godfather delighted in thinking of his house as a place where these sad children could feel free, that he'd spent his money building a theme park—perhaps I should say *a school*—because he wanted to teach us how to be happy, which for him meant learning how to live lightly, a goal that in my godfather's estimation could be achieved by doing things precisely because they served no purpose—hence the emphasis on useless skills—or, in other words, learning how to live without metaphysics, in the kingdom of this world, a concept best illustrated by one of the images that comes to mind whenever I think of him: it was Sunday morning, the second day of one of those wild weekends—I must have been seven or eight—and Arnaut and I were in the chicken coop, foraging eggs for breakfast, when all of a sudden a pack of feral dogs came running down the hill, and I looked at my friend, who at the time seemed to me the image of bravery, and saw that he'd gone pale, and all at once I was afraid, but then I turned and saw my godfather walking toward the dogs, wearing his jeans and leather boots and a white shirt that billowed in the wind, with a rifle in his hands, and I saw him raise the gun and take aim and shoot until two dogs were dead and the rest had fled, and then he walked to the coop and told us all was well and asked for our help with the bodies—the corpses were heavy, the blood had dried on the fur—but I wasn't scared, because in my godfather's world, everything was a game, there was no need to think twice—he certainly hadn't thought twice before purchasing six thoroughbred German guard dogs: five girls, with names like Iuna and Nina, and a single boy, his favorite, named after Odysseus's friend—or, if you prefer, consider another Sunday, some years later, when he invited all of our families for a paella lunch and had me help in the kitchen, and I watched him labor over the burning hearth, frying onions and garlic, chorizo and peppers, pouring white wine by the bottle, scattering hand-fuls of rice smuggled from Majorca—*the motherland*, where he wasn't born, and had never lived, and didn't die—ladling stock perfumed with saffron—*Did you know it's more expensive than cocaine?*—and nestling seafood with Andalusian names: almejas and mejillones, camarones and jaibas, and as he cooked, he played an album by Joan Manuel Serrat—*Catalunya's own Bob Dylan*—and sang along in that wide and rounded tongue, half Latin, half Spanish, half French, that so resembles the Occitan of the troubadours:

leu sui Arnaut qu'amas l'aura
e chatz la lebre ab lo bou
e nadi contra suberna

and though he was always out of key, my parents and the parents of the other children were charmed out of their usual decorum—*¡Ay Arnaut, el alma de la fiesta!*—and I noticed the way the women looked at him as he handed them plates of golden rice, and when I stood beside him as he addressed his guests before the feast began—*I'd like to thank my sous-chef, Mr. Bookworm*—I realized that I wanted to be a man like he was a man, but metaphysics has a way of intruding into the most lighthearted life, which is why I cannot forget how that Sunday ended: later that evening, my godfather got up from the table to go to the bathroom and lost his balance and fell, and as he collapsed, he held on to the tablecloth and dragged it down, along with the salad bowls, water carafes, and mussel shells, and for a moment he lay on the floor, blinking at the ceiling, his white shirt stained with wine and oil, and a stunned silence filled the room, until my godmother, livid with cold rage, muttering between clenched teeth—*I can't believe you, in front of everyone, you disgust me*—got up and walked toward him, very slowly, and helped him get up, and later that night I overheard a conversation in which my parents returned again and again to the word borracho, and the next time I went over to my godfather's, I began to notice the bottles of Cutty Sark—on his bedside table, near his corner of the couch—and the highball glass perpetually in his hand, always filled with ice and a liquid that cycled from amber to translucent, because, in a half-hearted attempt to pace himself by imitating Churchill, he'd let the ice melt and dilute the whiskey, and then one day on the school bus—I must have been twelve—my best friend announced his family was moving to a town three hours away, a decision that at the time seemed mysterious, though I since have learned that my godfather's import company had collapsed years earlier, something to do with NAFTA, and that at first nothing had changed, but he'd refused to get a job or sell the house, and at some point the situation had become untenable, and his wife had given him the first of countless ultimatums, and he'd decided on a change of air, a new house, a small town, a quiet life, and so the family moved to San Miguel de Allende, where my best friend learned and later taught me how to take a shot, roll a joint, and snort cocaine, all of which introduced a distance between Arnaut and me, a distance that grew even after his family returned to Mexico City—the San Miguel experiment did not help my godfather get sober, but it did drain the last remnants of his bank account, sometimes their landline would be down, and on a few occasions my friend inquired, while averting his eyes, if I wouldn't mind asking my mother for a thousand pesos for groceries—a distance that became insurmountable after I left for the United States and resolved never to look back, all of which perhaps explains my reaction when my father called to tell me that my godfather had died—he didn't go into details but I later found out that it happened in the office at the edge of the property, where he had locked himself with his whiskey after my godmother kicked him out, and that my best friend had been present at the last moment, and though we never talked about it at length, the one time we discussed it, he told me it happened in the afternoon: he'd gone to check on him and found him on the floor, conscious but disoriented, and he'd held him in his arms—*I stroked his hair*—but it was to no avail, and my godfather, his *real* father, had remained *agitated*, which is to say *terrified*, until the end; and so when my father asked me if I wanted to go to the funeral, I replied that I had schoolwork to do, which is to say that I was committed to a project of active forgetting, which is to say that I wanted to become an American, which is to say an amnesiac, which is to say I was a coward, and so I was not present when they buried him, but on the day of the funeral I couldn't stop thinking of one of the last times I saw him, a year before I left, when he decided to take his boys and me to eat gusanos de maguey, and we drove to a cantina and ordered grubs and guacamole and made tacos and washed them down with beer, and everything was great until we noticed my godfather was sweating and his lips were larger and his face had taken a purple hew, and when we asked if he was all right, he replied he was allergic to the grubs but loved them so much he still ate them once a year) was at the height of his powers.

Otra vez esta maldita felicidad

The best mezcal is made from tobalá, a type of agave native to the mountains of Oaxaca where my mother did her field-work. While some producers have devised methods to cultivate this particular varietal, the process is expensive and difficult: the cactus flourishes only in the wild. Unlike its more famous cousin, blue agave—the kind used to make tequila—tobalá is a very small plant, which means hundreds of specimens are required to make a batch of liquor. Every bottle of fine mezcal implies that an Indigenous laborer spent days wandering the sierra, foraging for tender desert plants. The recent mezcal craze has increased demand for tobalá to the point where scientists have warned that the plant is at risk of extinction.

Pruebe nuestra salsa habanera

The morning after the party, I walked to Arnaut's house, a spartan apartment above a row of squalid taquerias. There was no door on the ground floor, so people walked in and out as they pleased. As I climbed the stairs, I dodged a pile of human shit.

He answered my knock with a dazed smile. He told me he didn't remember the previous night. I gave him an unsparing summary. He offered me coffee and said he was sorry. I told him it was okay. Then I said what I'd come to say.

"I think you have a problem."

He lowered his head. "I know," he said, rubbing his rib cage.

"You okay there?"

"Yeah. It just hurts for some reason."

I noticed that a coffee table by the door was broken in half, its slab of solid wood cracked near the middle.

"Oh, shit," he said. "I must have fallen on it."

We headed out to get breakfast and sat across from each other in a cheap eatery. I ordered pozole and quesadillas. He ordered a beer.

"Seriously?" I said.

"You're right," he said, turning to the waiter. "Coffee is fine."

The soup arrived. I added a few drops of a salsa heavy with overripe habaneros. We ate in silence. When Arnaut finished his bowl, he cracked a tostada, slathered it with a whole tablespoon of the salsa, and swallowed it whole. Then he swallowed another. And another.

"What are you doing?" I said, horrified.

His face was bright red and his hair was soaked with sweat and he was crying. "It's the only way to beat a hangover."

When the waiter came back, Arnaut told him he did want the beer after all. I paid for the meal and excused myself.

Mexiconceptual

"It's hideous."

"Are you kidding? It's perfect!"

The Bear and I were standing in the mirror-plated museum that housed the eclectic trophies of a man who until recently had been the wealthiest person in the world. The curation of the temporary exhibit, a meditation on the history of silver in Mexico, was as chaotic as the traffic jam outside. A colonial dollar stood next to an ornate chalice that in turn stood next to a silver-lined hollowed cacao pod in which some eighteenth-century hostess had once served chocolate to her guests. According to the Bear, this lack of logic was the product of the owner's unorthodox collecting strategy. Rather than seek out a few select masterpieces, the man preferred to instruct his buyers to purchase in bulk. It didn't matter if it was second-tier stuff—he wanted one of everything, and often more than one. That, said the Bear, was what made the museum interesting: it was the world's last baroque cabinet.

"I guess I don't get it?"

"I'll give you a hint. It's the box."

The last case of the exhibit contained a cast of the museum building in pure silver. The curators had decided to show the model in its original packaging, which opened around the sculpture like a flower. On the back flap, in large silver letters, was written: BVLGARI.

Mirrey, quiero ir al antro

One day, walking around La Roma, I passed a nightclub that once enjoyed the patronage of my high school classmates: Club Rhodesia.

The name stopped me in my tracks. Suddenly I was back in Charleston, just hours after the church massacre, a reporter's notebook in my hand. I saw again the photograph of the killer: the scowl, the bad haircut, the flag of the Republic of Rhodesia stitched on his breast.

It was too late for a knock-and-talk, but I needed a story. For the past fourteen hours I'd driven through Lexington County, searching for the murderer's family. Two of my colleagues had stayed in Charleston, tracking down the victims. I was in Lexington because my colleagues were Black and Filipino, whereas in the judgment of my editors, I passed for white. The last address on my list corresponded to a clapboard house on a road with no streetlamps. The lights inside were off, but there was a truck on the lawn. I parked and took a few steps toward the house. Then I heard him.

"Stop right there," he said from the darkened porch.

"I'm sorry to bother you so late. I'm a reporter. I was hoping—"

He didn't reply. Instead, I heard the sound of metal scraping against metal. I raised my hands. For several seconds we did not move. He sat on his porch, holding a shotgun. I stood on the road, holding a notepad. The moon shone over the trees.

"You can leave," he finally said.

I walked to my car, hands above my head. After half an hour I pulled up by the side of the road and vomited. *You can leave.* Not a request or a command but a granting of permission.

They must have had no idea, I said to myself as I continued on my way, thinking of the wealthy, light-skinned Mexicans who'd founded the club. They must have thought it was just a cool name.

"Oh, but they knew!" Esteban said later, at a different nightclub. "Do you know what they did for opening night? They wanted Black waiters. You know, as a stunt. The earthquake in Haiti had just happened, so they went to Port-au-Prince and hired a bunch of people and flew them to Mexico City for the night. The funny thing is, they made them wear safari attire. Which, of course, is what the white settlers would have worn."

Oficina de naturalización

On the morning of my visa interview at the American embassy, I walked out of my father's house and was surprised to find Moisés still hadn't arrived. I looked at my watch, a Patek Philippe my parents had given me when I graduated from college, and saw all was well. We had plenty of time.

I set my backpack down and sat on the sidewalk to wait. Minutes passed—first slowly, then faster. I texted Moisés; he didn't reply. I began to grow nervous. We now had less than forty-five minutes to get to the embassy, which should've been enough, except that time in the capital had the bad habit of speeding up whenever you hit a traffic jam: the slower you moved, the faster the seconds ticked, such that you were exponentially late to wherever you were going. And if I was late to the interview, my visa wouldn't get approved, and if my visa wasn't approved . . .

I reminded myself that no amount of freaking out would make time run backward and tried to do the breathing exercises they'd taught us at the website after people started having panic attacks whenever we had to cover yet another mass shooting—but it didn't work. Instead I kept going back to what Moisés had said a few days earlier, about my wanting to be an American writer. When did that actually happen? At what point were you no longer a Mexican writer?

When the IRS began to consider you a resident alien for tax purposes?

When you stopped imitating Alfonso Reyes and started copying Joan Didion?

When you traded the crónica's artificial persona for the personal essay's mask of sincerity?

When you memorized the questions that the Department of Homeland Security liked to ask at the airport?

When you began thinking of yourself as "Latinx"?

When they finally gave you a green card?

And then, right as I was beginning to have a meltdown, Moisés arrived. I walked straight to the car and got in the back seat.

"To the American embassy, please," I said curtly. "We're running late."

Moisés started the car and drove down the street significantly faster than the speed limit. "I apologize. I know this appointment is important. I thought I'd made sure to come an hour before we had to leave, but I probably wrote the time wrong. I take full responsibility."

"Yeah, the interview is at eleven thirty . . ."

Moisés shot me a confused glance in the rearview mirror.

"That's what I thought."

"It's ten fifty-five. We're not going to make it."

"I'm sorry, joven Sebastián, but I'm pretty sure it's nine fifty-five." He pointed to the clock on the control panel of the car. "See?"

I looked at my watch, then at the clock, then at my watch again—and then it hit me. "I'm sorry," I said, the wave of relief immediately replaced by embarrassment. "My watch is still on New York City time."

Calle de amores

One afternoon, I dropped by the house where my father grew up and found my grandmother Luisa surrounded by a small crowd of great-grandchildren. She offered me whiskey and told me that she didn't like to sleep in the bed where she'd conceived her offspring anymore, preferring instead a comfortable reading chair.

The chair faced a large window that opened onto a courtyard near the back of the house. The courtyard was full of an indiscriminate profusion of plants: ferns, roses, orchids, dahlias, sunflowers, bougainvillea, and an immense rubber tree. The roots of the tree had broken the tiles that paved the floor. In those cracks grew other plants: dandelions, love grass, feverfew. Among the weeds, half-buried in the dirt, I saw the broken neck of a beer bottle.

"Each morning," my grandmother said, "I take note of every new petal."

This, I realized, was the proper way to wait for death.

"We might as well keep going," Moisés said. "Never a bad idea to be early."

We drove in silence for a while, then hit traffic on Reforma Boulevard. The sun, refracted on the glass of the skyscrapers, fell on the dusty palm trees and on the golden statue of the Angel of Independence atop its column, making it shimmer in the polluted air. Then Moisés cleared his throat.

"So," he said, in a tone that made me think he wanted to put my timezone faux pas behind us. "If you don't mind me asking—what did you cover as a reporter before you decided to get a masters?"

"The police, actually."

"And how much does a police officer make over there?"

"Depends on the city. In New York, the place I know best, a cop can take home ninety thousand dollars a year."

"But that's for bosses, yes?"

"No. That's a rank-and-file cop with some years of experience."

"Let me do the math." He reached into his suit jacket for his cell. "So, ninety thousand times twenty is . . . one-point-eight million pesos."

"What can I tell you? They have a union."

"Right."

We inched forward, then stopped again. An older man carrying a tray loaded with cigarettes walked up to Moisés's side of the car. Moisés rummaged through his pockets, lowered the glass, and handed him a fistful of coins. The man offered him a pack of cigarettes, but he refused it.

Then Moisés caught my eye in the mirror. "Do you know how much I make?"

"No idea."

"Some fifteen thousand pesos a month. About one hundred eighty thousand pesos a year. So that's, what, nine thousand dollars?"

We stopped at a traffic light. A troupe of shirtless teenagers rushed into the street from the sidewalk. Two of them began juggling machetes. A third took a drink from a gallon of gasoline, lit a match, and exhaled a cloud of fire. When the light turned green, the teenagers rushed between the cars for tips. Moisés lowered the window and handed the fire-breather a bill. I wondered whether he ever refused anyone.

"The real question, though," he said, gesturing at the teenagers with his head. "Is how much *they* make."

I turned to the window so he wouldn't see me blush. In the capital, five American dollars could buy a three-course meal and a beer. I was told high-end sex workers charged $150 per night. With my share of the rent for the two-bedroom in Crown Heights where I lived with the Shakespearean, I could afford a luxurious apartment downtown. And yet some of the Austro-Hungarians were as wealthy as the bankers of Manhattan. In America I was a petty bourgeois, or at least I could convince myself that I was. Here there was nowhere to hide.

"Anyway," Moisés said. "Can I ask you another question about those well-paid New York cops?"

"Sure."

"Are they any good?"

"In what sense?"

"As cops. Are they good at being cops?"

I wondered if I should tell him I'd spent most of my time as a reporter writing about police brutality. I didn't want to alienate him—I was desperate for him to like me—but I also didn't want to lie. Besides, he was a communist, or at least read like one. Maybe he, too, thought all cops were bastards?

"I mean, for what they pay them," Moisés went on, "you'd hope they'd be decent."

"They spend most of their shift arresting Black and Latino kids for petty shit like jumping the turnstile at the subway. And every few weeks they kill a civilian."

"Right. I read about the protests."

As he spoke, an Indigenous woman carrying a child in a rebozo walked up to my window—and all of a sudden I was a teenager again, at the height of the drug war and of my paranoia, when I began to lose touch with reality. I had been stuck in traffic in a car not unlike this one when a woman approached my window and pulled a gun from her rebozo. Except there was no gun. I'd seen something that wasn't there.

"Now can I ask you a question?" I said.

"Sure."

"Why haven't the poor killed the rich already?"

Moisés laughed. "Oh, I wouldn't know." He reached under his suit jacket with his right hand. "But I suspect it has something to do with this." He pulled out a Colt .45 and set it on his lap.

Su amable donativo llena las calles de música

The city center is home to a small army of organ grinders. They stand on corners, at major intersections, near tourist attractions and terraced restaurants, tirelessly turning the wheels of their instruments. They wear brown uniforms, halfway between bellboy and traffic cop. They are organized in a union. They are very polite when asking for tips. They are also going extinct. Many of their instruments were made in Austria-Hungary in the late nineteenth century. Replacement parts are difficult to find. The result is that Mexico's street organs have been slowly falling out of tune for more than a hundred years. Some grinders have fared relatively well. In certain streets you can hear mechanical renditions of "The Blue Danube" that are perfect save the two high notes at the end of each phrase, which are conspicuously missing. Others have not been so lucky. They serenade the capital with the sonic equivalent of an unrestored fresco or a half-collapsed temple—the dissonant death-rattle of an empire that refuses to die.

Favor de llenar su forma antes de formarse

At the American embassy I waited in a hanger-like building lined with rows of plastic chairs. Thousands of my fellow citizens fidgeted in limbo between hope and fear, fanning themselves with their immigration documents and making small talk.

"How many times have you been rejected?"

"Man, I can't even remember."

"And where are you going?"

"Louisiana, to work at a seafood-processing plant."

"And are you coming back?"

"Not if I can help it."

I moved down the row as the next seat became vacant. Eventually I reached the end of the line and was told to wait while a consular officer interviewed the person ahead of me. The officer was a few years older than me and clearly hated her job—this wasn't what she'd had in mind when she joined the State Department. Her voice dripped with condescension and suspicion.

"Have you ever been to the United States? Did you have a visa at the time? Did you overstay? Why are you not answering my questions? You don't speak English. You said in your application you spoke English. You are denied."

Then it was my turn.

"It seems you've lived in the United States for several years. You are aware, I'm sure, that the student visa you're requesting is not a path to permanent residency. Have you ever been arrested? Have you ever bought or sold drugs? Have you ever helped anyone who was in the United States illegally? Have you ever advocated for the destruction of the United States government? Okay, just one second. You're approved."

Misterioso asesinato en la UNAM

I accompanied my father to a birthday party. The host had gone all out—open bar, quesadilla buffet, and, of course, a cover band playing Buena Vista Social Club. The crowd was illustrious: television executives, celebrity academics, esteemed newspaper columnists, and a whole generation of folklorist poets. There were also politicians, both firebrand leftists and a former president of the conservative National Action Party. I spied the owner of the telecom monopoly, the guy who'd commissioned BVLGARI to make a replica of his own museum. He wandered around the garden, holding an iPhone over his head, in search of a signal.

I ordered a drink. Here they were, the Austro-Hungarians, in all their glory. Many were supposed to be sworn enemies. They called one another names on the Senate floor and in the pages of the metropolitan dailies; they went on television to denounce one another's ill-gotten wealth; they demanded investigations, appealed to commissions, took principled stances in public debates. Some even had the pluck to protest in the streets. Here, they clinked champagne flutes.

The scene reminded me of an incident I'd read about in the paper earlier that week. After an administrator at the National University was stabbed to death, a group calling itself

"Individualists with a Tendency toward Savagery" published a document claiming responsibility for the crime:

We executed this man to show we have no respect for hypercivilized life. We don't believe in "a better tomorrow." We aren't "revolutionaries." We are individual terrorists with egocentric, amoral, and indiscriminate objectives.

I wondered what would happen if the Individualists—clearly Russian majors high off their first misreading of Dostoyevsky—decided to strike here, bursting into the courtyard armed with Uzis and wearing black T-shirts emblazoned with the portrait of Mayakovsky.

"Party's over, fat cats!" one of them would shout, shooting into the air.

A Spanish-language cover of "Blitzkrieg Bop" would begin to play through the loudspeakers. There would be a glorious moment of chaos as dozens of heavyset oligarchs trampled one another in a futile attempt to escape. Near the end of the rampage one of the Individualists would point her gun at me. I'd raise my hands but also nod.

"Shoot me," I'd whisper. "I deserve it."

I shared my fantasy with the other guests at my table, who stared at me blankly.

"How's school going?" a man in his thirties asked.

"Hasn't started yet—I'm moving in a few . . ."

"Right, I forgot! You just graduated."

"Actually, I . . ."

"And how's Headmistress Mia?"

"Wait—what? From Colegio Tomás Moro?"

I realized then that he—and probably the whole table—thought that I was still in high school.

"Be careful, manito. I don't think she's a fan of edgy humor. I get you, though. The Ramones," he said. "I know the Ramones. So funny."

Los sueños de Dylan

The day before I was supposed to fly back to the United States, I got an email from Arnaut:

> *Hey, Sebas—*
>   *I'm sorry we didn't get to hang again before you left. I called you a bunch of times but I always got your voicemail. Anyway, I have some news. Turns out I'm moving to Australia next month. Gonna do* WWOOF *in the outback. The permit lasts only three months but I'm hoping I can figure out something more permanent once I'm there. It's all very last minute. I guess I just thought it would do me good to get away. You know, like you did. I'm excited! But also bummed. Because this means we probably won't see one another for a while. So I wanted to tell you that I love you. You're my brother. I'm so fucking proud of you. Those gringos at Iowa have no idea what's coming for them. Go West, young man! Just don't forget about us?*
>
>   *—Arnaut*

Visión de los vencidos

Among my father's books I found an anthology of what little Mexica literature survived the conquest. It was a useful volume: a generous selection with a scholarly introduction and literal translations of each poem. On my last day in the capital, as I killed time before heading to the airport, I decided to "translate" something into English. I picked a lament from 1521, the year when my ancestors destroyed the Aztec metropolis and began building Mexico City:

Our arrows lie broken on the ground	Their horses roam freely
Our houses no longer have roofs	The walls are dyed red
Maggots roam the streets	The walls are splattered with brains
The water is red	When we drink it tastes of salt
We beat the walls in anxiety	We make holes in our refuge
Our shields were once our refuge	They couldn't stop this desolation
We've eaten rotten bread	We've gnawed on salt
On adobe	On crumbled dirt
On mice	On lizards

Even on maggots

Weep O my friends	Tenochtitlan is lost
The water is rotten	The food is rotten
Such was the will	Of the Giver of Life

In Tlatelolco

By the time I finished I was rattled by guilt—not the tenuous pangs of privilege, but an almost ontological awareness that I was the heir of a cursed bequest. I opened the book at random and landed on some verses by Nezahualcóyotl, the poet-king:

Ica zonahuiyacan ihuinti xochitli
Tomac mani
Ma on te ya aquiloto
Xochicozquitl

I tried to make sense of the poem without looking at the translation, but I recognized only one noun, xochitli. Flower.

Salidas internacionales

The plane took off at midnight. The moon shone through my window, big and blue over the clouds. Below glowed millions of light bulbs, smaller than fireflies, brighter than stars. For several minutes they filled the horizon, spilling from the valley onto the slopes of the volcanoes. No matter how many times I flew in or out, the sheer size of the city continued to amaze me. It grew every year, swallowing villages and landfills, forcing rivers into plumbing. One day, I thought, it would cover the whole of the earth.

Part II

Iowa City

August 2016–May 2017

In which Your Correspondent moves to the Middle West, discovers that he has made a terrible mistake, attempts and fails to write a history of nostalgia, makes and loses a friend, feels discouraged by the imperatives of academic creative writing, ponders the conquest of Mexico, gets drunk on the night of the election and into a fight with a dubious Mexican, meets a musicologist, and in general is a waste of oxygen and space.

La pradera ominosa

On a bright morning in August, a few weeks after I returned to New York with my new visa, I loaded my belongings into a rental van and drove west. The rowhouses of Brooklyn gave way to the rust of western Pennsylvania and the endless suburbs of Illinois. I was saddened by the end of my relationship with the Shakesperean, but my sadness was tempered by excitement. A new life waited for me in the Middle West—one devoted to literature.

As I crossed the Mississippi, I recited in my head the list of essays I hoped to write. Of these, none excited me more than the chapters of a history of nostalgia in the mold of Robert Burton's *The Anatomy of Melancholy*; the point of which would be to refute the received idea that people who leave their home countries had a moral duty to feel a desperate desire to return to their native land. I didn't miss Mexico, and I resented the suggestion that this lack of nostalgia meant that something was wrong with me, when the opposite was true: nostalgia was a disease; its absence, a sign of health.

The book would open in Switzerland at the end of the seventeenth century, when a young physician coined the term *nostalgia* to describe the deadly affliction that struck the droves of migrants who in those days were moving from the countryside to the cities, then it would flash back to ancient Greece to discuss the rich etymology of the word *nostos*, only to fast forward to Napoleon's invasion of Russia and the American Civil War, when thousands of soldiers were diagnosed with fatal cases of the disease, and finally conclude with an examination of the birth of modern psychiatry. It would include considerations of Homer and Nietzsche, the contemporary craze for vinyl records, and the psychological pathologies of refugees; and it would be, I told myself, at once erudite and readable, giving way to a triumphant book tour and numerous awards, recognition from my peers, and the ultimate prize: American citizenship awarded on literary merit.

But then, as I entered Iowa City and drove through leafy streets flanked by Victorian houses that sweated in the humid summer heat, I began to have misgivings. Fuck the name—this was not a city. The so-called downtown, where the studio I'd rented sight unseen was located, consisted of a single commercial strip lined with bars whose black-and-gold logos, graced by an anthropomorphic hawk with a hypertrophic musculature, said everything one needed to know about the undergraduate fans of the university's mediocre football team. No matter. I'd come here to write. Better to have no distractions.

After getting the lay of the land, I headed to the closest Target and got towels and sheets and a mattress, then drove around town to pick up a desk, shelves, and the rest of the furniture I'd bought from departing students.

"In case you need to look up the assembly instructions, the model name is Skitsäng," said the novelist who'd sold me an Ikea bed, as he handed me the incongruously heavy box. "Two dots over the A. It's in pretty decent shape. Only thing is, it used to be black. Last winter I got cabin fever and wound up sanding it down."

"Cabin fever?"

"Yeah, dude. Donner Party shit. Be forewarned."

I drove back to the the center of town and parked in an alley next to the Pedestrian Mall, then wandered around on foot, looking for the address, until I found myself standing in front of a handsome brick building that wouldn't have been out of place in Baltimore or Philadelphia. On the ground floor there were two businesses: a boutique named after some tropical fruit that sold bright-colored dresses that I couldn't imagine anyone wearing and a space-themed pizza restaurant that reminded me of a Pixar movie, but which promisingly stayed open late and sold beer.

I made several trips back to the car to get the bed and the rest of my stuff, then punched in the code and dragged everything upstairs. I tried the door to my studio and discovered it was unlocked. I walked in to find a small but not charmless room with exposed brick walls, a hardwood floor, and four large windows that flooded every corner with sunlight. Not too bad, I said to myself as I began putting together my bed. All you need to be happy is a proper bookstore, a decent bar, and a handful of interesting people—and here you'll have all those things. Besides, do you want to be the coastal-elite asshole who complains about the indignity of living elsewhere than Brooklyn?

Tristes trópicos

The more advanced students of the program had organized a barbecue to welcome the new class. I went to the liquor store to pick up a bottle of tequila, then waited for my ride: a second-year student who'd served several tours as a marine in Afghanistan.

"We're pretty close-knit," he said as we drove over. "Many of us are working class, so we bonded over that. It's not like the fiction and poetry workshops. Most of them look down on us because they all went to an Ivy."

"Right," I said, wondering whether I should tell him that I'd gone to school in New Haven.

At the barbecue I found some thirty twenty-somethings clutching cans of Pabst Blue Ribbon and grilling hamburgers and hot dogs. Every single one of them was white.

Then another second-year student approached me, dragging a brown woman by the arm.

"Mayeli!" she said, with an enthusiasm that struck me as affected. "This is Sebas. You guys are both Mexican. You should talk!"

The second-year wandered away. I looked at Mayeli, who had short hair and a tattoo of the goddess Coyolxauhqui on her shoulder, and she looked at me—her eyes pausing on my watch, which I promptly buried in my pocket.

"Thank God!" she said. "I thought I was the only one."

We switched to Spanish and told each other about our previous lives. She'd been raised in California by an immigrant family, gone to Stanford on financial aid, and worked as a housing organizer in the Bay Area. Her favorite author was Cherríe Moraga. She wanted to write about her parents' deportation back to a small, violent town in Tierra Caliente.

We were in the midst of these disclosures when a third-year student—a tall, thin white girl in a flower-print dress—walked over to us. "Man!" she said, laughing. "It's been so long since I've heard Spanish! Time to do some ethnographic anthropology!"

I blinked, then looked at Mayeli, who stared at the white girl with disbelief. My first thought was that the newcomer didn't know what she was talking about—there was anthropology and then there was ethnography; they weren't the same thing. Or were they? I wasn't sure. Still, the comment struck me as evidence of stupidity, not malice. Mayeli, on the other hand, was horrified. She didn't say another word for the remaining time the girl stood next to us talking in circles about that time in college when she'd gone to Guatemala for a service trip.

"We were supposed to help these villagers build a drainage system," she said. "But we fucked it up—and then everyone got dysentery!"

After a while the girl lost interest in her anthropological subjects and wandered off. Mayeli drank a beer in one gulp and shook her head. "Chingada madre," she said. "¿A dónde nos venimos a meter?"

Los filisteos

"I just don't *care* about Nietzsche," said one of the second-year students, who I'd secretly taken to calling the Decanonizer. "Who wants to read about dead white males?"

It was the first time that my writing was up for workshop, and it wasn't going well. We'd finished discussing one of Mayeli's essays, which our classmates had liked well enough, except for the bits that were in Spanish, which they felt were "pushing them out" of the piece.

"I agree," said another student. "All this theory and history and stuff—why don't you give us a character we can identify with, or at least care about? Nietzsche isn't super sympathetic, and I don't get why you spend so much time describing his migraines. I'd much rather read about your life. Tell us about Mexico!"

I stared at my notebook. I'd spent weeks researching Nietzsche's medical history to make a facetious argument that his real illness was not syphilis but nostalgia. The essay reinterpreted his philosophy as his attempt to rid himself of the disease. I thought it was great, but now I was having doubts. To give myself courage, I picked up my pencil and wrote DON'T FALL PREY TO AMERICAN ANTI-INTELLECTUALISM in the margin of my notebook.

Balada de un hombre delgado

One day, walking home from the library, I noticed the brothers of a fraternity had hung a large banner over the littered porch of their rickety Victorian: MAKE AMERICA GREAT AGAIN. At first I was surprised—weren't college students supposed to be liberal?—but then I realized I shouldn't be. I hadn't followed the last months of the election closely, consumed as I was by the petty dramas of the program and my antiquarian research on nostalgia, but I knew that the faux city was a blue oasis in a bloodred state. The undergrads who moved here to drink and pretend to get an education came from places where reactionary ideas were as pervasive as the fertilizers in the tap water.

Then a young man in basketball shorts and a wifebeater emerged from the house and sat on a stained couch on the porch. He took off his baseball hat, wiped the sweat from his forehead, cracked open a beer, and reached into his waistband to scratch his testicles. I felt an impulse to strike up a conversation, or, more accurately, to interview him, to take out a notepad and put on a charming reporter's smile and interrogate him about his brothers' support for a candidate so clownishly unfit for the presidency—but the young man snorted and spit a glob of saliva the color of chewing tobacco in my general direction.

"What the fuck you looking at?"

"Nothing," I said, then turned around and continued on my way.

"That's right!" the frat bro yelled after me. "Walk away, you pussy!"

Perhaps I should be paying more attention, I thought as I passed Cactus III, one of several identical pseudo-Mexican restaurants that sold margaritas by the gallon. Like most of my former colleagues back in New York, I lived under the assumption Trump would lose. One of my old employer's rival news websites had even relegated coverage of his campaign to its entertainment section, a clickbaiting stunt I found annoying but not entirely unreasonable. The clown had many supporters, but the fury with which they chanted his racist slogans was proof they knew they were losing. The Mussolinian rallies that so unsettled reporters were the final tantrum of a silent majority that was never truly silent and was no longer a majority. They would not go gentle—they would kick and scream until the bitter end—but go they would, into the goodness of the night.

But would they? I wasn't sure anymore. The few articles I'd read made it clear that Trump's voters weren't just resentful old men in coal-mining backwaters but also respectable professionals, tech millionaires, nice ladies who hosted garden parties in the suburbs—even, as I'd just discovered, college students.

Like the fraternity brother who'd spat at me, these people were angry, and their anger lingered in the air. It was an atmospheric dread, a slight scent of catastrophe that made me terribly anxious whenever I thought about it, which is why I tried to think about it as little as possible. After all, much of that anger was directed at Mexicans—RAPISTS, he called us, BAD HOMBRES. I reminded myself I wasn't *that* kind of Mexican. I was an Austro-Hungarian. I had money, light skin, and elite credentials, and these advantages, unfair as they were, protected me from the hatred Trump incited and harnessed. I didn't have to worry, not for myself.

Or did I?

Preguntaréis, ¿por qué su poesía no nos habla del sueño, de las hojas, de los grandes volcanes de su país natal?

Fine, I thought one night in my studio after another bad work-shop, you want me to write about Mexico? You want me to be your tour guide, to educate you, to teach you a few things about my fucked-up country? Fine, I'll do it. But it won't be what you want. I refuse to give you what you want. I'll write you a god-damned history of Mexico, sure, the whole fucking thing—but

I'll do it in the voice of a seventeenth-century colonial aristocrat. Because that's what you take me for, isn't it? You think that my prose is too mannered, my diction too elevated; that I tell too much and don't show enough; that I'm a pedant and a know-it-all and a snob who went to an Ivy? You've seen nothing yet!

I, Sebastián Arteaga y Salazar, natural citizen of the Very Noble and Loyal City of Mexico, licensed bachelor of the liberal sciences, candidate for master of fine arts, and Your Imperial Mercy's Most Foreign Correspondent, hereby present a veridical chronicle of the history of Mexico.

The nature of the subject that Your Mercy has asked me to discuss, however, requires that I preface my relation with a warning. Your Mercy requested an informative report on the Mexican colonies of the United States, but I cannot pretend to have written anything resembling "the truth." That this course of action amounts to insubordination does not escape me. In my defense, Your Mercy, consider a strictly factual account of the birth of this star-crossed country:

In the seventh Serpent Day of the Year of the Reed, some thousand warriors from the city-state of Tlaxcala descended onto the Valley of Anáhuac and marched to the edge of the lake that in those days filled the basin. There, at the head of one of the bridges that joined the mainland with the floating metropolis of Tenochtitlan, they were met by several thousand of their all-powerful enemies: the Mexica, the rulers of an empire coeval with the Known World. For reasons that remain mysterious, the Mexica not only declined to destroy the invaders but agreed to host the small group of foreigners that the Tlaxcalteca had brought with them. Two years and nine months later, on the thirteenth of August of the Year of Our Lord 1521, one of those foreigners stood on the pile of rubble that had been the capital of the cosmos and declared that the New World now belonged to the archduke of Austria.

Four sentences, scarcely a paragraph, a beginning and an end with nothing to link them together. Thousands of pages have been written about the subject, Your Mercy, but this is a story where the facts are few; the interpretations, many; the difference between the two difficult to discern.

Consider, Your Mercy, the possibilities:

The foreigners were loyal Spaniards fighting for their German king. Or they were opportunistic privateers in search of Indian gold. Or pious Christians fighting for their Roman god. Or desperate men in search of something other than misery.

Their leader, Hernán Cortés, was a brilliant tactician, a gallant lover, and a diplomatic genius; or he was a fumbling commander, a bigamist uxoricide, and an avaricious arriviste. Most likely, he was a man of ambition whose only discernible talent, according to one of his contemporaries, was an undeniable facility for "the art of the novel," which he put to good use in his famous Letters of Relation, *where he presents a litany of lies with such literary skill that five centuries later, most who know his name still believe he single-handedly conquered the world.*

To consecrate what would have been a mundane slaving expedition into a holy quest from which there was no turning back, the novelist set fire to his ships as soon as he reached the mainland, watching in silent prayer as the galleons burned like so many autos-da-fé. Or he did not burn the ships but sank them. Or he did not sink them but ran them ashore and had them dismantled. The hulls, he wrote, were rotting. He wanted to save the nails.

In the decade before the novelist's arrival in Anáhuac, there were either seven or eight omens in the Mexica capital, which either included or did not include the sudden appearance of a burning star that outshone the sun, the ghostly wailing of a bereaved mother, and the births of an unusual number of Siamese twins. Or there were no omens, a possibility suggested by the fact that every known description of them dates from after the end of the war. Or there were omens but they were not unusual. Or they were unusual but not necessarily baleful.

That last question seems to have been on the mind of Moctezuma Xocoyotzin, the elected great speaker of the Mexica, who in the months before the end of his world gathered in the capital large numbers of astrologers and demanded an explanation for the signs. The emperor grew so enraged at the uselessness of his soothsayers that he had their families slaughtered before their unseeing eyes.

Then again, Moctezuma was no superstitious child but the most powerful man in the Known World. Why would he be afraid of comets?

The great speaker welcomed the Spaniards to his palace and immediately surrendered his vast domains because he was convinced that the arrival of the foreigners marked the fulfillment of an ancient prophecy: that the White God who'd granted his ancestors temporary stewardship over Anáhuac would one day return to claim his throne.

Or there was no prophecy and the great speaker opened the doors to the foreigners because his character, like that of all Indians, combined predilection for satanic rites with prelapsarian innocence, to the effect that he was at once angel, demon, and idiot.

Or there was indeed a prophecy but Moctezuma did not believe in it; he merely pretended that he did in order to lure the Spaniards into a trap that he then proved too cowardly to close.

Yet perhaps Moctezuma welcomed the Spaniards with all the honors due to a diplomatic embassy not because he wanted to kill them, which he could have easily done outside the palace or on the way to the palace or even inside the palace, but because dynastic struggles within the city-states of the Mexica confederacy had left his empire in a position of relative vulnerability to the republic of Tlaxcala, its foe in a decades-long cold war that threatened to turn hot, and parlaying with the enemy's strange new ally struck him as preferable to a tiresome conflict.

Or maybe the great speaker wanted to expand his vast collection of rocks, crystals, meteorites, and seashells, jades and emeralds, jewels of gold, ingots of silver, mirrors of copper and obsidian, fish, fowl, and flowers, cacti both fruit-giving and intoxicating, trees of dyewood, trees of perfume, trees of shade, tame ocelots, trained tapirs, hairless dogs bred to be small, birds of feather, song, and prey, frogs, salamanders, axolotls, snakes of many kinds, jaguars, leopards, panthers, tigers, apes and monkeys, dwarfs and giants, hermaphrodites, epileptics, idiots, seers of visions, savages, barbarians, and many other such marvels, monstrosities, and miracles, thinking that the pale strangers and the large deers they rode would make for a fine addition to the museum in which he collected samples of all of the things of this earth, over which he held power in the name of the gods.

On Labor Day, Mayeli invited me to accompany her on a visit to her parents in rural Mississippi. We'd been spending a lot of time together and become close, but I'd begun to feel anxious around her. Our budding friendship rested on her perception that I understood where she came from. And so I tried to keep the details of my background blurry, worrying that, were I to tell her who I really was, I risked losing the one friend I'd made in the program.

We drove for hours on the eerily straight highways of the Middle West, taking turns to read out loud from the Plutarch we'd been assigned for our History of the Essay class. I felt honored she trusted me enough to take me to meet her family. Her parents had returned to America a few years after their deportation, but they still didn't have papers, and she was understandably protective of them.

Around sunset we arrived at a well-maintained ranch house at the edge of a two-thousand-person town, where the rows of shuttered storefronts with sun-bleached signs gave way to untended overgrowth. Her parents were waiting on the porch. He was tall and taciturn, standing straight like an oyamel; she was short and restless, shifting her weight from one foot to the other. I greeted them in too-formal Spanish and noticed a bewildered look in the mother's eyes and a wry smile on the father's lips. They'd immediately recognized me for who I was. I hoped they wouldn't betray me to their daughter.

Mayeli and I spent most of the weekend helping at the family restaurant. On Friday and Saturday the clientele consisted of white Americans—Trump voters, I thought, supporters of a man whose main electoral promise was to launch a campaign of ethnic cleansing against people like Mayeli's parents. Ignoring the menu's offerings of mole and carnitas, they ordered Pantagruelian burritos drenched in a white sauce made with cream cheese and garlic power that they called "queso," which Mayeli's mother prepared with an air of disgust.

On Sunday, however, Mayeli's father woke up at three in the morning to make birria. When she and I arrived at the restaurant hours later, we found the place full of Mexican families. I brought bowls of steaming broth to the tables and noticed that many of the customers' eyes were glazed with exhaustion, as if they'd driven for hours. My friend's family business was the only Mexican restaurant for many miles, and these people flocked to it in search of not only food but also spiritual comfort. Through a culinary alchemy, Mayeli's family conjured a country within another, ferrying people across hundreds of painful miles so that they might spend a few moments in a familiar place where they weren't fugitives. In that moment, I realized, I was in Mexico, and I felt a bittersweet joy at the thought that I shared a bond with all those strangers.

But as I washed dishes at the end of the day, I was forced to admit that I wasn't one of them—not if I was honest in a way I hadn't been with Mayeli. I wondered whether she would have allowed me to witness the miracle if she'd been able to read me like her parents had read me.

Later that night Mayeli and I sat with her older sister and brother-in-law, drinking beers around a firepit in the backyard of the family's house. The sister's husband wanted to know how the program was going.

"Pensé que ibas a estudiar para cirujana," he said. "Pero eso de ser escritora también está chido."

"¡A ver cuándo escribes una novela de romance como las que me gustan!" the sister said.

Mayeli smiled, but I couldn't tell if with sadness, nervousness, or irony.

"¿Y qué?" the brother-in-law said. "Is it mostly chicanos like you guys?"

Mayeli looked at me and sighed, and I realized with panic that she'd figured me out, that perhaps she'd always known.

"No," she said dryly. "It's mostly white folks."

The next day the whole family packed into Mayeli's car to drive to another small town several hours away, where a relative was getting married.

"Yo manejo," her father said.

"No, papá, ¿cómo crees?" Mayeli said. "¿Con la licencia de California? ¿Y si te paran?"

"Aquí está tranquilo."

We drove out of the town and onto the highway. Mayeli's father asked me questions. We were training to become English teachers, right? Did people with our degree find jobs after graduation? And what was Iowa like? Were there Mexican folks around? Was there a place where you could get proper food? His daughter never ate enough. Especially since she'd given up meat. Which was very strange, if you asked him. Back in Guerrero, people saved to buy pork for Sunday, but here in America, where you could have meat every day of the week, where even beef was affordable, his daughter had for some reason decided that . . . .

Then we heard the siren.

Out of nowhere a police car appeared behind us. The bodies of everyone in the car tensed. I looked at Mayeli and saw she'd closed her eyes. Her father pulled over by the side of the highway.

A white officer from the State Police walked up to his window. "License and registration, please."

Mayeli's father handed him the documents without a word.

"Where are you heading?"

"To a family wedding, sir," Mayeli said from the back seat, suppressing her slight accent.

The cop looked at her, then at her father, then at her again. "All right. Just tell your dad to take it easy on the gas." He handed the papers back to Mayeli's father and walked away.

We drove on, a scrupulous five miles under the speed limit. The silence grew heavy. After a while I couldn't take it.

"El que mucho corre . . ." I said.

I waited for someone to finish the proverb so we could all laugh together—but nobody spoke another word for the rest of the drive. I tried to catch Mayeli's eyes, hoping to show her silent solidarity, but she made a point of looking away from me.

El pecado original

From my failed attempt to write a history of Mexico out of sheer spite:

> *The litany of possible interpretations goes on, Your Mercy. At any rate, all sources agree that relations between the Spaniards and the Mexica became tense as the mild Mexican winter gave way to the season of storms. Then, in July 1520, Cortés received news that the governor of Cuba had dispatched a small army to arrest him on charges of desertion and treason. The captain hurriedly left the city to meet with the newcomers, taking most of his men with him and leaving behind a small garrison at the command of Pedro de Alvarado.*
>
> *This Alvarado, a veteran of the slave raids that unpeopled the Caribbean, had earned a reputation for cruelty among men accustomed to mass killing. Hearing or imagining or inventing a rumor that a faction of Mexica noblemen planned a coup against their womanly king and his pale captors, he decided to take preemptive measures. Taking advantage of the distraction caused by the Mexica's monthly*

festival of sacrifice and dance, he commanded his men to close all the exits of the ceremonial plaza. In a matter of hours the leadership of the Mexica confederation lay dead from dagger wounds to the back.

It was at some point in the ensuing chaos that Moctezuma was killed. The most common version of the story has him standing at the edge of the roof of his palace, pleading with his people to lay down their arms and obey their new rulers, only to fall from a plebeian's stone blow. Contemporaneous Mexica accounts, however, suggest the great speaker died at the hands of Alvarado himself. The captain, panicking at the realization that tens of thousands had laid siege to the palace, thought that impaling the emperor on a pike and raising his desecrated body over the royal residence would frighten the city into surrender. The gesture, alas, only fanned the flames of what Cortés the novelist, in one of his least plausible choices, insisted on calling "the mutiny" or "the rebellion."

The events that ensued, Your Mercy, are thought to be well-known and yet remain mysterious. Cortés promised the men sent to arrest him more gold than they could carry and convinced them to make him their captain. He then returned to the city and, to his surprise, found it in a state of open war. His attempt to rescue the survivors among Alvarado's garrison was a disaster in which the Spaniards were all but annihilated, an incident which came to be known as the Sorrowful Night. To this day, Mexican school children visit the tree on which the Father of the Fatherland is said to have leaned to weep for his friends. I, for one, am of the opinion that the image of the defeated conqueror crying under a willow betrays the offices of a novelist who reaches for a cliché in a half-hearted attempt to make his character-narrator slightly harder to hate.

It was the birthday of one of the women in my cohort, and since I'd been nursing a hopeless crush on her, I decided to make an exception to my self-imposed solitude and go to her party. The house she shared with two women from the fiction workshop was crowded with aspiring writers who clutched red plastic cups filled with flat beer while they danced awkwardly or stood in small clusters, shouting tidbits of conversation to one another over the din of out-of-fashion hip-hop. The scene reminded me of freshman year in college. I thought about leaving before anyone noticed, but the host caught my eye and smiled and walked over to me.

"Sebas! So glad you're here! Listen, would you mind if I stand here for a bit? Ralph has been acting super creepy around me and won't leave me alone."

Ralph was the oldest member of our cohort: a forty-something recovering heroin addict who never came to class and talked nonstop about how he'd been kicked out of the Navy and lived on the street for a while. We'd been at Iowa for only a couple of months, but he'd already harassed every woman in the program.

"I'm sorry he's bothering you," I said, resigned to the part of stage prop.

"It's bad. The other night he came over uninvited and asked if he could sleep in my bed because it was late and he didn't want to be alone. I said no, obviously, but he wouldn't listen. In the end he said if I wanted him to leave, I had to give him some Xanax."

"That's insane."

"I know. A bunch of us are filing formal complaints. Hopefully that and the fact he's shown up to literally one class the entire semester will get him expelled."

Then another woman in the program walked into the house. My crush saw her, let out a yelp of delight, and ran off to meet her.

I sighed and headed to the front porch for a cigarette. On the darkened lawn I saw Mayeli talking with a fiction student. I thought of saying hello but didn't want to interrupt. I'd started treating her deferentially, as if she were wiser but also frailer than the rest of our classmates. This was the last thing she wanted, I knew, but I couldn't help myself. I was finishing my smoke when Mayeli raised her voice enough for me to hear her clearly.

"But he's *wealthy!*" she said.

My heart sank. I put out the cigarette, threw the butt into a flowerpot, and went back into the house for another drink.

Later, when I was about to head home, I bumped into Mayeli in a hallway.

"¡Comandanta!" I said, hoping my old nickname for her would somehow conjure a familiarity that was no longer there. "Ya me iba para mi casa, pero me da gusto que nos hayamos topado. ¿Cómo estas?"

"You going on foot?"

"Yeah," I said, switching to English. She never used Spanish with me anymore. "It's not far."

"I'll give you a ride."

She turned around and walked out of the house. I followed her across the lawn and noticed her steps were unsteady.

"Listen," I said when we got to the car. "Are you sure you're okay to drive? Maybe we can walk together and you can pick up the car in the morning?"

"No. Get in."

I tried to say I would prefer to walk but nothing came out. I sat in the passenger seat, biting my lip, and fastened my seat belt with shaking hands. Then Mayeli drove away from the party, much faster than necessary, down the pitch-dark streets of the residential neighborhoods of Iowa City, braking too hard and too late at stop signs—until we burst into a busier thoroughfare and ran a light and swerved onto the sidewalk to avoid a bus and almost hit a jogger.

"What the fuck?" the jogger yelled. She banged her fist on my window. "Are you trying to kill someone?"

Mayeli honked the horn until the woman went away. Then we drove on. Soon we were downtown, where throngs of drunken undergraduates were filing to their dorms at bar close.

"Okay if I drop you here?" Mayeli said.

"Sure," I said, breathing a sigh of relief. "Thanks for the ride."

She nodded but didn't say anything. I got out of the car, closed the door, and bent over to look at her through the half-open window. "¿Hablamos pronto?" I said.

She started the car and drove away.

La llegada del cometa

History caught me like it catches everyone: unaware. I was sitting at an overcrowded dive bar in the Middle West, three months into the MFA program for which I'd sacrificed my work visa, flanked by two classmates that I was tentatively befriending to compensate for my falling out with Mayeli: the woman I had a crush on and a man who was later accused of multiple sexual assaults.

The states on the map kept lighting up red. The crowd grew drunker. Someone started to sob. An older man laughed. The woman I had a crush on went home. The man who would be accused of sexual assault made jokes on Twitter. Everything was unreal, as if the world had ended and all that remained was a computer simulation in which the contrast between colors was slightly too high. I hated everyone around me—the ones who laughed, the ones who cried, the ones who stared at the heads jabbering away on the screen.

I went out for a cigarette. I figured by the time I came back, our fate would be sealed. At first I tried not to look at my phone for the handful of minutes it would take me to smoke, but soon I caved and opened Twitter. I felt compelled to say something, anything, a placeholder phrase that would not so much convey a thought as plead for a like, a retweet, anything that indicated someone remembered I existed—but I couldn't think of anything. After a while I tweeted something to the effect that, if the tide turned, I swore to go to the sanctuary of the Virgin of Guadalupe to offer flowers.

I went inside and found the room in disarray. Someone had done the math. We were past the point of no return.

"But has the AP called it?" I said to no one in particular.

At that very moment, as if I'd jinxed the odds, the heads on the screen interrupted the white supremacist they'd invited to comment on the events to announce that the Associated Press had called the race in favor of Donald Trump.

The room fell silent. Besides the affected diction of the talking heads and the occasional whimper, the only sound I could hear was the blood pumping through my punch-drunk head. I found some people I vaguely knew and invited them to my apartment to keep drinking. On the way there, as I chain-smoked and took swigs from a horrible bottle of acetone-sweet ouzo someone had brought, I checked Twitter and discovered that my stupid message had garnered a few retweets and a private reply from Mayeli: *You're going to be just fine. So maybe just shut up for a while?*

I took another swig of ouzo, deleted the tweet, and hoped my former friend was right.

"Fuck it!" said a novelist as he stumbled on my stairs. "If it all goes to shit, we'll all move to Mexico together! Right, Sebas?"

El invierno de nuestro descontento

Winter came. The sun rose late in the morning, set early in the afternoon, and shone behind a thick, gray veil that blocked most of its light and gave what little made it through a blue tint in which all faces seemed sickly. The snow fell heavy and dense and piled several feet high on the sidewalks. Walking to class felt like moving through a tunnel. Mole people, I thought as I put on several sweaters and wrapped a scarf over my face, we've become mole people, little helpless mammals who huddle in their lairs and emerge only when absolutely necessary, and then tremulous with fear.

Standing outside for the length of a cigarette was difficult: the wind burned the face, the joints ached with precocious arthritis. Large icicles formed on the cornices of buildings, hanging over one's head like broadswords. At dusk the undergraduates still flocked to the bars. Through my window I saw long lines of young women wearing nothing but cocktail dresses, wrapping their arms around their chests, shivering, on the brink of hypothermia. One night, as I trod through the snow on the way home from the bar, I found one of them unconscious in the alley behind my building. I called an ambulance, but then her friends appeared and dragged her away, her limp legs leaving a trail on the snow.

"Katieee!" one of them yelled, as if the passed-out girl could hear her if she spoke loudly enough. "Watch it with the Firebaaall!"

A few minutes later the ambulance showed up. "So they just took her away?" the paramedic said. "Do you know what dorm they're at?"

"Wouldn't want to narc on them."

"Sure, don't get them in trouble. Who cares if they choke on their own vomit?"

Mornings were hardest. I woke up earlier than I wanted, filled with a formless dread I found difficult to dispel. I went to class on autopilot and spoke more often and louder than I should have. Then I came home and drank and read Pound and Heidegger, reveling in their hostility to the reader. I became ingrown, like a toenail, incapable of holding a conversation, convinced everyone disliked me as much as I disliked them. I longed for New York, for my friends who worked at little magazines, for my job at the website, for the wonderful woman with whom I'd shared the apartment in Crown Heights.

I looked at my pile of philological articles on the meaning of *nostos* and at the Loeb edition of the *Odyssey* I'd borrowed from the library, and I realized that my project had failed: I'd come down with a bad case of nostalgia—not for Mexico, but for Brooklyn.

Los sinsabores del Verdadero Policía

The alumnus had done well for himself: starred reviews, an appearance on National Public Radio, a profile in the *Styles* section, an option with Netflix. Perhaps that was why Prairie Lights Bookstore had deemed it necessary to deploy its battalion of moody interns with instructions to plaster the faux city's astoundingly numerous bulletin boards with the flier promoting his reading: an amateur design in black and white, xeroxed at low resolution onto neon-red sheets of printer paper, in which the alumnus's name and the title of his memoir, *The Patrolman and the Penitent*, were printed in a typography that called to mind a "wanted" poster from the time when Anglos began settling the North American territories that a few years earlier had been part of Mexico.

I knew I hated him the moment I saw him at the bookstore

café, standing amid a gaggle of sycophantic students, inscribing copies of his book with lengthy dedications. He wore a Zorronian bolo tie and a white dress shirt under a red flannel that made me wonder whether he'd left the gallon hat at the hotel. He leaned back and lifted his chin as he listened, narrowing his eyes and nodding slowly, like some streetwise charro in a black-and-white picaresque starring María Félix. He pronounced certain words a certain way, but he blew his cover each time he said Día de los Muertos instead of Día de Muertos.

Then one of the moody interns clapped his hands and asked people to take their seats and silence their phones. I thought of going home but remembered that our professors had made it clear the program expected us to attend the events it funded, lest the taxpayers of Iowa complain their hard-earned dollars were going to waste. I cursed the day I left New York and sat in the back row, like some delinquent highschooler, ready to confirm my prejudices.

After a hyperbolic introduction by his old thesis adviser, the alumnus walked to the lectern, nodding in acknowledgment of the polite applause of the three-dozen people who'd come to see what the hype was all about. He cleared his throat and said he'd decided to read from the note to the reader at the start of the book, rather than from a representative chapter, which he realized was unorthodox. It was just that, after several readings where members of the audience had reacted negatively—no, he corrected himself, *strongly*—to what he had to say, he'd come to see the importance of giving readers a sense of the "place" from which he'd written the memoir.

There was a moment of silence. People shifted in their chairs. The alumnus licked his lips, took a sip of water, wiped his mouth with the sleeve of his flannel. He flipped through the pages of the book. He coughed. What, was he nervous? No way. He was bluffing—but wait, hadn't he gotten canceled? Yes, that was it. He was worried that someone was about to . . .

And then, all of a sudden, in a way that felt paradoxical, like a long-awaited jolt, the alumnus began not so much to read as to perform. He barely looked at the page (had he *memorized* the thing?) and spoke with a trained actor's just intonation and artful pauses, marking the accented syllables of each phrase (had he written the thing *in fucking meter?*) and modulating tone and timbre to highlight the weight of each sentence. The motherfucker, I realized with irritation, was talented. Which, of course, only made me hate him more.

When I finally managed to listen to what the alumnus was saying, however, the pleasure of hatred gave way to confusion. As it turned out, the name on the cover of his memoir wasn't the one with which his parents had christened him. Everyone else in the family was white, but his maternal grandparents had been Mexican—or more accurately *Hispanos*: his people had settled near Santa Fé centuries before Mexico even existed and therefore insisted on referring to themselves as *Spanish*—and he'd wanted to honor him by signing the book with a name in their language.

The gesture was the culmination of a decade-long journey that began right after college, when the alumnus went to Juárez to volunteer at a migrant shelter. The year he spent there opened his eyes to both grace and violence, but by the time he went home to Pasadena, he still felt green, ignorant of the world, unschooled in the ways of the border—the bleeding edge of the West, as he liked to call it, where the personal was geopolitical.

And so the alumnus hatched a plan. He'd enlist in the patrol. Ride a horse. Wield a whip. Wear a brownshirt. Not because he agreed with what they did. On the contrary: to blow the whistle on their crimes.

His girlfriend and the rest of his friends from Pomona College expressed concern. He told them not to worry, he wouldn't let them get to him, turn him into some sadistic pig, some little Eichmann carrying out criminal-categorical imperatives. No, he wasn't about to turn into a cop. He'd remain a mole. A spy. A double agent. A noble traitor.

Training was tough but he toughed it out. To his surprise, he came to enjoy it: running five miles on command, lifting his own weight ten times in a row, shooting at silhouettes under the Arizona sun—it made him feel like a man. But what surprised him the most was that he liked his colleagues. Their coarse camaraderie. Their roughrider humor. The no-questions-asked loyalty they extended one another. His friends at Pomona had it wrong: people didn't become cops because they were sadists but for the same reason they joined amateur soccer leagues. Yet there was also a deeper affinity at play. The fact that the Patrol felt less like a paramilitary bureaucracy than like a band of oath-bound brothers probably had something to do with the fact that many, if not most, of the alumnus's new coworkers were Mexican. Like his grandparents. Like him.

At first they were suspicious—what was this light-skinned college kid doing in the patrol?—but soon enough they began inviting him to baptisms, weddings, carnes asadas on football Sundays and Friday-night fights. The alumnus accepted their welcome with incredulous gratitude. His grandparents had died before his birth; he'd never gotten to experience his culture. Now there he was, bashfully accepting a dance with the quinceañera, making expletive toasts in Spanglish, singing along with the mariachis, firing his service gun into the sky. He'd always been Mexican. Now, for the first time, he felt like one.

But sometimes it got ugly. Like with the water bottles. The ones activists left at strategic points along the trails. No, he wasn't proud of it. It was true that it hadn't been him wielding the knife, technically speaking, but it was just as true that he'd gone to college and therefore read that German lady's book about that trial in Jerusalem, and so he was well aware that, when it comes to great crimes, declining to participate—*refusal by omission*, he called it in self-aggrandizing moments; *playing dumb*, he corrected himself in self-pitying moods—wasn't enough. He should have told his comrades they shouldn't do it. Even if the bosses said so. Because they knew, didn't they? What it was like. They'd learned all about it at boot camp. The stages of decline. First confusion. Then delirium. Then euphoria. Then exhaustion. Then the seizures and the arrests. Yes, he should have spoken out. Gone on TV. Denounced. Accused. Testified before Congress or the Hague. At the very least he should have resigned. He knew all that and it troubled his sleep even back then. But he couldn't quit. Not yet. He needed more evidence. It was a worthy sacrifice: the cleanliness of his hands in exchange for an exposé of his nation's cruelty.

But then he found them. The woman and her child. The unit was short a few men, so he'd been assigned a solo patrol. He went on horseback and saw them from afar, motionless under the half shade of a thorn tree. When he knelt before them, he discovered they'd been there for only a few hours. You could tell by their warmth: it still radiated from within. Nearby was an empty half gallon, the dirt beneath still damp. Someone had pierced it and left behind the plastic to ensure the dying understood they were being killed. Above, stark against the azure, three vultures circled the sun.

In the weeks that followed, the alumnus stopped sleeping. He spent whole nights with his laptop on his chest, letting the algorithmic tides carry him from one video to the next, trying to keep himself from weeping. He began to lose track of himself: one morning he woke up to find he had torn out his toenails.

He never attempted suicide, not actively, but he took to driving on highways in the small hours, speeding without headlights in the dark, hoping some unwitting trucker would do what he didn't dare. His mother begged him to see a doctor. His few remaining non-Patrol friends staged an intervention. His girlfriend left him.

After some months of increasingly erratic behavior, the bosses had him involuntarily hospitalized, in part to help him dodge charges, mostly to avoid liability. When he was released weeks later with a prescription for antipsychotics, he learned that the patrol had let him go with a medical discharge. To his surprise he felt relieved—and then he realized that his surprise was itself proof that, for all his promises to the contrary, he'd wound up becoming a True Policeman.

The alumnus moved back to Pasadena, working construction to pay rent for his mother's basement. After six months of physical exhaustion and maternal discipline, he recovered enough to put on a plausible show of adult functionality: a job at a nonprofit, an apartment of his own, a new partner, twice-weekly cognitive-behavioral counseling. But for all the therapy and the pills, he still couldn't sleep. Each time he closed his eyes, he saw their faces, sunburned and peaceful, the first timid flies already reckoning the way for the horde of creatures large and small that would soon break down their bodies into nutrients for the thornbushes of that land without rain.

When he heard of the migrant caravan, he knew at once he had to help. He wasn't sure how, but he was sure he had to atone. Make amends. Repair the harm. Then it hit him: His role would be to keep the record. Document the events. Preserve the tale for posterity. And so he got on a plane with little more than a camera and a notepad, and, upon landing in Chiapas, destroyed his American passport. Now he, too, was undocumented. The book he was holding in his hands, available for purchase at the door, was the account of what came next: his attempt to become another faceless figure in the crowd.

Las ilusiones de la no-ficción imperial

From my failed history of Mexico:

> *In the weeks and months that followed, there were arrivals of reinforcements from Cuba and Tlaxcala, diplomatic intrigues with disgruntled imperial vassals, amassing of armies at the shore of the lake, hurried construction of miniature galleons. There were burnings of bridges and freshwater aqueducts, cannonades and bombardments, skirmishes and night-raids, famine and thirst.*
>
> *More than anything else, however, there was pestilence. It's impossible to say how many perished from the plagues. The missionary friars count millions, though their apocalyptic sensitivities gave them reason to overestimate. A figure accepted by some modern historians has it that eighty-five out of every hundred men, women, and children living in the Mexican highland in 1519 died in the course of the war. One researcher estimates that the Indigenous population of central Mexico numbered about 1.5 million at the time of the invasion, dropped to less than 70 thousand by the turn of the century, and had grown to a mere 275 thousand by the time Father Hidalgo called for independence in 1810.*
>
> *The dead included the Mexica, of course, but also the Spaniards' Tlaxcalteca allies. The only ones spared were the emissaries of the White God. From this troubling fact one of the more subtle theologians among the early missionaries drew the uncanny conclusion that the Lord had unleashed the plagues to punish not the Indians but the Spaniards. Cortés*

and his men had made the portion of the earth that most resembled the Garden of Eden into a replica of hell. The Good Shepherd, in his infinite mercy, had brought home his herds and left behind the sinners, so that they might find, in each tangled mass of hair and bone, a premonition of Judgment Day.

But such subtleties came later. After eighty days of bombardments and no food or water and the ravages of the plague, Tenochtitlan capitulated to the invaders. Cortés then led a triumphal procession into the heart of the city. Above his head he carried a banner with the image of the Holy Virgin and the arms of the House of Habsburg. It's said that the novelist wept again when he climbed the half-destroyed Great Temple and gazed at the volcanoes over the immensity of the lake, not in joy at the knowledge that his name would be remembered but in sorrow at the certainty that the rest of his days would be but a shadow of the present moment.

But was there anything glorious about that day? August is the last month of Anáhuac's rainy season, Your Mercy, and the only time when temperatures climb above the usual perpetual springtime. The canals would have been at high water. The decomposition of a body produces noxious gases that become trapped in the anatomical caverns. This is why the drowning sink but the drowned float. Your Mercy, consider the stench.

Consider that there was nothing to eat and no potable water.

Consider the outbursts of anger and fear.

The picking of wounds.

The repetitions of prayers.

The grinding of teeth into dust.

The nightmares and the insomnia.

Consider the hallucinations: the Angel of Death, the Flayed Lord, the Wailing Mother, Sant-Iago Moorslayer, Tezcatlipoca the Avenger, the Adversary in his many forms.

If Cortés and his men are to be remembered with any super-latives other than those related to their cruelty, Your Mercy, it's as the authors of one of the most improbably successful cover-ups in the annals of genocide: the idea that the rulers of the metropolis that became Mexico City granted them sov-ereignty over their domains not by force of arms but because they recognized the Spaniards' superiority.

The lie proved so effective that a newer empire found uses for it. In 1878, the Federal Government of the United States commissioned an Italian artist to create a series of nineteen panels depicting the history of the young nation's eponymous continent. The third scene was to represent Moctezuma's sur-render to Cortés; the fifteenth, across the way, Santa Anna's submission to General Scott.

The message was crude, Your Mercy, as imperialists tend to be. Just as Austria outdid Rome when its armies entered the house of Moctezuma, now America outdid Austria by marching its marines into the same halls. The Valley of Anáhuac had been marked by Providence as a birthplace of empires. In taking it by force and raising the Stars and Stripes over the plaza where Alvarado murdered Moctezuma, America earned the right to rank itself among the victors. The righteousness of the enterprise was as self-evident as the proposition that all men are created equal.

The problem, Your Mercy, is that the whole thing is fake: Moctezuma did not surrender to Cortés. In truth not even the stone is real. The Frieze of American History *that adorns the Capitol rotunda is not a frieze, but a trompe l'oeil: a mural painted to look like a frieze. So it goes with most nonfiction, Your Mercy, including my own. The difference is that some of us admit to our fabrications while others build empires on optical illusions.*

¡Que vivan los Dorados!

The alumnus stood silent for a moment, making eye contact with members of the audience, holding the expression of a college-theater Hamlet. Then he closed the book with a clap and smiled like a priest telling his congregants they could go in peace. The crowd exploded in applause.

I sank into my chair and looked for Mayeli. She barely came to workshop anymore, let alone to optional but highly encouraged events. Every so often I'd run into her at Dave's Foxhead Tavern, usually on weekdays, usually in the early afternoon, but also, with increasing frequency, in the midmorning, when I'd head to the bar in hopes of hastening the end of another empty day by means of a self-aware flirtation with functional alcoholism, only to find her sitting by herself, on a corner stool at the edge of the bar, nursing a beer, staring out the grime-sleeked window, dying of nostalgia. I'd nod in greeting and she'd nod back but not look at me, so I'd order a PBR and a rye from the hostile barkeep and head to a booth near the back, where I couldn't see her and she couldn't see me. I'd open my book and pretend to read, holding on to the thought that, even if we couldn't be friends, we could at least sit at the Foxhead, alone and yet together—but moments later I'd hear her settle her tab and walk out of the bar.

Then I felt a hand on my shoulder and was reminded that I was sitting under the too-bright fluorescent lamps of Prairie Lights Bookstore, surrounded by people who I most certainly didn't want to think I was vulnerable to solipsism. I looked up and saw the smiling face of the youngest member of my cohort: a delightful kid from a rusty town in Michigan who wrote about Batman and *It Follows* and always shared his cigarettes and kept inviting me to play disc golf, and who often made me wonder whether the problem wasn't the faux city, the program, or my classmates, but myself.

"Hey, sadboi," he said. "All good? We've been yelling your name for a hot min. Some of us are going to the Fox with the man of the hour. Wanna come?"

"I should go home."

"And do what? Listen to the National?"

We stood around for a while, making small talk while the alumnus finished fake laughing with the head of the poetry workshop. Then we headed downstairs and onto the street and toward the Foxhead. All the while my classmates heaped praise on the alumnus—the power of his prose and his performance, the courage he'd shown by taking on such an urgent task at such great moral risk. It was a shame that some people couldn't see that. They had heard about the—how to call them?—*disruptions*. During his readings. And honestly? Maybe it wasn't their place, because the people behind the *disruptions* were for the most part "Latinx," whereas they were white, but somebody had to say it: it was unfair that people who hadn't even read his book felt they had the right—or, like, the *obligation*—to silence his voice.

We sat down at a booth in the bar.

"Thank you," the alumnus said. "I know it's coming from a place of solidarity, and that means a lot. Because, not gonna lie, it *has* been hard. At the same time? I'm okay with it. The folks who interrupt my events have every right to be mad. That's what the book is about. The immigration system is a dehumanization machine. And, shit, I was a part of that machine for nearly six years. And I know the fact I wrote a book about what I saw doesn't erase what I did. I used to think it would. Or at least hoped so. But I was wrong. Because, like, what right do I have to say anything about this shit? But I guess after a while I started to question if keeping quiet out of shame wasn't just another way to avoid it. Maybe it was the other way around. Maybe I had a duty to speak out, to testify on what I saw—and to do it *from* that place of shame. But before I could do that, I had to prove my commitment. To my readers, sure, but mostly to the migrants. And also to myself. And, shit, I don't know—maybe to God. I wouldn't call myself a Christian. But honestly? You can't spend a lot of time working in or around immigration without noticing that what goes down by the border sure as hell looks a lot like the Bible."

There was a pause in the conversation. I wondered if anyone would ask the obvious question, but a moment passed and nobody spoke.

"So you stayed for all of six years?" I finally said.

The alumnus turned to look me in the eye. "Almost twenty percent of my fucking life."

"Look at that!" said the delightful kid from Michigan. "We're down to our strategic beer reserves. Sebas, give me a hand?"

I got up from the table and walked over to the bar with him.

"Kinda cringe, right?" he said while we waited for the pitchers.

"Rather cringe."

"I was worried I was the only snake on the plane."

"It's a cringefest. A cringenival. A Bayreuth of cringe."

"Never mind. You and I don't belong to the same reptilian species."

"Thanks for defusing."

"No problem, sadboi. But play nice? Last thing we need is the program's large adult son complaining to the faculty about how rude we were to him."

By the time we made it back to the table, the conversation had moved on to the leitmotifs of the Iowa of those years: the challenge of navigating the intersecting vectors of bidirectional oppression of a white supremacist society; the Nonfiction Writing Program's second-child syndrome viz. the fiction and poetry workshops; the importance of decolonizing the canon, the classroom, and most importantly the cardiac chamber. I listened in silence, hurrying through rounds of rye, increasingly plastered and increasingly annoyed.

After some time, I went to take a piss, and on the way back stopped by the jukebox: a Precambrian machine that played CDs filled with idiosyncratic mixtapes of pirated music. I fed it a quarter, flipped mindlessly through the mechanical menu, chose the first track I recognized—LCD Soundsystem's "Dance Yrself Clean"—and returned to my seat.

Soon a vaguely tropical loop of percussion samples filled the room. A throbbing synth bass growled through the speakers on the first beat of each bar, rattling the bottles behind the counter. Then the vocal track came in and I realized with horror that now I'd been the one to blow his cover. Because I was enjoying it, wasn't I? I was getting a kick, a smug little hit of dopamine from the devious pleasure of gathering yet more evidence for the proposition that I was better than these Americans. I felt a wave of disgust at myself, but the self-hatred only made the kick hit harder. Who knew resentment could feel so good?

To my disappointment, however, nobody at the table seemed to realize what had just happened. By then the delightful kid and most of my classmates had gone home. The only people left at the table were the pseudo-anthropologist, who'd given dysentery to a bunch of Guatemalan villagers, the Decanonizer, a living white girl who didn't care about dead white males, and the alumnus, who was clearly going to sleep with either of them, although preferably with the Decanonizer.

"Don't get me wrong," said the alumnus. "It's obviously terrible. And terrifying. At the same time? Maybe it's what we need. To wake up. To shake things up. Maybe shit has to get worse before it can get better."

"Fuck yeah!" said the pseudo-anthropologist. "That's what I always say to the Mensheviks at the grad-student union meetings.

We can't just sit around waiting for the revolution to happen on its own!"

"Plus," the alumnus went on, looking at the Decanonizer, as if the pseudo-anthropologist had never spoken, "worst comes to worse? Like, at the very least? It's gonna make art punk again."

At that point I couldn't hold it anymore and burst out laughing.

"Right," said the alumnus. "I guess it's all really funny, isn't it? Fascism. Fucking hilarious. But to be honest, brother? I don't get the joke."

I waved my hand apologetically, trying to contain the spasms of hilarity. "I'm sorry," I said when I managed to stop laughing. "I'm not making light of it. It's just—well, not gonna lie—you're starting to sound like someone who doesn't stand to lose much from this . . . this . . . How to call it? This necessary tragedy! This wake-up call! This valiant effort at cranking up the dialectical locomotive! Because guess what, baby? That song and dance about the emergency brake? Fucking revisionist heresy! This is a world-historical rocket ship, honey boo, and it's either shoulder to the wheel or back against the . . ."

"Dude, that's bullshit," the Decanonizer said. "Nothing to lose? Buddy, maybe this is news to you, but I have a uterus. And, like, two hundred grand in student debt. Besides, guess what? Some of my best friends are Latina—actually, one of them is undocumented—and I fucking resent the suggestion that—"

"Do you mean Mayeli?"

"What? No. But so what if I did?"

"Mayeli is an American citizen."

"Look, boss, you need to check your privilege, okay? Because you don't know shit about me. Got it?"

"I'm sincerely sorry," I said insincerely. "But there's been a misunderstanding. I never said *you* sounded like you had nothing to lose—only that *he* did."

"That's even worse!" the Decanonizer said. "He's fucking Mexican!"

"Oh, don't worry, he's made sure it's impossible to forget that."

"You're being a jerk, Sebástian."

"Sebastián."

"Sorry?"

"Stress on the last syllable, s'il vous plaît."

The alumnus set his glass on the table slightly louder than necessary. "All right, compadre. You've had too much to drink, and you're starting to say things you don't mean. Time to go home."

"Fine. But can I ask you a question before I go?"

"Homey, you're making a fool of yourself."

"Why Emiliano?"

"What?"

"Your name. Why did you pick Emiliano? As opposed to, I don't know, Maximiliano."

"Listen, brother, so far you've been getting friendly advice, but keep it up and you might get something else."

"Was it because of Emiliano Zapata?"

"Who the fuck are you to gatekeep Latinidad, pendejo?"

"It's just so . . . basic. Don't you think?"

The alumnus threw his beer in my face. "It's my abuelo's name, asshole."

"Okay, sure," I said. I stood up, drops of lukewarm lager dripping down my hair onto my glasses. "But did Gramps fight with the Ejército del Sur?"

"Get the fuck out before I give you a puteriza, vato!"

I took off my glasses and wiped them on my shirt. "Putiza," I whispered as I put them back on.

"What the fuck did you just say?"

"The noun you're looking for is putiza. Or alternatively

madriza. But never puteriza. Nobody has ever said puteriza. Unless it's some Northern Mexican thing. But even then, it'd still be incorrect, because, as José Vasconcelos famously quipped, civilization ends where carne asada begins."

The alumnus slapped me across the face. I laughed and took a bow for the Decanonizer, then showed myself out.

El mes menos cruel

Then spring arrived all at once, with a burst of energy like the electric current of a defibrillator. The sky unfurled bright blue, uninterrupted by clouds, crisscrossed by songbirds. The sun returned and the air became golden, at once warm and reflective, such that everyone shone as if alight from within. Trees grew leaves overnight; flowers burst everywhere, like weeds, overcrowding their beds. Insects molted, hatched, metamorphosed: bees, waterbugs, fireflies and mayflies, spiketails and spreadwings. Deer appeared in unexpected places at inconvenient times, almost causing car crashes. One morning, heading to class on the footpath next to the Iowa River, I saw a red-tailed hawk dive from the heights at an impossible angle and strike a running rabbit.

In those heady weeks, I discovered the poets: bewildering creatures who spent months on a single line, floating through the world without effort, still shocked the taxpayers of Iowa had agreed to spend their hard-earned dollars to allow them to waste two precious years on a task both necessary and useless. I began sitting with them at the Foxhead, listening to their earnest conversations about Susan Howe and astrology. I caught myself staring at them with a mixture of desire and disbelief—who knew so many attractive people would be attracted to the same art form? To my surprise, they seemed to like me. The Middle West was a terrible place and America was going to the dogs, but now at least I wouldn't drink alone.

La calle de los mangos

"Okay, Sebas, so it looks like you're a Sagittarius, rising Leo, moon in Taurus. Which is crazy!"

I was sitting with a handful of poetry students in the living room of one of my new poet-friends, Constant Amadea Adler, who everyone else called Connie, but whom I insisted on calling Constant Amadea Adler, because someone with such a name simply could not be addressed in any other way.

"Seriously, though," Connie went on. "That combo is scorched earth. How do you live?"

"Look up his chart-siblings!" Preetha said.

"Leave my sister out of this, witches!"

"Easy, nonfiction boy," Connie said. "It's famous people who had your same chart. I got Marie Antoinette, which is both upsetting and totally spot-on." She clicked on a link on the website and burst out laughing. "Okay so this is perfect. Guess who's Sebas's astrological twin? Fucking Balzac! Which makes sense. Because if good old Honoré drank five gallons of coffee every night, our boy Sebastián sure loves his Adderall."

"Show some respect? I have a condition."

"Of course you do, Mr. I Wrote Fifty Pages On Homer Last Night Just For Kicks."

"You know what Sartre said on his deathbed?"

"Jesus, Sebas, stop it with the philosophers!"

"He said: Yes, I could have lived longer if I hadn't taken all that Benzedrine. But I wouldn't have written the *Critique of Dialectical Reason*."

"Never got to that one."

"It's incomprehensible."

"Right, because he wrote it on fucking speed!"

"More to the point—don't you take Adderall, too, Constant Amadea Adler?"

"Me? No, no. I'm a Concerta girl."

"Same difference."

"Nah, dude. You take a drug of abuse. I take psychiatric medication."

"Should we go to the Foxhead?" Preetha said.

"Um, yes please?" Bijan said. "Otherwise these two are going to keep winding each other up."

We walked out of Connie's house and headed to the bar. We got drinks and sat at a booth and proceeded to engage in the national pastime of MFA students: talking shit about the program.

"It's so annoying!" Charlie said many drinks later, brandishing her whiskey like a Molotov cocktail. "They *love* your work, think it's *fantastic*—so long as it's about the 'ethnic' food Grandma used to cook for you!"

"Oh my God, Charlie!" Connie said. "You're a fucking monster!"

"Like, for fuck's sake!" Charlie went on. "I'm a fucking $L=A=N=G=U=A=G=E$ poet! I'm into, like, syllabics and syntax and shit. I don't write about myself. You know why? Because I'm fucking boring! I'm an upper-middle-class half-Asian girl from the suburbs of Chicago. My parents are *doctors*! I went to *Dartmouth*! There is *nothing* interesting about *that*!"

"It's funny," I said. "I submitted a piece about food to get in. This essay about carnitas I wrote at the website. Identity content, they called it."

"That's what I mean!" Charlie yelled. "It's *clickbait*. And the people who play that game here? They fucking *suck!* They fucking suck and everyone fucking knows it, but nobody can fucking say it, because if you say it, you're saying their identity—not their writing, their *identity*—isn't fucking valid!"

She was loud. People turned to look at us.

"Charlie, you don't have to scream," Preetha said.

"I'm not *screaming*!" Charlie screamed. "And so what if they can hear me? They *should* hear me! It's fucking *true*!"

We fell silent. Charlie's rant had begun as a joke but along the way became serious. We didn't know how to respond. After a while Connie tried to restart the conversation: "Do you ever write about being Mexican, Sebas?"

"Of course he doesn't!" Charlie said. "Sebastián is my comrade in the struggle against the identity peddlers. He writes Borgesian shit about, like, Renaissance medicine. He's not trying to please the herd! Right, Sebastián?"

I took a sip from my whiskey. The truth was I'd begun an essay about Mexico City based on the notebook I'd kept when I went back to get my visa. I thought of lying but couldn't bring myself to do it. A moment passed, long enough for Charlie to realize what was going through my mind. Her shoulders sank. "Oh, no," she said quietly. "Et fucking tu, Brute?"

"I'm just trying it out? I mean, yeah, it's in the first person, but it's not, like, a *memoir*. It's about . . . capitalism? And colonialism! It's auto-ethnography, auto-theory, auto . . ."

Charlie scoffed. "You mean *autofiction*?" She finished her drink and stood up. "I need a refill. You can't possibly expect me to raw dog reality after this treason."

"Charlotte, honey," said Bijan. "You're a grown woman and can do whatever you want, but tomorrow you teach at eight and you've already had a few, so maybe . . ."

"Fuck off, Bijan!" said Charlie. She turned around and headed for the door and yelled: "I fucking *hate it* here!"

Aquí viene, en su palanquín, sobre un elefante

And then I received an email from a woman I'd known vaguely in college:

> *Hi Sebastián!*
> *You probably don't remember me, but we met in New Haven years ago. I'm writing because I just found out I was accepted by the doctoral musicology program at Iowa. I'm deciding between going there or returning to Yale, and I think it'd be good to get a sense of the place before I make up my mind. I'm visiting for a week later this month. I know this is a lot to ask, but I was wondering—could I crash with you?*
> *Best,*
> *Lee*

My first reaction was annoyance. My studio was tiny, and over the course of my time as a mole person, I'd become protective of it as a solitary refuge. Still, I didn't want to be rude, so I wrote back saying I was sorry, I just didn't have the space to host her, but would be happy to get coffee and talk about life in Iowa.

A few weeks later my phone reminded me I was supposed to meet Lee at Prairie Lights. I groaned—I was writing and didn't feel like talking to a prospective student. Still, I put on clothes and walked the block and a half between my house and the bookstore. I wasn't sure what she looked like, but as soon as I stepped into the coffee shop I saw a restless blonde sitting by the window, sipping ginger beer and reading. I wandered over and, without a word, sat across from her at her two-person table.

"Jesus!" she said when she looked up from the book and saw me.

She was pale and slight in a pre-Raphaelite way; she had gray-blue eyes surrounded by incipient crow's feet that gave her a world-wise air; and she had a long and narrow neck like some beautiful bird's. She was wearing what looked like a rather expensive vintage cardigan—the red wool faded into ocher over the decades—but underneath she wore a white men's oxford shirt, buttoned all the way to the top, that I immediately recognized as a budget item straight from the clearance rack at the Gap.

"Lee, right?"

She laughed loudly, almost unbecomingly, her chest shaking in spasms of delight. "Dude," she said, catching her breath. "That's so not okay!"

"I'm sorry."

"It's fine. It's just—there's a reason I don't watch horror movies!"

"What are you reading?"

She lifted the book to show me the cover: *The Glenn Gould Reader*. "I got here early, so I picked it up downstairs."

"And how is it?"

"All right! Gould's a charmer in his own prickly way. But he's also wrong about Mozart. Can you believe he recorded the piano sonatas just to prove they were bad?"

She laughed again. I felt silly for not having pulled out my inflatable mattress.

"So, you got into the musicology program?" I said. "Congratulations! It supposed to be very good, no?"

"Thank you! Yeah, it's a good program—not the best in the nation, but there's this one professor I'd love to work with. I just didn't want to accept without checking out the place first."

"Yeah, I did that. It was a mistake."

"So you don't like it here?"

"Not really."

"Why?"

"The town is too small. The winters are terrible. The food is bad. And the people—I mean, the poets are fun. And I'm sure the music school is great. But the folks in my program? They're philistines. Like—"

"God, are you always so insufferable?"

"Ouch."

"Don't worry, I'm just negging you."

"I just want to give you the real deal. So you can make an informed decision."

"But how can I be sure you don't think I'm a philistine and are telling me lies to keep me away? You wouldn't even let me crash with you!"

"I'm flattered you remembered me."

"I guess that means I should be offended you forgot me!"

Now I was the one laughing. I couldn't believe I was making such a bad impression. "So, you study music? Like an art historian of sorts?"

"I guess? I'm a bit of a dilettante. I play the piano, but I'm no pianist. I've done some conducting, but I'm no conductor. And I moonlight as a composer, but that's a secret, so don't go around blowing my cover!"

"A Jane-of-all-trades! And where are you living these days?"

"Colombia. Cartagena, on the Caribbean coast. Been there a couple of years."

"¿Y hablas español?"

"¡Claro, huevón! ¿A poco me tomas por una de esas gringas nefastas que se mudan a América Latina en busca de sol y hombres que sepan bailar y no se molestan por aprender el idioma? I forgot to tell you about my other dilettantish pursuit. I like to translate from Spanish. Mostly poems."

"That's so dope! I was always so confused by the fact that American literary kids don't seem to give a damn about translation."

"I know, right? That was what made me fall in love with Latin America. Turns out my niche hobby is your Super Bowl!"

We went on that way for some time, then we headed for dinner, then drinks, then a night-walk. The next morning, we had breakfast, then lunch, then dinner. Before I knew it, we'd spent her whole visit together. There was something early-modern about her—a brilliant energy that suggested a perpetual motion machine. Besides, she was fluent in Spanish. I found myself thinking that I'd never dated anyone who spoke my language, that our shared bilingualism meant there was something symmetrical about our conversations, something reciprocal, as if we were one another's double, or the negative of one another's film, or . . .

"¡Ay, pero que cursi!" she said, laughing at me, on her last night in the Middle West, the only one she spent in my apartment, as I delivered a version of that soliloquy. "Just don't start quoting from Aristophanes's speech, all right? En Cartagena yo tenía una pierna que se la pasaba explicándome las virtudes de la moderación. Que si el just mean y que si el error del exceso. And so, one day I got tired and asked why he was reciting *Aristotle for Dummies* to me. He was this kid from Medellín, lighter than most folks from Cartagena, so he turned bright red, but he was a slow learner, so he just started talking about Dionysus instead."

"Sounds like a charmer. Pero, ¿qué chingados quiere decir 'pierna'?"

"It's Chilean, actually. Picked it up from a one night stand. Short for 'peor es nada.' What you call the guy you text when it hasn't rained for months and the crops are failing and you have to think of the farmers. But if you're a girl, you say it only if you are trying to sound like you're not like all the other girls, which is something I try to avoid. It's funny, people tell me I compensate with my voice. Have you noticed how it gets lower in Spanish?"

"I'm too distracted by your caribeño accent. It's as if I sounded like an Australian rancher who spent his whole life in the outback."

She smiled and threw a pillow at me and headed to the bathroom.

"Admit it," she said as she brushed her teeth. "You were totally about to quote me some Plato." She spat out the toothpaste and caught my eye in the mirror, then went on. "Latin American literary boys are all the same."

I was about to reply but she took off her T-shirt and put on a clean one, and though she was still facing away from me, I caught a glimpse of the freckles on her shoulders, and all of a sudden I didn't have anything to say. Then she took her melatonin, informed me we weren't going to have sex, and climbed into bed next to me. I turned off the light and tried to sleep but lay awake all night. The next morning, as she packed her AeroPress coffeemaker into her mountaineering rucksack, I gave her an anthology of Mexican poetry with a dedication where I called her "my twin." Romance wasn't in the cards—so why not call her sister?

Hoja de ruta

"Have you given your thesis any thought?" Irina, the professor who led my workshop, asked during our end-of-term conference. "You don't have to submit a prospectus until next year, but better to start sooner rather than later. You mentioned something about nostalgia?"

"Yeah," I said. "That project is dead in the water."

Irina nodded. She'd been in the room when my classmates gently dissuaded me from writing about Nietzsche. "One of the most important things I learned as a student here was to ignore unhelpful comments. The workshop is not a focus group. You aren't trying to please everyone."

"I've just realized that the book I wanted to write would have been more at home in a PhD program . . ."

"That's possible, though I wonder whether you are idealizing doctoral studies. Your essays on nostalgia were quite literary. I'm not sure they would have flown in an academic department. But that's okay. Few people end up writing the thesis they had in mind when they applied. Do you have any other ideas?"

"Since everyone seems to want me to write about Mexico, I was thinking I could put together a collection of vignettes about the Mexico City elite and how they're all miserable. It'd be a mixture of history, sociological observation, autobiography, and political commentary. The idea would be to juxtapose themes and invite the reader to trace connections, like Ernst Bloch in *Traces* or Walter Benjamin in *One Way Street*. I even have a title: *Capital*."

"So long as the second volume isn't impossible to get through."

"Don't worry. I promise to put the critique of political economy in scene."

Manos y sueños

Lee and I started texting a few days after she left Iowa City to go back to Colombia. At first once a week. Then once a day. Then many times a day, at night, while out with friends, in class, on hikes, brushing our teeth, over books we forgot to read. Soon we were late to everything, wide eyed with sleeplessness, possessed by a peculiar graphomania, a compulsion to write to one another all the time, in every medium at our disposal: handwritten letters that took weeks to arrive, short emails in suspiciously polished prose, direct messages across Google Chat, Facebook, Twitter, and Instagram. Before long a web of words had grown between us: whole volumes' worth of writing, a small private library that soon became a private language.

Full disclosure, she wrote one night at four in the morning. *I'm starting to think we might have stumbled on something important. And I think I'd love the program at Iowa. At the same time . . .*

Three little dots bounced on the bottom of the app, where her next text would appear. Time stretched, slowed unbearably. I put down the phone. This was ridiculous. Romance via instant messaging was the stuff of high school, a long-gone rite from the dial-up era. I picked up the phone again but she still hadn't written, so I grabbed my cigarettes and crawled out of the window and onto the fire escape. It was the old, impractical kind—made of metal, painted black, rusty in spots, so narrow and precarious I couldn't imagine using it in an emergency—and yet I loved it, because it reminded me of Brooklyn.

Oh well, I thought as I leaned against the wall and lit a cigarette, suppressing a pang of nostalgia for New York. Wasn't in the cards. No point in lamentations. Be a good sport, old sport. Offer an off-ramp. Save face for you both. I picked up the phone from the windowsill and finished her sentence: *At the same time, Iowa sucks! You should go to Yale. It's almost certainly the better choice—and more importantly, it sounds like that's what you want, no?*

She tapped the little heart icon, indicating she liked the message, and I felt my noniconic heart sink. *Ay, huevón,* she wrote. *On the one hand, you're not wrong. I should go to Yale. It makes more sense, career-wise. And probably happiness-wise, too, judging from your horror stories. On the other hand? I was hoping you'd convince me . . .*

Fuck me, I thought. This is what I get for being reasonable, mature, not-insane. *I'd love to convince you,* I wrote. *But the idea of you taking me into consideration in such a big decision makes me nervous? What if you come here and discover I'm even more insufferable than you thought?*

I'm on the same page. I mean, I like you. A lot. But it does seem unwise to get involved if we're both going to have commitments in different cities.

A la verga, ¿sabes qué? Retiro lo dicho. Recanto. Me desdigo. Yale sucks. Iowa is amazing. Come live with me and be my love.

Right away, Chris Marlowe. Nothing makes me wet like pastoral rhymes.

It's a dope poem!

Is it?

And I will make thee beds of Roses / And a thousand fragrant posies, / A cap of flowers, and a kirtle / Embroidered all with leaves of Myrtle.

Yeah, that's what I mean . . .

I had given up all hope when, a few days before the end of the semester, Lee wrote to ask if I wanted to collaborate on a translation of a poem by Sor Juana that she wanted to set to music. On the appointed day I sat in my studio and opened the Google Doc where she'd pasted her first stab at the text.

Should I start making changes?

Yep.

Starting from the top?

Anywhere you like.

Nothing mortified me more as a reporter than watching my editor make changes to my copy in real time, but I was inclined to do anything she told me. Her compass hovered over mine for a moment. Then we were running down the page, rewriting phrases together, testing variants, trying out phonetic rather than semantic equivalences. By sunset we had a working version:

aggrieved by mortal wound
for love's offense I grieved
and worked the wound to widen
that night come quick
my soul in whole to loss devoted
sorrow to sorrow added and turned
and searched and found in life
death by thousandfold increased
but when my heart by blows
to sighs reduced gave sign
of last surrender
I by some prodigious fate
came back and asked
what lover higher pleasure knew?

I could do this all day, she wrote.
Me too. For more than a day.
    Actually, I was thinking—you know how you said you were planning to spend the summer in Mexico City? What if I joined you?

Part III
Mexico City

June 2017

In which Your Correspondent travels home for the summer in the company of his maybe-girlfriend, visits the sanctuary of the Virgin of Guadalupe with his mother, contemplates the history of Mexican Catholicism, learns quite a bit about eighteenth-century opera, hangs out with a neobaroque painter and a Bergsonian filmmaker, and experiences something like happiness.

Todas las flores

On the northeastern edge of Mexico City, a thousand feet above the highland and eight thousand over the sea, rises the Cerro del Tepeyac. Around the hill sits la Villa, a complex of churches dedicated to the Virgin of Guadalupe, the "Mother of all Mexicans." Each year millions of pilgrims climb the slope to ask for her intercession. Some want forgiveness, safe passage across the border, a blessing for a child, but most seek to be cured of an ailment of body or soul. Alcoholics and anorexics, diabetics and drug addicts, sufferers of dystrophia, leukemia, nostalgia—they all come for healing.

The streets around la Villa are lined with cheap eateries, budget motels, cluttered stores that sell rosaries, crucifixes, scapularies, effigies, prayer books, votive candles, and more flowers than would seem necessary to fulfill the needs of even a Third World megalopolis. The establishments range from tawdry boutiques to street stands consisting of a plastic stool and a few ten-gallon buckets. In the morning the buckets are filled with marigolds and calla lilies bundled by the dozen in cones of wet newsprint. By sundown the sidewalks are covered with a pungent layer of crushed petals.

On the day I accompanied my mother to la Villa, I walked up to a stand where I heard two women conversing in Nahuatl. They looked me up and down and one of them quoted me a price: for a bundle of marigolds, she wanted a fourth of the daily minimum wage in Mexico City—a tenth of the hourly minimum wage in New York. I handed her a bill. She rummaged in her apron pocket. I insisted she keep the change.

"Gracias, joven," she said.

"No, doña. Gracias a usted."

The woman smiled, amused by my formality. "¿Vienes a ver a la Virgencita?"

"Sí."

"¿Y qué le vas a pedir?"

"Que se mejore mi mamá. Está malita de cáncer."

The woman's expression turned serious. She handed me another bundle.

"Llévate dos," she said. "Y rézale mucho."

I tried to pay for the second bundle, but she refused my money.

"Igual te cobré de más," she said.

I walked back to the armored car, which Moisés had kept idling on a side street. I sat in the middle row, next to Lee, and turned around to face my mother and her best friend, Jana.

"She gave me two for one," I said as I handed them the flowers.

My mother took the bundle, brought it to her face, and smiled her chemotherapy smile, beatific and exhausted. I was glad to be of use to her. In the face of her disease, every pleasure was a victory.

Norteamericanos perdidos en Norteamérica

And so there we were, Lee and I, a few months after we'd reconnected in Iowa, together for the summer in Mexico City. I was nervous to go back home for so long, but the excitement of having time with her trumped my reservations. When she emerged from the arrivals terminal, carrying the same stupid rucksack she'd brought to the Middle West, my hands were sweating. Were we friends? Twins? Twins who had a weird crush on each other? It was all very confusing, but the confusion lasted less than a day. By the end of her first week in town, we could barely stop touching each other. We must have been extraordinarily annoying.

"And how long have you known her?" my mother asked as I helped her trim flowers in her kitchen.

"About three months."

"And she's a classmate?"

"No, she goes to school in New England."

"But she's your girlfriend?"

"Not exactly."

My mother set the scissors down. "So she came all the way here to spend the summer with you but she's not your novia?"

"Es mi pierna."

"¿Perdón?"

"It's a Pan-American thing."

My mother sighed and shook her head, less in disapproval than confusion. "Muy moderno el asunto," she said as she cut off the stem of a sunflower.

I gave her a kiss on the cheek and ran off to meet Lee at the apartment we'd rented. For the first few weeks we worked our way through the museums, occasionally heading to the Cineteca to see a film with Esteban. We'd even gone to Puebla with the Bear and his American girlfriend, Chloe. But now our days felt empty. One morning, as we walked down Avenida Álvaro Obregón, she suggested we find someone to translate for kicks.

"Un tipo raro, ¿entiendes?" she said. "Un espécimen que nadie se espere."

"How about Tablada?"

"Is he the guy with the knife?"

"Yes! Does he sound like a good project?"

"Oh, absolutely. He'll be a perfect third."

We set out to ransack the bookstores of Calle Donceles in search of José Juan Tablada, a fin de siècle vanguardist who, after spending his youth pacifying rebellions and singing the praises of General Díaz, traveled to Asia and came back to publish the first collection of haiku in any language other than Japanese, only to go to Paris, where he claimed to have invented the *calligramme* years before Apollinaire; and then return to the capital just in time to join the wrong side of the Revolution, a mistake that forced him to spend a decade of exile in New York; at the end of which he came back, yet again, to find that the revolutionary government had requisitioned his house and razed his garden, including the Japanese willow he'd bought as a seedling in Kyoto and lugged across the Pacific, and about which he wrote one of his most perfect poems:

Tierno saúz	Tender willow
casi oro, casi ambar	nearly gold, nearly amber
casi luz . . .	nearly light . . .

So far, though, we'd found only a handful of texts scattered across outdated anthologies. At the third bookstore we visited, Lee knelt before the shelf labeled Poetas Menores, Malditos, y/o Olvidados and ran a finger over the backs of the volumes, silently mouthing the names of the authors.

"Chico," she said, her voice dropping an octave to better round the wide vowels of Caribbean Spanish. "Esto es absolutamente fútil. Aquí no hay nada." She got up and dusted her jeans. "That said, they do have interesting stuff. Anarcocomunistas atacameños, protosurrealistas rioplatenses, una antología de lautremontianos suicidas y hasta dos que tres perroflautas neoinfrarealistas cismáticos. The deep cuts de la poesía marginal."

"But nothing by our guy?"

"Alas. Alas de cuervo."

I said I'd check the Mexican literature section and, if I had no luck, we'd call it a day. I walked deeper into the bookstore, which occupied the cavernous ground floor of a crumbling colonial palazzo but nonetheless felt claustrophobic. Rows of wooden bookshelves stood three or four feet apart, rocking whenever a brave soul leaned a ladder against them. The air smelled of damp grime. Near the windows, in the few corners where sunlight reached, I saw dancing clouds of disintegrated books. After a few false turns, I found the sign that read LITERATURA MEXICANA and confirmed Lee was right. Volume XCIII of the state-funded edition of the collected works of Octavio Paz stood next to a paperback titled *México en las profecías de Nostradamus*, which itself leaned on *Poetas religiosos del virreinato*, on top of which rested a scholarly monograph on the hydrology of the Valley of Anáhuac.

I was about to give up when I heard her calling me. "¡Joven Sebastián!" she said, poking fun at the formal diction of Mexican Spanish. "¡Muy estimado y muy talentoso y muy querido joven licenciado don Sebastián 'El Sin Apodo' Arteaga y Salazar!"

I walked toward her voice, making wrong turns in the labyrinth of bookshelves, until I found her, standing a half-foot taller than me, with her sunglasses perched above her head, and holding a thick hardcover over her shoulder like a brick.

"Why are you such a troll?"

"Troll? Me?"

She handed me the complete works of Tablada, the 173rd copy of an edition of two hundred the National University had put out in the fifties. "Guess who directed the project? An abbot! As in, a monk-daddy! I suppose it makes sense—our guy was a bit of a reactionary, wasn't he?"

We paid for the book and wandered around Calle Donceles until the sky turned ominous. We ducked into a coffee shop to avoid the rain and set to work on the poem. By the time the sun returned, we had a version that satisfied us:

GLANCE OF
YOUR FIRST PASSION
YOUR FIRST GLANCE I STILL FEEL IT LIKE A KNIFE IN THE HEART

"THE KNIFE"

J.J. TABLADA

When we walked out of the coffee shop, we found the rain had washed the pollution away. In the distance, at the end of the street, we could make out the snowcaps of the volcanoes.

"¡Mira, huevón!" Lee said. "¡La fucking región más transparente del aire!"

I turned to face her. It was true. Through her eyes the city looked different.

El señor barroco...

Too short to provoke terror and too thin to inspire tenderness, the Bear looks nothing like a bear. If anything, his bony frame and patchy beard suggest a malnourished cub in a Renaissance menagerie, or one of those tree-dwelling creatures whose air of permanent bewilderment suggests they, too, are baffled to have been placed in the same genus as grizzlies. He wears small, round glasses like Velázquez, a white Panama hat like Gauguin, and a felt cape like Toulouse-Lautrec; he carries himself with an elegance so anachronistic it begins to seem feminine; and yet the most eccentric aspect of his self-presentation is that none of it is affected. The Bear is earnest to the point of being incapable of irony but also self-reflexive enough to realize people see his idiosyncrasies as an insincere persona.

The result is that the Bear—perhaps the purest specimen of creole to be found in contemporary Mexico—goes through the world perpetually afraid that people will find him ridiculous and is constantly hurt by the discovery that they do. Consider the incident that led to the end of his undergraduate studies at the Art Institute of Chicago. During a critique at the end of his first semester, a teacher suggested he might want to try making something that wasn't a figurative canvas—an installation, perhaps, or maybe a conceptual piece. The Bear replied he was a painter, not a con-artist. The teacher said that the Bear was entitled to his opinions, even if they were reactionary, but that having a wide range of tools at his disposal, even if he didn't use all of them, would make him a better artist.

"Well," the Bear replied, "I own a gun and I know how to shoot, but that doesn't mean I'm going to kill my mother, right?"

What followed is a matter of contention among historians of art, but most sources agree that the argument escalated into a fistfight, which the Bear lost, which is not surprising, considering he looks nothing like a bear. My friend didn't help his case when at his disciplinary hearing he argued that the very fact the dean was worried he might shoot up the school underscored the importance of taking a stand against conceptualism—for what was Columbine if not the logical conclusion of the pernicious fetishism that animates contemporary performance art, that nihilistic ascription of magical powers to actions that, for all their artificial sacralization, occur outside any recognizable ritual context and are therefore devoid of meaning?

The incident cost the Bear not just his diploma and his student visa but also his inheritance. His father, a sadistic banker, was pleased to receive this confirmation from the academy that his son was a talentless dilettante. He wrote the Bear out of his will, refused to let him live in his house, and cut off his allowance, forcing him to sleep on friends' couches until he saved enough to rent a rooftop studio in a crumbling part of La Merced. After some years, the banker decided to allow his son to use the family summerhouse in the resort town of Valle de Bravo for one weekend every two months, a gesture that the Bear first considered a misguided attempt to mitigate the punishment but that he later came to see as a cruel joke.

"But the worst part," the Bear said to me once, "is when I tell people that I sacrificed everything for the baroque, and they laugh and pat me on the back. As if all of this were a goddamned performance piece!"

... y la dama barroca

> ... *that famous musician who delivered us from the plainsong of Lully, which we'd been chanting for more than a century, and who wrote so much unintelligible visionary stuff and apocalyptic truths about the theory of music, none of which ever made sense either to him or anyone else. He left us a certain number of operas where there is some harmony, scraps of song, some disconnected ideas, noise, flights, triumphal marches, lances, glories, murmurs, victories that leave one breathless, and dance tunes that will last forever.*

So went Denis Diderot's description of Jean-Philippe Rameau, the composer who'd captured Lee's attention for the better part of her two years in Cartagena. When she first described his opéra ballets—four or five hours long, divided into vignettes with little in the way of unified plot, disinterested in psychology, unafraid of the *deus ex machina*, "basically the eighteenth century's Marvel movies"—I worried I'd gotten more than I'd bargained for. But then she proceeded to inform me that she, too, found most of his work boring and had even fallen asleep during a performance of *Les Indes galantes*, the opera that later supplied most of the music for her and her ex-boyfriend's stage adaptation of *The Kingdom of This World*, Alejo Carpentier's magical-realist novel about the Haitian Revolution.

"Think of me as the editor he needed and never had," she once said of Rameau, Carpentier, or the ex-boyfriend, I forget which.

Even at the time, though, I wondered whether she didn't see herself as something more complicated, something forbidden and exhilarating: a ghostwriter, a restorer or renewer, a forger or plagiarist, an artist in her own right, liberated from the traps of the ego and the temptations of self-doubt by the irony of pretending she was nothing but an amanuensis, Gordon Lish disguised as an administrative assistant. In short: a translator.

Para Philip Larkin

I have a picture of my mother when she was my age. She has high cheekbones, a sharp and elegant nose, and a small mouth with thin lips that refuse to smile for the camera. She wears large glasses with thin frames, her curly hair long and studiously frazzled. She could pass for an Italian intellectual from the 1970s—except that, underneath her corduroy jacket, she wears a huipil.

My mother came of age at a time when a generation of creoles rediscovered their country's Indigenous heritage. Instead of pursuing law or business, as their parents wished, they enrolled in the Faculty of Social Sciences and the National School of Anthropology. Then, armed with structuralism and a basic command of Zapotec grammar, they set out for the sierra. They conducted interviews, recorded oral histories, wrote elegies for dying traditions. For all their critical theory, they remained untroubled by the ways in which their wealth and light skin complicated their interactions with the people who were both their subjects and their hosts. They lived in dirt-floored huts and ate boiled beans and tortillas, convinced that this mortification of the flesh brought them closer to the common people.

Years earlier, when I took the train from New York to Washington twice a month to visit her in the hospital, my mother told me about waking before dawn to help her host family harvest maize. She described huddling under coarse blankets when winter spread a wet shroud on the mountains. She told me about participating in rituals involving sacred psychoactive plants and Catholic liturgy mixed with the worship of goddesses whose skirts were made of serpents. But she also told me about watching children die of curable diseases and feeling the agonies of shame when her hosts served her portions twice as generous as theirs. Most painful to watch, she said, was the way men treated women. Girls as young as twelve were given in marriage to much older men. They bore child after child, sometimes giving birth in the milpa, carrying the newborns in their rebozos alongside their older siblings. They were, she said, no different from livestock: commodities to be bartered, capital to be exchanged.

When my mother returned to the capital, she decided to use her training not just to describe Indigenous societies but also to improve them. She joined an NGO and went back to the sierra with a backpack full of condoms and anatomical diagrams. I never asked her whether she saw the ways in which her work came uncomfortably close to the legacy of eugenicists who time and again have tried to deal with poverty not by redistributing wealth but by encouraging poor women to have fewer children. I didn't ask because I worried she was going to die—though perhaps I should have asked precisely for that reason.

Whether or not she considered such questions, my mother failed in her endeavor. After a few months of fruitless work, she returned to the capital, tired and disillusioned. By then the young criollos who used to stay up all night talking about the need to abandon gemeinschaft and return to gesellschaft were concerned with attaining the trappings of bourgeois respectability: a salary, a mortgage, a marriage. They wouldn't have used this term, but they were becoming neoliberals. In that atmosphere my mother's radicalism shriveled. She straightened her hair, started wearing makeup. She traded her huipiles for pretty dresses and high heels and parleyed her expertise in statistics into jobs at a political consulting firm and later at a bank. When she came home at night to a three-bedroom apartment too large for a single woman, she began to wonder whether Engels hadn't been wrong, whether the path to fulfillment didn't in fact run through the traditional family.

And then, at one of the countless weddings she attended that year, she sat next to a bespectacled lawyer who talked too fast and listened too little. She dismissed him as a pedantic bore: he insisted on debating the relative merits of Heidegger and Foucault while the rest of the guests danced.

"Half of the history in *Discipline and Punish* is made up," the lawyer said. "Not very disciplined, if you ask me!"

"Your guy was a straight-up Nazi!"

"And yours supported the ayatollah!"

"Who at the time was seen as an anti-colonial liberator!"

"I'll admit I always had a soft spot for the shah."

"So you're into Nazi philosophers and hand-me-down Romanovs? Got it."

When he offered her a ride at the end of the night, she turned him down with a laugh. But then he asked for her number and to her surprise she gave it to him.

The lawyer would later become my father. In those days he was a lowly bureaucrat tasked with hammering out minor details of the North American Free Trade Agreement. Despite his soporific job, he made veiled references to Nicaragua, implying he'd played a role in securing funding for the Sandinistas. He seemed to have read everything. Above all else, he was funny, if sometimes at his own expense. Before long they were engaged.

I like to think at the time of their wedding, my parents' relationship was one between equals. In their marriage portrait they seem elated: two youngish intellectuals from good families, urban professionals who left behind their radicalism for a quiet life together. They look so boring and yet so promising. There have been times when, looking at that picture, I've felt something like envy.

But there's a reason most comedies end with a wedding while most tragedies begin with one. My father turned out to be ambitious. Soon he was barely at home, climbing the ranks in the government. Left alone to care for her brood, my mother quit her job. Bored and restless, she poured her energy into our education. When my teacher suggested I might benefit from repeating the last year of preschool, my mother grew indignant. For months she sat with me each day, patiently walking me through the Montessori method until I was the best reader in the class. The problem was that she insisted I become equally excellent at math, fencing, the piano, and horseback riding—a set of skills fitter for an Austro-Hungarian dragoon than for a Mexican boy. Each time I failed to meet her expectations, she grew furious.

"No hay nada peor en el mundo," she'd say, "que el talento desperdiciado."

Contraneomemoria

Esteban's documentary was the product of years of work. Every few weeks, whenever they could get away from their jobs, he and a small crew traveled across Mexico, shooting footage of whatever they found. When they'd amassed enough material—two hundred hours of film—they divided each sequence into scenes three or five minutes long, then classified the fragments according to criteria that included narrative function (beginning, middle, end), theme (work, leisure, violence, the absurd), affect (lighthearted, anxious, humorous), and color palette (warm, cold, bright, dark). With the help of a software engineer, they wrote an algorithm that used the audience's answers to a multiple-choice questionnaire distributed in advance of each screening, to select a number of fragments from the archive and arrange them into a coherent ninety-minute narrative.

The result was a film that was never the same; each time Esteban showed it, *Drift* was different. What did not change was the will to change, the method for making meaning. The logic was alternation and parataxis: the jump cut, the primary device. You'd see the beginning of one sequence, then the start of another, then yet another, then a set-piece, then a long shot, then a still photograph, only to return to the continuation of the first sequence, then the second, then the third. The effect was disorienting—that was the point—and yet the film made sense. The contrast between strands illuminated hidden aspects of reality.

On the night Lee and I saw it, the film began with a panoramic shot of a barren field at sunset:

A wind scatters clouds of drought dust into the air. In the

center of the frame, we see a shack with mud walls and a tin roof. We get closer, then inside, and discover two men at work in the dark. Squatting over bare dirt, they grind and mix powders of different colors. We look at their hands: old leather, gnarled wood that sparkles silver. After some time one of the men grabs a hollow reed from a pile and begins pouring the compound dust into the shaft—and only then do we understand we're witnessing the making of fireworks.

And then, in an eyeblink, we are in a Tijuana dressing room bathed in red and tenuous light, interviewing an exotic dancer about her earnings; in a butchery, watching the disassembly of a cow; in the sunlit midst of a historical reenactment of Cinco de Mayo, holding back laughter as dozens of people dressed in nineteenth-century military uniforms try and fail to hold their poses for a tableau vivant; in Michoacán, facing three subsistence farmers who sit on plastic chairs and hold archaic rifles as if they were plows or brooms and explain their decision to organize a militia to defend their fields from the cartel; in a working-class cantina at closing time, the waiters dragging unconscious patrons into the dawning street; in the women's bathroom at the Faculty of Philosophy and Letters, where someone is writing a list of names on the wall.

We see a group of Wixárica perform a ceremony of drunken dance and song that culminates in the slaying of a goat, the bottle of firewater passing from hand to hand under the desert sky's merciless clarity, everyone dressed in white cotton and colorful ribbons, spinning, vomiting, drinking more, spinning again, the drums and the shakers keeping a rhythm that ebbs and flows according to a pattern we cannot decipher.

We see an old man with missing teeth, standing at the edge of a cliff, playing a detuned guitar with missing strings, and singing about a broken bridge. In the background, white like an elephant in the sun, rises the president's latest inauguration: a gleaming concrete bridge.

We see a field of marijuana and the torso, but not the face, of a man holding a Kalashnikov, who patiently explains the influence of moonlight on the psychotropic potency of *cannabis indica*.

A factory line where women on the far side of middle age put together cardboard boxes with astonishing speed while someone off frame reads a novel aloud.

A group of soldiers dozing in the back of a truck.

A young woman picking strawberries.

A street protest in Oaxaca.

A group of schoolgirls playing hopscotch.

A teenager sniffing paint thinner.

Two young men kissing in a park.

A cemetery covered in marigolds.

After an hour and a half, having revisited most of its characters and locations at least once, the movie returns to the field where it began. The men with silver hands have built an elaborate contraption from their powder-filled reeds: the thin-boned frame of a fantastical palace, the outline of a miniature cathedral. At nightfall children gather. One of the men lights a torch, walks to the structure, and releases the artificial stars.

There was a stunned silence—then applause. One of the festival organizers dragged Esteban onstage to answer the audience's questions. Someone asked about the algorithm, another about Dziga Vertov, a third about Guy Debord. Then an older woman took the microphone. "Forgive me, dear," she said. "I'm just a pensioner with too much time on her hands. I don't know anything about art films."

"Neither do I," Esteban said.

"I feel like I just watched five different movies thrown together in a blender! And I get that's on purpose. It's supposed to be confusing, right? But I can't help wondering—what would you say your film is about?"

Esteban stared at his shoes, nodding as he listened. Then he looked up and caught the woman's eye. "I'm going to try to give you a real answer," he said. "I'm not sure what the film is about. Not anymore. But when I first had the idea—" He turned to the festival organizer. "It's a long story. That okay?"

The festival organizer gave him a thumbs-up.

"All right. Don't say I didn't warn you."

The film, Esteban said, was about time. Synchronized watches and standardized timezones made us think it was homogenous and universal, but this was an illusion designed to facilitate capitalism. Before the railroad schedule and the hourly wage, people intuited that time wasn't the same everywhere and always, that we should speak of times in the plural. After the Industrial Revolution, however, this plurality of times was replaced by a master timeline: the time of the factory and the office, of the bureaucrat and the general, of the all-powerful state. And yet, even if we convinced ourselves that every minute of every hour in every part of the world was equivalent to every other, time nonetheless remained heterogeneous, multiple, less a river into which one couldn't step twice than a maelstrom without a center.

This was true everywhere, of course, but in Mexico the turbulence of temporality was especially apparent. Here it was obvious that time worked according to different laws, depending on the context: there were places where it moved slower or faster and people for whom it advanced in a straight line or looped back on itself. Wasn't it true that parts of the country still lived in the sixteenth century while others existed in the future? Didn't reality here sometimes feel like a continuous stream and others like a discontinuity of fragments? In Mexico, eras nested within eras, cycles contained cycles. Times clashed, crossed, interrupted one another. Some were wheels; others, arrows; others still, mirrors or telescopes. That was why history—all history, but especially Mexico's—was less a line of successive events than a fractal of chaotic echoes. The only way to tell it truthfully was to find a form that induced in the spectator something like chronological vertigo.

"Sure, dear," the old woman said. "But what is your film trying to say?"

"It's about Mexico. Next question."

The old woman dismissed him with a wave of her hand and began heading to her seat. "Your flick's a mess, kid."

"Like Mexico."

"No, dear. It's messy like an artsy movie. But sure. Tell yourself whatever you need to hear to keep going. Maybe one day you'll learn how to make a flick that someone would actually want to watch. Or, you know, some manners."

La obra es el epitafio de su concepción

As it often happens with artists forced to dedicate most of their energies to the production of merchandise, it's impossible to spend any amount of time in the Bear's orbit without hearing about some of his countless unrealized projects:

Guardia nocturna: *A full-size remake of Rembrandt's* Night Watch, *in which besuited Federal Police bodyguards replace the shooting company of Captain Banning Cocq.*

El chile barroco: *A parody of the overuse of national clichés in Mexican contemporary performance art, in which the Bear and an assistant—myself—conduct extensive research to identify the hottest chile grown in Mexico, purchase two such peppers at a traditional market, ingest them whole at the Zócalo, and then walk into the cathedral in the throes of capsaicin agony, the idea being that the physiological effects of the spice would compromise our ability to repress our Catholic upbringing, thus allowing us to experience the baroque not through the mediation of late-modern nihilism but as the colonial subjects that we secretly remain.*

<u>El burro por delante</u>: *A series of landscape watercolors produced while traveling from Mexico City to Veracruz on foot and with no companion save a donkey. Something was supposed to happen to the donkey at the end to the journey, but neither Esteban nor I remember what.*

<u>Perdóname padre</u>: *A large-scale canvas in which the Bear's grandfather sodomizes the Bear's father, who in turn sodomizes the Bear.*

Los salvajes

Lee opened the upright piano at my parents' house and played a major chord that came out sounding like Stockhausen. She sat down on the bench and played a second chord, then another, grimacing at the dissonances. "You need to get this bad boy tuned. The thirds are, like, howling fifths."

"That's too bad. I was looking forward to my private concert."

She smiled but didn't look up and kept playing tentative scales, her thin, long fingers almost freakish as they crawled through the octaves, searching for a well-tempered key. Little by little cacophony cohered, tonality emerging from the miasma of notes like a constellation from unfamiliar stars.

"Well, well, well," she said in a mock seductive tone. "Andas con suerte, joven Sebastián. C-sharp minor seems to be in good enough shape. And, through the magic of transposition, we can pretend G-sharp is D natural, which gives us . . ."

She lifted her hands but kept the pedal down, leaving the harmony unresolved, the last chord suspended in the air, and turned to look at me with a devilish grin, theatrical and almost devious, then snapped her fingers metronomically, counting a cut-time beat for an imaginary orchestra, and bent low over the keyboard to play a stylized march—two interlocking broken chords, one on the minor tonic, the other on the dominant seventh, followed by a descending run down the scale:

—at first almost inaudibly, her fingertips grazing the keys, then faster, louder, her torso swaying with the rise and fall of the melody, as if the music emerged from her whole body, as if playing the piano were a kind of dance, until all at once she was playing presto, fortissimo, staccato, the theme barely discernible beneath the mordants and appoggiaturas, the filigrees and thrills, ornamentation so excessive it was no longer embellishment but essence, content as well as form.

"¿Bacán, no?" she said after the final cadence.

"Chingón, diríamos aquí."

"Chimba, dirían allá."

"Is it Rameau?"

"Obviously."

"From the opera?"

"Yes. But not originally. It's a fun story."

"I'm all ears."

"So it's 1725, right? And JP is this small-time clavichordist who's written a well-regarded treatise on harmony but not much music of note. One day in November he goes to the Italian Theater in Paris, as he does, except this time the program is unusual. Turns out that, a few months earlier, these French colonizer dudes from the Compagnie des Indes encountered the Mitchigamea Nation while exploring the Great Lakes. And, like, the Frogs are worried that the Brits and the Spaniards are eating their lunch in North America, right? So, the explorers make friends with the chief, Agapit Chicagou, who'll later give his name to the city, and invite him and other Mitchigamea leaders to come to Paris, thinking the splendor of Versailles will convince them of allying themselves with France rather than Spain or the UK. So Chicagou and company sail to Europe, where they meet Louis XV, who at the time is, like, a fucking tween, then spend several weeks getting paraded up and down the salon circuit, where they take a liking to wine and macaroons and talk political philosophy with Voltaire wannabes. But they also get taken to the opera. And they fucking love it! The Compagnie des Indes dudes notice that and smell a chance to make a buck. 'Listen,' they say to the Mitchigamea. 'We've shown you our music and dance. Only fair you show us yours!' And so, on the day Rameau goes to the Italian Theater, Chicagou and company perform their dances of war and peace. And JP is blown away. When he gets home that night, he sits at the clavichord and writes the piece I just played."

"That's wild."

"Isn't it? The wildest part is that 'Les Sauvages' becomes JP's

'Smells Like Teen Spirit.' The year he publishes the sheet music, the French aristocracy goes through this weird Native American craze. Countesses start wearing feathered headdresses to masquerade balls, all to have the appropriate costume—LOL pun unintended—to dance the tune of the season. So, a few years later, when the original production of *Les Indes galantes* is a total flop, JP decides to tack on a whole new act at the end of the opera. The scenario is what you'd expect: Two Native kids are in love, but the girl is also being pursued by two European soldiers, a Frenchman and a Spaniard, and given that the motherfuckers have just conquered the place, it looks like she'll end up with one or the other foreigner. But then the colonizers realize that the love between the 'Indians' is as pure and uncorrupted as the forests of the New World, so they magnanimously allow the kids to get married. The climax is their wedding song—a duet for soprano and tenor based on the keyboard piece."

"Did you use it for the Carpentier adaptation?"

"Duh! It's the best part of the opera."

"I guess I'm wondering what you did with the racism . . ."

"That was the point." She began playing again, syncopating the rhythm, adding accents on the offbeats, turning the arpeggios into percussive chords, until the piece was no longer a march but a danzón. "Take a celebration of colonialism and flip it upside down. Inside out. Daniel wanted to make a ballet based on a novel about a slave revolt and asked me to suggest the music. So of course, it had to be *Les Sauvages*."

El pintor de la tarde

Though the Bear sometimes manages to sell one of his neobaroque canvases, most of his meager income comes from several scrupulously legal gigs which he nonetheless insists on referring to as "cons" or "rackets." Historically, these moneymaking schemes have included dog-walking, interior decoration, drawing lessons at the elegant homes of his mother's more compassionate friends, and art workshops at the sort of aspirational private school that peddles counterfeit class markers to newly wealthy parents.

But the most reliable and profitable of the Bear's rackets has always been that of "court painter"—i.e., commissioned portraitist to the younger generation of the Austro-Hungarian elite. My friend's canvases hang in the condos and penthouses of dozens of twenty-something bankers, architects, corporate lawyers, and full-time trust fund administrators. These clients seem to be attracted in equal part to the Bear's style (which in society portraits translates into paintings realistic enough to be seen as depictions of their owners yet weird enough to read as Serious Art) and to his prices (which are, as my father once tactlessly put it, "surprisingly cheap"). For the equivalent of four hundred American dollars, the Bear's high school classmates can purchase a painting in which an ever-so-slightly deformed version of themselves stares back with an anxious, unsmiling expression on a greenish, nauseated face.

These portraits prove surprisingly difficult to interpret. Are they remakes of the late-medieval *memento mori*? Political mirrors in which the rich may contemplate the thousand sordid images of which their souls are constituted? The snobbish insult with which an old family's disinherited scion expresses his resentment for parvenues and arrivistes? The more thoughtful among the Bear's patrons understand that this unnerving ambiguity is precisely what constitutes the artwork for which they've paid. Those who vaguely remember some of the names they learned during the six drunken months they spent in Florence defend their purchase to skeptical visitors by saying it is an "interesting" juxtaposition of the mannerisms of El Greco and John Singer Sargent. The rest, alas, are wont to complain the paintings are ugly and wonder whether the Bear paints the way he does simply because he lacks the skill to do otherwise.

It was with these last clients in mind that the Bear instituted a few nonnegotiable clauses for all portrait commissions: his full fee must be paid in advance; he retains buyback rights if the patron does not like the painting; and the sitter agrees not to see the canvas until it's finished.

"I made the mistake of letting Esteban take a peek," the Bear told me as he began the preliminary study of my portrait. "Ever since, the motherfucker hasn't shut up about how I made him look fat."

La reina de la noche

The video showed the soprano from below, from the perspective of the musicians in the orchestra pit. She was young, brown, and beautiful, and she had large fine eyes, a full mouth, and barely any makeup—a welcome rarity in opera. Her costume was a simple white tunic that suggested, with intentional ambiguity, both a Grecian isle and a sugarcane field. She paced amid lines of white linen hung to dry, nervously folding and unfolding an embroidered shawl, also white, all the while singing, half to herself, half to an old woman who unbeknownst to her was her master in disguise:

> ¿Se puede amar sin libertad?
> ¿Qué es el amor esclavo
> sino un sortilegio vano
> sin cuerpo ni realidad?

Eventually the old woman—a heavyset white tenor wearing a too-tight kimono and something that approached Kabuki makeup—joined the soprano in a contrapuntal duet, their voices crossing and turning around each other like two ballroom dancers or a pair of trapeze artists flying high without a net, in a controlled chaos that induced vertigo and made me gasp for breath. What was this impossible contradiction, this harmony in cacophony? The musical effect was intensified by the fact that the two voices were arguing opposite points. The tenor-disguised-as-an-old-woman sung an inverted version of the soprano's soliloquy:

Se debe amar sin libertad.
¿Qué es el esclavo sin amor
sino un suspiro de dolor
sin corazón ni voluntad?

The result was a dialectical fugue, a juxtaposition of binary contraries—soprano and tenor, man and woman, white and Black, master and slave—that negated and yet defined one another. It was philosophy and music and drama all at once, and it was magnificent.

Just when I thought it could not get any better, a dozen dancers emerged from behind the linen hung to dry: men and women, all of them shades of black and brown, all of them dressed in white cotton, all of them moving in intricate patterns that made me think of arabesques or vines in the columns of baroque churches, twisting and entangling their limbs with one another in impossibly contorted compositions, only to separate suddenly, as if a terrible force tore them apart, and throw themselves into the air, lifted and then dropped by an invisible wind that I immediately realized was the merciless wind at the end of the fifth canto, the harsh wind of heterosexual love in a patriarchal world, where no man or woman could look at each other eye to eye, where someone was always in charge, where those who served wondered if it were possible to love without freedom and those who ruled replied it was precisely the lack of freedom that necessitated love.

Toward the end of the number, as the duet dwindled into a reprise that was and was not the original theme, the camera panned down and to the left to show the musicians. I caught a glimpse of Lee in the center of the pit, facing the charangos and violas da gamba, conducting in the old style, from the keyboard of an upright piano that should have been a harpsichord, keeping the whole thing together with wide arpeggios and the clack of her flamenco shoes.

El llamado de la ley

And then my father fought with President Felipe Calderón and was sent away to be Mexico's ambassador to London. The move was supposed to be punishment, exile in a golden cage, but it had an unexpected effect on my family's life. Forced into withdrawal from the intoxicants of power, my father began to resemble his former self. After a few years of strolling together through Hyde Park on Saturday afternoons, my parents remembered that they liked each other. When I saw them during school breaks, they seemed happy.

But then, six years after they left Mexico City, when they were living in Washington on a different diplomatic appointment, my father came home with what he said was excellent news: he'd been nominated to fill a vacancy in the Mexican Supreme Court. My mother feigned elation, walked across the carpet, then burst into tears. He was confused. Why couldn't she share his happiness? My mother tried to explain she'd been miserable in Mexico. My father shook his head, said he had to make some calls, and locked himself in his study.

Shortly before his confirmation hearing, she was diagnosed

with cancer. Her doctors said there was a 95 percent chance she would die within five years and recommended she stay in Washington to receive treatment. Nevertheless, my father decided to continue with his confirmation process.

"Do you realize how much you are going to regret this?" I said to him one afternoon as he drove me to the Washington train station.

"I'll come every weekend," he replied. "And then, when she gets better, she can finish her treatment in Mexico."

When we got to the station, I shook his hand firmly and wished him luck at his hearing. Sixty thousand people had signed a petition for the government to rescind his nomination, arguing his role in the drug war disqualified him for the court; the Senate nonetheless confirmed him with an overwhelming majority. As my mother began chemotherapy, my father moved back to Mexico City and swore to uphold the Constitution.

She joined him in Mexico a year later, shortly after I started school in the Middle West, having beaten the statistics she'd studied so assiduously in university. For six months she wore herself out, setting up the new house, running from one reunion to another, attending boring luncheons with the spouses of the other justices. Then, just when she was beginning to feel at home again, she went to the hospital for a routine scan. Her cancer had returned.

Around that time my mother grew close to one of her nephews, a rock singer who put his affection for psychedelics to good use by leading groups of American tourists on peyote-gathering trips. One day he invited her to meet his teacher, a Wixàrica curandero who would heal outsiders for a small fee. He gave my mother a prescription: Go to the Tepeyac. Bring her flowers and an apple.

As it happens with sensitive and intelligent people who had the misfortune of attending Catholic school in the wealthier districts of western Mexico City, the Bear's self-conception alternates between megalomania and self-loathing. One day he seems convinced the studied neglect to which his peers subject him is proof of their limitations, the next he walks through life avoiding all glances as if he were some kind of metaphysical leper.

The causes of the Bear's hyperbolic judgments of his own worth are unique to his labyrinthine psyche, but I'm confident a significant portion of his neuroses can be traced to the long, unhappy years he spent at the Colegio Vista Hermosa. I didn't know the Bear at the time—we met when we were seventeen, after he transferred schools—but I have no difficulty picturing him in the institution's bright orange uniform. Everything about him must have been an affront to the vigorous, gregarious, unreflective masculinity that was supposed to be the governing ideal for bourgeois Mexican boys. He is physically small and emotionally large; he shows no interest in cars; he takes no pleasure in the humiliation of others. On top of everything—and this alone might have put him beyond the pale—he just can't get into soccer.

Such qualities would augur the Bear a difficult childhood in any number of places, but in Austria-Hungary they guaranteed him decades of misery. This is because the Mexican elite, usually so hypocritical, is more honest than the American ruling class in at least one respect: it feels no need to go through the motions of meritocracy and pretend, against all evidence, that the children of wealthy and powerful people grow up to become wealthy and powerful not because they are the children of their parents but because they are talented and hardworking. The Bear's classmates pummeled him and called him a faggot every bit as much as they would have at Eton or Andover, but my friend, unlike his equivalents in the First World, couldn't count on the traditional allies of nerdy kids.

In the first place, the Bear's parents—his father in particular— saw the world through an aristocratic ethos that understood quirks and idiosyncrasies not as the manifestation of an individual essence as frail and unique as a snowflake, but as concerning evidence that their son was incapable of performing the only task required of young men of his station who wished to remain in the class of their birth: to get along with their fellow oligarchs. Most of the Bear's teachers, for their part, came from the college-educated middle class and thus felt no desire to coddle the one kid among their students who referred to Schopenhauer as "Schopenbaby," because my friend's intellectual curiosity didn't alter the fact he was just as wealthy as those among his classmates who treated their instructors like servants.

And then there were the priests who ran the colegio. The Catholic Church implanted in the Bear the ingrown suspicion that people around him treated him awfully not because they were awful but because *he* was. The priests of El Contadero, committed to confirming their wealthy parishioners' delusions about their own moral perfection, had little use for the concept of original sin. This theological vacuum left my friend with the worry, impossible to dispel, that the awfulness that made him deserving of torment was not the product of some inherent human flaw but the fact that somewhere along the way the Bear must have done something so heinous that redemption seemed all but impossible.

The coup de grâce was the fact that redemption was in fact always possible, but only if the Bear repented for his transgressions. After years of introspection, however, the Bear remained unable to pinpoint what he'd done to deserve the torments to which everyone from his father to his so-called friends subjected him throughout his childhood, never mind ascertain whether he'd done it only once, whether he'd done it again and again over the years, or even whether he was doing it right then, in that very moment, as he painted a nude portrait of Chloe, his white American girlfriend, and listened as she explained, for the thousandth time, that the antique crucifix earrings he'd gotten her for her birthday were not only an anti-Semitic assault on her heritage but also another example of his alarming unwillingness to check his class privilege, because how was she—a "middle-class" Jewish girl, the daughter of a psychiatrist and a university provost, the granddaughter of people who escaped the Holocaust—supposed to understand the fact that the earrings were pure seventeenth-century silver, if not as a transparent indication that the gift was a symbolic purchase of her body?

El tema internacional

In theory Lee went to Colombia on a Fulbright Fellowship to study the musical structures of Afro-Caribbean dances. In practice, though, her research consisted for the most part of going out at night to dance cumbia.

"I never partied in college!" she said to me once on a walk around Chapultepec. "So, I had all these unused party-credits in the party-bank and decided to splurge. That's how I met Daniel. He was this tall, muscular guy—I'd been watching him dance and thought he was hot, but hot in that aggro way hot guys have of being hot, and that was enough of a turnoff that I wasn't going to try to catch his attention. But then he came up to me and took my hand without a word and started leading me. And at first I was, like, whoa, buddy, who the hell do you think you are? But the thing is, he was such a great dancer you just had to follow him. It was like swimming in the sea—the wave overtook you, and you had no choice but to let go."

They went to bed together that night, which Lee said wasn't special. In those early days in Cartagena, she brought home someone different almost every time she went out—only to wake up in the morning to find herself alone in bed. This baffled Lee: the urgency with which her one-night stands fled her apartment at the crack of dawn, as if they feared if they stayed longer, she'd try to trap them.

"Seriously, though," she said. "Why are you Latin American fuckbois always convinced you're so irresistible that any girl you bone will wind up falling in love with you? Like, jeez, I just thought you were hotter than your friend! But when I woke up after that first night with Daniel, he was still there. He wound up staying for the weekend, then for the week, then for a month. And, not gonna lie, that gave me pause. It was obvious I had more money than him—a fellowship in dollars goes a long way in Colombia. And that was awkward, I guess? But I was so in love with him. With the way he lived so comfortably in his body. How he was in control of every single tendon. And he didn't speak English, so I got to practice my Spanish. Plus, he knew all the good places to hear music and all the good nightclubs. Y, bueno, pues, Daniel es muy moreno—I'm not sure a blond gringa on her own would have been welcome in some of those spots. I figured it was all part of my research into Caribbean musical culture. And he knew it and he hated it, but I didn't know it at the time. I sure would find out, though."

Para Violeta Parra

And there I was, stuck in traffic in an armored car with my mother; her best friend, Jana; a bodyguard; and my maybe-girlfriend, about to participate in a ritual to which none of us had any right. We got out of the car and walked to la Villa. Along the way we saw crowds of pilgrims. Some carried large wooden crosses in penance for heavier sins. Others didn't walk but advanced on their knees, leaving rivulets of blood on the asphalt.

Our first stop was the new basilica: a hideous building erected in 1976 that resembled an airport terminal or the set of a science fiction movie. We stood in line to ride a mechanical walkway that ran in front of the altar, hoping to catch a glimpse of the miraculous image. I tried to induce in myself the shudder I'd once associated with the divine, but it was difficult to feel anything holy in a place so much like Penn Station.

We then headed to the old church: a baroque construction from the seventeenth century. My mother and Lee walked in, but I stayed outside with Jana. She took out a pack of cigarettes from her jacket, lit one, took a long drag, and exhaled through the nose. I was desperate to ask her for one but didn't dare. I'd quit when my mother was diagnosed. She didn't know I'd relapsed.

After some time, the others walked out of the church—my mother short and dark, Lee tall and pale. I got the sense they liked one another, but I never knew with my mother. At least this one spoke Spanish.

"Very well," my mother said in her too-formal English. "I am ready. Shall we head to the summit?"

I offered my mother my arm and she took it, and we began to climb the stairs to the sanctuary. I tried to go slow and support her weight, and at first we advanced at a reasonable pace, but after a few steps my mother paused and let go of my arm and walked to the edge of the stairs to sit down on a bench.

"Forgive me," she said. "I only need to catch my breath."

I nodded and waited with Lee and Jana for what was probably less than ninety seconds but nonetheless felt like an eternity. Then my mother got up from the bench and took my arm again and we climbed on, pausing to rest every few minutes, and as we got closer to the sanctuary, time itself seemed to slow to match the tentative rhythm of her steps, the intensity of her effort, and her evident mortality. Her difficulty took me by surprise. She was so adept at pretending to be well I forgot she was ill. The joke was it wasn't cancer that made her breathless, but the treatment. The paradox struck me as deeply Catholic, deeply Mexican. The path to love leads through suffering. The price of health is sickness. The meek shall inherit the earth.

Detrás de cada gran hombre

The show was Daniel's master's thesis in dance, which perhaps explained why his name was the only one printed on the promotional posters. The truth, however, was that Lee had put as much work into it as he had and that most of the major ideas for the performance, from the choice of Carpentier and Rameau to the decision to arrange the music for an ensemble that mixed baroque and Caribbean instruments, had emerged from the long conversations that punctuated their life of dancing and sex.

"I've spent nights and nights trying to untangle it in my head," Lee said to me once. "Whose idea was whose. It drove me crazy for a while—I really didn't know which parts of the show were mine and which were his. It didn't matter when we were together, but after we broke up . . . It's not that I wanted him to credit me—okay, that was part of it, fine—but more that I wanted to know, for my own sake, whether I could think of the opera as mine, too, as opposed to just his."

To me, at least, the question of who was responsible for what seemed settled from the first minute of the video of the show. *Les Indes galantes* was as much a ballet as it was an opera, and the same was true for Lee and Daniel's adaptation of *The Kingdom of This World*: the opera was hers, the ballet was his. But then, as the video progressed, I began to see what Lee meant. The dance was inseparable from the music and the words: take any element out and the whole thing fell apart. The show belonged to both and neither of them: it had emerged from the negative space between their minds and bodies, almost like a child.

"Wait, so he didn't give you credit?" I asked.

She sighed but didn't look at me and instead stared at the screen, where Daniel, playing Macandal the Sorcerer, lifted a young dancer off her feet, wrapping his arm around her waist like a vine on a tree.

"He thanked me in the acknowledgments of the written portion of his thesis," she said. "And he singled me out for special applause at the end of each performance. So I guess in a sense he did credit me? But I still felt like he hadn't? It's hard to explain. I used to think it was a weird combination of righteous indignation at what was clearly patriarchal nonsense and plain old ugly artistic jealousy. But for a while now I've concluded that yes, he should have given me a lot more credit. Especially considering how things ended."

Que elegancia la de Francia

Lee and I got out of the cab in a derelict corner of La Merced, not far from the witch-market, and walked up and down the deserted street under an overcast sky, past the steel rollers of the warehouses, looking for the address the Bear had given us, until we found a squat apartment building with bare cement walls painted red but sunbaked ocher. We rang the doorbell and then the Bear emerged, panama hat and all, a picaresque grin on his face.

"¡Ah caray!" he said as he looked us up and down. "¡Qué elegantes!"

He opened the door and showed us in with his arm. We followed him into a dark, damp courtyard, or rather a tall and narrow chute, water dripping down walls green with moss and black with mold, blind windows open to nothing but other windows, the patch of gray sky half blocked by white laundry hung to dry.

"This way," the Bear said, pointing to a steep spiral staircase half-hidden in a corner.

We climbed up, half-tripping in the dark, until we got to the rooftop, where he led us to the cinderblock shack that he called, a bit aspirationally, "his studio." He unlocked the door and we walked in to find a cramped room, unfurnished save for a mattress and a table with a hot plate. Piles of books, sketches, and canvases in various stages of completion leaned against the walls. The cement floor was covered in paint splatters and takeout containers. The air stank of turpentine and sweat.

"I usually boil my water to save a penny," the Bear said as he poured drams from an unmarked bottle into murky glasses that once held votive candles. "That bottled stuff? Might as well be Veuve. But I just ran out of propane, so I'm afraid I can only offer you mezcal." He pulled out the rusty folding chair from beneath the table. "And I'm further afraid," he went on, offering the seat to Lee, "that I only have one throne."

Lee sat down but didn't say thanks or even look at the Bear. That gave me pause, but I decided it was nothing.

"I know you came here hoping to purchase a fine Afghan rug," the Bear said. "But maybe I can cajole you into taking a look at my other wares? Some portraits, perhaps? I get the sense that they are—how to put it? Easier to like."

He rummaged through a pile of paintings, extracted a wood panel, and set it against the wall across from us. The picture depicted a young woman, naked from the waist up, against a gold background that called to mind a baroque altarpiece. The sitter had very pale skin, very short hair, and very sad eyes. She seemed to be looking at someone behind us with a paradoxical combination of numbness and terror.

"Wait," I said. "Is that who I think it is?"

"That's a relief," the Bear replied. "I know I'm always saying photography is a form of blindness, but I'm glad she's recognizable."

This was no portrait: this was biography. The way the woman's fingers pressed into the skin of her forearm, the thin band of darkness between her barely parted lips, the greenish-blue shades beneath her insomniac eyes—each detail was a chapter in the tale of María the Beautiful, María the Reckless, the Sorrowful, the Cruel, the Mad.

"I haven't seen her since high school," I said. "Is she better now?"

"I suppose you could say that," the Bear said. "Two weeks after our last session, she swam out into the ocean in Puerto Escondido and drowned herself. That's why I have the portrait. Never came to pick it up."

He was about to say something else when a high-pitched whistle pierced our eardrums.

"Finally!" the Bear said. "The propane guy!" He lifted the mattress from the floor and extracted a ziplock filled with bills. "I'll be right back," he went on, then ran out of the room.

I turned to Lee to ask what she thought of the painting—and discovered she was staring at the wall, clenching her jaw, obviously furious. I realized that she hadn't spoken a word since we arrived at the Bear's, and that I'd fucked up badly by failing to notice. "Is something wrong?" I said, though I already knew the answer.

"He's from one of the wealthiest families in Mexico."

"Okay, hold on—"

"He's from one of the wealthiest families in Mexico and he mocks me for trying to look like my parents aren't broke."

"But when did he—"

"You seriously don't know?"

"I'm sorry, I just—"

"¿Qué elegantes?"

"Oh, that?"

"It was the same at Yale. The rich kids didn't give a fuck if their clothes looked like shit. They were rich, so they could afford to look poor and still fit in at their rich-person school. But guess what, Sebastián? It's not that I love thrifting and vintage clothes. It's that my family has no money."

"He was paying us a compliment!"

"But why use that word? It's obviously ironic."

"I think the register in this particular context is more playful-hyperbolic than—"

"Not in the mood for translation theory, Sebastián."

"I'm sure the moment he finds out he'll offer you the most baroque apology imaginable."

"Oh God, please no. I'd die of awkwardness. It's not that big of a deal—I'm used to it. But real talk for a minute, joven Sebastián?"

"Always, güera Lee."

"Do you have any idea how long it's going to take me to pay off my credit card after I bought a plane ticket to come see you?"

El Indio Fernández dirigía con pistola

"So how did it go in LA?"

"They were speechless. Some cried. One of them even asked: 'Is this . . . cinema?'"

We were sitting in the backroom of el Mirador de Chapultepec, snacking on pork rinds and drinking mezcal in anticipation of one of those leisurely Mexican lunches that put American three-martini affairs to shame.

"They said we were shoo-ins for the Golden Palm," Esteban went on. "The Golden Bear. Maybe even one of those little statues of El Indio Fernández they hand out as party favors. They agreed to make the documentary available for screening in every global market and committed twenty mil for the sequel."

"So it flopped."

"Catastrophically."

"Wait, I'm lost," Lee said. "You went to California?"

"Last week," Esteban said. "For all of two days. Lovely place but not my jam. The light is weird. The fruit is huge but doesn't taste like anything. People have perfect skin. No way any of it is real."

"That checks," Lee said. "I grew up there and can confirm it's all a simulation. But I want to hear more about your Hollywood adventure!"

"There's not much else, I'm afraid. I went, I saw, I failed. All rather predictable. No way the gringos were going to buy a weird Mexican flick about how time is out of joint."

"Right. Because Americans are philistines. You boys never get tired of that bit."

"What are you talking about? Some of my best friends are Americans!"

I shot Esteban a pleading glance, then looked at Lee, who was laughing a bit too loudly. I reached over the table and took her hand. "But you know we're never talking about you, right? Because there's obviously exceptions—no, it's the other way around. Most Americans are good. The problem isn't Americans but America, not the people but the state, the impersonal, imperial machine that . . ."

I stopped. Lee was laughing louder than ever and now Esteban had joined her. "Don't be silly, joven Sebastián," she said. "Do you really think I'm that fragile?"

"Yeah, my boy," Esteban said. "It's just friendly banter among friendly citizens of friendly sister republics. Nobody would take it personally!"

"Exactly!" Lee said. "It's not like you boys would take offense if some California girl were to say that most Mexican men are neurotic machistas whose unresolved mommy issues compel them to be mean to the women they like, right?"

"Take offense?" Esteban said. "Never! Besides, the hypothetical gringa would be telling the truth. We very much like the lady in question. Or at least one of us does."

"Aw, Esteban, I like you too! Too bad I'm sleeping with your friend. But eyes on the prize, huevón. How did you wind up in LA? Doesn't seem very like you."

"It wasn't my idea. It was my guy's."

"Your guy?"

"My guy. My man in LA. A manager-agent type. This charming art bro who wears nice suits and is an absolute Hollywood shark, sniffing the water for blood money, but also a beautiful boy who loves film. Some months ago someone showed him a pilot I wrote, this narcos-and-NAFTA number about Nazario Moreno— remember him? That batshit drug lord from Michoacán. The one who was obsessed with the Crusades and all that. Anyway, it was magical-realist hackery. *The Wire* meets *One Hundred Years of Solitude*. *The Godfather* meets *Memories of Underdevelopment*. Pablo Escobar meets Tyler Durden, or the Unabomber, or maybe Jesus, or rather that guy who wrote *The Book of Mormon*—except they're all Mexican. I wrote it only because this producer I know said it was stupid neither of us was getting rich while all the streaming companies were sinking millions into cartel telenovelas."

"It's better than he's making it sound," I said. "The idea of telling the story of neoliberalism through the biography of the craziest narco Mexico ever produced always struck me as too good for TV."

"I'll grant the title was pretty good," Esteban said. "*Free Trade.* Your boo came up with it. He has a knack for titles. If he were smart, he'd market himself as a title doctor and make boatloads of money, but instead he insists on writing the stuff that goes below the title. Anyway, Art Bro liked the pilot well enough that he asked to see more of my work. I sent him a couple of scripts I had in the drawer, plus a few episodes of the stupid political sitcom I directed last year. Commercial crap. Mercenary merchandise. But right before I sent the email, I decided to also show him the kind of stuff I was actually interested in making. I ran the algorithm and sent him a brand-new cut of *Drift.* And, well, Art Bro loved it. Said it was an important work of art, the sort of thing people would still be talking about in thirty years. He even thought the streaming services might be interested. I was skeptical, but Art Bro was enthusiastic, so I agreed to fly to LA and show the thing to the executives."

"Who didn't like it," Lee said.

"Who didn't get it. Which was a disappointment, but not for the reasons you think. It had nothing to do with them being American."

"Don't try to bluff me, Esteban. I learned lie-detection juju back at Langley."

"I'm being serious for once. I never thought they'd offer us a deal. But Art Bro had given me hopes that they'd at least understand what I was trying to do. That they would be cynics who knowingly back mediocre shit because it makes money rather than idiots who think *The Sopranos* is our century's *Crime and Punishment.*"

The waiter walked over to our table and handed us oversize

menus. "What can I get you, dama y caballeros? ¿Róbalo a la sal? ¿Chamorrito para taquear? ¿El famoso tribilín de la casa?"

"Bring us escamoles, please," Esteban said. "And another round of mezcal."

"I'm fine, actually," Lee said, lifting her glass. "Still working on the second."

"The puritan ethos!" Esteban said after the waiter left. "Fascinating. Do you believe in predestination, Lee?"

"Busted! I grew up in the Bay Area, which is not quite New England, but my parents were strict Calvinists. My dad read me Jonathan Edwards's sermons as bedtime stories. It fucked me up—I can't even have three rounds of hard liquor before lunch on a Tuesday without worrying about my eternal soul."

"Wait—is that for real?"

"Obvio no, Esteban."

"I'm impressed. Takes a troll to troll a troll."

"Nothing like four years on scholarship at Yale to teach you self-defense. But you were about to regale us with hot Hollywood gossip."

"So I arrive in LA, right? And I meet Art Bro at some ridiculous tiki bar, where he explains he's leased a little theater to show the film to the streaming executives. Says they are intrigued, excited, pumped. Says he has a hunch this might be big. After a while we get to talking about Fritz Lang and wind up getting rum drunk on mai tais and going to some party at someone's mansion. The next morning I wake up on a park bench somewhere in Los Feliz with a horrible hangover. I look at my phone and realize the screening was supposed to start five minutes ago. I try to call an Uber—but there're no available drivers. So I reconnoiter the terrain for a cab or a bus or a random motorist whose vehicle I might requisition—but the street is deserted. So I look up how long it would take me to walk to the theater—and then I really start to panic, and not just because by the time I get there my Hollywood career will be over. The mai tais must have done a number on my gastrointestinal tract. I'm moments away from shitting myself."

"Delightful!" Lee said. "Nothing like a bit of scatology right before lunch to open the appetite."

"I'm sorry the appetizer you ordered against the advice of the cook isn't to your satisfaction, ma'am. But fine. Let's talk about something else."

"Era pura cábula, Esteban," Lee said. "Puro cheste."

"You mean chiste?"

"Right, yes. Chiste. Thank you. Please finish the story?"

"If you insist. After discovering my bowels are on the brink of a nuclear meltdown, I try to remain calm enough to think rationally. The most urgent crisis is clearly the intestinal one, so I look around for a store or a restaurant where I might use the toilet . . . And then I see it, bright green and ridiculous, abandoned in the middle of the sidewalk. A close relative of the tricycle. A toy for a child too young for a bike or a teenager too uncool for a skateboard. Only the dimmest tech luminary in Palo Alto could ever convince himself that it could serve as a mode of urban transportation. Un patín del diablo, pues. But what's the word in English?"

"Scooter?"

"Yes! With a lawnmower motor attached. I try to get it to work, only to discover I'm supposed to get a stupid app and pay a preposterous registration fee. So I just stand there, sweating in the sun, clenching my sphincter, waiting for a satellite to pass. At long last I manage to get a signal—and before I know it I'm rolling down the sidewalk as fast as the thing can go, which is about as fast as a sprinting six-year-old, dodging civilians, biting my lip to keep my bowels from exploding. By the time I get to the theater, the streaming people have been waiting for an hour, so they're straight up livid when I insist on stopping by the bathroom instead of starting the screening right away. I run into the first stall and slam the door and at last relieve myself. But the relief doesn't last long. Because, of course, I've clogged the toilet. And, of course, it won't stop flushing. I try to shut down the water pipe but can't figure out how. So I pretend it never happened and go back to the theater, run the algorithm on my laptop, and give a quick introduction. Then we show them the movie. They seem interested, but when it's over it becomes obvious they're at a loss. One of them clears his throat and thanks me for coming all the way from Mexico City. Says the film is 'super smart' and 'really deep.' But then he starts talking about the changes he'd like to see. And it's all downhill from there. Because apparently the fellow had a hard time following the jump cuts. And, sure, he doesn't care that he doesn't always know what's going on when he's watching Godard. But truth be told? He never managed to finish *Histoire(s) du Cinema*. At which point I cut him off and say I want to make sure I'm getting it right. They want the film to be less confusing, yes? Precisely, he says. We're in the business of popular entertainment, and confusion isn't entertaining. I was about to reply in rather impolite terms, but Art Bro caught wind, looked at his watch, thanked the streaming people for their time, and said we had to run to another meeting. The executives head out—and then, to my delight, we hear one of them yelling from the hallway: 'What the fuck? Do you have any fucking clue how much I paid for these fucking sneakers?'"

"Perfection!" Lee said, laughing again. "Lazarillo would be proud."

"What can I tell you?" Esteban went on. "If you can't beat the gringos, you can at least shit all over their Jordans."

A decade after the destruction of Tenochtitlan, when the process of colonization had entered its "spiritual" phase, the first archbishop of Mexico, Juan de Zumárraga, presided over the inquisitorial trial of an Indigenous man named Martín Ocelotl. The accusations were serious: Ocelotl, a "necromancer" who claimed to be one of the soothsayers Moctezuma summoned to his palace to interpret the portents that preceded the arrival of the Spaniards, had engaged in polygamy and heresy. He'd travel from town to town, dressed as a Catholic priest, and preach that two of Christ's apostles—whom he imagined as Mexica deities: half men, half jaguar—were soon to arrive in New Spain and deliver the Indigenous people from the grip of the Spaniards. Ocelotl, it goes without saying, was burned at the stake.

It was in this context of violence and syncretism that Nuestra Señora de Guadalupe appeared on December 9, 1531. According to a Nahuatl manuscript discovered a century later, the Virgin showed herself to a recent Indigenous convert named Juan Diego and commanded him to ask Zumárraga to build a church for her atop the Tepeyac. The archbishop agreed to see the Indio but dismissed his story. The notion of the Virgin Mary speaking Nahuatl was laughable; the project of building a church on a hill where pagans worshipped the mother goddess Tonantzin, borderline heretic.

Juan Diego went home dejected. But when he passed near the Tepeyac, the Virgin appeared again. She instructed him to climb to the summit, collect flowers, and bring them to Zumárraga. Juan Diego did as he was told and, since he didn't have a bag, carried the flowers in his cloak. The archbishop yelled at him never to come back, but Juan Diego unfurled his cloak and unleashed a torrent of red Castilian roses—a variety unknown in the New World. Imprinted on the coarse fabric was a likeness of the Virgin. The image was similar to traditional representations of Mary save for one detail: the mother of God had brown skin. The archbishop fell to his knees and ordered the construction of a chapel on the Tepeyac.

The hill became a beacon for Indigenous Christians, who flocked in droves to see the dark-skinned Virgen de Guadalupe. They called her Tonantzin: our mother whose skirt is made of serpents. To accommodate the growing number of pilgrims, the Church erected a second chapel and a larger temple at the base of the hill, designated by the Vatican as a basilica second in holiness only to Saint Peter's in Rome.

One problem here is that the image of the dark-skinned Virgin appears to have been based on the banner, made in the monastery of Guadalupe, that Cortés carried when he marched on Tenochtitlan:

Taxonomia de la fauna austro-húngara

Esteban had just finished relating the sad tale of the auteur and the art bro when the waiter came back with our food and drinks.

"This looks delicious!" Lee said. She spooned a dollop of escamoles onto a tortilla, sprinkled a bit of green salsa on top, and took a bite. "So buttery! Some kind of corn, I assume?"

"It's ant eggs," Esteban said.

Lee stopped chewing and brought a napkin to her mouth. "Right. Of course. Should have known. Too bad I'm a stupid gringa." She got up from the table. "One minute, please." She turned around and walked to the bathroom, breaking into a jog after a few steps.

I turned to Esteban. "You need to be nicer to her."

"I'm being perfectly pleasant."

"I get it. You hate Americans. But she's my partner."

"For reasons unknown."

"She's brilliant. And kind. And gorgeous."

"And a gringa."

"I didn't realize you were such a xenophobe."

"Let me rephrase. She's an anthropologist."

"So is my mother."

"Your mother knew not to fuck her subjects."

"So you can't be interested in other cultures if there's an erotic element to the thing? Because in that case I'm just as bad."

"Your interest in America is a life project. Her interest in Mexico is participant observation. It makes sense you can't see that. You're, like, neurochemically in love with her."

"Now you're just being cruel."

"I've just watched this kind of movie before. And I'm afraid the conventions of the genre are such that shit's unlikely to end well for you."

I was about to reply but Lee came back to the table. "My apologies, gentlemen," she said. "Insect protein is a work in progress for me."

Esteban cleared his throat. "Lee, querida," he said, still looking at me. "I'm starting to worry I might have offended you. Si ese es el caso, quisiera ofrecerte una discul—"

"¡Cómo crees, Esteban! Nothing wrong in reminding Americans that we're less sophisticated than we think. Especially because many in the US assume Mexico has no high culture. But it's not like the kids at Tisch are making algorithmic documentaries about the nature of time, right?"

"Flattery will get you far. But I'm afraid you've got it wrong. Mexicans are also philistines. At least the rich ones. You should meet our private school classmates."

"Yeah," I said, relieved to change the subject. "Our school was a den of fascists. The headmistress stood by the front gate every morning, assessing the capillary state of the students. If she determined your hair was too long, she pulled you aside, sat you down on a stool in her office, and tamed your hair with a fine-tooth comb until you looked like a Hitler Youth. And if you persisted in your ways, she personally gave you a haircut."

Lee made herself another ant-egg taco, looked at it with determination, exhaled deeply, and took a bite. "Catholic school," she said as she chewed. "Dodged a bullet there."

"Ah, but there's the rub," Esteban said. "It was supposed to be a secular institution. The founders were hippie-dippie liberals who wanted an 'educational community' inspired by Thomas More's *Utopia*. But they were soon dethroned by the most imbecilic kind of creoles—the sort that get a dispensation from the pope to marry their cousins. Soon they were offering the catechism as an extracurricular."

"But were the kids actually Catholic? Did they save themselves for marriage?"

"Yup," I said. "Everyone was super repressed. Freud would have had a field trip."

Esteban laughed. "Maybe *you* didn't fuck, Sebas. But the

popular kids sure did. They felt awful guilty about it, though. So you had to get wasted first. If you wanted to have sex or even get to third base, you had to make sure that the next morning both you and the girl in question were able to pretend not to remember what happened."

"Fantastic," Lee said. "I'm sure nobody ever got hurt."

"It was a mess," I said. "And, like, this is obviously nowhere near as bad as sexual violence, but what really bothers me is that they were also so *lame*. It was like they'd never once had a thought in their lives."

"In fairness our classmates were especially bad," Esteban said. "If you go to the south of the city, you can still find enlightened bourgeois who harbor intellectual ambitions, though they don't belong to quite the same class as the kids your boo and I went to school with. But the people who run things? They've been thoroughly lumpenized. I blame NAFTA. It made rich Mexicans want to become American—and not just any kind of American but the dumbest possible type: white suburbanites from Texas or Florida. The sort of people they met on their Easter trips to Disney World or the outlets in San Antonio. They failed, obviously—I'm thinking of the girls who'd wear Abercrombie & Fitch to school without realizing they were cosplaying the American middle class rather than their peers in the one percent. But along the way they lost their tradition. These people used to spend their fortunes building cathedrals. Now they buy time-shares in Las Vegas."

"But then where did you boys come from?" Lee said. "How did this drunken teenage wasteland populated by wealthy, rape-y Catholic illiterates decked in Abercrombie produce people like you two?"

"Well," Esteban said. "There're different categories of fancy Mexican."

"They overlap but remain distinct."

"Sort like the Neanderthal and the Cro-Magnon."

"There're fresas, who are rich, most often Catholic, and invariably clueless, but for the most part harmless. Except for their accents, which are known to cause aneurysms."

"There're mirreyes, who are thickskulled and ostentatious and possibly closeted and certainly dangerous."

"Pipopes, who come from Puebla, by which one means the provinces as a whole, and give themselves cosmopolitan airs by supporting Real Madrid."

"Juniors, who are the nepo babies of someone in the cabinet."

"Narcojuniors, who are the nepo babies of someone in Sinaloa."

"Igualados, who bought their own furniture."

"Progres, who are fresas who read *Open Veins of Latin America*."

"Whitexicans, who are fresas who wish they were American."

"And then, of course, there's the criollos, who are almost always fresas, occasionally pipopes, and every so often mirreyes, but never whitexicans."

"Whitexicans are criollos who've forgotten who they are."

"Criollos are whitexicans who can quote Quevedo."

"Mirreyes are criollos who didn't get the memo about the Revolution."

"Fresas are criollos who can't tell a Monet from a Manet."

"The progresía wish they were igualados."

"The narcojuniors wish they were juniors."

"The pipopes wish they were mirreyes."

"And the famous Austro-Hungarians?" Lee said.

"The Austro-Hungarians are an old-money species of the criollo genus who can tell you about how Grandpa fought against Juárez."

"And sometimes against Moctezuma."

"Kind of like the Mayflower people, except that instead of Puritans they were crypto Jews and crypto Muslims from Andalusia and Extremadura who came to the New World after the going got rough in Spain."

"Though some of them are Basque or Catalan."

"And a few are French."

"And a handful are actually Austrian."

"But rarely if ever Hungarian."

Lee laughed her loud, disarming laugh. "Okay, so let me see," she said. "You two and the Bear are criollos, specifically Austro-Hungarians, rather than igualados or pipopes. Sebas is also a junior, but not a narcojunior. None of you are mirreyes, though you all have mirrey-esque moments, and you would implode if someone mistook you for whitexicans. Is that more or less right?"

"Close enough."

"And your Abercrombie-wearing classmates would be whitexicans who wish they were American?"

"Pretty much," I said. "That's a big part of why I left."

Esteban laughed and finished his mezcal.

"What's so funny?"

"Where did you go when you left?"

"Oh, come on! It's not the same."

"Maybe. But you, too, wish you were American. It's the most creole aspect of your personality. Had you been born in the seventeenth century, you would have wanted to be Spanish. A few decades ago you would have died to be French. But you were born in the nineties, so your innermost desire is to become a gringo. A New York intellectual rather than a Texan barbarian, sure, but a gringo nonetheless. Nothing to be ashamed of. Just don't go around pretending you're any less colonized than our beloved classmates."

Para Roberto González Echevarría

As the summer was ending, I wrote an email to my teacher:

Dear Irina,

I hope that you are doing well and that the break has proven restful. I'm writing today because I've been considering a change in the direction of my thesis. I still want to write about Mexico, but it occurs to me that rather than focus on capital in the capital, I should center the project around an exploration of the baroque both as a style in art and an ethos in life. I've come to see "baroqueness" as a central aspect of Mexican and Latin American culture—one that sets it apart from the "realist" worldview I associate with the United States.

So what is the baroque? It's a way of looking at the world in which interpretation is primary, in which there's no representation that isn't already interpreting what it represents. Realism seeks to portray the world as it appears; the baroque, to imbue it with as much meaning as possible. This is why it loves excess and proliferation, why it prefers hybridity to purity. Where realist art proceeds by subtraction, removing everything extraneous until only the diamond core remains, the baroque advances by addition and multiplication. New York, the ultimate realist city, is on a rectilinear grid; Mexico City, by contrast, is amorphous, irregular, even monstrous. Realism is metaphorical, singleminded, diachronic; the baroque, allegorical, digressive, synchronous. Realism is a sonata; the baroque, a fugue—or an opéra ballet.

I want to explore this distinction in several ways. First, I want to profile the life and work of three artists—the Bear,

a painter; Esteban, a filmmaker; and Lee, a composer-con-
ductor—who have little in common save that they are baroque
and my friends. Second, I want to think about the Virgin of
Guadalupe, the central symbol of Mexican Catholicism and
a prime example of baroque hybridity. Third, I plan to write
about my friends' favorite cantina, El Centenario, a place that
seems to embody the "popular" side of contemporary Mexican
baroque. In terms of form, I think the short vignettes in the
style of the German modernists can still work—it's not a
coincidence that Benjamin wrote his doctoral dissertation on
baroque mourning plays. As for the title, I'm not yet convinced,
but maybe it could be called "The Great Theater of the World,"
after the Calderón drama.

What do you think? Does this sound halfway interesting?
No need to write back right away—you should enjoy your
summer! I just wanted to put this in writing, lest the idea
run away from me. Thanks again for everything, Irina. See
you in the fall!

Best,
Sebastián

Y tú te vas, jugando a enamorar . . .

"All right, folks, that's it, thanks for coming, you don't have to go home but you can't stay here," Lee said. She paused the video on her laptop several minutes before the end, just as the dancers and singers came onto the stage to take a bow.

"Wait—I want to see them clap for you!"

"Well, as the poet said, you can't always get what you want."

"Come on! Let me bask in your glory!"

"Not gonna happen."

"What I mean to say is that it's amazing, Lee."

"Stop before I spontaneously combust."

"I'm serious. You made something extraordinary."

"Your credibility diminishes with each additional compliment. But thank you. It meant a lot to me at one point, and it was good to share it with you."

"So there's no way I can convince you to let me watch you take a bow?"

"If you really want to? It's just that fucking Daniel did something really shitty when I went on stage, and I'd rather not look at it again."

"Is it stupid I want to punch him?"

"It is stupid. Worse, it's man-stupid. But I kind of like it. He'd beat the shit out of you, but that's what makes it charming."

"Hey, there is heroism in defeat! And glory!"

"Forget it. I changed my mind. It is stupid you want to punch him."

"What did he do?"

"It's embarrassing."

"It's hard to embarrass yourself in front of someone who likes you as much as I do."

"Ever the charmer, huh?"

"I'll be here all week."

"Promise not to judge? Because it really is dumb. So, he calls me to the stage, right? And I climb out of the pit, shaking and sweating from two hours of conducting, and he gives me a big kiss on the lips in front of everyone and—"

"That isn't embarrassing at all!"

"Yeah, but that's not it. Can a girl finish a story for once? So he kisses me, right? And I turn around to face the audience and take my bow. And while that's going on he's standing behind me, next to the principal ballerina, this friend of his from the conservatory. And at the time I had no idea it was happening, and I only learned about it when I watched the video for the millionth time—but he reached out to hold her hand."

She fell silent. I waited, then realized nothing else was coming.

"That's fucked up," I said, a beat too late.

"See, this is why I didn't want to tell you."

"No, I'm sorry, I just—"

"It's such a tiny fucking thing. It upsets me that it upsets me."

"We don't get to control what affects us, though . . ."

"Since we are in full-disclosure mode, I might as well tell you he cheated on me. With her. For months. While we were all working on the thing together."

La novena maravilla

When we made it to the top of the cerro, I was disappointed to find a chapel no larger than a classroom. The carvings on the frontispiece were crude. The frescoes were uninspiring. The candles were not even candles but small electric lights. This was not some grand baroque cathedral, no triumph of art and science. A shrine, I thought, full of skeptical spite.

My mother let go of my arm and walked into the church. I began to follow her, but Jana stopped me.

"I think she needs a minute," she said.

My mother marched to the altar and looked around to make sure no priests witnessed her heretical act. She discreetly placed an apple at the feet of the Virgin and took a seat on the front pew.

I turned around and walked away from the church, toward the edge of the cliff. I leaned on the handrail and looked out on the valley. It had rained two days before but by then the citizens of the capital had again managed to saturate the atmosphere with ozone and heavy metals. The volcanoes were barely visible on the horizon. For a moment I wondered whether I could see them only because I knew where to look, whether I was seeing the mountains or remembering them.

Then I felt a hand on my shoulder. It was Lee's. I turned to face her, and there, in the distance, panting from the climb, sweating through his suit, surrounded by his bodyguards, hurrying up the last few steps, I saw my father, all of two hours late.

Suelta

"Is this a good idea?"

"Why wouldn't it be?"

"There's a metal detector at the door!"

It was Friday night at the height of the storms and the heat—the handful of weeks when the city felt tropical, almost Caribbean, the prudish reserve of the highland briefly replaced by the shamelessness of Mérida, or perhaps Havana, or even Cartagena—and the Bear, Chloe, Lee, and I were standing outside Salón San Luis, an old-school cumbia club in La Roma.

"There's a live band," the Bear had said earlier that evening, when we were sitting in my and Lee's apartment, trying to decide what to do with the night. "And disco lights. And waiters who try to scam you. And sinister-looking fellows in sharkskin suits. And aging ladies of the night. It's classical, canonical, colossal—a temple of tropicália!"

"Sold!" Lee said. She got up from the couch. "Just let me change real quick."

"Wait," Chloe said. "Are we dressing up?"

The two disappeared into the bedroom. I turned to the Bear. "You know I hate dancing, right?"

"Is that because you can't dance?"

"It's a chicken-or-the-egg thing."

"It's the decadence of the creoles, that's what it is. Or are you going to tell me don Luciano Fernando didn't know how to lead a lady?"

"Sorry, Herr Grünewald, but I'm not sure I follow—what does the Mexican-American War have to do with . . ."

"How do you think he got the gringos to spare the silver mines? By dancing with their wives!"

I was about to reply but then the girls returned—and the sight of Lee shut me up. She'd put on eyeliner and had her hair up, and she was wearing a black dress that grasped her midriff and reached halfway down her thighs. She saw me looking at her and smiled and turned just enough for me to see the dress was backless.

"I'll call a cab," I said.

When we got to the club, though, I was forced to confront the fact that the Bear had brought us to a mob joint.

"So what if they have a metal detector? It means they take security seriously."

"It means that people try to sneak in guns!"

The Bear turned to the bouncer. "Discúlpelo, maestro. El señorito se largó al gabacho de chamaco y regresó todavía más fresa de lo que se fue."

"Me vale verga si se fue al gabacho o a Francia o a chingar a su madre," the bouncer said. "Are you coming in or not?"

Lee stepped forward without a word, opened her handbag for the bouncer, paid the cover, walked through the metal detector, and turned around to look at me—and before I knew it, I had followed her and she had taken my hand and she was guiding me down a long, dark hallway, a soft red glow filtering through the door at the end, the blare of the music growing louder, first the kick drum, then the bongos, the congas, the claves, the brass, and finally the female singer's luscious voice—and then Lee pushed through the door and all at once we were in an echoing hall bathed in multicolored light, the band in matching sequined suits playing on a raised stage over the dance floor where dozens of couples swung and swayed and turned and twirled in one another's arms, exuding sweat and pheromones.

We wandered around past tables where men with undone neckties and the air of union bosses or agents of the Ministerio Público drank whiskey sodas and teased one another, until a waiter waved us down. "If you want a table," he yelled over the band, "you gotta get bottle service."

"I forgot this is a den of thieves," the Bear said. "Tráiganos bacacho blanco. Y cocas de lata. Y hielo. Y un chingo de limones."

"¿Y de botana? If you get a bottle, you gotta get food."

"Is there a surcharge for the air too?"

"There's guacamole, pickled eggs, pickled pig's feet . . ."

"Nothing pickled, for the love of God," the Bear said. "Guacamole is fine."

The waiter shuffled away just as the song was ending. The people on the dance floor clapped, took bows, kissed one another on the cheek or the hand or the mouth, scoured the room for a new partner. There were twenty-something couples who'd clearly taken lessons, middle-aged men in bureaucratic shirt-sleeves, grand dames in vertiginous heels, shop girls in short skirts, graying gentlemen wearing ostentatious watches, retirees reliving the seventies, hipsters cosplaying the thirties, thin-limbed bank tellers on Tinder dates, busty schoolteachers letting loose for summer break, lawyers, nurses, clerks, butchers and butches, femmes and twinks, hairdressers, seamstresses, waiters, line cooks, drunks, cops, crooks, cranks—the citizens of that other, secret city that hid beneath the melancholy capital and emerged only at night, looking for trouble and pleasure.

The waiter came back with our rum and a plate of depressing

guacamole. The Bear poured everyone his version of the Cuba libre: a highball's worth of liquor topped with the juice of three limes and a dash of coke.

"Are the girls over there working?" said Chloe, nodding toward a table where six or seven older women in rococo makeup disregarded the no-smoking signs.

"Yup. Ficheras. They dance for tips."

"Just dance?"

"It's a beer-in-a-paper-bag thing. And a dying trade. In a few years these ladies will join the typewriter repairman and the humble painter in going the way of the dodo."

The ficheras must have noticed us staring, because one of them put out her cigarette, got up from the table, and walked toward us.

"Shit," Chloe said. "We pissed her off."

"Chloe, flaquita, te prometo que estas señoras están más que acostumbradas a que la gente se les quede viendo. They're tough as hell."

"That's what worries me!"

"You're right, she's about to slice our throats with her nail extensions."

The fichera got to our table and sat down on a free chair, a cloud of perfume trailing after her. "Hey, handsome," she said to the Bear. "Saw you looking. Wanna go for a spin?" Before he could reply, she took him by the hand and led him to the dance floor.

"Did she just steal my boyfriend?" Chloe said.

"Right under your nose," Lee said.

Then the singer tapped the microphone, sending feedback through the speakers. "Evening, beautiful people!" she said. "I'm Paloma Contreras, and the snazzy fellows behind me are La Sonora Sacabuche. Let's hear it for the boys!"

The crowd cheered and whistled and applauded.

"That's right!" the singer went on. "La Sonora Sacabuche son amantes de las musas como los de antes, no como los de ahora, que todo lo hacen con autotune. And to thank you for your discerning patronage, they've prepared a special instrumental number for tonight. Beautiful people, I give you La Sonora Sacabuche's take on Juan Sebastián Bach's *Little Fugue in G minor*, arranged for cumbia ensemble by the famed teenage maestro, the legendary wunderkind, Sinaloa's very own Mozart, Alansito Espinosa, here on the synths!"

"No way!" Lee said. "This can't be happening—"

Before she could finish her sentence, the guiro counted in the beat and the accordionist stepped forward to play the subject of the fugue.

"That's it," she went on. "You're coming with me." She took my hand and lifted me to my feet.

"Your Honor, I have a bone spur," I said, half-heartedly resisting.

"Sebas, they're playing baroque cumbia!"

"And the last guy was a ballet dancer!"

"¡Pobrecito! ¿Te caíste del columpio y te raspaste la masculinidad?"

By then we were in the middle of the dance floor, the couples swerving to avoid us as the different voices chased after one another, the stately organ piece translated to the language of the dance hall.

"Are we starting ex nihilo?"

"I'm afraid so."

"How the hell did that happen? You grew up in Latin America!"

"That's why I left. To avoid dancing."

"It's all about feeling the rhythm. You count the first three beats, then pause on the fourth. Un, left foot back; dos, right foot across; tres, left foot across—*and*—cinco, right foot . . ."

"Is that a Zen koan?"

"Maybe it'll be easier if we do it together." She took my hand and put it on her waist. "Don't look at your feet. Look at me."

I raised my eyes and saw her smile with mischief and found that I could no longer resist, that I had no choice but to draw her close, until there was nothing between us but the cotton of her dress and the fabric of my suit.

"Can you feel it?" she whispered.

I nodded.

"Then let go. Suelta."

Efectos secundarios

One afternoon in early August, my mother asked me to accompany her to chemotherapy. I replied I'd be delighted, which was the wrong note.

"Should Lee join us?" I said.

My mother's face tensed into an imperceptible frown—one of her eloquent ambassadorial gestures, subtle enough for diplomatic denial and yet unambiguous enough for back-channel negotiations. "I don't know, Sebastián. Nobody looks good in that chair."

"You look great everywhere, Mamá."

"Don't get me wrong—she's a delight. But as you know I've always been a bit private when it comes to this sort of thing."

I smiled, but I was secretly annoyed. She had every right to decide how she wanted to deal with her illness, and that included who got to be around when she was vulnerable. But I remembered the deep bond she'd formed with the Shakespearean during her first round of treatment, when the actress and I took the train from New York together every month to spend a few days with her at the house in Washington or at the hospital in Baltimore, how sometimes she'd asked her to come to medical appointments to which I wasn't invited, how she'd cultivated a strange sort of intimacy with her, as if they were both members of some secret society, a Great Order of Womanhood whose members shared a feminine familiarity so private that it could be expressed in the presence of men only through a silent language of significant glances. Her refusal to allow Lee to participate in her care, even in the smallest of ways, meant that she had decided to keep her out, to exclude her from the sorority of the heart. She would never say so, of course, and she would always treat her with warmth and kindness, but she'd made it clear that she would prefer it if another woman bore her grandchildren. It was subtle, even elegant, but it was also rude.

I texted Lee to let her know she couldn't come, then went downstairs to pack a lunch that my mother almost certainly wouldn't touch: an apple thinly sliced, a thermos of white tea, a slice of pumpernickel smeared with avocado and sprinkled with black sesame, a smoothie made with oat milk and bananas and enriched with peanut butter, protein supplements, and the instant chocolate-drink powder she'd loved as a child, as well as napkins and a bamboo fork and spoon that, unlike the metal kind, wouldn't react with the drugs and sting her mouth.

I picked up the insulated lunch box and returned to her bedroom, where she was folding a thick blanket into a tote bag containing a large water bottle, a bar of Toblerone, a powerbank, a phone charger, a tin of high-CBD weed gummies a friend of my sister's had smuggled from San Francisco, and heavily annotated copies of Stefan Zweig's *The World of Yesterday* and Sándor Márai's *Portraits of a Marriage*.

"Well," she sighed, looking at her loadout on the bed. "I suppose I'm ready?"

"Ready for battle!"

"What did we say about military metaphors, Sebastián? Haven't you read your Sontag? Surely it must be on the syllabus for your master's program."

I laughed and offered her my arm. She took it and we went down the regal spiral staircase while she held on to me with one hand and the railing with the other. We walked out of the house, got into the armored SUV waiting outside, and asked the bodyguards to drive us to the American-British Hospital—a private institution where the cost of a night's stay far exceeded the average monthly wage. All through the drive we talked about the books she was reading. She was in a Mitteleuropean phase, she explained, and had already worked her way through all of Joseph Roth's fiction and most of Freud's case histories.

"They read like novels!" she said. "Domestic drama of the highest quality. Jane Austen could never. So far *Dora* is my favorite. The family dynamics feel so familiar, even though he's writing about a very different culture."

"I always thought our people were more Austro-Hungarian than Mexican."

She laughed at my joke, which triggered a long fit of a loud, dry cough that scared the life out of me and made me think of Settembrini and Naphta.

"Who's next?" I asked when the attack subsided, trying to keep my worry and the guilt I felt for having caused the fit from showing in my voice.

"Rilke's *Malte*," she said. "And Musil. Though I'm a bit apprehensive about that one. It's been a minute since I sat down with a proper modernist epic rather than with frivolous feuilleton stuff."

"I'm not sure I'd call Freud frivolous."

"Oh, but I'm reading him in such a frivolous way! I'm not interested in clinical technique or the structure of the mind. I'm just here for the gossip."

We arrived at the hospital and got out of the SUV at the reception bay, which looked less like the entrance to a sanatorium than the gate to a luxury hotel. We stepped into the lobby—a large, well-lit space with vast windows and tall ceilings, decorated in a tasteful, subdued style, featuring elegant yet functional furniture in muted earth tones, that made me think of the world's largest first-class airport lounge.

Guided by the instinctive muscle memory known only to people who repeat the same process countless times, my mother walked straight to a little machine not unlike the Global Entry kiosks at US immigration checkpoints and scanned the barcode on the patient ID that hung from the lanyard around her neck. The machine pulled up her profile, which included her name, address, picture, diagnosis, and allergies, as well as a list of her past and future appointments, the medications she was taking, the names of the doctors responsible for the various aspects of her treatment, and the outstanding balance on her account. It then printed out a small piece of paper, the size and texture of a credit card receipt, with her schedule for the day: chemotherapy at twelve-thirty in the infusion lounge on the fifth floor, then additional blood work in the lab in the basement, then a thirty-minute conference with her oncologist at his office in the top floor, and finally a fifteen-minute meeting with her pain-medicine specialist on the second floor.

We got on the elevator. "They want to switch me to fentanyl patches," she said.

"OxyContin doesn't work anymore?"

"It works fine. But they think I'm being stoic. Pretending to be in less pain."

"That does sound like you."

"Maybe, but it also raises a philosophical question. How did they gain access to my inner life? What happened to the opacity of the subject? Surely I know more about my sensations than they do! Besides, complaining all the time is a bit undignified, don't you think?"

"Mamá, you have cancer. You're allowed to complain."

"The women in the sierra also got cancer. But they didn't get fentanyl. Not even morphine. Just medicinal herbs. And they didn't complain."

The elevator door opened, and we walked into the infusion lounge: a room the size of a restaurant, filled with orchids, and divided into semiprivate booths outfitted with a large reclining chair upholstered in pale-green fabric, a foldable table, and a handful of smaller seats for the patient's guests. It looked like a spa, save that the green chairs were surrounded by IVs and heart monitors, and that the folks sitting in them didn't exactly have the air of people taking a day off to get a facial and a massage.

We found seats in the waiting area. "God, they look awful," my mother said. She stared at the patient directly across from us, a woman whose body had shrunk to the size of a malnourished prisoner of war, her yellow skin pulled taut over the angles of her skull, her whitening hair so thin it looked like a newborn's.

"You're nowhere near that bad, Mamá."

She let out a scoff, then immediately composed herself. "I know I don't look like a corpse, Sebastián. But I also know that's where I'm heading."

"I'm sorry. I'm just trying to cheer you up."

"I don't need cheering up. I'm already quite cheery."

"It's okay to be scared, Mamá."

"That's the thing, Sebastián. I'm not scared. You should give it a try."

A nurse carrying an iPad and wearing a concierge's smile walked over and asked to scan my mother's ID. She led us to a booth facing the windows, which opened to a spectacular view of the hazy Valley of Anáhuac.

"Please, make yourself comfortable, señora Arteaga y Salazar," the nurse said. "Clara will be with you shortly to collect your blood samples."

My mother took out the blanket from her tote bag, sat down on the chair, and wrapped it tightly around her body with a series of practiced movements. "Must it be Clara? She's a charming young lady, but she never finds my veins, and leaves my arm all purple."

"Of course, señora. Would you prefer to work with Martina today?"

"She's a bit older, no? Knows what she's doing. Yes, please, if at all possible."

A few minutes later a large matron in her sixties appeared in the booth, pushing a little metal cart that reminded me of the ones used by flight attendants, except that instead of miniature wine bottles and trays of microwaved chicken, it was loaded with needles, glass tubes, latex gloves, and disinfecting wipes.

"Good afternoon, señora," Martina said. "How are we doing today?"

"Very well, Martina, thank you. Especially now that you're here. They wanted to have Clara poke me. She's a sweetheart and extremely competent, but you know young people. They're still learning, mostly by trial and error."

Martina laughed. "I suppose I've had a bit more practice, yes," she said as she put on a pair of gloves.

"Just don't tell her I said that, please? I quite like her."

Martina gently took my mother's left arm, lifted the sleeve of her loose-fitting blouse, and wiped her skin clean with disinfectant. "Don't worry, your secret is safe with me. But you do have rather shy veins, señora Arteaga y Salazar. They like to hide from us. Open and close your fist a few times for me, please?"

My mother did as she said, and then Martina grabbed one

of the tubes, affixed a needle to it, and plunged it into her flesh. She bit her lip and closed her eyes but didn't flinch. The nurse repeated the operation several times, until her little cart was crowded with vials filled with my mother's blood.

"That wasn't so bad, was it, señora?"

My mother had gone pale. "Not bad. Not bad at all."

Martina wheeled the cart out of the booth. My mother pressed a button on the chair to recline the backrest and sank into the fabric. She closed her eyes and took several deep breaths. "I'm fine," she said. "Just a little dizzy."

I reached for the lunch box and opened the zipper. "Should you have the apple? Or can I get you a Coke from the vending machine? We don't want your blood sugar to drop after they exsanguinated you like that. Full-blown medieval-monks-misread-Galen shit! Next time they might as well bring out the leeches. Clearly your issue is an excess of ill humor. Trust me, I would know."

My mother laughed, then had another coughing fit. "I'll save the apple for later. But you're a funny kid, hijito."

She took a sip of water and pulled out her Zweig to signal she didn't want to chat for a while. I stared out the window and tried to find the volcanoes in the smog, making an effort to conjure the strange, almost comforting familiarity that hospitals offer those who spend a great deal of time in them, hoping to keep at bay the dread that seized me anew each time I discovered, yet again, that my mother wasn't some ethereal spirit beyond the reach of disease and decay, but a creature of this black earth, an amalgam of water and proteins, a handful of throbbing arteries, a bundle of churning organs, a soft, leaky, imperfect machine, vulnerable to the blind will to power of its own rebellious cells, fallen mitochondrial angels who would rather reign in hell than serve in heaven.

Because, for all my insistence to the contrary, I knew that my mother was in fact heading to the same place as the woman with the hair of a newborn. The same was true of everyone, of course, but my mother was heading there faster and more visibly than most. Spending time with her meant brushing against death, feeling her soft, cold touch caress the back of the neck. Death had become her maid-in-waiting, her chaperone, her witness. She was keenly aware of her presence, and she was courageous enough not to hide from her. On the contrary: she had become conversant with death, addressed her with informal pronouns and in familiar terms.

In recent months, it seemed to me, she had even begun cultivating something like a friendship with her—a friendship grounded on mutual respect and reciprocal promises of kindness and facilitated by my mother's visceral understanding of finitude and fatality, of the futility of lamenting the very thing that makes us human, of the obvious and undeniable truth that death is an integral part of life, of the less obvious but more urgent truth that, while we have no say in terms of time, manner, or place, we are in fact endowed with the freedom to choose how we confront our fate.

I often wondered whether the difference between our attitudes toward death didn't have something to do with the fact that she'd spent her life studying and practicing the Day of the Dead and other related traditions, whereas I'd fled to a country where people were so terrified of dying that they were simply incapable of thinking about the subject, let alone speaking about it, even when it was staring them in the face.

Whatever the reasons, the truth was that, even if my mother wasn't afraid of death, I was afraid of losing her. She knew that, of course. She could read me like an open book, even or especially when I tried to hide from her. Sometimes I wondered whether

her displays of courage weren't a performance staged for the benefit of the people who loved her or whether she downplayed her metaphysical fear and her physical pain for our sakes, not only to put us at ease but also to model for her children how to contend with the human condition, to teach us how to live by example, transforming even her illness into part of her lifelong pedagogical project.

These thoughts were going through my head when another nurse showed up pushing a similar cart, though this one was loaded with bags of saline solution and small glass bottles tinted an opaque brown that made me think of a homeopathic pharmacy or a nineteenth-century apothecary, each of them containing a different poison—a designer toxin that killed a little to stave off death.

"All right, señora Arteaga y Salazar," the nurse said. "We're going to start if that's okay with you."

"Please do, Priscila. Shoot the horse already."

The nurse loaded a saline bag on the IV drip, then inserted the catheter into the bulging plastic port that my mother's surgeon had implanted under the skin near her clavicle, where large veins were easily accessible.

"We're going to start with the anti-nausea medication," the nurse said. "Your file says that your new treatment is giving you trouble with that, right?"

"I wouldn't call it trouble. More like an inconvenience. A slight discomfort."

"Even so, if we can make it go away, we will. This infusion should take about an hour. I'll be back then to start with the oncological medications, okay?"

My mother nodded and the nurse left.

"The nurses here are so nice," I said.

"They usually are. At least when they're not overworked, poor things. In America at least they had a union."

"These ones seem especially attentive."

"Well, sure. This is a rather fancy hospital. Fancier than Hopkins, even. I suppose if you can't compete on cutting-edge care, you can always compensate with customer service. Especially if the clientele you're hoping to attract consists of people willing to spend a fortune to avoid setting foot in a public hospital—you have to make them feel like they're flying first class. It's the same with private schools, at least the ones in this country. The academics are lackluster at best, but the facilities? They're as flashy as the ones at Exover."

"You mean Exeter? Or Andover? They're two different schools."

"We should have sent you there. It would have been a bit more expensive than the Colegio Tomás Moro, but at least you would have learned some math."

"You're never going to forgive me for flunking calculus, are you?"

"It's unforgivable. Even writers should be numerate."

"Hard as it is to believe, Mamá, I can actually count to one hundred."

"I doubt that. But more to the point, arithmetic is not enough. At the very least, a cultured person ought to be able to produce a proof of the Pythagorean theorem from memory."

"Can *you* prove that the angles of any figure with three sides always add up to one hundred and eighty degrees, Mamá?"

"Of course not! But I'm not a cultured person, Sebastián. I'm just a housewife. Essentially illiterate."

"An illiterate housewife who reads Freud for fun, can design complex statistical models, speaks fluent Spanish, English, Italian, and Zapotec, and just so happens to hold a doctorate in anthropology."

"I'm not fluent in Zapotec, Sebastián. Or for that matter Italian—the other day I tried to read the new Ferrante in the original and couldn't make sense of it. And I never finished grad school. Thirty years later I'm still ABD."

"What if you finished the dissertation now? Wouldn't that be a fun project? And then you get to have a thesis defense and wear the funky robes and style yourself Dr. Arteaga y Salazar—the whole song and dance!"

My mother smiled and looked out the window. "That would be fun. But I'd have to go back to the sierra for at least a few months. And to tell you the truth, I'm not sure I'm well enough to walk from the house to Chapultepec. Let alone conduct fieldwork in rural Oaxaca. It was hard enough when I was twenty-five."

"What if you went after finishing this round of treatment? You know, when you feel better."

She closed her eyes and smiled again. "Yes. You're right. When I feel better."

I was about to say something else when the nurse returned. She took one of the brown glass bottles from the cart and secured it to the IV, hanging it upside down, then pierced the thin metal lid with a needle connected to the bag of saline solution, and adjusted the mechanism that regulated the rate at which the toxic chemicals dripped into my mother's veins.

"Just to remind you, this is the first of three medications," the nurse said. "Each should take about two hours, so six in total. My records say you prefer to start with the roughest drug, so that's what I've done."

"Thank you, Priscila. Better to swallow the bitter pill first, don't you think?"

"I know you've heard this many times before, but you may feel some discomfort. It's nothing to worry about—just standard side effects. But if you start to feel faint or like you might pass out, or if your heart starts beating too fast or too slow, or if you get a fever, or if your eyes, nose, or mouth starts to bleed, or if you vomit more than three times in an hour, or if you vomit blood even just once, or if you start to feel a pins-and-needles kind of pain in your arms, legs, neck, or torso, or any kind of pain on the left side of your chest, or if you experience anything off or unusual or especially unpleasant, please call us. You can press the leftmost button on the armrest at any time, and either I or one of my colleagues will be with you right away. Okay?"

"Much appreciated, mija. But I can't believe they make you repeat that epic each time I visit. It's like the security announcement before you fly. Everyone knows it by heart but still must go through the motions."

The nurse giggled, a bit artificially. "I wouldn't know, señora. Never gotten on an airplane." She smiled with compassion, this time sincerely, and left the booth.

My mother returned to her book, so we didn't speak for some time. Then, after a while, she asked me to pour her a cup of tea from her thermos—the treatment messed with the nerves in her mouth: cold and even room temperature liquids were difficult— and sank deeper into the chair. I placed the cup on the folding tray, but she didn't touch it. Minutes passed. Her face grew pale. Her breathing quickened. Sweat pooled on her forehead.

"It's rather odd. You can feel it in your veins. Like they've replaced your blood with whatever they put in air-conditioners."

Arnolfi resucitado

One night at El Centenario near the end of the summer, the Bear offered to paint a portrait of Lee and me. He said he'd give us "the art lovers' special": two for the price of one and a half.

"How's that supposed to work?" I said.

"It's simple arithmetic," the Bear said. "My regular fee is eight thousand pesos. So, generally, if I painted two portraits, you'd owe me sixteen thousand doubloons. But since you are lovers of art, artsy lovers, and soon to be lovers depicted in art, not to mention you're all right, as far as human beings go, and seeing also I really could use some pocket change right about now, I'm willing to—"

"But it doesn't make sense. You are still making only one picture."

The Bear threw his hands in the air and looked around the cantina, as if searching for a witness to confirm it was in fact insane the world expected him to work under such conditions.

"I mean, it's still more labor," Lee said. "He's got to paint two different figures. It's not like every square inch of canvas is the same."

"Thank you!" the Bear said. "Maybe I should call it *Art Lover with Still Life of Philistine.*"

I took a drink. Why the hell not? The peso was plunging, and I was in love. "You know what? Fuck it. Let's do it. What do you say, Lee? We split the cost?"

"What you should be talking about is how you're going to apportion the exorbitant profits when you sell it in twenty years," the Bear said. "Don't worry, I won't take offense."

Lee stirred her drink, even though by that point it was just half-melted ice. "I guess I'm not sure? Let me think about it?"

"Ah shit," the Bear said. "I should have known not to ask you both at the same time. Now it's like one of those horrible scenes when some foolish criollo decides to propose to his girlfriend in the middle of some family thing and she turns him down in front of Grandma. Very unpleasant for everyone involved."

"You're Grandma in this scenario?"

"More like the wolf."

The incident with the painting forced me to confront the fact that Lee would soon leave for New England for her PhD while I went back to my MFA in the Middle West, and though we'd talked about visiting one another, it was not at all clear whether we'd remain in some sort of relationship or become the twins we were always supposed to be. One night over dinner we tried to decide what to do. We discovered our feelings about the situation were reciprocal but reversed, as if we were mirrors reflecting each other. Each time one of us expressed a desire to solidify what existed between us, the other began to scan the room for emergency exits, which caused the one to take a step back, which caused the other to express a desire to solidify things. But this emotional fractal didn't trouble us much. The reciprocity of our confusion was a deeper and more honest mutuality than any falsely shared certainty. It made us anxious, of course, but so did everything else. We congratulated ourselves for not being like all those other dull, sublunary lovers—but the fact remained that in two weeks there would be a thousand miles between us.

I'd almost forgotten about the portrait when the Bear dropped by our place unannounced, as he did, and proudly he'd found the solution to all our problems. "A diptych! A lovely portrait of a bour-geois marriage from some merchant city-state in sixteenth-century Flanders. One of those places where they let people get divorced."

The painting showed us from the waist up, standing next to each other against a green-blue background with expectant expressions, our eyes fixed on the same point, as if scouting the future. The Bear rushed to finish on time for Lee to take her half. We decided each of us would keep his or her portrait, because we were modern people with no illusions about romance, and it'd be odd to have an oil painting of an ex hanging in the house. As for the question of our relationship, we agreed to "play it as it lay," as Lee put it. Why give a name and the attendant rules to something that wasn't part of any class other than itself?

Still, the paintings looked better together.

"You should go find Lee. I'm making you be so rude to her by asking you to come here and abandon her in a foreign country."

I looked up from my book and saw that in the hour or so since my mother and I had spoken, she had gone from translucent pale to a seasick green. There was no way I was leaving her in this state. "Don't worry about her. She's a resourceful lass."

"Thank you, hijito, but your father should be here soon, and you've already done your part. We've had such a lovely chat and a few solid hours together. That's all I could ask for. Last thing I want is for you to waste your vacation among moribunds."

I looked at my watch. My father was supposed to relieve me at the hospital an hour ago. "When you say it like that, it sounds like spending time with you is a chore. And it isn't. It's a pleasure, Mamá."

She smiled, but her expression changed immediately into a grimace of disgust. She swallowed and clicked her mouth. She took a deep breath, then another. "Will you pass me the emesis basin?"

"The what?"

"The half-moon-shaped metal container. Should be on the table."

I turned to the table but didn't see anything that resembled my mother's description. I scanned the booth, opened the drawer on the small cabinet by the green chair, got on my knees to peer under the table—but I couldn't find it. "I'm sorry, Mamá, but I don't know where it—"

Then I heard her dry heave and realized that "emesis basin" was just a fancy name for "puke bucket." I got on my feet in a panic and looked for anything that could work—and then I saw a small plastic trash can in the corner of the booth. I grabbed it and held it before my mother, who bent over it and began contracting in what struck me as inordinately violent spasms. Seconds later her mouth opened as wide as it could and a torrent of acrid yellow bile rushed out of her throat, splattering the sides of the trash can and her own face, making an awful sloshing noise. The torrent stopped for a moment, and I began to move the waste bin away, but my mother reached for my hand and held it like a passenger on a shipwrecked ocean-liner would cling to driftwood, her fingernails sinking into my skin and almost drawing blood, then began heaving again, this time for much longer, several minutes, until the torrent began anew. We repeated this operation a third time, and then she let go of my hand. I put the trash can down and grabbed a tissue from the table and wiped the droplets of vomit off her face.

"See, this is why you should have left."

"Mamá, I went to college in the US. It takes a bit more than a little throwing up to scare me. Do you think they have wet wipes somewhere? I think I got it all off, but I wouldn't want you to have to smell it."

"Don't worry. I can't smell anything anymore."

Then we heard someone knocking on the booth partition and turned to see a young man wearing a labcoat and a wide grin that revealed a set of impeccably white and perfectly straight teeth.

"Afternoon, Laura," the young man said. "How are you feeling?"

My mother's face lit up, though it still retained a greenish tint. She gestured with her hand, first at the newcomer, then to me. "Sebastián, I'd like you to meet Dr. Eric Ward-Maldonado. He's one of Dr. Graue's residents—and don't tell him I told you, but he's also my favorite. He has a pleasant bedside manner, as you can see."

I looked again at the young doctor and confirmed that the fellow was, in fact, almost comically handsome: tall and muscular, with green eyes, an angular nose, and a thick mop of messy black hair that was a bit too long for a clean-cut professional, but which gave him a boyish air that surely charmed more than one sixty-something lady patient. "A pleasure, Doctor," I said.

"And Dr. Ward, this is Sebastián, my eldest boy. He's visiting from Ohio, where he's attending the famous Writers' Studio!"

The doctor lifted his eyebrows. "That's very impressive! I'd heard about a similar school in Idaho, I think—or was it Indiana? Illinois? But I hadn't heard about the one in Ohio. Must get a lot of snow out there, huh?"

"Tons of it."

Dr. Ward nodded politely to signal that our little exchange of pleasantries was over, and it was time to get down to business. "So, Laura, Dr. Graue asked me to stop by and ask you a few preliminary questions before your conference with him later today. How's the new treatment treating you? Still lots of nausea?"

"A little, but nothing to write home about."

I shot her an exasperated glance. I wasn't about to interject—this was between her doctor and her—but the nurse had told us we should call her if she vomited three times in an hour, as she had just done in less than ten minutes.

"Really? Because I don't mean to spy on you, but I couldn't help hearing you heaving just now."

"I'm much better now, Dr. Ward. Just had to let it out."

"I wish I could make it go away, but the cocktail that we're giving you seems to be doing what it's supposed to, and Dr. Graue thinks it's best to stick with it for as long as it continues to work, even if the side effects are difficult, rather than risk tumor growth while we try other approaches. I'm sure he'll be happy to tell you more about his reasoning when you see him."

"That makes perfect sense, Doctor."

"That said, I'm not happy about the vomiting. We can't give

you another dose of the intravenous antiemetic just yet, but there are other things we can try—and also other things *you* can try."

"Such as?"

"Have you considered cannabis?"

My mother burst out laughing. "Dr. Ward, I'm scandalized! Are you trying to turn me into a drug fiend? I haven't smoked since I was in graduate school. But my daughter's friend did bring me some gummies from California. She says they're mild and designed for medicinal use."

Dr. Ward looked around theatrically, as if making sure nobody was within ear shot, then bent in closer to my mother and spoke in a stage whisper: "Well, don't tell anyone I said this, especially not Dr. Graue—but I think it might be a good idea to eat a couple of those before each chemo session, and to keep some around for the second or third day after each infusion. For now, I'm going to have one of the nurses stop by with some nausea pills. I'm also going to think of a few longer-term options so we can go over them with Dr. Graue. Sounds good?"

"Sounds perfect, Doctor. Thank you."

Dr. Ward gently placed a hand on my mother's shoulder, then walked out of the booth and across the infusion lounge toward the nursing station, my mother following him with her eyes.

"We should introduce him to Inés."

"Mamá, are you trying to ship your doctor and my sister?"

"I just think he's a nice, gentle, good-looking boy with a respectable profession and a promising career!"

"Sounds like *you* want to run off with Dr. Ward, Mamá!"

"What? No way! I'm old enough to be his mother."

"Are you familiar with the term cougar?"

She laughed and was about to reply when we heard a familiar voice calling out from the elevators: "¡Laura, mi vida!"

I turned around and saw my father approaching us, carrying an impractically large flower arrangement in a glass vase. "At least he showed up," I said.

My mother let out a sigh and raised an eyebrow and nodded. "On the one hand, I get it. It's not like he can miss oral arguments. The future of the republic, etc., etc. On the other hand? I'm his wife. And I have cancer."

By then my father had made it into the booth. He left the flowers on the corner of the table and leaned in over my mother to give her a kiss on the lips—but she turned away from him. "What's wrong?" he said. "Is it that I was late?"

"No, silly. It's that I just threw up."

"Didn't they give you anti-nausea medicine?" my father went on as he reached out to shake my hand without looking at me.

"They did. It just doesn't work so well."

My father shook his head and sat down next to my mother, in the chair where I'd been sitting. "They should figure something out. They can't have you vomiting all day."

"Dr. Ward says a nurse will come soon with some pills that ought to help."

I stood up and said I was going to the bathroom, annoyed that my father felt entitled to complain about my mother's care when he couldn't even show up on time. When I came back to the booth, I found him standing by the windows, looking out on the city with an encrypted cell phone next to his ear. I repressed a pang of fury and instead sat down next to my mother, in the same chair, and began chatting with her about the difference between THC and CBD. After a while, however, my mother began to turn green again.

"I'm sorry, hijito," she said. "Don't think I can make conversation just now."

"That's okay, Mamá," I said. I got up and grabbed the trash can and brought it closer, setting it on the floor next to the green chair. "Do you want some water?"

She shook her head—and then, without the usual warning heaves, her torso bent involuntarily, her diaphragm contracted, and the yellow fluid came out again. I rushed to grab the trash can and held it in front of her face, managing to catch most of the liquid—but some of it still fell on the blanket and her blouse. My father must have heard the noise, because when I looked up, he was standing right behind me with terror in his eyes, trying to reach over my shoulders to help me hold the waste bin and feel that he wasn't completely useless.

After a while the vomit subsided, and I put the trash can down again. "We need to get this off you," I said as I began unwrapping the blanket from around my mother's body. "You brought a change of clothes, right?"

"Where the fuck are the nurses?" my father asked.

"I'm sure they're coming."

"They should be here already. They should have been here a long time ago."

"I can press the button," my mother said weakly.

"You shouldn't have to press a button. It's their job to make sure you have everything you need."

"They're overworked," my mother went on, sounding a little out of it. "Poor things. They don't even have a union."

My father stood up and smacked his thigh with his hand. "That's it. I'm going to get them. And then I'm going to talk to their supervisor. This is unacceptable."

"Alberto, please," my mother said, reaching out her hand as he walked past her. "That's not necessary."

I looked at her and saw she was not just green with nausea but also red with anticipatory embarrassment and mortification. I got up and hurried after my father, who was walking through the infusion lounge with brisk, decisive steps, resolved to stop him before he could make a scene—but before I could reach him, he'd made it to the nursing station.

"Are you having staffing issues this shift?" he asked, loud enough that I could hear him but at least not shouting. "Because my wife just vomited all over herself. You were supposed to bring her anti-nausea pills. What's the problem?"

I stepped into the nursing station and saw a group of three nurses, including Martina and a girl who I assumed was Clara, sitting around a table with half-eaten sandwiches in their hands, looking up with rabbit eyes at a former attorney general and current Supreme Court justice, who clearly hadn't the slightest idea of the extent to which almost everyone in the country was terrified of him.

"Papá, they're on their break," I said, putting a hand on his shoulder. "They'll be with us when they can. Let's let them have lunch in peace."

"I don't think so," my father said. "They have a duty of care. And one of their patients needs care. Lunch can wait."

Martina nodded, wiped her lips with a napkin, and got up from the table. "Of course, Justice Arteaga y Salazar. I'll fetch la señora's medication right away. Please accept our apologies."

"Thank you, Martina," I said, as kindly as I could.

"Yes, thank you," my father said, then turned around and walked out of the station.

I caught up with him and put a hand on his shoulder again. "Listen. You can't do that."

"Do what?"

"Abuse the nurses. Or any kind of subordinate, for that matter."

"I didn't abuse anyone. I politely asked them to do their job."

"They were having lunch, Papá. And it makes Mamá uncomfortable when you start acting like a petulant asshole."

"What's making her uncomfortable is the nausea that their negligence is causing her."

"They're not causing her nausea. The chemo is."

He didn't reply. We walked back to the booth, where my mother had somehow managed to change her blouse without anyone noticing and without anyone's help, all while wearing a catheter attached to a surgical implant.

"What can I tell you?" she said with a wink when I asked how she'd done it. "One gets lots of practice in Catholic school."

We sat down and chatted for a while. Then, when I was about to leave to go meet up with Lee, my father looked at his watch. "It's been thirty minutes."

"Thirty minutes since what?"

"Since that nurse said she was getting your pills right away."

"Oh, that? Don't worry."

My father didn't reply and instead walked over to the armrest of my mother's chair and pressed the button several times to call a nurse.

"Don't think they'll come any faster if you press a hundred thousand times," my mother said.

She had just finished speaking when Martina appeared in the booth, carrying a tray with two paper cups: one with pills and one with water. "I'm sorry to be so late! The pharmacy couldn't find the medication."

My father looked at her with venomous eyes. "Why the hell are you making excuses?" he said, getting louder as he went on, until he was yelling. "The pharmacy had nothing to do with it. You just couldn't be bothered. You had to finish gobbling down your chow."

Martina froze where she was, her eyes open wide.

"Are you familiar with the concept of duty of care? Because guess what? You have it. And you're being derelict about it. You should be ashamed of yourself!"

"Alberto . . ." my mother pleaded.

"What if it hadn't been a nausea pill, huh? What if it had been something more urgent? She could have died! You could have killed her!"

Martina opened her mouth to say something, took an involuntary step back, and accidentally tipped the vase that contained the flowers my father had brought, which fell and shattered on the ground, spreading water and petals and shards of glass on the floor. My father looked down at the mess—and then he lost what remained of his restraint.

"Look what you've done! You're useless!"

I turned away, unable to bear the embarrassment, and to my distress saw that the entire infusion lounge, nurses and patients, was staring at us.

"Do you realize you could get sued?" my father kept yelling. "Is that what you want? To lose your job? Because that's sure what it looks like! It's unbelievable! You—"

Then another loud voice interrupted my father: "Alberto!" I turned in that direction and saw the venerable figure of my mother's octogenarian physician, the head of oncology at the American-British Hospital and of the Faculty of Medicine at the National University, distinguished member of the Mexican Academy of Sciences and the National College, and a lifelong friend of my paternal grandfather: Dr. Urbino Graue.

"Dr. Graue," my father replied. "I'm glad you are here. There seem to be serious issues with your staff."

The elderly doctor approached, walking slowly with his cane. "What the hell do you think you are doing, young fellow? You're screaming like some mannerless arriviste."

"Doctor, your nurses are being negligent."

"In the care of our dear Laura? Never. Especially not Martina here, who is one of the best in the business and the pride of this hospital, and who deserves to be treated with respect. Even by a justice of the Supreme Court."

"Dr. Graue, I assure you that . . ."

"What would your father say, Alberto? And your mother?"

My father was about to say something but stopped himself. He was one of the most powerful men in the country and he knew it, but before a man whom he'd been taught to respect from earliest childhood, he reverted to meekness.

"I'm very sorry to do this, Alberto," Dr. Graue went on. "But I'm afraid I'm going to have to ask you to please leave the infusion lounge. There are delicate patients here, and I cannot allow this kind of outburst."

My father lowered his head and nodded. "Of course, Dr. Graue. You're right. Please accept my apologies."

"I'm not the person you owe an apology to, Alberto."

My father raised his eyes and turned to Martina, trembling with humiliation. "Doña Martina," he said, "le pido una disculpa sincera por mi comportamiento. Fue completamente inaceptable y lo lamento profundamente."

Martina was standing there, still holding the tray with my mother's medicine, shaking a little. She looked at Dr. Graue, then at my father, then at the oncologist again.

"Thank you, Justice Arteaga y Salazar," she said. "I, too, should have been more careful."

My father flashed a tense smile, then turned to my mother. "I'm afraid I have to go."

"Better that way," she replied. "I don't want you here anymore."

He leaned in to kiss her—but she again turned away. He put a hand on my shoulder and squeezed it a little, then shook Dr. Graue's hand, bowed to Martina, and walked away as fast as he could without running.

"I'm sorry I had to kick him out, Laurita," Dr. Graue said. "I must go do a few rounds. But I'll see you later tonight, yes?" He grasped Martina's hand for a moment and left.

The nurse set down the tray on the table. "You should take these now, señora. They'll help."

"Where are you from, Martina?"

"Oaxaca, señora."

"That's what I thought. Serrana, yes?"

"How did you know?"

"I spent some time in the mountains."

"That's very nice, señora. What were you doing there?"

"I was living with a family to learn about their lives."

"The university sent you?"

"That's right."

"¿Y qué? ¿Lee rneo xidza, señora?"

My mother's face illuminated. "Yes. A little. I'm very rusty, though. But I do want to say—Wexhixhe yote doli xkia kiebe. And I mean it, Martina."

Martina smiled. "Rnaban xhixhero kati no rban giel wxhixhe." She picked up the tray from the table and went on in Spanish: "I'll ask one of the janitors to clean up the mess, all right? And I'll be back later to start the last infusion."

"Dioxklé, Martina," my mother said.

The nurse left. My mother sighed and returned to her book.

"What did you say to her?" I asked.

She smiled and raised her eyebrows but didn't answer.

Part IV

Mexico City

September 2017

In which Your Correspondent travels to Mexico for a wedding, gets in a car crash, interviews a traumatized bodyguard, outlines a phenomenology of the cantina, competes with his best friend for American attentions, ponders the rise of neoliberalism, considers the biography of a messianic cartel boss, recalls the paranoia of his childhood, attempts and fails to confront his father's role in the national catastrophe, and in general is reminded of the reasons why he moved to the United States.

El eterno retorno

A few weeks after I returned to the United States, I received an invitation to the wedding of Aviva, one of my few Mexican friends from college. The news made me melancholy—many years earlier I'd been in love with her—but it also gave me an excuse to get out of the Middle West. I booked flights to stay for a week and counted the days with anticipation. But on the first day of my visit, heading to El Centenario to meet Esteban and the Bear, I passed a newsstand and caught a glimpse of the tabloid Ludwig and Darwin used to read—and felt ill.

Lleno de mi, sitiado en mi epidermis

Moisés was on vacation, so the Federal Police sent another officer to drive Esteban and me to the Bear's summerhouse in Valle de Bravo. I protested and said we were perfectly capable of getting there on our own, but my father's head of security threatened to quit if I got my way. The town was too close to Michoacán.

I stepped out of my parents' house and found a tall man with large hands leaning on an armored Passat and staring at his smartphone. He started when he saw me, as if I'd caught him in something. He put his phone away, squared his shoulders, and nodded. I nodded back and walked to the car.

"Afternoon, licenciado," he said, in a tone so stifled I wondered whether he'd memorized a script. "I'm Captain Pedro Campeador. I'll be your escort this week. It's a true pleasure, señor."

He tried to take my backpack. I resisted for a moment, then handed it to him.

"Pleasure's all mine, Pedro," I said. "But don't call me sir, please."

I reached for the door handle but he grabbed it first. I got in the car and was overwhelmed by the air freshener. On the floor, beneath the driver's seat, I saw a tactical bag, an assault rifle protruding through the half-open zipper.

Pedro started the car and drove away from my father's house. We picked up Esteban and took the avenue that would lead us out of the city. After a half hour of silence, Pedro turned on the radio.

"Do you like classical, sir? I find it relaxing."

"Me too," I said. Stravinsky wasn't soothing, but I didn't want to be difficult.

"I used to listen to norteñas," he went on. "But lately I've been trying to get into classical. You know, to set an example for my kid. It's important, to set an example. Plus, the doctor recommended it. Said it'd help me relax."

I nodded but didn't reply. The air freshener was making me lightheaded and *The Rite of Spring* was making me anxious, and it was all Pedro's fault. We drove west until we hit a traffic jam. The opulent houses of Las Lomas rolled by so slowly that we didn't seem to be moving. After a while, Pedro began muttering to himself and tapping his fingers on the steering wheel. Less than a mile from the expressway, he switched on the car's police siren and began pushing his way out of the avenue.

"We'll take the callejuelas for a while," he said. Dozens of irate drivers blew their horns at us. "That way we'll get in front of the accident or whatever is causing this."

"Whatever you think is best," I said in Spanish, then turned to Esteban and went on in English: "I hate it when they do that."

"Do what?" he said without looking up from his book.

"The siren. It's for emergencies."

"Whatever."

"I'm serious. It's low-key corruption."

By then we'd gotten off the avenue and were driving down a narrow street. I turned to the window, basking in self-righteousness. After a while the edges of the houses began to blur together. I wondered whether we were speeding but then realized the effect came from the bulletproof glass, so thick it warped the contours of things. I tried to focus my eyes and saw flowerpots on windowsills and sneakers hanging from wires and dogs rummaging through trash bins. I felt dizzy. I looked up, trying to calm my nausea, and saw a tangle of improvised electricity lines and the protruding iron bars that supported the walls of the houses, black and rust-red against the white-gray sky.

Then I heard the bang.

Pedro screamed and slammed face-first on the steering wheel. The car swerved. We crashed into a van. I closed my eyes and smelled burnt tires and held my breath for the next gunshot.

El reino de este mundo

Three hundred miles west of Mexico City, past the volcanoes of Anáhuac and the plain of Toluca, at the end of a highway that turns into a dirt road that leads into a village of tin-roofed houses without running water, a boy of eight is sitting in a cornfield with a metal spoon in his hand. It is the season of knife-fights. The heat is an audible tension, like sparks on a live wire or static on a broken radio. All that remains of the harvest is a congregation of mummified cornstalks. They stand tall around the boy, brittle and bent like broken old women, watching him hold the spoon before his eyes and concentrate his will into an impossible imperative. The spoon does not bend. But many years later, when Nazario Moreno finds himself surrounded by his enemies and comes to the realization that the time has come for him to die for the second and last time, he will remember the distant afternoon when he hid in the milpa to escape his mother's blows and discovered he'd been touched by the divine.

Mexicanos al grito de guerra

"No need to be awkward about it," Esteban said the day before the wedding. "She invited us both."

He had a point. It'd been years. Besides, neither of us had been involved with Aviva for very long.

"I guess it's what she always wanted," he went on. "But I'm still surprised she decided to keep the kid."

It was late for lunch and early for dinner and the weather was cooler than usual, so the terrace of Contramar was almost empty. We'd ordered ceviche and beer and finished them both but Claire—Aviva's maid of honor and a good friend of mine from college—still hadn't shown up.

"Are you sure she has the address?" Esteban said.

"I texted it."

"Her phone doesn't work here."

"It said she'd received it."

"We need her. She's our buffer."

I was going to say something, but the waiter interrupted me. "Another round, gentlemen?"

"No thank you," I said.

"Don't listen to him," Esteban said. "Three mezcales, please."

The waiter nodded and walked away. I looked at Esteban. "Did you just order me two drinks? Or do you now chase liquor with liquor?"

"Relax. One's for the American."

"It's not even four!"

The waiter came back and placed a plate with orange slices and chile salt in the center of the table and a glass in front of each seat.

"You have a patriotic duty to get drunk tonight," Esteban said.

I sighed and took a drink. The liquor tasted of smoke and red dirt. "It's very good," I admitted.

"I thought it was too early."

Then a car pulled over in front of the restaurant terrace and a woman with dark hair and pale skin got out and walked toward Esteban and me. I hugged her. Esteban kissed her on the cheek and pulled out a chair for her.

Claire scoffed in mock outrage and sat down. "A shotgun wedding? Chivalrous men? What's next? A duel?"

"Shall we toast the bride?" Esteban said.

Claire picked up her glass. "Is this for me?"

"It's for the traffic jams. They get on your nerves."

"Well, to Aviva!" Claire said. She threw her head back, drank the whole glass, and burst into coughs. "Jesus Christ!"

"You're supposed to sip it," Esteban said. "That thing where you put salt on your hand and lick it and squeeze a lime into your mouth? It's a corporate ploy to sell you guys rubbing alcohol."

Claire let out a laugh I recognized from college. It had a hint of irony in it, as if she wanted to let on that she knew that she was letting herself be led astray. "So, what are we doing tonight? It's you guys' Fourth of July, right? Aviva's stuff tomorrow doesn't start until late."

"Why don't we go to El Centenario?" I said.

Esteban frowned. "¿Neta? ¿Quieres traer a una gringa a la cantina?"

"Hey!" Claire said. "I understood that!"

"I'm kidding. We'll show you some local color."

The names of the bodyguards I had as a teenager were Ludwig and Darwin, but they were as Mexican as mezcal and regret. Their father, a landowner from Chiapas, christened them hoping they'd pursue the arts and sciences. Instead, the two brothers became cops in a country where the police are feared and reviled. Their suits were boxy, half a size too large. They smelled of cheap cologne, raw onions, and cilantro. They were very polite. In their spare time, they watched Sylvester Stallone movies, played cards, and read a tabloid called *Alarma*.

The newspaper was short and wide. Images covered every page, full-color photographs printed in cheap ink that smelled sour and stained your fingers. A raindrop was enough to dissolve the pulp and send the reds bleeding into the blues and the blacks. If you set the paper on fire, as I did on indolent afternoons, the chemicals in the ink burned a supernatural green.

The photographs on the front page always depicted at least one body. Sometimes, a headless torso on the side of a rural road, its genitals mutilated. Others, a group of men in working clothes, hands tied, blood flowing from gunshot wounds in the back of their heads. Others still, a teenager in the rear seat of a car, mouth open in surprise.

Ludwig and Darwin kept the paper on the armrest of the bulletproof Passat where the three of us spent a substantial portion of our days. I often browsed it when we were stuck in traffic. On a cloudless afternoon in September, a few years before I left for America, the front page showed a man dangling from an overpass. We were leaving my parents' house in El Contadero, my electric guitar in the trunk. I noticed a blue Sentra across the street. Inside, looking at us intently, sat five tattooed men.

A few days later I wrote again to Irina:

Dear Irina,

Hope you are well! I'm in the middle of a brief visit to Mexico City, where I've had a series of conversations that made me think that perhaps I shouldn't write a thesis on the baroque, but instead on the relationship between politics and literature in Mexico. Remember the piece about the conquest I submitted to workshop last semester? How it had this running bit about how Cortés was a novelist? I was thinking I could write about a few other Mexican historical figures who were also writers and readers of one sort or another. Like Maximilian von Habsburg—more than anything else, he was a Romantic. Or Nazario Moreno, this narco who also happened to write a bonkers autobiography.

The point would be that politics is first of all a matter of interpretation—of storytelling, of rhetoric. This is true everywhere, but what makes Mexico special is that there, unlike other countries, this work has fallen on oddly literary writer-politicians who have a peculiar relationship to facts: they see them not as the source material of interpretation but as its end product, which is why they often say they write nonfiction when in fact they don't. The working title is now "Arms and Letters," after Don Quixote's famous dilemma, the idea being that in Mexico those two professions are one and the same.

I realize the concept is vague but I hope it will become clearer as I write. Perhaps we could meet sometime next week and talk in person? Writing a book that captures something of the contradictory phantasmagoria that the word "Mexico"

denotes for me is proving more difficult than I anticipated.
Thank you for your patience, Irina, and see you soon!

All the best,
Sebastián

Lo nuestro es cosa mejor

On a thoroughly gentrified block, across the street from a coffee shop that sold Belgian, Spanish, Mexican, and "Maya" hot chocolate, between an upscale sushi restaurant and a corporate convenience store, on the ground floor of an art-deco building whose apartments were all Airbnbs, there stood my friends' favorite cantina—an establishment whose clientele used to consist of taxi drivers and retired boxers, and which later became an artists-and-editors joint.

The sign above the entrance read: EL CENTENARIO: DESDE 1939, but as far as I knew, nothing significant happened in 1839. This raised a question: The centenary of what? A private anniversary? A grandmother's birth, a family's arrival in the capital? Hubris—the founder's declaration that their business would last a century? A reference to the coins that General Díaz put into circulation on the hundredth anniversary of Mexico's independence from Spain, unaware that the Revolution was about to put an end to his dictatorship?

I prefer to read the sign as a commentary on the cantina's peculiar effect on its patrons' experience of time. At El Centenario watches fall out of sync. An hour lasts a year—until it's over, when it seems to have lasted a minute. Nights become eternal but fade from memory, such that the previous afternoon blends with the next morning. For the old men who play dominoes on the corner tables, the cantina offers centuries' worth of experience payable at closing in the currency of regret. El Centenario may have been founded in 1939, but on any given night it has been serving drinks for all of a hundred years.

El Centenario isn't a bar any more than a public house or a biergarten is. Cantinas tend to be well lit, often with the ugliest fluorescent lights. There are no loudspeakers; if there's music, it's because a busker wandered in. Pool tables are unheard of, but dominoes and dice are available behind the bar. These differences may seem superficial but reflect a deeper distinction. Cantinas and bars both sell liquor, but only the alcoholics among their clients treat booze as an end in itself rather than as a means to another, more elusive intoxication. In bars this other drunkenness is the tantalizing possibility of going home with a stranger: the dim lights and loud jukeboxes let drinkers convince themselves that the person on the next stool is interesting and attractive.

The atmosphere of cantinas, by contrast, seems designed to discourage flirting. This is not to say that there's no eroticism at El Centenario—or that women are safer there than elsewhere—but to suggest that romantic interactions in cantinas have a flavor of surprise. A glance across the table, a sudden encounter in the men's bathroom, a farewell peck on the cheek that stumbles to the mouth—these moments are as common here as anywhere else, but the patrons of El Centenario seem to experience them as the fulfillment of a possibility so remote that they might have written it off as impossible.

Ya viene el cambio

I was ten years old when the Mexican government first determined the threats against my father were credible enough that my family needed a permanent escort of armed men. The millennium had come and gone and Mexico had just held its first democratic elections. Anxious for fresh names, the new government asked my father, then a private lawyer, to head the intelligence agency. The morning after he accepted, I found several men in dark suits outside our house.

"Who are you?" I asked.

They looked at each other in silence. They'd trained to protect me from people who wanted to kill me, not to explain why I needed protection.

"We are your father's escort," one of them finally said. "We're here to make sure nothing happens."

As the years passed and my father rose to higher positions, the bodyguards multiplied. At first my siblings and I each had one, then two. My mother started with five, then seven, then eventually had ten. By the time my father became attorney general, he had twenty bodyguards. When we went out as a family, we were surrounded by two dozen men, ten assault rifles, and several live grenades.

On the day I met Ludwig and Darwin, when I was thirteen, their commander told me they were the finest of the federales and their job was "to make my life easier." There's no question they succeeded in their first task: they didn't tell my parents when I skipped school; they helped me buy liquor; they drove me home from parties at ungodly hours. But they also sat two rows behind me when I took a date to the movies, waiting to see whether I'd work up the courage to make a move. They forbade me from driving to the beach, strolling in the street, and sleeping over at friends' houses. They insisted on calling me sir, but they could have sold me to the Sinaloa Cartel for more money than they could ever spend.

Capture el instante en un instante

The photographer usually wanders into El Centenario around midnight and doesn't stay long. Unlike the flower vendors and the beggars, he doesn't insist when a table turns him down. Sometimes he seems almost relieved.

"How long have you been doing this?" I asked him one night.

"Forty years," he said. "I had an uncle back in Oaxaca. He taught me the ropes. Then I came to the capital and started working the cantinas. It used to be good money."

He took a small cardboard box from his messenger bag, placed it on the table, and extracted an aluminum pouch the size of a postcard. The text on the wrapping had faded but enough remained to see it was written in Cyrillic characters.

"They don't make these anymore," he said as he tore the pouch and loaded the film into the camera. "Some months ago I found a few boxes in the flea market in Tepito. A friend keeps telling me there's this Chinese guy who has whole crates, but nobody knows where to find him."

He lifted the camera to his face and pointed first to the Bear, then Esteban and me. "Draw closer," he said. "And smile."

The flash was brighter than I'd expected. I worried I'd closed my eyes. The photographer opened the camera with a brusque pull at a lever and took out the film. He held it from a corner with two delicate fingers, like a butterfly collector examining a specimen.

"And when you run out?" Esteban asked.

The photographer raised an eyebrow but didn't answer. He waved the film through the air, produced a stick of glue and a piece of cardboard from one of the countless pockets of his utility vest, touched the back of the photograph with the glue, and pressed it onto the cardboard.

"All right, young men," he said. "That'll be a hundred pesos."

I handed him a bill. He took it with a smile and slid it into yet another pocket.

"Thank you for supporting the arts," he said. "It's developing, so don't touch it for a minute."

He turned around and walked out of the cantina. Seconds later an image began to appear on the film. Colors emerged on the edges and advanced inward: the white and blue tiles on the wall, the Bear's red sweater, my brown hair, my gray jacket. Then, when Esteban's face should have appeared, the process stopped. As if a portion of the past had been removed from the future. As if a hole had opened in the fabric of time.

"¡Puta madre!" the Bear said. "The film's expired."

El detective salvaje

I opened my eyes and looked out of the window. The crash wasn't serious, just a bent fender and a broken headlight.

"Must have been firecrackers," Esteban said.

I looked up and saw a man getting out of the van. I turned to Pedro but he was already out of the car, walking on the road toward the other driver.

Then I saw the gun.

"On the ground!" Pedro yelled. "Get the fuck on the ground!"

The man's eyes opened wide. He raised his hands, fell to his knees, and lay face down on the pavement, between the bumpers of his van and our car.

"Why the fuck did you do that?" Pedro screamed, pointing the gun at the man. "This is a police vehicle, motherfucker!"

I looked around. Cars had stopped to gawk. A crowd assembled on the sidewalk. A woman was filming on her iPhone. I had a flashback to my days as a police reporter. This wouldn't end well.

"Vamos a valer verga," Esteban said.

I saw he was dialing on his cell phone. "Are you calling the cops?" He kept dialing. "Don't," I said.

He turned to face me but his eyes drifted past me. I followed his gaze and saw a man about our age standing in the midst of the crowd, staring at us through the bulletproof glass, a machete in his right hand.

I didn't know what to do, but I had to do something, so I got out of the car and walked to Pedro. He heard the door close and turned to me. His hands were trembling. A vein throbbed on his forehead. He looked not terrifying but terrified.

"Sir!" he yelled. "Get back in the car!"

I heard the murmur of the crowd and sirens coming closer and the sobs of the man writhing on the pavement, and for the first time in the two decades I'd been around bodyguards, I decided to break the unspoken code that binds the sons of powerful men with the powerless men who guard them.

"Captain," I said. "Please don't make me call the ministry."

Pedro closed his eyes. He wiped the sweat from his forehead. He took a deep breath. For a moment I worried he was about to shoot himself. But then he exhaled and opened his eyes and looked at the car, the man on the pavement, the crowd on the sidewalk. He caught the glance of the young man with the machete and held it for a moment. Then he put his gun in its holster.

We got in the car. He turned on the siren. We drove away.

For a while nobody spoke. I counted the rate of my heartbeat and thought of what I'd say to the police and the journalists when they inevitably showed up. Minutes passed, then an hour. By the time we left the city I felt calmer. Then Pedro broke the silence. "Please don't mention it to your father, sir. I have a kid."

Pedagogía del oprimido

From the first chapter of *Me dicen el más loco: diario de un idealista*, the posthumous autobiography of Nazario Moreno:

In youth I knew cruel poverty. I wore rags and ate beans—boiled,

never fried; lard was luxury. My child mind imagined that
the rich had white bread, not tortillas, Coca-Cola instead of
water. But we had no sugar for our coffee. Only work and
hunger. My father, a drunkard, had two wives and preferred
the one who wasn't my mother. He beat my mother, and my
mother, bitter, beat her children—me more than the others,
for I was restless and loved to fight. There were days when
I fought ten times: first the children of neighboring towns;
then, no strangers left to fight, cousins and friends. I walked
around with blood and dirt on knuckles and shirt, on forehead
and lip. Blood and dirt everywhere—color of mud, texture of
dried shit. Naïf that I was I hoped to grow strong and make
money. Never again river-water. Always white bread and
Coca-Cola. Lard always. Pork throughout the week. Each day
the feast day of a saint.

Los cuerpos como banderas

She kept her hair short and wore trousers. She sang songs men
had written for women but kept the pronouns unchanged. She
smoked and drank without coyness, such that over the course of
her long career her voice transformed from an operatic alto into
a hoarse lament that was even more beautiful.

My favorite recording of her is an original setting to music of
an old poem by Alfonso Camín about the most famous prosti-
tute in Havana. The instrumentation is simple: an obstinate bass
drum, an aching guitar. She sounds terrifying and irresistible, like
a forest fire or a tidal wave:

> Ponme la mano aquí,
>   Macorina,
> Ponme la mano aquí.

Put your hand right here, Macorina. Put your hands on me. Touch me, Macorina. Touch me where I say. The words are simple but difficult to translate. On the page they read as crass lechery haunted by violence; on her lips they become a paradox: power exercised by someone whom desire has rendered powerless.

Chavela Vargas recorded her first album in the early 1950s, a decade after El Centenario first opened. It's not entirely impossible that she wrote the music for "Macorina" on one of the small tables near the back.

Modernidad y justicia social

I realized I was in trouble one night while I watched TV at my father's house. The talkshow host was interviewing a neoliberal politician about Donald Trump's threats to impose tariffs on Mexico, perhaps even cancel the North American Free Trade Agreement. The politician gesticulated as he spoke, eyes wide with disbelief. I couldn't help feeling sympathy for the man. He was a member of my father's generation of Mexican statesmen—people who bet all their chips on a worldview in which the United States and Mexico were partners.

The Mexican elite once shared the Latin American Left's traditional hatred of the United States. To my grandfather's generation—Francophile admirers of Mitterrand le philosophe—the North American ruling class was a coterie of barbarians crass in manners, crude in taste. Their rulers were tradesmen: either avaricious bourgeois who soiled themselves in finance or opportunist parvenues who leveraged a picaresque gift for social climbing into Hollywood moguldom. And so my grandfather and his cousins sent their sons to schools where French was the main foreign language, which only served to make English the subversive choice. Tired of their forebears' piety, my father's generation embraced

American culture. They revolted against the staid Hegelianism of their teachers, looking for inspiration first in Chomsky, then in the Chicago School. When the Soviet Union began to collapse, they felt vindicated. History had ended. America had won. Their fathers had been proven wrong.

My father's classmates then applied for student visas, just like mine, and flocked to the great universities of the United States, where they discovered the lucid beauty of quantitative economics. What a rush it must have been to realize the alchemical secret to turning shit into gold was written in the language of interest rates! When they returned to Mexico City with their doctorates, they began to lobby furiously for economic integration. They envisioned NAFTA as the first step toward a partnership that would eventually resemble the European Union, with free movement of capital, commodities, and labor. That last point was crucial: if Mexico was to sacrifice its autonomy for trade with the United States, it needed guarantees that its citizens would be allowed to go where the market called them. Otherwise, the alchemical spell would misfire: some people's shit would be turned into gold, but what little gold most Mexicans had would be turned back into shit.

The Socialists, the nationalists, the Zapatistas, even the old -school reactionaries warned my father's generation against bargaining with the devil. The neoliberals replied in earnest that they believed Mexico and the United States could work together as friends. Their classmates, teachers, and wives were American and fond of Mexico. Why would the United States as a whole be different?

The debate was never in good faith. Democracy was a decade away; the Left was toothless; the old Francophiles had retired. The three countries of North America signed the treaty with fanfare. The Mexican economy grew, but not at the pace the neoliberals projected. The richest man in Mexico became the richest man in the world, but the poor remained poor. In some senses they were poorer than ever. Their corner stores now sold American cigarettes, but their young people were gone. Some of them sent enough money that the streets of small towns across Mexico were soon lined with large labyrinthine houses, built without architects, in garish vernacular styles that aspired to opulence—but many more came back with nothing, broken, telling confusing stories about predawn raids and freezing detention cells.

As the years passed even the neoliberals began to suspect something was wrong. Again and again my father's generation of politicians called their American classmates, by then senators and governors. Hadn't they sat through the same seminars, listened to the same exaltations of laissez-faire borders and freedom of movement? Hadn't they made a deal? The Americans demurred, misquoted Burke on gradual change, said they were about to step into a meeting.

I sat in my father's TV room, watching the economist all but tear out fistfuls of his own hair. I looked at his face, at the large, deep-set eyes that are the marker of my people. The problem was his generation of criollos refused to see themselves as colonials. They didn't realize that their classmates at Harvard and Chicago treated them nicely not because they saw them as equals but because they were light-skinned curiosities in well-cut suits, distinguished guests from a quaint but insignificant country. With Indigenous people and mestizos, it was a different story. The Chicago Boys' belief in individual freedom didn't extend to people with dark skin. Their economics was not the objective science they claimed it to be, but a political instrument designed to justify imperial expansion—a postmodern American equivalent of sixteenth-century Spanish Catholicism.

I turned off the TV. The Americans had let me go to Yale

because they wanted me to become a translator, a go-between. I was supposed to go back to the capital, leverage my last name into a position in the highest levels of government, and advocate for American interests. Instead, I held on to my visa as if for dear life. And now I'd given it away in hopes of becoming a writer. I lay down on the couch but couldn't sleep. My earliest memories were of watching American films, coveting American toys. The band I formed with my high school friends had played covers of American songs. For better or worse I was a child of NAFTA. And then, as I lay in the reddish darkness of a city I barely knew, wondering what judgment awaited me as a foreigner in my own country, I realized I was talking to myself in English.

Guerra, guerra en el monte, en el valle

Everyone at El Centenario was already drunk. Against my protestations, Esteban ordered a bottle of mezcal, saying it was cheaper that way. For the next few hours, he and I took turns pontificating about colorful episodes of Mexican history. Claire listened with a combination of amusement and exasperation. The mezcal was acrid and tasted of gasoline but gave me a warm feeling.

I stepped outside to smoke. When I came back, I saw Esteban lean over and kiss the American. I felt my face grow hot but told myself it was better this way. In theory Lee and I weren't a couple, but we talked on the phone almost every day. I stopped by the bar to order quesadillas and brought them to the table. They pretended nothing had happened and I followed their lead.

Then the head waiter turned up the volume on the television. The din of conversations died, and all eyes drifted to the screen, which showed the balcony of the National Palace and a clock counting down. When the hour struck, President Enrique Peña Nieto emerged, a flag in his hand.

"¡Asesino!" someone shouted.

"¡Ratero!" another countered.

"¡Hijo de puta!"

"Ask your slut of a wife what I did to her pussy last night!"

"Do you need ointment for your asshole after the gringos did you so good?"

"Resign and kill yourself while you are at it!"

Then an aide appeared behind the president and held a microphone to his mouth. The cantina fell silent.

"Mexicans!" the president said, his voice echoing through the city as thousands of speakers repeated his words. "Tonight, we honor the men and women who died so we may have a fatherland!"

The air at El Centenario grew thin, as if everyone held their breath at once. The only sound was the clinking of glasses and the televised murmur of the crowd at the Zócalo. Then the president took a deep breath and called the heroic roll.

"¡Viva Hidalgo!" he bellowed.

"¡Viva!" the crowd responded.

"¡Viva Morelos!"

"¡Viva!"

"¡Viva Zapata!"

"¡Viva!"

"¡Viva México!"

"¡Viva!"

"¡Viva México!"

"¡Viva!"

"¡VIVA MÉXICO!"

"¡VIVA!"

The president waved the flag and the cathedral bells tolled and fireworks burst and car horns blared and dogs howled and shot glasses shattered and gunshots fired into the sky and all of Mexico cheered as if we'd won the World Cup. Then he handed the flag to his aide and raised his right hand, tensing it across his chest with the palm parallel to the ground. The nation rose as one and, precariously holding its drunken balance, saluted back.

Lo que el César no sabe . . .

When I was a teenager, my father took me out to dinner once a month at a French restaurant frequented by politicians, where we would order confit de canard and a bottle of Bordeaux and refrain from talking about anything important.

A few weeks before the incident with the blue Sentra, on the way to the restaurant, I read in *Alarma* that a teenager my age had been found in a car not unlike mine. His father, a famous businessman, had paid a large ransom. It made no difference: the kidnappers still brought the boy to a dark alley, tortured him, and shot him in the face.

"Papá," I asked over crème brûlée. "Have you ever received a death threat?"

He took a sip of scotch. "Not a single one."

Años de peregrinaje

At age sixteen Nazario concluded there was nothing for him in Michoacán and decided to go to the North. He crossed the border without documents and settled in Redwood City, California, where he found landscaping work. The pay wasn't bad but the days were long, and he hadn't come to America to break his back in the sun. He heard there was money in drugs, laid his hands on some marijuana, and enrolled in a public high school to sell it to the students. After some time he got a permit that allowed him to cross the border at will. He began traveling back and forth between the United States and Michoacán, selling American cars in Mexico and Mexican weed in America. He then "stole a wife"—the term is his—and bought a few acres of land near Apatzingán, at which point he found himself in possession of everything he wanted and yet unsatisfied. So, he resolved to become a drug lord.

Y tu mamá también

After the national anthem was over, we ordered another bottle. Esteban said he was going to buy cigarettes. When he walked out of the door, Claire moved to the seat next to mine. I thought of Lee. In theory we weren't a couple.

Then Claire put my hand on her thigh. "¿Ponme la mano áqui?" she said, misplacing the accent.

I kissed her. She leaned back and laughed. "You Mexicans!" she said, then leaned back in.

When Esteban returned, Claire went to the bathroom.

"You know she kissed me first, right?" he said.

"You mean you kissed her."

"A technicality. And Lee?"

"We aren't a couple."

"You sure seemed like one."

"We're playing it as it lays."

"What does that even mean?"

"None of your business. What do we do now?"

He finished his mezcal and shook his head. "I guess we'll have to see where the night takes us."

He is old, or seems to be, but perhaps it would be more accurate to say he is old fashioned. It isn't the gray hair that dates him but the pomade, the whiff of cologne, the Windsor knot on the fraying tie. And then there is the anachronism of his profession, which is older than gramophones and pianolas, banking and religion. From sundown on Friday to sunrise on Sunday, he wanders the cantinas of La Condesa with a guitar in his hands and a rose in his lapel. For less than a dollar he will sing a song for you. Any song. He knows them all by heart.

He usually looks embarrassed when he approaches a table to offer his services, but once he begins to sing, all traces of shame disappear from his face. He knows that he is a midwife for emotions in a city as congested with feelings as it is with diesel trucks, that his work is as essential to public health as the sterilization of stray dogs and the delousing of schoolchildren.

The troubadour has a ballad for every occasion, but he's most emotionally nuanced when he sings about unrequited love. He knows love lost, love unattained, love that never existed. He can sing anger or regret, self-loathing or good riddance, jealousy as suicidal fury or as masochistic voyeurism. He understands the bitter pleasure of picking at old wounds but also the wild joy of willful forgetting.

This precision of expression has a powerful effect on the troubadour's listeners. Sometimes, when he holds a dissonant chord for a few bars longer than expected, it's as if the gap between words and feelings disappears completely. In that moment, especially if it's after midnight and everybody has been drinking, some listeners burst into tears—and not the modest droplets of cinemas but the ugly outpourings of funeral homes.

These moments of emotional release are possible because the troubadour's repertoire is the poetic equivalent of communal pastures and public baths. The songs he sings do not merely give voice to his listeners' inner lives: they shaped them, gave them form. When the troubadour plays and the crowd sings along, the regulars of El Centenario hear their innermost aches in another's voice and are thus reminded they are not alone.

Yet the larger part of this catharsis comes not from the individual's communion with the crowd but from the intensity of the relationship between the singer and the person who requested the song. When he sings, the troubadour looks at his patron straight in the eye, holding an unblinking gaze that would be out of place in any other setting. The result is a sudden intimacy more reminiscent of a confessional or a brothel than a concert.

One night the troubadour walked up to the table where I was sitting with friends. Over the next half hour, they took turns requesting songs. I hummed along, trying not to call attention to myself. But then it was my turn.

"What's it going to be, boss?" the troubadour said.

The whole table turned to me. I ransacked my brain. What was the name of that song about passports? I could hear it in my head—a haunting, halting minor tune over a syncopated rhythm, a tentative voice tying syllables together with slurring ligatures: No soy de aquí, ni soy de allá . . . The milonga evoked a waterfront bar in Buenos Aires rather than a cantina in Anáhuac, but I couldn't think of anything else. "What about that Facundo Cabral tune? The one about not being from here or from there?"

My friends jeered. "An Argentine?" Esteban said. "Really?"

I turned red and looked at the troubadour. His smile widened. "Sorry, boss. Don't think I know the chords."

Childhood of poverty, migration to America, empirical discovery of basic economic concepts such as inelastic demand and the correlation of risk and profit—on the surface, Nazario's biography follows the same template as the stories of any number of Mexican narcos. The difference is that he loved books: the Bible and the evangelical theology of John Eldredge, self-help tracts of both the mystical and the business-friendly varieties, popularized accounts of the Mexican Revolution, anthologies of Maya myths, treatises on alchemy and astrology, summaries of the Platonic dialogues, *The Prince*, *The Lord of the Rings*, *The Da Vinci Code*, *The Art of War*, *Quotations from Chairman Mao*, and the Egyptian *Book of the Dead*.

It should come as no surprise, then, that Nazario turned out to be something stranger and more terrifying than a mere criminal capitalist. The question then becomes whether to call him a politician, revolutionary, or cult leader. While all those terms are appropriate, none captures the mixture of brutality and charisma with which he acquired and wielded power, much less the double consciousness that allowed him to commit mass murder while regarding himself as a compassionate man. Prophet comes closer, but the positive connotations of the word would require one to modify it with the adjective *false* or the phrase *of death*. And so perhaps it's best to describe Nazario as what he undoubtedly was—a writer of not inconsiderable powers:

> *There is an old adage that says every people has the rulers it deserves. I would add that every government has the criminals it breeds. For the truth is that those of us who are born without the favor of a saint must suffer and wage battle. For the wretched of the earth there is no path and no door, no school and no trade. Nobody cares—not the Church, not the state,*

not our fellow men. And so I ask the journalists and the politicians and all those who persist in foul calumny and call me unfeeling and evil, all those who say in print or in speech that I fancy myself a god or a saint: What did you expect? What did you expect from a child who grew up with the world as adversary, walking alone on dusty mule-trails through half-starved villages, with no companion save misfortune, grief-sick and resentful, embittered and diminished, seeing in each face nothing but hopelessness and the encroachment of death? What did you expect from a country ruled by a government corrupt and dishonest that cares not for its people, their life and liberty, their works and days, their foolish pursuit of unreachable happiness? What did you expect from a culture that has become barren, that has forgotten the importance of blood and soil, of family and birthplace, that worships American gold at the expense of Mexican brother and sister? Let us be honest for once. The man who breaks the law out of hunger and pride never acts alone. You are all my accomplices.

No te malviajes

"I'm pretty sure they're safe," the Bear said.

"Pretty sure is a pretty low bar."

It was sunset. We were sitting on the terrace of the Bear's family's house in Valle de Bravo, staring at a little plastic bag containing three brownish pressed pills. Esteban reached over the table and grabbed the bag, took out a pill, and downed it with beer. He passed it to the Bear, who also swallowed a pill, then offered the last one to me.

"No pressure," he said. "But you're being a total wuss."

I took the bag from his hand and threw the pill in my mouth—and then within the hour we discovered that we couldn't sit still, and that we were grinding our teeth, and that our hearts were racing, and that the lights were brighter and the sounds louder, and suddenly it was absolutely imperative that we go on a walk, so we left the house and climbed down the hill and headed to the town, where we discovered that smoking cigarettes felt better than usual and that someone was following us and that maybe we were having heart attacks and that if we weren't in fact dying, then the only possible explanation for our present state was that we had unwittingly ingested not a small dose of MDMA but an untold amount of methamphetamine, in which case it would be safe to assume that more than one person had died in the course of the production and distribution of our kick, which in turn meant that we should feel guilty, but it was difficult to feel anything, in part because we were exhausted, which made sense, considering that the sun was already high in the sky, which in turn made us wonder whether we shouldn't eat something, but the truth was that we didn't feel like eating, and so perhaps the thing to do was to keep walking around the narrow streets of the charming town, past the whitewashed walls of the houses with their band of red paint near the ground, and invent a pastime to distract ourselves from our racing hearts, and after some time we decided we should translate a poem into English, so we returned to the Bear's house and sat on the terrace and after much argument agreed that *Death without End,* José Gorostiza's book-long epic about a glass of water, was an ideal candidate, given the circumstances, so we looked it up on the Bear's phone and got ahold of a pen and a notepad, and by the time the sun set again we had the first few lines:

> Full of myself, besieged inside my skin
> by an intangible God who drowns me,
> belied perhaps
> by his radiant atmosphere of lights,

which overcasts my overspilling consciousness,
my wings shattered into shards of air,
my clumsy crawling through the mud;
full of myself—too full—I find myself
in the astonished image of water,
which is nothing
save a ceaseless tumbling
of fallen angels
plunging into gravity's immaculate delight . . .

El hombre se descubre en sus silencios

On our last day in Valle de Bravo I stood on the Bear's terrace and looked down on the lake. The water was gray and the sky was white and on the other side of the basin rose dark green mountains. Slow damp clouds were falling into the valley, turning the air into mist.

"Looks like it's going to rain," the Bear said. "We better get going."

I nodded, grabbed my backpack, and headed to the gate. When I walked out of the house, I found Pedro on the driver's seat of the car he'd crashed, staring at the lake through the bulletproof window. I wondered what had happened to him. Then I wondered why I wanted to know.

The Bear, Esteban, and I loaded our things into the car, and we headed back to Mexico City. As we drove up the mountains, Pedro cleared his throat and took a deep breath. "Sir. About the other day . . ."

"Don't worry. We'll come up with a plausible story and stick to it. How's that?"

"Thank you, sir. I've been a bodyguard for only two weeks. I'm not used to this kind of service."

I nodded, pleased with my own magnanimity. Then Esteban scoffed.

"What?" I said in English.

"Nothing."

"What?"

"Low-key corruption?"

"He could lose his job."

"He could have killed someone."

"So I should get him fired?"

"Do whatever you want. I don't care."

"Clearly you do."

"I just think hypocrisy isn't a good look."

I turned away and looked out the window. I began to second guess myself. Maybe I shouldn't ask Pedro. I wasn't a reporter anymore, but perhaps I was a hypocrite. After an hour of agonizing, I decided to go for it. "Pedro, what were you doing before you were assigned to bodyguard duty?"

He caught my eye in the rearview mirror, then looked back to the road. "I was part of a tactical assault squad, sir."

He started to say something else but hesitated. I felt my face grow hot and wondered whether I should apologize. I turned to the window to avoid Pedro's eyes and saw timid raindrops hitting the glass, storm clouds forming in the distance. I told myself it was the insomnia. Every night since I'd come back, I'd had nightmares. In America I slept well. I closed my eyes and rested my forehead against the cool glass. Maybe if I slept through the drive, I'd feel better when we got to the city.

But then, just as I was drifting out of consciousness, Pedro started talking again. "Yeah," he said. "My boys and me? We busted some heads. For sure."

There was something different in his voice. He sounded loose, almost pleased. I sat up and looked at him in the rearview mirror and saw he was smiling.

"You should have seen us. All cocky and proud. We'd show up at la maña's safe houses real early in the morning and we'd knock on the door and give them a chance to surrender and then we'd hit them with everything we had until every last mañoso was in handcuffs or in a bag. And let me tell you, sir, we were damn good at it. We had it down to a science, three simple steps: show up, knock-knock, bang-bang." He laughed, then went on, speaking faster, almost tripping on his words. "That's right. We were tough as nails. And don't get me wrong, sir, we weren't perfect, we might have gone in a little too hard on a mañoso or two, I'm not going to sit here and pretend that never happened. But at the end of the day, we went home knowing we were some damn fine federales."

He fell silent. I wondered if it'd been condescending to think he'd feel compelled to answer my questions. Maybe he was dying to talk.

"Why did you decide to join the force?" I said.

"Like most people, I guess. My daddy was a cop in the old highway patrol, before the reorganization. He didn't want me to join, though. Said it was a shit life. So I started lawyer-college. Figured it would be the same thing but in a suit. But the truth is I had the bug, wanted a piece of the action. And besides, I wasn't good with books. So one day on my way to school I said fuck it and went to the academy instead, and before I knew it I was in Sinaloa."

"So you were fighting El Chapo?"

"And the brothers Beltrán. Those were the good years, sir, the golden age, the days of glory. I mean, don't get me wrong, señor, it was fucked up; those fuckers weren't kidding around. They were businessmen. They weren't going to let us into their shit without making a scene. You could almost say I understand them, not that I condone them, just that I understand. Still, it wasn't too bad. We stayed in hotels and had Sundays off. We got to see our families every couple of months. The pay was always late but it arrived sooner or later. Hell, sometimes we even got to go on TV to show off all the shit we'd found on the mañosos, all the coke and the meth and the guns. And, I mean, sure, you had to wear a balaclava, for your own safety, especially after the papers published the photo of one of the boys who killed the elder Beltrán, and then the mañosos showed the picture around until they figured out who he was, and then they showed up at his house and killed his wife. But still, your kids knew it was you in the mask, and even though they couldn't tell their friends about it, I like to think it made them proud. So yeah, señor, what can I tell you? Sinaloa was no bed of roses, no sir, but it was what we signed up for. And besides, the seafood was great."

He paused to hand a bill to a tollbooth attendant. He pocketed the change and drove on but didn't start talking again. I figured there was no harm in asking at this point. "And then what happened?"

"They sent me to Michoacán."

"And what was that like?"

"Like an American movie. Like Vietnam. Like hell. We lived up to our knees in mud. The army had helicopters, armored trucks, but we weren't soldiers and the roads were shit, so we had to walk everywhere. There were no markets, so we ate crap from a can, or places to stay, so we commandeered people's cabins. They weren't happy about it, but it's not like the bosses gave us tents. The worst was the nights: either boiling or freezing. Plus you never knew when you would go for them or they would come for you. After a while we were all crazy from no sleep."

He rummaged in the pocket of his suit and handed me a cell phone. "Here. Take a look."

The cracked screen showed a group of men in tactical gear

standing at the edge of a ravine in an oyamel forest. They were posing like a soccer team, the ones in front crouching and the ones in the back standing straight.

"There we are," Pedro said. "My boys and me. We look real silly with those smiles, don't we? Truth is we were scared shitless. You could hear the rat-a-tat of the point-fifties in the choppers and the bra-ka-ka of the Kalashnikovs on the hills. But we wanted a picture for our kids. Guess that's the joke."

He stopped. I knew where this was going but couldn't resist. "What's the joke?"

"The joke is that a few minutes later they came for us. Los hijos de la chingada. They knew the terrain. Came at us from above. Mowed down all of them. All of my boys."

La noche sin fin

On a cloudless night in September five years after I left for America, a group of police officers held forty-three college students at gunpoint in the same small town Mayeli's parents had risked everything to leave. The officers loaded the students onto cattle trucks and forced them to march up a wooded hill under a starry sky, until they reached a clearing by a river. There, the police handed the students to the members of a small-time cartel. As the sun rose, the traffickers lined up the students. One by one, they shot them in the head.

The narcos doused the bodies with gasoline, covered them with old tires, and set them aflame. The bodies burned for hours, well into the afternoon, until only smoldering ashes remained. The men shoveled the ashes into black garbage bags, which they threw, still open, into the river. The ashes dissolved like dried flowers crumbled into a dust so fine it disappears in the wind.

When the government that nominated my father to the

Supreme Court finally allowed reporters to visit the scene, all that was left to photograph was an empty field of grass with specks of blackened earth. There were no bodies to put on the front page. There were also few facts to put in an article. The story I just told used to be the government's version, but it has since changed countless times—and shown to be as riddled with lies as Cortés's account of the conquest. A team of international experts has uncovered evidence that the Armed Forces and the Federal Police also participated in the massacre.

The Austro-Hungarians of the capital experienced the drug war as paranoia—a vague, unsettling suspicion that something was wrong, that dark forces were secretly planning their demise. By contrast, the poor in the provinces experienced the war as terror. Where paranoia is diffuse, terror is concrete: the butt of a rifle, the texture of ropes tightening around one's wrists, the desecrated body of a loved one, an empty field by a river.

Such is the way of the world: the rich write novels; the poor just die.

Laurel de victoria, sepulcro de honor

After Claire came back to the table, we spent an hour making nervous small talk about the wedding. When the head waiter announced last call, we looked at one another in silence. I wondered whether we were all thinking the same thing. I thought about saying it but decided to see if one of them would say it first. After a while I couldn't take it.

"I'll get the check," I said as I got up. "We'll settle up later."

When I came back, they were kissing. When I sat down, they kept kissing. When we got in a taxi, they were still kissing. When we got to Esteban's apartment, they headed to his bedroom, and I lay out on the couch. I took off my shoes and turned off the lights but was too nauseated to sleep. I got up and poured myself a glass of water. I scribbled a few incoherent notes on the ways in which NAFTA provides historical proof that the concept of national independence is nothing but a liberal fallacy. Then I vomited in the sink.

The next morning, I woke up with bright sun on my face and no idea of where I was. I got up slowly, trying not to make sudden movements, and headed to the kitchen. I made a pot of coffee and scoured the cabinets in search of aspirin. I sank on a chair and noticed my hands were shaking. Then Claire emerged from the bedroom wrapped in a sheet and locked herself in the bath. A few minutes later Esteban came out in his underwear.

I handed him a cup of coffee. "Did you two have fun?"

He tried to take a sip but burned his lips. "No, my boy," he said. "We were too drunk." He groaned and collapsed on the chair next to mine. "Probably better this way." He pressed his thumbs into his closed eyes. "Sleeping with an American on Independence Night counts as high treason."

"Do you have any aspirin?"

He pointed to the bathroom. Behind the door, we could hear Claire dry-heaving and wet-retching.

"Good thing we have another party to go to," I said.

"Shit!" Esteban said, as if he'd only now realized. "Aviva's getting married!"

A breeze came in through the window, carrying the echo of the military parade downtown. Hundreds of miles away, deep under Oaxaca, immense rocks were shifting.

La venta es un castillo

The waiters at El Centenario wear an immaculate uniform: black dress shoes, black dress pants, white dress shirts, black aprons, white or black hair slicked back with water and gel. Their studiously exaggerated decorum betrays that the cantina's pretense to elegance is less an attempt to assuage the class anxieties of its clientele than an elaborate joke on the rich. The youngest must be in his late forties; the oldest must be at least eighty. They are attentive, even obsequious, but their solicitude is tempered by their obvious amusement at the expense of their clients. They've been here forever, seen it all. They know the hearts of men, their infinite capacity for folly. They look upon their customers with the ironic compassion with which minor deities once regarded mortals, sighing and shaking their heads and whispering to themselves, "There they go again."

El camino a Damasco

A few years after his marriage, Nazario's ambition drove him to return to the United States. This time he settled in McAllen, Texas, where he became involved in the methamphetamine trade. Against his better judgment he began using his own product and grew reckless, leading all-night revivals in storefront churches, preaching under his own name, attracting attention. Eventually his luck ran out and he was arrested and imprisoned. When his sentence was over, he was deported and spent several years wandering the villages of Michoacán, preaching the gospel and "studying the philosophies of the ancient Egyptians, Indians, Chinese, Greeks, Hebrews, and Aztecs." Then, as he stumbled home on a summer morning after a week-long bender, he received a revelation that God had chosen him to bring his Kingdom to earth.

He recruited a small group of disciples and told them that it was their duty to fight the evils of both the cartels and the government. Soon after, he received a second revelation and came to see that God wanted him to fight fire with fire. He then procured a cinder block shack in an out-of-the-way place—and gallons of industrial solvents, and large plastic barrels, and enough pseudoephedrine to treat a family of congested elephants, and a quarter ton of fertilizer—and began building the first of countless methamphetamine laboratories.

Nazario's extravagant displays of power attracted the attention of President Felipe Calderón, who hailed from Michoacán and became hell-bent on reclaiming his home state for the republic. In October 2006, Calderón strode onto a stage at an army barracks outside Apatzingán, wearing a military uniform even though he was a civilian, and declared his administration was now at war with the drug cartels. He said the civilian security cabinet—chiefly my father, then attorney general, and Genaro García Luna, a career cop who'd been appointed public security secretary—would coordinate the effort, but the Armed Forces would also take a leading role. The police, he explained, were too poorly equipped and too corrupt to stand a chance against the cartels. The good news was the conflict would be quick. After a few months of decisive action, the people of Mexico would know peace.

In the years that followed, the country plunged into darkness. The tense equilibrium which gave the old drug-trafficking organizations an incentive to keep a low profile collapsed. The cartels ceased to behave like commodity exporters and started acting like factions in a civil war. Bodies piled in the streets—soldiers and gangsters, yes, but also sex workers and shopkeepers, farmers and migrants, truck drivers and schoolchildren. My father and García Luna differed on the appropriate response. Eventually their disagreement became an ugly personal feud. By 2009 the two men refused to speak to one another—an unsustainable situation, considering they were supposed to be coordinating a war. Presented with a choice, Calderón decided to keep the plainspoken cop over the sibylline lawyer. That's when our family moved to London.

A decade later, García Luna was arrested in Texas on charges of accepting millions from the Sinaloa Cartel. At the height of the period that came to be known as "the democratic transition," though, the government's inability to defeat the cartels seemed inexplicable. Desperate to have something to show for his efforts—and under pressure from his American friends—Calderón embarked on a frantic campaign to capture or eliminate the bosses of the most notorious cartels.

In 2010 the president held a triumphant press conference to announce the Federal Police had killed Nazario Moreno. In a strike of public-relations genius, Nazario didn't disprove his adversaries' willful error. Instead, he wandered Michoacán surrounded by his retinue of knights, letting himself be seen by the people, a warlike messiah returned from the dead.

Nazario soon defeated or absorbed his local competitors and came to dominate the drug trade in several states. His genius, however, was not in military strategy but propaganda. His organization, la Familia Michoacana, was less a smuggling ring than a political movement that mixed agrarian communitarianism with regional chauvinism. Their goal, Nazario claimed in billboards and newspaper columns, was to rid Michoacán of the "foreigners" who tore the region's social fabric and stole the wealth of its people—a nebulous collection of enemies that included other cartels, transnational corporations, and the Mexican and American governments.

The message resonated with many in Michoacán, one of the poorest states of Mexico. With their support Nazario became the de-facto ruler of an area the size of West Virginia. La Familia collected taxes, built roads, and funded schools and hospitals. It set up courts of justice where its judges sentenced "antisocials" such as rapists and thieves to punishments ranging from public humiliation to execution by hanging. Eventually the organization expanded its business beyond drugs, taking control of Michoacán's rich mines and fertile fields to export iron ore to China and avocados to the United States.

This last development suggests Nazario's rise to power is best understood as the ultimate consequence of neoliberalism. The North American Free Trade Agreement realigned Mexico along a north-south axis and created incentives to move all valuable commodities toward the United States. At the same time, the treaty forced Mexican farmers to compete with the industrialized agriculture of the Middle West, which, despite the US government's breathless celebration of free markets, remained subsidized. Millions of Mexicans, many from Michoacán, were forced to emigrate to the North, where they found themselves marginalized by the law and excluded from lucrative work. Predictably, some turned to the drug trade. When they returned home, they discovered that the collapse of the old state apparatus from the days of one-party rule had left a vacuum of services and therefore authority. It's no surprise they decided to fill the gap.

But attributing the phenomenon of la Familia to international politics and economics risks obscuring the fact its members were responsible for their actions, even if we were all their accomplices. The exact number of their victims is unlikely to ever be known, but even today, years after Nazario's downfall, villagers keep discovering mass graves: fifty, sixty, ninety bodies in the same shallow ditch. On more occasions than anyone can count, Nazario's men dragged dozens of people out of their beds in the middle of the night, lined them up, and shot them in the head.

Para Patrick Iber

One afternoon, between my trip to Valle de Bravo and Aviva's wedding, I went through the bookshelves in my father's study, looking for his copy of the essays of José Lezama Lima. I thought the Cuban poet's manifesto, "La expresión Americana," where he offered a modernist defense of the baroque as the highest manifestation of Latin American culture, would be useful for my thesis. Instead, I stumbled on a hardcover edition of Harold Bloom's *The Western Canon*. I thought I recognized it, so I took it from the shelf. I was right: there, on the first page, was a handwritten note, in English and signed by an American diplomat, thanking my father for his willingness to join "the global fight against drug-trafficking."

It must have been 2007 or 2008, when it was still possible to pretend Calderón's offensive against the drug lords was something other than a disaster. A high-ranking US delegation had traveled to Mexico to meet with their "partners" and coordinate binational anticartel efforts. On their last night in the country, my father invited them over for dinner. He did that frequently, bringing political allies—and occasionally adversaries—to the house. Part of it was atavism: the exquisite courtesy of the creoles, that neurotic compulsion to display hyperbolic hospitality. But the dinners were also a choreographed performance designed to charm the guests and advance my father's goals. On such nights the whole family was called to service. My mother would cook a feast: red snapper stuffed with plantains, angel-hair pasta with lime zest and scallops and pine-nuts, wafer-thin shells of dark chocolate tempered in the shape of a tulip and filled with cardamom mousse. My younger siblings were summoned to meet the guests and show off their impeccable manners before obediently retiring at bedtime. I, being a little older, was sometimes asked to join the dinner table, with instructions to ask intelligent questions.

That evening with the American delegation went well. The guests were Bush-era neocons—not the faux-Texan, anti-intellectual type, but the kind who read Leo Strauss in college: the perfect audience for our little troupe. And indeed, the Americans were impressed. In their minds Mexico was a barely civilized place. They didn't expect the Austro-Hungarians.

"I was told you are a bookish man," one of the Americans said to my father as he handed him *The Western Canon*.

"Thank you," my father said. "Bloom is one of the great American minds of his generation. Sebastián loves his anthology of the best poems in the English language. Don't you, Sebastián?"

I nodded, filled with adolescent embarrassment.

"Would you recite some of 'Crossing Brooklyn Ferry' for our American friends?" my father said. "Or maybe a bit from 'When the Lilacs Last in the Dooryard Bloom'd'?"

"I would prefer not to," I said, praying for a stroke.

"A shame," my father said, turning to the Americans. "But let the record show that in this house we are Whitmanians."

At the end of the evening, the leader of the delegation—a tall man with a drill sergeant's jaw, the broad shoulders of a high school quarterback, and the spilling gut of a desk-bound bureaucrat—stood up and clinked his champagne flute with a spoon. "I'd like to propose a toast," he said. He waited until he had everyone's attention, then went on: "We live in an age full of dangers. Hidden dangers. All over the world there are dangerous people in the shadows. Islamic terrorists. Drug traffickers. Dictators who threaten the innocent with weapons of mass destruction."

"That's right!" said another American who'd had a little too much to drink.

"It wasn't always like this," the leader of the delegation continued. "A generation ago the enemies of freedom were out in the open. Nazis. Communists. And so our grandfathers fought them in the open. But the challenge we face is different. The wars we must fight are different. The war on terror. The war on drugs. These battles are as important for the survival of the free world as the fight against Hitler and the Soviets. But many don't see that. Our grandfathers were celebrated as heroes. We, alas, have to accept the fact our fight is thankless. Which is why I raise my glass for Attorney General Arteaga y Salazar. We thank you for your hospitality, Alberto. And we thank you, too, for your courage, and the courage of your family. Because the kind of war we must fight comes with risks. Risks that affect not just us but also our loved ones."

The American paused again, then turned to look at me. "Sebastián," he went on. "You should be proud of your father. What he's doing isn't easy. And, as I'm sure you know, because you're an observant young man, it's also dangerous. The enemies of freedom don't like it when good men challenge them. But good men must step up anyway. And for that they need the support of their families. You, Sebastián, and your lovely mother and siblings, are very brave. The risks you're accepting by standing with your father are scary. But you are doing the right thing. Because your father, Sebastián, is working to make the world a better place. He's lucky to have a son who understands."

I stared at him—at the splat of sauce on his white shirt, at the miniature bald eagles on his too-wide tie, at his Neanderthal chin—and felt a surge of disgust in the bottom of my gut, as if I'd smelled something rotten.

"I'll wrap up before I bore you to death," the American concluded, raising his glass. "To Alberto! And to his family!"

My father bowed his head in thanks and raised his flute. "And to Mexico's greatest friend," he said. "The people of the United States!"

Para Heinrich von Kleist

The day after I returned to Iowa from Aviva's wedding, I climbed onto my fire escape for an afternoon cigarette, beer in hand, and opened Twitter on my phone to try to figure out which among my old colleagues at the website had been laid off after a sudden drop in traffic caused by a tweak in Facebook's algorithm.

Then I saw the headlines.

I called my mother but she didn't pick up. Neither did my father. Or my sister. Or my brother. Or the Bear. Or Esteban. I kept calling, one after the other, always in the same order, and as I listened to their voicemail greetings, I was struck by how calm I felt when I realized that, except for the Bear, all of them lived in either La Roma or La Condesa, the two districts of the capital most vulnerable to earthquakes.

Eventually my father texted me. So did my mother. A few minutes later I got a message from the Bear. He and his girlfriend Chloe had run into my siblings on the street. *Chloe's building collapsed,* the Bear wrote. *But we are okay. Your brother was even able to save his kitten. It's crazy tho—smoke everywhere.*

I picture them huddled on the sidewalk: the Bear with his scrawny beard and Panama hat, Chloe in her overalls and sunglasses, my sister with her pink hair, my brother holding on to his overweight cat.

But I still hadn't heard from Esteban.

I texted the Bear asking if he knew where he was. He didn't reply. A quarter hour later I got a call from my sister.

"Mom and Dad are coming to meet us," she said. "It looks like everyone is safe."

"What about Esteban?"

She fell silent. In the background I heard sirens. "I don't know. The Bear went looking for him."

I later learned that the Bear had made his way through streets lined with debris to Avenida Ámsterdam, where he saw Esteban's ancient Mac sitting on top of the rubble, and that he then spent several hours talking to neighbors, gawkers, police officers, firefighters, rescue workers, emergency medics, wailing mourners, army engineers, television reporters, city employees, volunteer diggers, terrified tourists, injured bus drivers, soldiers, and priests, asking all of them if they'd seen Esteban. As if they knew him. As if they'd be able to recognize his body.

El búho de Minerva no vuela salvo al anochecer

One morning shortly after the earthquake I went through the voice memos on my phone and found a five-hour-long recording I'd made one night in 2014, a few months after the massacre of Ayotzinapa. I pressed play and heard my father reiterate his agreement to speak on the record, then the sloshing sound of scotch falling into tumblers.

"Can you tell me about your role in the drug war?"

"I'm not sure that's the right term. But sure. Where should I start?"

"I was thinking we could start by talking about Calderón's speech."

"The one in Michoacán?"

"Yeah."

The recording then went quiet for a moment. Next there was the sound of someone knocking on a door, then the squeak of a sliding chair, then indistinct words between my father and the housekeeper. I held my headphones over my ears, trying to make out what was being said—something about orchids. Then I heard another round being poured and the voice of my father, clear once again.

"We can begin there if you like. But to properly answer your question we'd have to go back much further."

He then began listing the factors that had set the stage for the tragedy.

He told me about the American efforts to close the navigable waters between Colombia and Miami, which he said forced cocaine shipments to move on land and through Mexico.

He told me about the end of the American ban on the sale of assault rifles, which he said dramatically increased the firepower of Mexican traffickers.

He told me about the coming of democracy to Mexico, which he said dismantled the network of unofficial agreements between the old authoritarian government and the cartels.

All the while he spoke with the calm eloquence of a man who has brushed with history and has come to understand that people make it, but not under conditions of their choosing; that the names in history books do not refer to individuals but are ciphers for unfathomable forces; that if it hadn't been him, it would have been someone like him, because we are not autonomous agents so much as beings-in-the-world.

But then we began to argue.

He insisted that what was happening in Mexico was not a war but a matter of criminal justice, cops and robbers rather than soldiers and insurgents.

He insisted that he never used the word "guerra" to describe the conflict.

He insisted that the press had invented the term to blame the government for a disaster that was in fact the product of world-historical dynamics beyond the control of any individual actor.

He insisted on this point even after I opened my laptop and read out loud several instances in which he'd used the word during interviews with better reporters than me.

Que te agarre confesado

That day long ago in September, Ludwig, Darwin, and I were heading to band rehearsal at my friend Pablo's house, ten minutes away from my place. We passed one of the bodegas that lined the streets of my old neighborhood. It occurred to me I shouldn't show up empty-handed.

"Could we stop to pick up some beer?" I said.

The bodyguards did not answer. I looked over my shoulder. The blue Sentra was behind us. I tried to remain calm. To distract myself, I started reading *Alarma*. One of the featured stories was a profile of a cartel member dubbed El Pozolero—the Soup Cook. The Federal Police had found several vats of acid in his backyard. Chemical testing revealed that he'd used them to dissolve more than a hundred bodies.

Then I heard a familiar click: the parts of an assault rifle snapping into place.

Ludwig made a sharp turn. My head banged on the armored window. I closed my eyes and heard angry car horns and the roar of the engine and Ludwig calling for backup. I heard the rasp of tightening Velcro as Darwin put on body armor. Then we came to an abrupt stop. I opened my eyes. There was a wall in front of us. We'd reached a dead end.

La vida es sueño

Though he always denied it, there's reason to believe Nazario began using drugs again after his first death. How else to explain the delusions of grandeur that convinced him he was the reincarnation of Hugh de Payns, the twelfth-century French nobleman credited in several chronicles as the inaugural grand master of the Poor Fellow-Soldiers of Christ and the Temple of Solomon, better known as the Knights Templar?

Then again, it isn't difficult to find reasons why Nazario would have identified with the founder of a transnational army of warrior-monks. Like Payns, he saw himself as a defender of order against the threats of the infidels; like him, he understood spiritual ends cannot be accomplished without material means—the Templar order, after all, became one of the most important financial institutions of medieval Europe. In the most generous interpretation, the Knights Templar offered Nazario a model for a political entity that could compete with nation-states without becoming one. In the least generous, Nazario's fascination with the order had nothing to do with political theory and everything to do with the search for eternal life.

Whatever the particulars of Nazario's reasoning, the fact is that in 2011 the organization formerly known as la Familia began calling itself los Caballeros Templarios. Nazario wrote his own version of the order's code of conduct and required his men to attend seminars where they read and discussed the text. He held extravagant initiation ceremonies in which he wore a suit of armor and brandished a broadsword. He went as far as ordering the priests of the towns under his control to display statues of him in Templar regalia alongside the effigies of the saints.

Un desplome de ángeles caídos

"I dropped to the ground and played dead," Pedro said. "That's what they tell you to do at the academy. At the time it sounds ridiculous. You're lying there on the courtyard, pretending to pretend to be dead, and you know in your heart there's no way it's going to work, right? But the thing is, it worked. The motherfuckers never came back to check. My guess is they didn't have time. They were trying to fuck up as many of our teams as they could. Break the perimeter. Create distractions. Open a path for their boss. Maybe that's why they had the mule. I don't know. Who the fuck knows? Does that answer your question?"

A few decades ago, most cantinas denied entry to women. These days the crowd at El Centenario is evenly split across genders, but the establishment retains something of its old identity as a place where men constrained by masculinity can allow themselves to speak the truth.

There's something ritualized about these conversations of unmasking, to the point that Mexican Spanish has a specific word to describe them: *netear*, the verbal form of *la neta*, a slang term for *the real deal* that itself derives from *neto*, as in a bottle's net content of liquor. At El Centenario, men who are engaged in this ritual are easy to identify. They arrive early, always in pairs, and sit at one of the secluded tables in the back, away from eavesdroppers, as if they already know what to expect from the night.

They will begin in pretense, making small talk about politics or soccer. Then, as empty glasses accumulate on the table, one of them will make a tentative overture with an oblique comment on the general bitterness of life. The other man will lean in and ask if everything is all right, but the first man will shake his head and order another round.

"It's nothing," he'll say.

"Come on, now," his friend will insist.

"It doesn't matter. Who gives a fuck?"

This coy dance will continue past midnight. Then, when they've had enough to drink to be able to claim to have forgotten the conversation by the following morning, the levy will burst.

"La neta is I cheated on her," he'll say. "She knows. And I'm sorry but can't say it or don't want to say it but wish I wanted to or could. It's still going on and I want it to stop but I don't want to stop. She wants to leave and take the children and I don't care if she does. But I wish she would stay."

He will go on, slurring his words, talking in circles. His friend will nod but say nothing. The head waiter will announce last call and the first man, terrified by the prospect of leaving without confessing the whole truth, will get to the point.

"Pero la mera neta is I, too, want to leave. I want to say goodbye or rather not say goodbye. It's not like they'd understand. Every day when I wake up I think about it. I'd take no baggage and leave early and go far. I'd change my name, live alone, talk to no one. That's all I want. To not give a shit about anyone and know that no one gives a shit about me."

The head waiter will ask the men to leave. The one who listened will call a cab for the one who confessed and tell him she'll forgive him; he just has to say he's sorry and mean it, like he did just now. The man who confessed will then hug his friend or fall into his arms or throw himself into them. Perhaps he will start crying. Perhaps he will kiss his friend. Perhaps his friend will kiss him back.

The taxi will arrive. For a moment the two men will think about leaving together, early in the morning, without saying goodbye. Then the one who confessed will go and the one who listened will stay. He'll light a cigarette and worry that someone saw the kiss. Then he'll go home to his wife.

A la nada, pero juntos, y eso ya es algo

Darwin cocked the assault rifle. He looked at his brother, who nodded emphatically. He opened the door of the car and walked back toward the intersection. His shoulders were hunched forward, concave around his thorax, as if to shield his heart; he seemed more likely to curl up into fetal position than to return gunfire. Still, he walked down the long and narrow road, past half-finished houses painted in pastel colors, under the bright, polluted sun of Mexico City, which makes everything seem discolored, as in an old photograph. He walked slowly, becoming smaller and smaller, until he turned the corner and disappeared. I thought that I would never see him again, and that I would never see my parents again, and that I was going to die a virgin, and that I would never write a novel.

Vale verga la vida

And then there's the detail that pushes the tale of Nazario, already full of fiction, into the realm of what Alejo Carpentier called "the marvelous real" and later came to be known as "magical realism"—the mule. After the fiasco of the press conference, the Mexican government redoubled its efforts against the grand master, deploying a kill-or-capture operation that involved several hundred marines, thousands of soldiers and Federal Police officers, and five Black Hawk helicopters purchased secondhand and at low interest rates from our American allies. At the same time, the people of Michoacán grew tired of the Templar's reign of terror and organized citizen militias to expel Nazario's soldiers from their towns. In March of 2014 the government and its allied militias surrounded the last remaining Knights at the top of a mountain in Tierra Caliente. Nazario then grabbed his Kalashnikov, got on the mule, and headed downhill to die like a king.

La vida empieza donde se piensa que la realizada termina

Three hours later Esteban sent a mass text: *I'm OK. My phone was dead but I'm alive. Sorry I scared you.*

I was so elated that instead of saying I loved him I asked where he'd managed to find a working outlet.

At El Centenario, he replied. *They stayed open the whole time.*

El regreso del Cid

But there's another version of the story about the mule. During the final months of his life, as the Mexican military closed in on him, Nazario's meth habit sent him into a violent psychosis. Mad with sleeplessness and paranoia, he began executing his bodyguards on suspicion of being spies, assassins, or demons trying to tempt him. The remaining Knights grew tired of the grand master's antics and began whispering mutiny, conspiring for regicide. On the afternoon when their enemies surrounded the camp, they killed their leader and, for reasons that remain mysterious, carved out his eyeballs with a spoon. The gesture surely gave them much satisfaction, but it did nothing to alter the fact that the most elite soldiers in the Mexican security apparatus were still firing on them with everything they had. And so the Knights took Nazario's body, tied it to a mule, and sent him down from the mountain for the marines to see.

Una presencia ausente

Darwin came back five minutes after he left and collapsed on the front seat. In the rearview mirror I saw his eyes were shut. He sighed, loosened his tie, and let go of the assault rifle.

"It's all right," he said. "They were construction workers."

Ludwig nodded and started the car. When we got to Pablo's

house, my friends were upset I was late. Then they realized my hands were shaking.

"What happened?" one of them said.

I tried to reply but my voice deserted me.

"What happened?"

"Nothing. Nothing happened."

Nocturno de México

We didn't speak for the rest of the drive back to Mexico City from Valle de Bravo. I stared out of the window and saw the pouring rain refracting on the red and white lights of the traffic jam. The sun had set but most of the streetlights were broken, so the avenue was dark. After a while the rain stopped and the traffic eased. We got to Esteban's building, unaware it would collapse less than a week later, and parked across the street.

"What time is it?" the Bear said. "I'm starving."

"Let's go to El Centenario?" Esteban said.

My friends got out of the car, but I stayed in. "Come with us?" I said to Pedro.

He looked at me on the rearview mirror. "I don't know, sir. It's not allowed."

"One drink? We won't tell anyone."

Pedro looked at his watch and sighed. "All right. Just one."

We walked to El Centenario and ordered tacos and beer and talked about American movies and the inexorable decline of the national soccer team. Then, many rounds later, Pedro told us about his seven-year-old son.

"He's learning the piano," he said. "He's been at it for only a year but he's already really good. And it's not just me. His teacher says so too. Says he has potential. Says if he keeps it up, he could make it into the Conservatorio. And I don't know shit about classical music, but I know that when he plays it's beautiful. The other night I couldn't sleep, and I got up to get a glass of water and there he was, with his headphones plugged into the keyboard, practicing in the dark. I sat next to him and asked him what he was playing, and he said Mozart. I asked him if he could show me, and he said he didn't want to wake up Mom but I could wear the headphones while he played. So he put them over my ears and he started to play a tune that made me think of when I was a little kid and I'd play hide-and-seek with my cousins, and after a while I got worried I was going to cry, and I didn't want him to see me like that, so I took off the headphones and told him it was real pretty and made me think of children. He said that made sense, because Mozart had written the melody when he was seven, just like him. I said it was late and he had school in the morning. He said he was having trouble sleeping, so would I mind if he practiced a little longer? I said all right, but is it okay if I sit with you? He said I could but only if I gave the headphones back. I said sure and he took them off me and put them on, and then I sat with him and watched him play in silence."

¿Eres o te haces?

A week after the earthquake I got an email from Lee:

Dear Sebas,

Thank you for your kind words about my work. You give really good compliments—so good, in fact, I sometimes don't know how to take them. All the same, I was happy to hear that you liked the sketches for the song cycle. Sor Juana makes a wonderful collaborator, particularly for a one-woman show.

It's weird to consciously set out to compose something entirely new, something entirely mine. Do you know what I mean? That impulse to consciously or unconsciously close off all possible avenues to becoming an artist. Translator, editor, collaborator, mistress, muse—anything but creator, anything but autonomy.

Sorry for brain-vomiting. Sometimes I don't know what I'm saying.

Also—and we can obviously talk about it more on the phone once you are settled back at Iowa—I was thinking: Would you agree that "playing it as it lays" has outlived its usefulness as a metaphor? It's getting silly, coming up with names for you when you come up in conversations: friendly-boy, lover-boy, pierna . . . We are a couple, Sebastián, in everything but name. And I, for one, think that offers an exciting possibility.

Love,

Lee

Part V

Iowa City

January–April 2018

In which Your Correspondent returns to the Middle West, is asked to prove he can speak English, ponders the life and work of a seventeenth-century astrologer, remembers his grandfather, applies for a green card, fails to steer a student away from danger, considers a generous offer, makes a fateful mistake, and worries his time in America is coming to a close.

Para Cosme del Rosario Bell

After spending the winter break in Mexico City on my own (Lee had gone home to her parents in California), I returned to Iowa, where the snow was at its peak and the cold air vibrated with uncertainty. Over the previous months, the Trump administration had formed a task force to identify naturalized citizens eligible for deportation, announced it would no longer allow foreigners who enrolled in Medicaid to become permanent residents, and repeatedly refused to issue passports to citizens of perceived "Hispanic" descent. It'd also begun to imprison children in concentration camps, though that last news item was so insane it was easier to pretend the concentration camps were not concentration camps and the children were not children.

I had nothing to hide, but was I sure I had met the criteria to file my taxes as a nonresident alien?

Did I check that the lady from the Office of International Students and Scholars remembered to initial the document that authorized me to teach two different courses instead of two sections of the same class?

And what about that time in New York, when I dragged poor Carlos to that god-awful party in the yuppie wastelands of Greenpoint, where, unsatisfied with getting into a cocaine-fueled shouting match about whether it was racist to apply North American racial categories to people from the Dominican Republic, I proceeded to let the host borrow my phone to request a re-up from his dealer, a moonlighting bike messenger who called himself "the Cheesemonger," and who months later found himself in the crosshairs of the district attorney for Kings County, who proceeded to drop surprisingly substantial charges on poor him and then use his testimony to secure indictments against a number of people associated with the call history on his cell phone, including a corporate lawyer, an art dealer, a burned-out rock star, miscellaneous finance bros, a college kid, and a coterie of elderly heiresses from the Upper East Side, the idea being to combat the unfounded accusations, heard in so-called "activist" circles and in certain corners of the yellow press, that the hard-working prosecutors of the proud borough of Brooklyn focused a disproportionate amount of their not-inconsiderable investigative resources on criminal cases against poor people of color, and sure, it'd been years, and none of the Greenpoint yuppies were ever arrested, and there was no reason to think even a rookie prosecutor would be foolish enough to build a case off a single text message, especially considering that the famous monger, that indolent, unprofessional motherfucker, hadn't even bothered to reply, much less deliver the package in question, but who was to say the public-relations people on Jay Street wouldn't at some point conclude that the only surefire way to improve the DA's dismal approval numbers among key demographics of the electorate was to please both the white xenophobes of Borough Park and the Latinx Socialists of Sunset Park by hanging a foreigner with decadent tastes and a fancy degree and a polysyllabic last name out to dry?

That my fears were ridiculous didn't make them any less terrifying. The Trump administration's immigration policies changed by the day; what was once allowed became illegal without warning. Each week brought a new leaked memo from the Department of Homeland Security proposing additional rules and regulations—confusing changes to the definition of unlawful presence and duration of stay, new penalties for minor infractions that could result in deportation and a ten-year ban from entering the United States. My foreigner's anxiety, as I came to call it, was an infinitely complex and mortifying version of the irrational suspicion that assaulted me once a month as I crossed the Pentracrest on my way to class: I'd become convinced that I'd left the Bialetti on the stove, and that the stove was on, and that it was only a matter of time before the pressure in the pot hit critical, transforming the charming espresso maker into an IED. I'd run back to the apartment, ready to find it covered in shrapnel and coffee grounds, only to discover the pot in the sink.

El arte de perder

A scene from a baroque drama: Moctezuma plays cards with four bearded foreigners. The newcomers have been his guests for almost a year, but they show no intention of leaving. At first their persistence was simple impoliteness; later it became frank insolence; now it threatens to blur the line between sovereign and subject. The crisis is acute. The courtiers dissemble no longer. The corridors echo with whispers about obsidian daggers, murmurs about well-aimed stones, variations on an impossible question: Why did he let them in?

The whispers reach Moctezuma, yet he has no answers. For months on end, he spent whole nights in the darkness of his divination cave, but the prophetic vision never came. To the emperor's surprise, the fact that the present and the recent past exceeded his understanding brought him peace rather than despair. He could not identify the final moment when salvation was still possible. Here was proof that the debacle was not the product of his blindness, but of the will of the gods. There had been omens. The vassal states were restless. There were too many questions. He needed time to think. What else could he have done?

But this clarity arrived too late. Until then Moctezuma had

lived in purgatory. Bored and isolated, overwhelmed with guilt and shame, fearful of his friends as of his enemies, less the Spaniards' host than their prisoner, the emperor came close to taking his own life. The invitation to join the card table saved him, in part because games of chance are a balm to cornered minds, in part because earning the foreigner's esteem, even as entertainment, afforded him protection from his regicidal counselors, but mostly because watching the Spaniards play confirmed Moctezuma's suspicion that Cortés and his men were not deities but beasts.

The rules of the card game were simple enough that even a child could have devised a winning strategy after a few hands, and yet, in almost every round, the Spaniards made mistakes so glaring that the emperor was forced to conclude they were no better than idiots. For reasons that remain mysterious, however, the emperor lost every hand he played. Each time the Spaniards embraced their gilded prices, yelling blasphemies and mocking the native idiocy of their host, the lord of Tenochtitlan smiled an inscrutable smile.

Para Jo Livingstone

"All right, so I've got your contract, your immigration papers, and your form from the Office of International Students and Scholars," said the English Department registrar. "You're pretty much set."

I smiled, but in my head I cackled like a mad scientist about to unleash his dreaded creation. Oh, yes, I was ready to teach, to shape the young minds of a gaggle of hatchling writers, to remedy some of the shameful lacunae in their bildung, to rescue their still-impressionable spirits from the self-lobotomizing temptations of the Yankee mistrust of erudition, to convert them from semi-barbarous tailgaters into sophisticated aesthetes, modernists in the making, future vanguardists who in due time would rescue North American letters from their self-satisfied provincialism, unleashing an era of literary vitality the likes of which hadn't been seen in these United States since the days of Bad Old Ezra Pound, a detestable fellow, no question, but also a great *teacher*, an *educator*, a *pedagogue* of such talent that he'd managed to single-handedly transform a country-bumpkin doctor from godforsaken New Jersey into none other than William Fucking Carlos Fucking Will—

"There's only one thing missing," the registrar went on. "Your English proficiency test."

"Pardon?"

"Your test. All instructors whose first language isn't English need to take it. There's a written portion and then you have to prepare a mock class for a panel of evaluators."

"But I obviously speak English. I'm speaking English with you right now."

"I know. It's silly. Why don't you write to Professor Bouvard? He might be able to make an exception."

I went home and sat down to write an indignant email to the English Department chair:

Dear Professor Bouvard,

I hope this email finds you well. I'm writing today because it has come to my attention that foreign-born instructors are required to take an English proficiency test before we are allowed to teach. I'm sure I don't have to explain why I find this requirement insulting. I may be Mexican, which is becoming more and more of a stain in this country, but I have studied the English language since I was six years old. I went to college in the United States, at a school where the language of

instruction was English, where among other subjects I studied
English literature, and from which I graduated with honors.
I have published hundreds of journalistic articles, all of them
in English. When I applied to the program, I submitted near-
perfect TOEFL scores and was admitted, presumably, on the
strength of my writing in English. What is more, over the past
semesters I have participated in class discussions in English
here at Iowa, and I have no doubts my teachers can attest
that I've never had trouble understanding them or expressing
myself. I would like to think that these facts constitute proof
that I am proficient enough in the language to teach intro-
ductory courses. And so I would like to ask you, respectfully, to
please waive the test.

Yours,
Sebastián

But then, as I reread the email looking for typos, I began to
second-guess myself. Was I being difficult? Was it such a big
deal? I decided to rewrite the email, lest I come off as arrogant
or uppity:

Dear Professor Bouvard,
I hope this email finds you well. I'm sorry to bother you, but
it has come to my attention that, as a foreign-born graduate
student, I'm required to take an English proficiency test before
I'm allowed to teach. While I understand the university has a
valid interest in ensuring that all instructors can communicate
effectively with their students, I was wondering if it might be
possible for the department to waive the exam in my case. As
you may be aware, I submitted passing TOEFL scores when
I applied to the MFA program, and as far as I know, such
results are valid for two years. Perhaps it might be possible to

*use that test as evidence that I'm qualified to teach? I would be
happy to discuss this matter with you in person and to provide
you with documentation—college transcripts, publications,
testimonies from faculty members here at Iowa—that attests
to my language skills. Thank you for your attention and please
accept my apologies for the hassle!*

All my best,
Sebastián

That's better, I thought. They are more likely to be helpful
if they don't feel attacked. I went out for a cigarette in the cold
winter air and came back to find Bouvard had written back:

Dear Sebastián,

*Thank you for your email. First, I'd like to apologize on
behalf of the department. We face a version of this issue every
year, and we don't like it one bit. The policy requiring foreign
instructors to take a proficiency test is problematic, to say
the least, but it's also codified in state law, so unfortunately
there's nothing I or anyone else at the university can do. My
understanding is that the requirement wasn't put into place
with English teaching assistants in mind, but because undergraduates complained that STEM instructors sometimes didn't
speak enough of the language to teach effectively. That said,
in the past we've waived the written test on the strength of
the instructor's standardized scores, so we should be able to
do that in your case. As for the mock class, the law requires
the university to record a video of the session and send it to the
Iowa Department of Education for review. You could decline,
of course, but I'm afraid that doing so would mean forfeiting
your assistantship and with it your tuition scholarship. If I
were you, I'd take the mock class as an opportunity to rehearse a*

*lesson plan for your first week of teaching. Please let me know
if you have any questions. And again, I'm sorry.*

Best,

Dr. FDB Bouvard

No, bueno, I thought, pues chingo a mi madre. Of course the
test was codified in law—this flavorless corner of the Middle
West, where people take pride in their own "niceness," was also
the place that kept electing Steve King to Congress—and of
course it was the undergraduates who complained, those hard-
drinking, corn-fed provincials who couldn't be bothered to learn
anyone else's language.

I read the email again, feeling my face flush with anger. So
dear Professor Bouvard—himself a French immigrant, as he liked
to point out—thought the test made sense when the instructors
were mathematicians from East Asia, but not when they were
Mexican writers? Oh no, they didn't like it one bit. They thought
it was "problematic"—just not problematic enough to do anything
about it. No, I thought as I went downstairs to smoke again, this
isn't problematic—this is *racist*.

Still, I felt unsure about using that word in a situation where
I was on the receiving end. I was Mexican, sure, but I was an
Austro-Hungarian. The position I occupied in Mexico was
closer to that of Dutch Afrikaners than to that of Black South
Africans. The only difference between me and the descendant of
Botswana's colonizers was that my people settled in Mexico a few
centuries earlier, such that at this point it was difficult to argue
we were anything other than Mexican. To think that fact put me
on the same boat as Indigenous people, or even mestizos, was to
miss the point entirely. Then again, if that was true, why was I
so bothered by the test?

I lit my cigarette, shivering from the cold, and called Lee. We'd formalized our relationship a few weeks earlier, and our daily phone conversations had become my favorite part of the day.

"Well, well, well! If it's not don Sebastián 'el Sin Apodo' Arteaga y Salazar!"

"Am I interrupting?"

"Not at all. I'm in the middle of writing a dumb paper about how chandé rhythms don't fit in Western notation, but I could use a break. How are you?"

"Pissed. Turns out I have to take an English proficiency test before they can officially hire me as a TA."

"What? Because you're Mexican?"

"I guess? Though apparently they do it to everyone whose first language isn't English, so maybe—"

"Sebas, that's fucked up. I'm so sorry."

"Thanks. That's actually what I wanted to ask you—do you think it's racist?"

"Obviously!"

"But, like, if I were French, they would still make me take the test . . ."

"But you aren't French, Sebas. You're Mexican. Why the hell do they admit people of color if they are going to make them jump through hoops to prove they can do what they admitted them to do?"

"I'm not sure I count as a person of color . . ."

"But they think you do, right? They probably count you toward their diversity goals. And that's what matters, no? It's not how you perceive yourself, but how others perceive you."

"It's just that back in the day, when I was covering the Freddie Gray uprising in Baltimore, I interviewed this Black librarian who thought I was Greek or Israeli and was totally surprised to learn I was Mexican. She said something that stuck with me: 'If the cops stopped you here, you'd go through the system as a white boy.' And, like, that's it, isn't it? That's the bar. Anything else is posturing."

"I mean, sure. But a Baltimore cop would probably treat an Asian person different than a Black one, so maybe it's not so simple? Like—"

"I just think it'd be dishonest. Like, Mayeli is a person of color. Your ex is a person of color. But me? It's like when they talk about Sor Juana like she was some kind of oppressed Latina—the woman owned slaves, for fuck's sake! Or when they say that Frida Kahlo, who was as German as—"

"Okay, fine! I get it. I'm sorry. I didn't mean to tell you how to feel."

"That's not what I meant—I really appreciate the support."

"Anytime, joven Sebastián. I should probably go, though. I'm supposed to present at the seminar tomorrow and I'm nowhere near finished."

She blew a kiss into the phone and hung up. I went back upstairs and fixed myself a whiskey. Lee was right. This was bullshit—though what did it mean that I'd had to hear it from her before I gave myself permission to really get mad? I brushed the thought aside and instead focused on revenge. I'd teach the mock class, sure, but I'd pick a subject so arcane that the evaluators would be forced to confront the ridiculousness of the exercise. But what should it be? Chaucer in Middle English? I still remembered the lines I'd had to memorize in undergrad—but no, it had to be something even more difficult. I sat down with my drink and then it hit me: *Beowulf!* In the Old English, with the funny little runes and all. I didn't know Old English, of course, but I was willing to bet neither did the evaluators.

A few days later I waltzed into the classroom where the exam was to take place and found three middle-aged white people holding clipboards and an aging video camera pointed at the whiteboard.

"Good morning!" I said.

"Good morning," the evaluators replied in unison, like school-children.

"Ready when you are."

"Great!" one of the evaluators said. "The test will last half an hour. For the first twenty minutes, you'll go through a lesson plan on your subject, which I take is—let me check—English, yes?"

"That's correct!"

"Excellent. Then, once you are done, my colleagues and I will take ten minutes to ask you questions on the material. You won't be evaluated on the content of your lesson, only on your language abilities. Sounds good?"

"Sounds perfect!"

"Please, go ahead."

I turned around and began writing on the whiteboard:

Hwat! We Gardena in geardagum,
þeodcyninga, þrym gefrunon,
hu ða æþelingas ellen fremedon.

"So," I said, turning to face the evaluators. "Can any of you read what's on the board? It's English, so it shouldn't be too difficult!"

One of them did so without hesitation. She then folded her hands and said: "But it's *Hwæt* with an æsc, not *hwat*. It doesn't matter, though. The Iowa Department of Education cares only about standard American English."

Habla de ti mismo y por añadidura hablarás del mundo

"So you want to change your thesis project yet again?" Irina said. She and I had gone for a walk around campus. She seemed concerned.

"Not a great look, I know. It's just—writing a history of Mexico through the lens of the permeability between art and power and their ambiguous relationship to truth . . ."

Irina took a long pull from her coffee, as if refueling her patience. "What's the new idea?"

"Narrow the scope. Concentrate on a single stratum of Mexican society: the creoles, the descendants of the Spaniards, the children of the baroque. The Austro-Hungarians. My people. For now, I'm working on an essay on an astrologer from the seventeenth century who I think put his finger on the 'creole condition' better than anyone. Next up are my grandfather and José Vasconcelos, the 'cultural caudillo' of the Mexican Revolution. After that, I'm not sure."

"And I suppose you have a title? You always seem to have a title."

"I do," I said, a bit embarrassed. "'The Horses of Empire.' You know, because a criollo can also be a thoroughbred without a pedigree."

We fell silent and made it back to the English-Philosophy Building. Irina turned to face me. "Look, Sebas," she said. "I have faith in you. But I worry you're trying to do something impossible, which is to write a book that contains the essence of a country. Perhaps the thesis should be less about the creoles in general than about one creole in particular. To justify juxtaposition one must explain the juxtaposer."

El amor que mueve el cielo y las estrellas

The next day I got an email from my mother:

Dearest Sebastián,
I was very happy to get your message—though I was also sorry to hear about the English test. It's very silly of them. But

try not to get too upset? It won't change anything and will only make you feel worse. Save that energy and use it to write!

Here things are OK. Some weeks chemo is rough. I've managed to keep enough hair that, if I cut it short and style it right, you can't even tell. I'm supposed to start a new treatment next week—this novel thing where they use your own immune system to attack the tumors. Dr. Graue thinks it might help with the ones in my lymph nodes. I'm feeling hopeful! I hope you are too. Sometimes I worry that you worry too much. You have since you were little. I wish I could reassure you like I used to back then.

What else? I'm reading Proust for the first time since graduate school. I loved it then but never finished it, so I figured I'd pick it up where I left it—and guess what? The bookmark was still there! A receipt from the artisanal crafts store Jana and I opened right after I came back from the sierra. I've told you about it, haven't I? It lasted less than a year and we wound up owing money to the bank, but we had a lot of fun. When we closed, we were left with boxes and boxes of ceramics. A lot of it broke over the years, and whatever was left got lost in one or another move, but I still have a Talavera serving dish—the real stuff from Puebla. If you ever come home, you should take it for your apartment.

Things with your father are better. Much better. We've talked a lot. We're finally making sense of our story, contrasting our different versions until we figure out how they fit together. He has apologized for many things, and I can sense he means it. I've apologized, too. I'm not without fault—nobody is when it comes to these things. It might be strange to say, but this is the reason why I'm grateful for my illness. It has given me the courage to confront what needed to be confronted. It has opened my eyes to what really matters.

Your brother and sister are both well. Inés is dating a new boy, and though unfortunately he isn't the good Dr. Ward, he's nonetheless a very sweet American kid who cherishes and respects her. Álvaro is now on his third term at King's College—he's thinking of writing his thesis about racial identities in revolutionary Mexico. You should call one another more often! Arnaut's mother asked about you—apparently he's still in Australia. I had the piano tuned so Lee can play next time she comes to visit.

I love you with all my heart, hijito.

Always,
Laura

Los modernistas en el sótano y las estrellas en lo alto

"The first thing you need to know about Ezra Pound," I said as I paced the classroom, "is that he was the most influential American poet of the twentieth century. The second thing you need to know is that he was a fascist. And what's complicated is that you can't separate his politics from his poetics. For instance, as the trigger warning on your syllabus notes, one of the poems we read for today, the one about Renaissance painting and monetary theory, is explicitly antisemitic. And yet..."

I paused. The students were watching me, but were they bored? Confused? Offended?

"Well, that's it, isn't it? There's an 'and yet.' Which is wild! How could there be an 'and yet' about fascism? But I'm afraid that's precisely what we have here. Because it's possible to dislike Pound's poems *as poems*, and not just as political statements. But what isn't possible, at least if we're talking in good faith, is to deny that this inexcusable person was essential to the development of American literature. And if we want to understand

American literature—as we presumably do, seeing as we want to write literature in America—we have to figure out why so many intelligent people thought his poems were *good*. So, let's hear it! What makes these weird little machines tick?"

A young woman with sunglasses and a Frappuccino—the only Black student in the class—raised her hand.

"Yes, Zoraya!" I said.

"I don't think we should be discussing Pound's writing in literature terms. Who cares if the poems were influential? They're racist."

It was the third week of the semester, and this was the first time she'd spoken. I nodded enthusiastically, trying, perhaps a little too hard, to convey that I took what she said extremely seriously. "Thank you, Zoraya. You're right: Pound and his poems are racist. And that may well mean that they aren't literature but something else. Historical documents. Examples of hate speech. Linguistic violence that ought to be locked in a special section of the library. But I suppose I'm trying to suggest that, actually, yes, a text can be racist and still be literature."

"Yeah, not buying that," Zoraya said. "There's nothing beautiful about racism."

"But we don't study art *only* because it's pretty, right? A racist poem can't be beautiful, agreed, but it could still be interesting and worth reading. If nothing else, we'd do well to know our enemy, don't you think?"

Something happened behind her sunglasses. "If you want to assign Pound in a class about, I don't know, racism in white American literary culture, then sure, put the bigot on the syllabus. What I'm saying is we shouldn't treat this shit as literature. Especially not in a writing class. How is all this stuff about creepy white boys doing rape-y shit in twelfth-century France supposed to help me, specifically, become a better essayist?"

I fidgeted with my chewed-on pencil, trying to find a response that wouldn't lead me into a minefield. "You know what, Zoraya?" I said. "You're right. I shouldn't have assigned Pound. He isn't a useful model for you guys. And if you wanted to read the modernist canon, you could have enrolled in a class about that instead of a writing workshop. As you know, this is my first time teaching, so I'm kind of learning on the . . ."

"Really? You're falling for *that*?"

I turned to face the voice, and realized with alarm that it belonged to the lanky white boy whose incredulous grin betrayed he'd only recently discovered that all it took to become terrifying was to cut his hair, wear combat boots, and button his black polo all the way to the neck.

"Billy, right? Would you mind explaining what you mean?"

"I just think it's interesting that you're letting cancel culture win."

Zoraya twisted in her chair to face him. "Nobody's getting 'canceled,'" she said, drawing air quotes around the word. "He's allowed to teach whatever he wants. It's just that I'm also allowed to say what I think about what he teaches."

"Oh yeah? What happened to diversity?"

"You want *diversity* for *fascists*?"

"No, that's what *you* want. Everyone knows all the real fascists are on the left. The Open Society Foundation. The Cultural Marxist International. Antifa? The biggest fascists of them all. Whatever you want to call yourselves, you don't want diversity. You want monotony. You think we shouldn't read anything that isn't spoken-word poetry by half-blind non-binary Cherokee lesbians who need to process the fact that their neighbors declined to post the BLM yard signs they handed out."

He was finishing that speech when Zoraya got up, picked up her things, and walked out of the classroom.

"Okay," I said, fighting back panic. "Okay, okay, okay. Gimme a minute, okay? I'll be right back. In the meantime, no sudden movements!"

I ran out into the hallway but didn't see Zoraya. There were even fewer Black undergraduates at Iowa than in the MFA programs. Last thing she needed was a Tucker Carlson impersonator in her first workshop.

I was debating running out of the building and trying to find her, when a bathroom door down the hall swung open, and she came out. "Zoraya!" I stage-whispered. "Do you have thirty seconds?" I trotted over to her. "Listen, I'm sorry about that. Could you drop by my office hours later today so we can talk about what happened?"

Zoraya laughed. "Sure," she said. "I'll swing by. That was only ten, though."

"Ten?"

"Seconds."

"Oh. I'm sorry about that."

"It's okay." She paused. "It's probably thirty now."

I did an IRL version of the praying hands emoji, and she turned and walked away. Back in the classroom, students were putting on jackets and hoisting bags over shoulders. A collective walkout? Would they drop the class en masse and report me to the Dean of DEI, leaving me to be booted from the MFA program and soon thereafter the country?

I cleared my throat and asked people to take their seats. My voice was far too loud. In response, there was a general murmuring about the time. I looked at my watch but then remembered I'd decided to no longer wear it, then at the clock on the wall. A minute past the end of class.

As they filed out, Billy approached me. I snapped my briefcase shut. "Please don't do that again," I said. "You're allowed to say what you think, but you're not allowed to disrespect your classmates."

"But I didn't disrespect her!"

"I disagree. And more importantly, so does she."

I walked into the hallway. He went after me.

"Wait! Professor Salazar!"

"Not a professor. Just a TA."

He followed me silently down the stairs and out of the English-Philosophy Building. As we walked down the front steps, he let out a world-ending whimper. "I just don't know how to deal with—"

"With what, Billy? Your Black classmates?"

He turned bright red. Suddenly he seemed younger. "No. With my anger. I was just looking forward to talking about Pound. Nobody else teaches him. So when she decided to bitch about including him? It pissed me off. I get mad all the time. But I don't like getting mad like that. I just don't know how to stop."

I looked at him—his bad shave, his stupid polo, the sweat pooling on his forehead—and felt a wave of compassion. I lit a cigarette. "Okay," I said. "Let's talk about Pound."

Todo es traza e invención

The story about Moctezuma's game of cards is fiction but not mine. I came across it in a short volume published in Mexico City at the end of the seventeenth century, under the title:

THEATER OF THE POLITICAL VIRTUES
Which Constitute a Prince
As they were Displayed by
THE ANCIENT MONARCHS
Whose Countenances now Adorn

THE GLORIOUS ARC OF TRIUMPH
Which the Very Noble and Loyal
CITY OF MEXICO
Has Erected to Welcome His Excellency
THE VICEROY

The author, Carlos de Sigüenza y Góngora, was one of those colonial geniuses who remained Renaissance polymaths long after their metropolitan peers had hardened into Enlightenment specialists. To his embarrassment, his friends in Mexico City knew him as the Doctor of Anáhuac; to his disappointment, his enemies in Madrid didn't know him at all. On the rare occasions when posterity deigns to remember him, it's either as the lifelong friend of a far superior writer, Sor Juana Inés de la Cruz, or as the author of:

Philosophical Manifesto
AGAINST COMETS
Which Are Therein Dispossessed
OF THE IMPERIAL POWER
That They Long Wielded Over
THE TIMOROUS,

an astronomical essay characterized by acrobatic prose and outdated science, in which Sigüenza, in his capacity as cathedral professor of astrology at the Pontifical University of Mexico, makes a courageous case against the common superstition that comets are omens of disaster.

I first read the *Manifesto Against Comets* on a packet of loose sheets photocopied from a copy of a copy that I foolishly threw away. Ever since then I've looked for the text, but to my astonishment the only copy to be found in any academic institution in the US rests in the rare-books library of an Evangelical college that refuses to loan materials to secular researchers.

In any event, my quest for *Against Comets* led me to one of Sigüenza's "letters of relation" to metropolitan Spain, a long and digressive account of the great Indigenous uprising of 1692. The text is a prime example of the journalistic correspondence that flourished in the American colonies of the Spanish Empire, a genre that begins with Columbus and includes the narratives of the conquistadores. It's the archetypical form of creole literature: an informative account of recent developments in the colonies, addressed to the mercy of an imperial reader with only a passing interest in the underdeveloped corners of the realm, written under duress—one rarely refuses the viceroy—and with virtuosic bravura that crackles with barely suppressed resentment. But the letter of relation might also be the origin of the Latin American crónica, that chimerical crossbreed of the journalistic essay and the essayistic fiction.

Sigüenza writes in the elevated diction expected of all baroque writers, but he does so with both feet on the ground, from the street rather than the library. He doesn't bother distinguishing between history and current events; he isn't afraid to moralize or editorialize, nor, I suspect, to exaggerate, misquote, mistranslate, or falsify. More than anything else, Sigüenza-the-cronista is incapable of limiting himself to the confines of his assignment. If the journalist is a man on a mission and the essay is a mission in search of a man, the cronista is an astrologer turned reporter who just can't help telling the Spaniards about the comets:

> *In the Year of Our Lord, 1692, on the twenty-third day of August, which month, in this Very Noble and Loyal City of Mexico, is the season of storms, the Sun fell into Eclipse, as the almanacs and prognostics had predicted. Were Your Mercy not*

a Man-at-Arms, but a Man of Letters well-learned in Astro-
nomical Problems and Astrological Matters, I would now
proceed to tell here, in the most precise Mathematical terms, of
the thousand Fair and Prodigious Things which on that day
I did by God's Grace observe. For that Mexican Eclipse was
one of the most complete ever witnessed on this Earth.

It came to pass in this manner. Shortly after the third
quarter of the morning's eighth hour, we, the Citizens of
Mexico, found ourselves in the midst of a Night not Good
but Evil; for truly, Your Mercy, no darkness ever did seem
so Tenebrous and Fearsome as the Impenetrable Horror
which did descend upon our Valley, where it remained for
the expanse of half of an hour's quarter. The Dread of the
Phenomenon exceeded all Prognostications; such that, on
the very instant in which light's absence filled the Firma-
ment, those Birds caught in flight fell from the sky, the Dogs
commenced their howling, the Women their fainting, and the
Children their crying.

In the Plaza de Armas, the Indias who habitually sell
fruits, vegetables, and other minutiae abandoned their
market-stands and ran, with the celerity which comes only
from Grave Fear and Mortal Fright, into the Cathedral;
wherein they threw themselves into Paroxysms of Prayer,
causing the bell-warden to sound the toll of Alarum and
Rogation; in which course of action he was soon followed by
the bell-wardens of most of the countless Churches, Chapels,
and Shrines of this our Noble and Loyal City, producing a
Great Cacophony that, together with the Darkness and the
cries of the People and Beasts, unleashed great Confusion,
and, for many, much Anguish.

Meanwhile, I, Your Mercy's Most Obedient Servant, was
filled with great Joy, and even greater Gratitude to God,

who had granted me the Grace of witnessing a great Event that, while rare, is known to take place in particular places and at particular times, according to particular patterns, the regularity of which is proved by both Faith and Reason and thus cannot be denied; though it is true that there are few Astronomical Observations describing the Nature of the Phenomenon, even in the most learned of volumes, at least those available on this side of the Ocean Sea; which Unfortunate Lacunae I, being of the sort of Temperament which seeks out in Physical Matters great declarations of God's Magnificent Irony, felt compelled to correct.

And so there I stood, Your Mercy, in the center of the plaza, still and silent while others quivered and cried, armed with no weapons save my Sextant, my Quadrant, and that device which the Natural Philosophers of your European Lands, so blessed with the wealth of Science and Learning, call Tele-Scope, *after the Grecian words for* Fore *and* Sight, *contemplating the Sun . . .*

Para Kiese Laymon

"Nope. Nein. Niet. Totally wrong."

"You just don't want to admit you're old. Which, I get. Confronting your own mortality? Heavy."

"Interpol *does not* count as 'classic rock,' Zoraya!"

"Maybe it's not classic rock. But 'Evil'? Definitely counts as an oldie."

"That's it. I'm dead. I've died. This is my ghost speaking. You, young scholar, are a stone-cold killer."

"It's okay to cry. And on that note," she said, raising herself slightly out of her chair.

"Hold on," I said. "I very much enjoyed our conversation, but we should maybe talk about what happened in class? Only if you want to."

"Don't know there's much to say? I mean, yeah, it was exhausting. It *is* exhausting. But I have no idea how you're supposed to handle Billy. That's your job, old man. Not mine."

El abogado del diablo

The breaking point arrived in February, when I read that the Trump administration was considering a new rule that would require companies wishing to hire "specialized nonresident aliens"—the category of foreigners who qualified for the visa I had in New York—demonstrate they'd made a good-faith effort to put America first by only hiring immigrants if they were willing to pay them a minimum salary that far exceeded the going rate for someone with my experience in my field. Besides, I still had three semesters left in the program, plenty of time for Trump to decide that Optional Practical Training— the yearlong work permit issued to foreign graduates of US universities and the traditional springboard into a more perma- nent immigration status—was the only thing standing between good American citizens and good American jobs, or else that the very notion of a work visa was an unpatriotic affront to the American worker.

Time was running out: each passing month under the nativist administration made staying in the country more difficult. I had to act soon and decisively. And so I wrote to a number of wealthy foreigners I knew from college, asking if they could recommend an immigration lawyer who might be able to help me with an application for permanent residency. Money wasn't an issue, I made sure to tell them. This wasn't the time for privilege-scruples. The life I'd built over the previous nine years was under threat:

I was ready to leverage all advantages available to me, no matter how unsavory. I told myself that the end justified the means, that I wasn't asking for anything unreasonable or untoward—just the certainty that I wouldn't have to leave the country that most of the people I loved called home.

That same afternoon I spoke on the phone with a fellow Yale alumnus, a former English major with a Beacon Hill accent who ran an immigration law firm that catered to hedge funds, but who occasionally took on writer-clients to "feel less like a sell-out." He asked me a few questions about the three short years that constituted what he called my "journalistic career" and concluded I was a strong candidate for a program that allowed "aliens of extraordinary ability" to sponsor themselves for permanent residency. He then quoted his fee and offered me a discount on account of my "artistic profession."

"Thank you so much," I said, even though the discounted rate was still in the five figures. "I feel better already."

"Yeah, man, I get it," he said. "These are dark times. The good news is you're the kind of immigrant they want—highly educated, highly skilled, with a demonstrated history of employment and no criminal record. You should see some of my pro-bono clients. They're desperate, and unfortunately with good reason."

"I can only imagine."

"I don't even remember the last time I won a deportation proceeding. But seriously, you can relax. In less than a year you'll be the proud holder of a brand-new green card, and you'll never have to worry about US immigration again. Right now, though, I need you to focus on gathering your materials. We need to convince the government you're so good at what you do it's in America's interest to let you live here. Think of it as applying to college, but on steroids. I'm going to need a wide sample of your best writing, glowing letters of recommendation from luminaries in your field—Pulitzers, MacArthurs, Guggenheims—and a comprehensive list of every honor, award, prize, and fellowship you've ever received, no matter how small."

"The gifted-and-talented dog-and-pony show."

"Exactly. And don't be afraid to brag—you won't get points for modesty. Don't lie, obviously, but exaggerate. You're auditioning for the role of rising star."

I thanked him again and hung up, feeling an uncomfortable mixture of relief and guilt. It would be great to no longer live from visa to visa or worry about inadvertently violating the terms of my status, but I was all too aware the only reason I'd be able to breathe easy was that I had money and connections. Nothing in my history made me more deserving than Mayeli's parents—and yet they drove five miles under the speed limit while I could pick up the phone and have a Yale Law graduate advocate on my behalf.

Trobar clus

Sigüenza's *Theater of the Political Virtues* seems to follow the conventions of early-modern statecraft handbooks so stubbornly that it becomes tempting to dismiss it as courtly flattery: smoke and mirrors, bells and whistles, dancing bears, candlelight and gilded wood—the charms of an Ariel, performed with a mocking smile for a duke from across the sea. And yet the *Theater* is also a work of revolutionary originality. Taking a cue from Plutarch, Sigüenza presents a series of biographies of exemplary kings, each of whom embodies a different virtue the new viceroy ought to emulate. The difference is that the leaders in question aren't Pericles or Marcus Aurelius but Huitzilopochtli of Brave and Constant Faith; Acampich, Hopeful in Adversity; Huitzilihuitl the Lawful; Iztcohautl the Prudent; Axayacatzin, Fortress of

Fortitude; Moctezuma, Emblem of Magnanimity; Cuauhtémoc, Righteous in Defeat.

Sigüenza was telling the Habsburg vicar that the people he was to rule weren't savages, but human beings capable of reaching the highest summits of the spirit. And yet the Doctor of Anáhuac doesn't praise the Mexica on their own terms, only through favorable comparisons with Western historical figures. Upon closer inspection it becomes clear the Doctor is less interested in praising the virtues of the "Indians" than in publicizing those of his peers.

Like every colonial elite, the criollos of New Spain resented their metropolitan cousins, whose laws excluded them from the highest spheres of wealth and power. Betraying their underdeveloped sense of proportion, they began to identify with the grandeur of the pre-Columbian past—though never, tellingly, with the Indigenous present—sincere in their conviction that the fact the Spaniards treated them as second-class citizens brought them close to the people their grandfathers had massacred.

When Sigüenza says the Mexica emperors were worthy of the viceroy's imitation, he means that being born in the colonies—as Moctezuma had, but also, and more importantly, the Doctor of Anáhuac—is not a stain but a virtue. As their resentment mutated from self-pity to self-regard, Sigüenza and his peers came to see their creole condition as an addition rather than a subtraction from their Western identity. From the Valley of Anáhuac, which they grew convinced was the center of the world, metropolitan Spain was but a dusty corner of Europe, a backwater populated by ignorant hicks that one unfortunately had to please. The *Theater* is less a prefiguration of postcolonial theory than the muttered protest of a second son who harbors the secret certainty he's better than his older brother.

After our conversation about Pound, Billy had taken to following me after class. And though I didn't love the optics of this Proud-Boy-in-training—this *Proud Infant*—as a teacher's pet, I'd thought it my duty to try to reach him. I'd even offered him a deal: if he read a book I lent him, I'd read anything he gave me. The next week, I handed him Orwell's *Homage to Catalonia*, which I hoped would give him a template for how to be bookish and political yet also reasonably macho. I figured he'd give me Jordan Peterson in return, but to my horror he brought something much closer to my heart: *The Will to Power*.

We headed to our usual spot in back of the building and sat on a bench facing the Iowa River. The distant sky of the Middle West was changing colors: behind us it was still blue, but before us it had turned purple. I took out my cigarettes and offered one to Billy.

"So there's rosy-fingered dawn," he said as he exhaled. "But is there rosy-fingered dusk?"

"Homer? I thought we were talking Orwell."

"We can do both."

"What class is Homer for?"

"Just for myself. I'm trying to read the Western canon. Get to know my heritage."

I lit my cigarette, bewildered that he really seemed to believe that he had a close cultural connection to Bronze Age warlords from the Eastern Mediterranean.

"There's actually a group I want to start here. It's called Defenders of the West. There's chapters at colleges and universities all over the country. Maybe you could be a faculty sponsor or something."

"No way that's happening."

"Why not? You're always talking about, like, Plato and—"

"First of all, I'm not a member of the faculty. I'm a graduate student. They only reason they have me teach solo is that the university is going broke because the Republicans in the state legislature think we're brainwashing you guys into becoming suicide bombers."

"I mean, you kind of—"

"Second of all—Defenders of the West? Sounds low-key fascist."

"Ah, the f-word again. Classic SJW move. Step one: make a rule about how you don't argue with fascists. Step two: declare that anyone whose ideas you don't like is a fascist."

I took a long drag. I really wasn't cut out to be a teacher.

"What's so fascist about the West?" he went on. "You're all about that shit. Or are you one of those people who think we shouldn't read Nietzsche because he was an antisemite?"

"The book you brought me isn't really by him. After he became disabled, his Nazi sister cherrypicked his unfinished notes, took out the bits where he railed against Germans, Germany, mass politics, crowds, messianic leaders, antisemites, and—"

"That's what I mean!"

"—pretty much everything we now associate with the Western tradition."

"Oh."

"What I'm trying to say is—you're not reading Nietzsche. You're reading fascist propaganda. Have you checked out *Ecce Homo*? It's all about how his philosophy isn't about, like, conquering Poland. It's about finding a way to live with chronic illness. The Übermensch is just a migraineur who chooses to Übergang instead of Untergang."

"Wait—what?"

"Never mind. What did you think of the Orwell?"

"I don't know . . ."

"It's right up your alley! *He* was a defender of the West! That's what anti-fascism is all about. Standing up and saying: ¡No Pasarán! to the people who want to destroy everything good about—"

"He was a communist."

"So?"

"Communists are America's enemies."

"So are fascists."

"Compared with Stalin and Mao—"

"Orwell was a Trotskyite—he . . ."

"—Hitler was pretty good."

El cinturón del oxidente

I stood in line to pick up my rental car, stomping my feet against the cold. It was five in the morning in late March, and while the snow was starting to melt, the hours before dawn were still bone-rattling. For once, though, I was happy to put up with the windchill. The commission from *The National Republic* had felt like the first cigarette after a failed attempt to quit. Still, getting authorization to get paid to do reporting while on a student visa had proven so stressful that I doubted I'd do it again.

After I got the keys to a beaten-down Subaru, I went through my plan of attack and reviewed the notes from the interviews I'd already conducted. The assignment was simple enough: profile the leader of the local nurses's union who was running in the Democratic primary for governor.

"I think nurses are so cool," I'd said a couple of weeks earlier to her communications manager, a rather cute girl with short hair, a Teamsters bomber jacket, and the very career-appropriate name Alex Press, as we smoked cigarettes outside the candidate's trailer. "My mom has cancer, so I've gotten to watch them do miracles."

Alex took a long drag and shook her head as she exhaled through the nose. "Cancer? And you're sucking on death-sticks? What the fuck is wrong with you, man?"

I stopped at the Kum & Go—I would never get over the name—for a half-gallon of iced coffee, washed down the absurd dose of instant-release amphetamines that some sleep-deprived resident at the university hospital had prescribed me just to get me to go away, and drove out of town. The campaign stop I was covering was the annual Spring Parade celebrated in Merlow, a town of some twenty thousand people an hour and a half from the faux city. The place had been prosperous in the midcentury but had gone into decline in the seventies, when the coal ran out and the meatpackers moved. The county, which had been a union town and a Democratic stronghold, drifted to the right. In 2016 almost 70 percent of its residents voted for Donald Trump.

I headed south on US 218. The sun rose to my left, illuminating the landscape, but there was nothing to see. There were no cities, no mountains or rivers, not even trees. Only the rectilinear highway and an endless expanse of yellowish emptiness: thawing land that had once been a prairie of long-grass and bison, but which had been so denatured with the fertilizers and pesticides required to maximize the yield of genetically modified seeds that it was now best described as a biotechnological factory.

I found myself thinking of a story Charlie had told me months earlier. A group of fictional kids were driving to Chicago. One of them needed to pee, but they were on the stretch of I-80 where there aren't any rest stops, so they pulled over in the middle of a cornfield. While the boy went off to piss, a girl got out of the car to stretch her legs. She walked to the edge of the field, tore out a cob, bit into it, like it was fruit rather than biomass, and shattered her front teeth.

By the time I got to Merlow the sun was high in the sky. It was a brisk day without clouds, the air already electric with spring. I wandered down a wide avenue lined with handsome gray-stone buildings—a hotel, a theater, a bank—which conjured images of a capital in miniature: a small, proud city of prosperous burghers, unionized hog-butchers, and Lutheran farmers come to market in their Sunday best. The scene before my eyes, however, didn't match the architecture: the din of exchange was absent; the store-fronts locked and the locks rusted; the streets full of sunlight yet empty of people, as in a painting by Giorgio de Chirico.

But then, as I approached an intersection, I heard a joyful racket of accordion, brass, and snare. I turned the corner and found myself before a technicolor cornucopia: crates of ripe-red tomatoes and wet-fresh cilantro, night-green jalapeños and noon-yellow habaneros, sun-soft mangoes and avocados, pyramids of onions, ziggurats of limes, plums, prunes, papayas, and picayas; strips of candy made of tamarind, marzipan, and amaranth, gar-lands of garlic, hoja santa, and epazote, piloncillo and achiote, hierbabuena, verbena, jamaica, anís, and canela, bundles of chile costeño, chipotle, mulato, pasilla, guajillo, and long, narrow ribbons of lottery tickets, fluttering in the breeze, vibrant like Tibetan prayer flags.

I walked into the store, hoping to talk to one of the "Latinx voters" the candidate I was profiling was desperate to attract. The door closed behind me, ringing a little bell that called the atten-tion of the middle-aged brown man sweeping the floor. He looked up, raised his Chicago Cubs hat, and smiled a bit too widely. "Can I help you find anything?" he said in unaccented English.

"I'm afraid I'm not a customer."

The man's smile faded. "Sir, if you're from Homeland Secu-rity . . ."

"No, señor, ¿cómo cree?"

He twisted his head and narrowed his eyes, less with suspicion than with bewilderment. "Así de güerito, ¿dónde aprendiste a hablar como chilango?"

"¿Pues dónde más? En Chilangolandia. En el Defectuoso. En la Gran Tenochtitlán."

The man burst out laughing, though I got the sense he was amused by the situation rather than by my jokes. "¡Mira nomás! ¿Qué anda haciendo un güerito chilango en este pinche pueblo jodido en este pinche estado fregado en este pinche país olvidado de Dios?"

He told me that his name was Edwin Mendoza and that he'd come to Iowa from Puebla thirty years ago. He hadn't heard of the candidate—the campaign had yet to reach out to his people. This negligence struck him as a mistake, because he wasn't a citizen and thus couldn't vote, but that wasn't true of many Mexican folks in the area. There were more of them now than there used to be, and some white people in Merlow weren't happy about that, even before Trump. But after the election things had gotten ugly. Every week he heard someone he knew had been detained or deported.

"Me trae malos recuerdos," he said.

"¿Recuerdos de qué?"

"De cuando se llevaron a medio Marshalltown."

He then described the morning in December 2006 when dozens of ICE agents stormed that town's pork-processing plant. The rumors. The panic. The people hiding in cornfields and basements. How he'd driven to the plant to find out what was happening. How he'd seen agents in anoraks and sunglasses load more than a hundred of his neighbors, still drenched in pig blood, into buses waiting to take them to a place from which nobody came back.

"That's why I moved here," Mendoza went on. "That town was haunted. But now it's started again. And it's worse than ever. Folks are afraid to go to work, to church, to take their kids to school. It's bad for my business, because people worry about going to a store that sells Mexican products. Any Mexican place, really. It's no way to live. I'd go back to Puebla, but you change so much living here that, when you return, your people don't recognize you. So if your magazine can get a message to the people in charge, I'd ask that you tell them to please stop the raids."

I chatted with him for a bit longer, then walked out of the store and found the city transformed. Hundreds of people had gathered along the avenue, standing with arms crossed or sitting on folding chairs, grabbing beers from coolers. The sound of a marching band drifted in from behind the corner, and all at once the crowd was cheering and throwing confetti for an American procession: the six-year-old Queen of Spring with her crown of flowers and her creepy makeup, the high school drum line in their circus uniforms, the balding mayor in a borrowed convertible, the firefighters on their giant toy trucks, the cops on their Iraq War Humvees, the Daughters of the American Revolution, the Friends of the Iowa Prairie, the Rotaries, the Odd Fellows, the Historical Preservation Society, the Girl Scouts, the Future Farmers of America, the UAW workers and their long-shot candidate, the American Legion, the Veterans of Foreign Wars, three Lutheran denominations, two Evangelical churches, the owners and employees of the regional bank, the dry-cleaner, the auto-parts store, the landscaping firm, the steakhouse, the diner, the burger joint, the red-sauce joint, the movie theatre, the funeral home, the dive bar, the gun range, and not a single business, association, or institution that could have been mistaken for Mexican.

And then, closing the parade, I saw a delivery van crowned with a giant plastic sombrero covered in red dots that looked like smallpox scabs but were supposed to be slices of pepperoni. Hence the legend in cactus-typography on the side of the van: THE ORIGINATOR OF THE PIZZA-TACO.

From the essay on creole identity:

... but the last morning of that first Thanksgiving break my freshman year of college didn't find me in a nostalgic mood. I woke up with a stupefying hangover and saw I'd missed several calls from my father. When I called back, he instructed me to stop fucking around and go see my grandfather, who'd been dying to die for years and was finally getting his wish.

I tried to get out of it by saying, not without reason, that the old man was unlikely to recognize me. My father chastised my lack of filial piety and assured me that, thanks to the good offices of the distinguished Dr. Graue, don Raúl would be alert when I arrived. Defeated, I asked Ludwig and Darwin to drive me to the old house. On the way I made a mental list of everything that was wrong with me. I was not studying law. I had left our country. I hadn't been confirmed Catholic. I was wearing a wrinkled suit.

When we finally arrived, I found my grandmother waiting at the gate. "We were expecting you for breakfast."

I grinned apologetically. She shook her head and touched my cheek and ran her fingers through my shoulder-length hair. "You need to get it cut. You look like an anarchist."

She pushed the gate open and took me by the arm, as if she were rescuing me from the firing squad. She guided me through corridors adorned with Ming vases and rare seashells, past the interior courtyard filled with blooming bougainvillea. I hadn't been to the house in a long time, but every corner was familiar from years of hide-and-seek. I remembered hiding in her closet, amid the naphthalene and the gowns; in the studio, beneath don Raúl's mahogany desk, where I once kissed my cousin Isabel; in the cellar, where I liked to tell my American friends my great-grandfather had harbored priests during the Revolution, even though he'd done nothing of the sort.

We arrived at the antechamber of the master bedroom, where an elderly nurse asked us to wait while she cleaned his bedsores. I slouched on the corner of a sofa, my grandmother perched in the center. I glanced at her hands, which were interlaced over her lap in a studied gesture. I tried to picture her as a young woman, when her parents sent her to New York for a year after she'd graduated from high school, in theory to polish her English, in practice so she could have a moment of freedom before her marriage. She and her sister made a splash in Manhattan with their blank checkbooks and their alluring accents and their Park Avenue address. They must have felt so alive, those two well-bred criollitas, letting their hair down for the first and last time.

After the brisk air of Central Park, though, the solemnity of Chapultepec proved oppressive. Terrified of dirt and germs, my grandmother took to washing her hands every half-hour and to wearing gloves from morning to night. Her skin, trapped in moist leather and burned by abrasive soaps, rotted away.

"I hear you have a fiancée. When am I going to meet her?"

I replied that Kirie, the woman I dated in college, was my girlfriend, not my fiancée, and that I didn't know when she would be able to visit.

"It's important we get to know her before the ceremony. I don't want to see her for the first time at the cathedral. But tell me, is it true she is Oriental?"

I sank into the sofa and was about to tell her that Kirie's father was half-Chinese, half-Japanese, and that her mother was half-Swedish, half-Lithuanian, but the nurse returned and gestured to me. I looked at my grandmother. She shook her head. "This is between you and him."

I walked into the darkened bedroom. My grandfather lay on the same bed on which he had been born, a crucifix over his head, plastic tubes protruding from his nostrils. A white gown had replaced his dark suit but his expression remained the same: a sad, somber drooping of the left eye, a bitter tension on the lips. He was larger than the last time I'd seen him, his abdomen almost monstrous under the white sheets. I remembered him walking slowly through the halls of the house, his cane marking the irregular rhythm of his gout-swollen steps. The sound was a warning to stay quiet in one's hiding place. He didn't like children running around his library.

The nurse handed me a chair. I sat down by the bed.

"You are Alberto's son, yes?"

I nodded, trying not to react to his rotten breath.

"I hear you are studying abroad. Where are you again?"

I answered, with the insecure snobbery of an abejorro among wasps, that I went to school in New Haven.

"Why not the École Normale? Or at the very least the Sorbonne?"

I replied that my French wasn't good enough.

He shook his head. "A real shame. Nothing like a French education. They train the intelligence there, not just the brain. And what is it that you study?"

I bit my tongue and wondered whether I should lie. "Literature," I whispered.

He was overcome by a violent cough, and for a moment I feared I might have killed him. I'd grown up under the impression that those Arteaga y Salazar born too late to enjoy the life of an idle landowner in Durango were supposed to practice one of three professions: law, banking, or the priesthood.

Among these, even banking was considered undignified, too bourgeois, too concerned with money. The men in our family were supposed to maintain order in the world, whether it was the sacred order of the Church or the secular one of the state, a task that had become especially important since the Revolution. It was not that my grandfather lacked an appreciation for literature—his library was one of the best in the city; his seminar at the Faculty of Law spent more time on Cervantes than on legal theory—but that don Raúl saw reading and writing less as vocations in themselves than as the natural byproducts of a public life. His generation of creoles was born during the Revolution, but its members remained nineteenth-century creatures, and not unconsciously but out of a prideful choice. The idea of a "professional writer" must have struck them as a devaluation of art into a means of making a living, or else as a notion as frivolous as a career in the theater.

Don Raúl's cough subsided. He spat out a mouthful of yellowish liquid into the chamber pot by the bed. "Do me a favor," he said as he wiped the phlegm off his beard with the sleeve of his gown. "Go to the library and bring me a pen and a Quijote. "

"Which edition?"

He shook his head and waved his hand as if he were swatting a fly. "Whichever you like! I'm dying. What does it matter?"

I walked out of the bedroom and crossed the hall into the library where I spent my childhood reading by sunlight. I headed toward the literature section and climbed to the top shelf, where my grandfather kept his hundred or so copies of Don Quijote: *cheap paperbacks, illustrated hardcovers, even a leather-bound edition from the seventeenth century. I chose a humble copy, printed in Republican Spain, and climbed down* from the shelf. I opened one of the desk drawers and found at least three-dozen fountain pens. I took one and returned to the bedroom.

"You have a lot of pens," I said as I sat by the bed.

He made a noise that might have been laughter. "What can I tell you? I wanted to be a poet." He took the book from my hands and struggled to remove the cap of the pen. "I produced only two sonnets," he went on as he began writing on the first page. "One to your grandmother, the other upon the death of Pope John XXIII. They were formally perfect but lacking in content. I destroyed all the copies."

He gave me the book with shaking hands. The pen fell on the sheets, spilling black ink over his bloated abdomen. His face grew softer. "I'm glad you have chosen a literary career. Law is the highest office after the priesthood, but letters, too, are an honorable profession. Keep this Quijote. Beware the Congregationalists of your university." He brought my head close to his. "Remember you are Mexican." With two fingers he made the sign of the cross of my forehead. "I'm tired. Go with God."

I didn't gather the courage to look at the inscription until a few weeks after I returned to New Haven, when my father called to tell me that don Raúl had died. I pondered whether to go to church but decided against it. Instead, I brought my Quijote to the center of the Silliman College courtyard. Ankles buried in snow, I opened the book to read out loud the last words that my grandfather had left me. The first page was covered in indecipherable scribbles.

The day before spring break Lee wrote me an email:

> *Dear Sebas,*
>
> *My plane to Colombia is about to take off, so I'll keep it brief. I've decided I'm willing to try an open relationship for the remainder of the semester, until we see each other in the summer. We can talk about the details later, but I think it would be easiest for me if we didn't tell one another about our escapades. This is all new to me, so I'm not sure it will work out, but it seems worthwhile to give it a shot. I love you, Sebas. I'll write again from Cartagena.*
>
> > *Yours, always,*
> > *Lee*

Well now, I thought, this is unexpected. I'd suggested we try non-monogamy shortly after we formalized our relationship, but Lee was skeptical and asked to table the discussion for a while. I wrote back to thank her for the trust she was granting me. Later that week I went to a party and came home with Charlie.

Perded toda la esperanza

And then, one morning in April, I got a call from my blue-blooded lawyer. He told me that, although there had been no official policy changes, the Trump administration had begun denying virtually all applications for "extraordinary ability" green cards.

"It's remarkable. I have a client from China. Also a Yalie. Brilliant guy. Double majored in econ and art history, then did a MPhil in PPE at Christ Church and an MBA in Palo Alto—and he just got rejected. The legislation says 'extraordinary ability' is measured through 'sustained achievement through time.' But what does that mean? My client sold a tech start-up for ten figures. But it was only one start-up. And wouldn't an extraordinary person in his field have sold, I don't know, three? Ten?"

He went on for some time. Eventually I got the message and asked if I should withdraw my application.

"Well, lawyers should never tell their clients to give up. But, to be candid, unless you get married to a citizen, your chances of becoming a permanent resident while Trump is in office are next to nil. If it's any consolation, it's not just you. Ninety percent of my clients have decided to drop their cases."

I thanked him and asked him to let me know if anything changed, then hung up. I felt a hollowness in the chest, a tightening of the trachea. I sat at my desk, stunned into stupor, listening to the muffled sounds of the street outside my apartment, where the American people went about their day in blissful ignorance that the end of the world had begun.

I still had options, of course. I could apply to a PhD program and ride another student visa for five years or try to get one of those two-year permits they sometimes gave to artists. Or I could look for another job in journalism and hope someone was willing to pay me enough to meet the new eligibility criteria for specialized-alien work permits. Even if everything went well, though, the respite would be temporary. A new visa would simply mean delaying the inevitable: the dreaded moment when I'd run out of stopgaps and have no choice but to face the fact that I'd built a life in a country where I didn't have the right to live.

The shape of my biography was not the product of my will but of the infinite chain of accidents that had led to my birth in one country and not another. Identity, which so many of my friends understood as self-expression, was not the field of freedom but its limit: the tailored straitjacket history wove for each person. Mine was cut of softer fabric than most people's, but even with its looser fit it nonetheless constrained my freedom of movement.

La revancha de los pedantes

"It's not about love!" Zoraya said. "It's about imperialism!"

We were discussing the chapter of *Love in the Time of Cholera* where the characters go on a joy ride in a hot-air balloon and wind up flying over fields littered with dead workers. As supplementary materials, I'd asked my students to read the diplomatic cables in which the United States had threatened the Colombian government with a blockade if it refused to break a strike at a United Fruit plantation, as well as a short historical article on the Banana Massacre. I wanted to suggest to them that the second term in "magical realism" was as important as the first—but instead the conversation had degenerated into a circular argument on what the book was actually "about."

"It's about how white America oppresses Latinx people," Zoraya went on. "About how American racism doesn't respect America's borders."

There was a moment of silence. I could sense the discomfort of many white students. But that was okay. Most of them harbored an unreflective patriotism that they'd do well to shed. But then, to my dismay, Billy spoke up: "Are you saying you'd rather live in some Third World country than in America?"

"Yeah, Billy. I'd rather live almost anywhere else than *white* America."

"There's no white America. Just as there's no Black America. There's only America."

I turned to Zoraya and discovered she was also looking at

me. "Okay, folks," I said. "I think we can suspend this discussion about whether the American nation is an integral whole or a mismatched collection of contradictions. What did you think about how time works in this passage? The characters don't just see the aftermath of the Banana Massacre, but also stuff that happened much earlier, in the colonial period. What's the conception of history that's . . ."

"Yeah, no," Billy interrupted. "Don't think we can move on just yet."

"Please don't derail the discussion."

"There's a question you need to answer."

"Billy, we're here to talk about García Márquez, not—"

"Do you agree that America is the greatest country in the world?"

I froze. Who was the audience here? Billy? Zoraya? The Dean of DEI? The one in charge of enforcing the new legislation forbidding teachers at Iowa public schools from suggesting that the US was fundamentally racist? "I guess it depends on what you mean by great? Do I think the US is the most powerful country in the world? Yes. Do I think it's the best country in the world? No."

"But then why do so many illegals want to come here?"

"Don't talk about people that way, Billy. Human beings aren't contraband. Let's go back to *Love in*—"

"They break our laws when they come here, though. Why don't they do it the right way and come legally? Why don't they get in line?"

I closed my eyes and took a deep breath, trying to contain the surge of anger expanding in my sternum. "Because there is no fucking line, Billy!" I said, louder than I should have. "Do you have any idea how hard it is to immigrate to the United States? Take me for example. I've lived here for almost ten years.

Went to school here. Have worked here. Never got in trouble. And I was just told I probably won't be able to stay once my student visa runs out. Imagine what it's like for people who flee their countries because they're hungry, or because if they stay, they risk being tortured and killed by a drug cartel, or by paramilitary death-squads funded by *your* government. Because guess what, Billy? The novel we're reading is damn close to nonfiction. It's mostly America's fault that all those countries are fucked up."

"Yeah, whatever. The poor little brown children are all dying of diarrhea. Too bad."

I closed my eyes and held on to my desk, trying to keep myself from saying something I'd regret. "That's it," I managed after a while. "Get out of my classroom. Do you even listen to yourself? You're talking about people who—"

"That's funny. You sound different when it's just you and me smoking by the river. So which one is the real one? Salazar or the other Salazar?"

"This has nothing to do with me. This—"

"Oh yeah? It's not about you, Professor Salazar? I saw your watch, dude. Before you took it off. You think we couldn't tell? So let's hear it. Why did you want to come to America if you weren't shitting yourself to death?"

I waited for an ingenious reply that would both humiliate and force him to confront the stupidity of what he was saying, but for the first time in my life I was at a genuine loss for words.

"See, that's what I mean. You'd rather make shit money teaching in America's armpit than be some rich big shot in Mexico. You know why? Because America is the greatest country in the world. And that's because it's a country built by white people."

I looked at my students, who were frozen in place, staring at me expectantly, waiting for me to dispel the evil their classmate had conjured; then at my apprentice, my fellow reader of Homer and Pound and Nietzsche. It wasn't that he'd disappointed me or that I'd failed him as a teacher. No, the origins of the rage boiling in my stomach were far less lofty. I'd read Levinas and Arendt and Fanon and Foucault; I'd cut my teeth among the monsters of the Yale Political Union; I'd attended Brooklyn reading groups devoted to the *Grundrisse* and *Anti-Oedipus*—and yet I'd just lost a speech-and-debate match with a child.

"You know what, Billy? You're always saying us libtards are too scared to engage with your ideas. So let's do it. Let's dance."

I then asked him to explain what he meant by *white*, *people*, and *country*. Each time he attempted a definition, I asked him to in turn define the words he'd used in his definition. Before long he was trying to account for *human, culture, nation, race, knowledge, belief, meaning, freedom, truth, good,* and *justice*. After a while he started to cry.

"What's the matter, Billy? You don't know what words mean?"

"I do know what words mean," he mumbled.

"Right, because you read the Western canon! Here, Billy, get up. Come to the whiteboard. We're going to play a little game."

He shook his head.

"Fine. We can play a different game." I turned around to face the board and wrote: Δίκη, πόλις, ἔθνος. I turned back to him and went on: "Tell me, Billy. Can you read what's on the board? I tried this same trick the other day with Old English, which I don't actually know. But I do know ancient Greek. You too, right? You're a *Defender of the West*! Who came up with that name, by the way? Because it's corny as hell. Almost as corny as your poems."

I paused and looked at the clock on my phone. The class had been over for more than ten minutes, but nobody had left. "Well, Billy, I'm afraid time is running out. But if you don't mind, I have one last question for you. Do I count as white?"

He didn't reply. Instead his crying intensified from droplets of rage into ugly tears of humiliation. I couldn't care less. I was enjoying his pain.

"Sorry, Billy, didn't quite catch that. Would you mind speaking up for the class?"

"I don't know."

"You don't know?"

"No, I don't. I'm sorry."

I walked to his desk and stood over him. "That's right. You don't know shit."

He broke into sobs. Child-sobs. Loud and unembarrassed. I felt a jolt of sadistic pleasure, then looked around the classroom and saw that every other student, including Zoraya, was staring at me in terror.

Para Rüdiger Campe

In the fourth chapter of the *Phenomenology*, Hegel's epic tale of humanity's philosophical coming of age, the Spirit encounters the Other. By this point the Spirit—Hegel's name for humanity as both individual and collective—has advanced from its brutish origins into an intermediary stage where it's already capable of self-referential cognition but nonetheless remains less than human. It's only after the Spirit meets another being like itself, a mirror that is also its negation, that it becomes aware of its own mind.

This awareness, however, is terrifying. The Spirit feels threatened by the Other, which it sees not as a sibling but as a rival. The two consciousnesses are drawn into conflict, at which point they kill each other, in which case history ends, or the one subdues the other, in which case the two consciousnesses become, respectively, Lord and Bondsman.

Hegel maintained that the dialectical dance of these two forms of the Spirit has the counterintuitive effect of deepening the subjectivity of the Bondsman rather than that of the Lord. This is because bondage, in its most general definition, consists of being forced to recognize the Other as a sovereign self-consciousness while the Other denies a reciprocal recognition. Transformed into a mere means by virtue of being forced to work for the Lord, the Bondsman's existence becomes a constant affirmation of the Other's status as an end-in-itself.

The result is that the Bondsman splits into two: a self-consciousness that knows itself to be sovereign, and a consciousness-of-the-Other that knows only the sovereignty of the Lord. The two subjectivities look at each other from across an abyss of contradiction: they are one another's negation; they are based on incompatible premises; they simply cannot coexist. This unstable situation brings about the metaphysical equivalent of a nuclear reaction: a process of sublimation by which opposites are reconciled. The Bondsman's antithetical selves clash in a violent struggle in which they are both destroyed, but through which a third entity comes into being. This new self is the Unhappy Consciousness: a mad and maddening mind that knows itself to be at once weaker and wiser than the Lord.

From that point and until the Haitian Revolution—the same that Lee and Daniel adapted for the stage—the Bondsman exists in a state of perpetual alienation, trapped in a cage of self-knowledge and unfreedom where pride and self-hatred engender resentment—but also, if we are to believe the *Phenomenology*, the first examples of what we know as "culture." It is the Bondsman, not the Lord, who first becomes a human being.

That's why I often find myself thinking of Hegel when I return to Sigüenza. Neither Lords nor Bondsmen and yet both at once, at the same time colonizers and colonized, the creoles don't fit into the neat binary of the dialectic. For all their efforts to convince themselves they were victims rather than beneficiaries of the conquest, Sigüenza and his peers remained invested in convincing their European masters they were exactly like them. Uncomfortable with the substantive identity of their caste, the descendants of Cortés sought an adjective that could define their difference from the Spaniards as accident rather than essence. They found it in *Indiano*, a shapeshifting word, at once antonym and modifier of European, that for some time circulated in the Hispanic New World as a near-synonym of the term preferred by the creoles' Anglophone peers: American.

The two words have atrophied—they are, as Nietzsche might say, coins that have lost their stamps and are now regarded as metal rather than coins—but I like to imagine there was a time when they denoted less an accident of geography than the paradox at the heart of every colonial elite's self-conception. American and Indiano once meant the same thing: *creole*, Lord-in-Bondage.

El hijo pródigo

The day after I made Billy cry, Bouvard called me to his office to let me know my teaching assistantship was suspended pending an investigation into my conduct in the classroom. He reassured me I wouldn't lose my tuition scholarship even if I was found unfit to teach. The Department would just find something else for me to do.

"A research assistantship, for example. Do you know Professor Eich? He's in poli-sci but has an appointment in English for complicated reasons that have to do with the fact that he speaks German. Not many German speakers at the UI. Anyway, he's working on the history of the political theory of money and could use some help."

"Sounds fascinating. I'd be delighted to assist with archival research, fact-checking, or translation of primary sources. In fact, I'm sure I could make a conceptual contribution to Professor Eich's work, seeing that I'm familiar with the central Marxist texts, and that—"

"Look, Sebastián, I appreciate your enthusiasm. But you don't understand. Eich needs someone to review two hundred and fifty thousand images of ancient coins and record their inscriptions. That's it. We're sending you to the basement. You can't scream at a student for thirty minutes about how he's an idiot for not knowing Greek."

"That's not—"

"You'll have the opportunity to tell your side of the story to the investigators."

He gestured to the door. I got up and headed for it.

"Oh, by the way," Bouvard went on as I turned the knob, "I'm afraid that, so long as the investigation is ongoing, we can't pay you."

I jerked around to face him. "And how am I supposed to cover rent?"

Bouvard looked around his office, as if a spy could have been hiding in a corner. "Tu parles français, n'est-ce pas, mon fils?"

"Pas tout à fait, professeur. Mais j'y arrive."

"Bien. On ne sait jamais qui est à l'écoute dans les universités américaines. Mais on peut toujours être certain que personne ne parle une autre langue que l'anglais."

I stood at the door, still holding the knob, unsure what I was supposed to say or do.

"Écoutes bien, jeune lion," Bouvard went on. "La fragilité des étudiants américains est absurde. Ridicule. Tu comprends. Tu viens de l'Amérique Latine, une région civilisée. Et à propos d'argent—tu viens d'une famille, dirons-nous, éminente, n'est pas? Je suis sûr que ton bon père peut te prêter quelques centimes."

I tried to come up with an appropriate reply, but I couldn't remember how to conjugate the verbal phrase *go fuck yourself*, so I limited myself to a nod and a smile and walked out of the office. On my way home, I texted my father to ask if we could talk. He called right away.

"¡El Gran Sebastián! To what do I owe this honor? How are you, hijito?"

"Hola, Papá. Todo bien, gracias. ¿Y tú?" He began to reply but I interrupted him. "Actually, I'm sorry, but I'm calling to ask for your help."

"What happened? Do you need a lawyer?"

"No, Papá, I don't need a lawyer."

"If you think you might need one, you definitely do."

I gave him a quick summary, twisting the facts a bit to make myself look more reasonable.

"I'm relieved," he said. "I thought you were about to tell me you'd been arrested for running over a toddler while high on methamphetamine."

"Do you really think I do meth, Papá?"

"You live in that part of the country. At any rate, it's bullshit. How much do you need per month?"

I told him what I got paid by the university.

"You live on *that*? I'll tell you what. Until they sort things out, I'll send you twice what you made as a TA. Hazard pay for dealing with American idiocy."

Para Natalia Reyes

I was heading to the Kum & Go to pick up cigarettes when I saw a poster on a bulletin board advertising a Prairie Lights event with Andrea de Olivares, the New York-based conceptual poet who'd recently become America's favorite Mexican writer.

I stood before the poster, seething with resentment. Olivares didn't know it yet, but she was my nemesis. Following Clausewitz's advice, I made a point of keeping tabs on her activities, setting up Google Alerts not just for her name but also for common monolingual-American misspellings. I clicked on almost every link the algorithm served me. Months earlier, for instance, I'd read an interview with the *Draft* where she spoke at length about the reasons why she loved living in Harlem—and delivered a brutal blow with the sort of sangfroid known only to those who grew up in Mexican embassies: "But what I love most about Manhattan is that it offers a bubble outside of the literary world."

I got to the front of the line and bought two packs of American Spirits and a handle of Jim Beam Rye. Both of our fathers had been ambassadors, both of us had gone to school abroad, both of us had enjoyed the encouragement of literary luminaries whose interest in nurturing our precocious gifts had nothing whatsoever to do with their friendship with our parents. And yet, even though she was less than a decade older than me, she was the author of a half-dozen celebrated books, whereas I was the author of such classics of digital journalism as "How To Talk About Cinco de Mayo Without Sounding Like A Gringo."

Olivares was already being called one of the most celebrated writers of her generation—which was also *my* generation. With the notorious exception of Heriberto Yépez, who had written in his blog that Olivares was "an AI hologram engineered in the R&D laboratory of the Latinx Studies Department at Stanford and then polished at the Wylie Finishing School," the consensus among critics on both sides of the border was that her last book, *Anti-Antigone*, should have been a shoo-in for the Pulitzer or at least the National Book Award. It was too bad that, since Olivares wasn't an American citizen, she was ineligible for both prizes.

And sure, fine, whatever—I had no issue admitting that her books were good, perhaps even great. If nothing else, they were better than my own books, which for all their merits suffered from the minor defect of not existing. No, the problem was that, with the possible exception of myself, Olivares was as far removed from the experiences of the impoverished people about whom she wrote as any living Mexican—and yet the bookstores I frequented in Brooklyn insisted on displaying her books on staff-picked shelves under such headings as *Our Favorite Women Writers of Color*, a category that usually included Claudia Rankine, Layli Long Soldier, and bell hooks—but also, with increasing frequency, Clarice Lispector and Alejandra Pizarnik.

This misclassification was grating because, before coming to America, Olivares had made a name for herself as a junior critic at *Libros Liberales*, the reactionary magazine founded by acolytes of Octavio Paz, where she'd published such juvenalia as an essay lamenting the Swedish Academy's decision to award the Nobel Prize to a "spokesman for the subaltern" by the name of Derek Walcott.

At home, as I poured myself a rye on the rocks—my second—I found myself hoping her new book would flop. *Green Card Marriage* was on every list of new-releases-to-watch, but the title made it clear that Olivares's canny strategy of appealing to the guilty conscience of white liberals had gone too far. I could picture it already: devastating reviews, a change.org petition, mobs banging pitchforks against the door of her publisher. Her downfall would pave the way for my ascension. The Americans wanted a Mexican writer who could make them feel smart and cosmopolitan. Why shouldn't it be me?

But then, as I went out on my fire escape to smoke, I began to wonder whether I was being unfair. Maybe the experience of being demoted from creole oligarch to racially ambiguous immigrant had been enough to raise Olivares's political consciousness. I'd have to attend her reading and ask her a few questions.

On the day of the event, I headed to Prairie Lights early to secure a front-row seat. I took out my notebook to review the questions I'd prepared: *Do you think that writers, and particularly writers from a place as unequal as Mexico, have a responsibility to be upfront about their class position? Do you still think Derek Walcott was a "spokesman for the subaltern"? What do you make of Wendy Trevino's "Brazilian is Not a Race"?*

It was good that I'd arrived an hour before the start time: Maggie Nelson, Leslie Jamison, and even Jonathan Franzen had all stopped by—but none of them had attracted half as many people. What was most puzzling, however, wasn't the size of the audience but its composition. Besides the usual mix of undergraduates and MFA students coerced into attending, faculty members eager to rub shoulders, and elderly white folks with nothing better to do, a substantial portion of the crowd was composed of brown women of all ages—teenagers with pink or blue hair, young mothers carrying infants, even a handful of abuelas. I recognized one of them: the bubbly girl who worked behind the counter at La Regia, a restaurant-cum-grocery-store-cum-Western-Union on a suburban strip-mall just outside town that was probably the only Mexican joint run by actual Mexicans in the vicinity of the faux city.

When the appointed hour struck, however, Olivares was nowhere to be seen. Ten minutes passed, then forty-five. The white Middle Westerners—whose meager culture consisted in little more than a strict etiquette, enforced through passive aggression, that valued punctuality above all else—began to whisper in tones of indignant incredulity. The undergraduates who'd long-since signed their TA's attendance sheets started going to the bathroom never to return. The MFA students, aware they'd have a harder time sneaking out, scrolled through Insta-gram and swiped on Tinder with resigned expressions. Only the brown women seemed unfazed, and continued chatting in more animated tones than were usually heard in the academic corners of the faux city.

By the time an hour had elapsed since the reading was sup-posed to start, the bookstore manager was pacing back and forth across the room, running her hands through her hair, mumbling inaudibly, looking at her watch every few seconds. Here was incontrovertible evidence that Olivares thought she was too good for the Middle West: she had no qualms inflicting a panic attack on the manager of one of the last independent bookstores between Chicago and San Francisco. Then one of the brown women's babies began to cry. I turned around and saw her walk out of the bookstore, rocking the infant in her arms—and realized with glee that Olivares's snub was in fact much worse. Never mind the bookseller: she had just stood up a group of people who very much resembled the working-class women who populated the books that had made her famous.

Maybe there's an essay here, I thought. A-plot: an account of the reading-that-never-happened, with the bookstore manager and the brown mothers as central characters. B-plot: a cool-headed vivisection of Olivares's reactionary juvenilia that would enlist Gayatri Spivak and Sayak Valencia to demonstrate that she profited from pretending to let the subaltern speak.

And then, to my immense disappointment, the poet appeared at the end of the stairs, arm in arm with the classicist-turned-lyric-essayist who ran the Nonfiction Writing Program. She had gray-green eyes, an oval face, and unblemished olive skin that called to mind vineyards and the scent of tarragon. When she smiled her lips parted to reveal a charming gap between her teeth, and her face lit up with a warmth that I could tell induced in everyone she encountered an irresistible desire to please her.

The bookstore manager grabbed the microphone to announce that the event was starting. Then the Decanonizer got up from her chair and walked up to the lectern.

"Good evening, pals!" she said. "Tonight I have the great privilege of introducing one of the most exciting writers working in the United States: Andrea de Olivares. Born in Mexico City, Olivares is the author of two collections of poems, a book of essays, a novel, and two trans-genre works of documentary verse. Though her earlier work was concerned with philosophical problems around the nature of selfhood—Olivares holds an undergraduate degree from the École Normale Supérieure, where she studied with Alain Badiou—in recent years she has turned to more political questions. Her best-known work, *Anti-Antigone*, a polyphonic account of a group of women who are trying to locate the bodies of murdered relatives, appeared in Oprah Winfrey's and Gwyneth Paltrow's yearly book-recommendation lists. Tonight she will read from her forthcoming book, *Green Card Marriage*, a long poem assembled by running the text of the US Immigration and Naturalization Act through Markov-chain software. The recipient of a faculty fellowship at All Souls' College, Oxford, Olivares has shown us that literature committed to social justice can also be formally adventurous—that Latina writers can also be experimental. Please join me in welcoming her to Iowa City!"

The crowd applauded politely. The Decanonizer left the lectern and Olivares took her place.

"Thank you for that way-too-kind introduction!" she said. "The bit where you called me a 'Latina writer' could use some workshopping, but that's fine—you're in the right place for that, from what I've heard." She smiled at the Decanonizer, who had turned bright red, and gave a nod of acknowledgment to the head of the program. Then she began to read very slowly, like an oracle receiving messages from Hades:

> Cruelty in good faith:
> a ceremony battered
> by loss or renunciation
>
> satisfies the requirements
> of evidence: testimony credible
> under oath of candor.
>
> The citizen spouse enjoys
> exceptions, status,
> minor immunities;
>
> the spouse abandoning
> a foreign country
> is a resident enemy.
>
> Witness the union
> of war and law:
> the territory of identity.

The poem then shifted to more narrative material: first scenes from the Brooklynite life of a troubled marriage between a Mexican woman and a white American man, later flashbacks to the woman's disordered life—sex, cigarettes, psych ward—as a philosophy student in Paris. After some twenty minutes of this, Olivares stopped reading but didn't move or say anything, her eyes fixed on the lectern. Eventually the audience realized there was nothing else coming and promptly broke into applause.

"Thank you for listening to all that!" Olivares said. "I was told I'm supposed to take a few questions—but maybe it's too late for that, seeing that I showed up a million years late?" She turned to the bookstore manager, who gestured for her to carry on. "Aw, shucks! I was hoping to run out the clock. Let's get it over with, shall we? Who wants to throw the first stone?"

I felt an oncoming stroke. Shucks? Really? What, had she grown up aw-shucking corn in Depression-era Nebraska?

Then one of the young brown mothers raised her hand. A moody intern walked up to her and offered her the microphone. She handed her child to the woman to her left and stood up.

"Hello!" she said. "Good evening to everyone. I am sorry for my English—it is still more-or-less, especially if I must talk in front of people."

Olivares smiled again, though this time in a different way—more sincere and less transparent. "¿Cómo te llamas?" she said.

No mames, I thought. Was she really trying to pass off class condescension as ethnic solidarity?

"Jane, señora de Olivares. Jane Preciado."

"Mucho gusto, Jane. Pero, por favor, no me digas señora ni me hables de usted. Dime Andrea, ¿va? Y que no te de pena hablar en inglés. Esta gente no habla español. Ni francés. Ni alemán. Ni nahuatl ni zapoteco ni mixe. Ni ningún otro idioma que no sea el suyo. Y luego ni ese lo hablan bien. Además, ¿te digo la verdad? A mí también me da pena hablar en público. Por eso llegué tarde: por el tráfico, sí, pero también de las puras ñañaras. Me tuve que echar un tequila para agarrar valor. Nomás no seas malita y le vayas a decir a alguien que ya vengo enfiestada, ¿ok? Porque, aunque no lo creas, de esto como."

A wave of laughter ran through the Spanish-speaking members of the audience. I wondered where she had learned to talk like that: ñañaras, malita, enfiestada. Surely not in 1930s Nebraska!

"Okay, está bien, Andrea," the young mother replied. "Muchas gracias. Pues mira, solo te quería decir que leí tu libro, el de Antigone. Y, bueno, pues, ¿qué te digo? Lo sentí. Lo sentí bien, pero bien fuerte. Lo que pasa es que mi prima, allá por Irapuato, pues hace como tres años que no sabemos nada de ella. Nada de nada. Ni adonde está, ni quién se la llevó, ni qué le hicieron. Y pues los oficiales y los soldados nos dicen y nos dicen de que si la andan buscando, de que si ya les dieron nueva tecnología, de que si es cuestión de tiempo, de que si ya mero, de que si en una de esas se fue con el novio, o se perdió en la droga, o se vino pa acá, pa'l Norte, y de que si luego sí pasa que gente que lleva años y años sin que nadie sepa adonde andan, que ya los dieron por perdidos, que ya les rezaron sus novenarios, pues de que si luego sí pasa que esa gente de repente se aparece por su pueblo, así como si nada. Y pues, bueno, Andrea, ¿pa' que te engaño? No nos hacemos ilusiones. Sabemos que lo más seguro es que nos la mataron. Y que en una de esas eso fue lo menos feo de todo lo que le hicieron. Pero igual nos gustaría encontrarla. Para darle cristiana sepultura. Porque es bien, pero bien feo, ¿sabes? No poder despedirse. No saber si pedir que nos la regresen viva, como se la llevaron, o si pedir que Dios la reciba en su Santa Gloria, para que pueda estar con su mamá y con su abuela, y con su hermano, el que mataron los soldados, y su papá, el que se murió en Minnesota de pura soledad. Y bueno, pues cuando mi sobrina—la que está yendo al college en California, allá en Berkeley, una escuela bien famosa, seguro tú has dictado cátedra allá—bueno, pues cuando me mandó tu libro, me dijo que me iba a identify with it, ¿sabes? Y pues yo no sé mentir, Andrea, hubo muchas partes que no entendí, porque como te decía el inglés todavía me cuesta, además de que tu libro, bueno, yo de libros no sé nada, pero pues tu libro, como que es diferente, ¿verdad? Como que es raro. Pero con todo y todo, la verdad es que mi sobrina me dijo la verdad. Porque me gustó harto. Así que fui y le saqué copias allá con el notario y lo fui repartiendo entre las paisanas de acá, del Johnson County. Porque no es nomás mi prima, ¿sabes? Casi todas tenemos alguien extraviado. Que no lo encuentran. Que no lo enterraron bien. Y pues tu libro nos hizo sentir que no somos nomás nosotras, ¿verdad? Que somos todas. Y, bueno, pues me da harta vergüenza, porque deberíamos haberlo comprado, porque pues ese es tu trabajo, y aquí siempre decimos que, trabajar de a gratis, ni pa'l marido. Pero la verdad es que luego nuestra economía se pone bien difícil. Y bueno, pues, cuando supimos que ibas a pasar por acá, pues todas dijimos que íbamos a venir a darte las gracias en persona. Porque si no podemos comprar tu libro, lo menos es decirte que aquí en Iowa te queremos mucho, y que aquí tienes tu casa, y cualquier cosa que necesites, porque nos regalaste algo bien, pero bien precioso, que es sentirse que la vida de una no es nomás de una."

I turned around and saw that the Mexican women in the audience were nodding solemnly. I had spent two years in the Middle West trying and failing to make friends with the faux city's vanishingly small Mexican community—and now this standard-issue, garden-variety SRE diplobrat showed up with her sappy little soap opera disguised as performance art, her literature as installation, her reheated refried rehash of century-old pseudo-dadaist nonsense—and boom, voilà, presto, the local chapter of the Selena Quintanilla Association of Middle-Western Paisanas showed up en masse to thank her for letting them see themselves in literature.

"Anyone else?" Olivares asked.

I raised my hand in way that conveyed an easy authority—a hand, and a question, at once casual and inevitable. But the moody intern walked past me without making eye contact and handed the microphone to someone in the standing-room section in the back: none other than my student, or former student, Zoraya.

"Hi there!" she said. "Thank you for that. That was so powerful. I feel I've got to burn some sage or something."

Olivares laughed a laughter so organic and sincere that it couldn't possibly be real. "I'm so glad! 'Desperately in need of an exorcism' is exactly where I want to leave my readers."

"I do have a question though," Zoraya went on. "You know how you said the bit where the TA who introduced you called you a 'Latin American writer' needed some workshopping? Can you explain what you meant?"

Oh, yes, I thought. Yes, yes. Yes! Ha-ha! Go forth, my padawan! To the breach, my courageous gakusei! Remember your years of training: Ethos! Logos! Pathos! Cry havoc, meine junge Kulturkriegerin, and release the hounds of war! I turned to look at the terror in Olivares's eyes, but to my surprise I found her smiling an even warmer smile.

"What's your name?" she said.

"Zoraya."

"Nice to meet you, Zoraya. Are you in the MFA program?"

"I'm a sophomore."

"That's awesome, Zoraya! Okay, I'm going to do that annoying thing where you answer a question with another question. Do you know where the term 'Latin America' comes from? Not from 'Latin America.' It comes from France. The French came up with it in the nineteenth century to justify why they, and not the US, should call the shots in the part of the hemisphere that had been colonized by the Spanish and the Portuguese. That's why they had to go all the way back to ancient Rome: the French were not Indigenous, obviously, but they also weren't Spanish or Portuguese, or even American. Why should they have say over a part of the world they had no connection to? Because, as the champion of the Romance-language-speaking peoples of the world, which is one of the most ridiculous concepts anybody ever came up with, it was France's duty to defend the Latin nations from the expansionist threat of the Anglo-Saxons of North America. It's that dumb."

"Wow," Zoraya said. "I had no idea!"

"But it's actually more complicated than that," Olivares went on. "Because the TA who introduced me didn't call me a 'Latin American' writer, which would have been ideologically suspect but at least accurate. No, she called me 'a Latina.' And here's where it gets sticky, Zoraya. Because, to tell you the truth? I'm not sure I even know what that word means. But insofar as I can hear it in everyday situations and have some sense of what is being conveyed, I think you could say that it's a name for someone who has roots in the former Spanish colonies in the Americas, but either was born in the United States or has lived here for a long time, such that their closest cultural ties are not to their ancestral homeland but to diasporic communities. And since wealthy people in 'Latin America' tend to be light-skinned, and since light-skinned migrants tend to have a much easier time assimilating to mainstream American culture, which is to say to white culture, and since this in turn means that wealthy immigrants, at least those from 'Latin America,' don't tend to form diasporic communities—well, then it follows that 'Latina' most accurately describes not just a person with roots in 'Latin America,' but a racialized person with roots in the lower socioeconomic strata of that region. And I'm very much not that, Zoraya. That's why I wrote this book. I got tired of being asked to participate in panels of 'writers of color.' Not because I don't enjoy their company— au contraire!—but because the kinda awkward truth is that I'm actually a white lady. A white lady from Mexico. Does that make sense, Zoraya?"

I turned to my former student, ready to find her taking aim for her sniper's shot, but to my disappointment she was nodding pensively. "That makes sense," she said. "But you just read us this dope poem about how you had to marry that awful white boy just to stay in the US! Not many white ladies have that experience, do they? Also, do you ever worry about writing about economically disadvantaged women, like you did in your other book? Because you're, like, hella bougie, right?"

Olivares burst out laughing. "That's right, Zoraya. I'm haute bourgeois, as my friends from the Rue d'Ulm would say. So, to answer your second question first—no, I don't worry about that. I don't think you have to have lived through something to have the right to write about it. What you don't have the right to do is write about stuff you don't know about. I spent almost ten years researching *Anti-Antigone*. I spoke to hundreds of buscadoras. I still don't know nearly as much as they do, but I do think I know enough to write a book of poems about their stories. When white American authors write annoying stuff about Mexico, it's because they don't know enough to know they don't know enough to avoid making fools of themselves. As for your other question—well, Zoraya, I'm afraid I lied to you. I've never been married. And I'd never get married just to get a green card. Can you imagine the mess of mixing business and pleasure like that? I did this thing where, if you win enough fancy awards, they'll just give you one for free. Well, not for free, it's extremely expensive, but you know what I mean. My latest book is what is known as a 'persona poem.' Have you encountered that term in class?"

Zoraya shook her head. We were supposed to talk about that when we discussed Pound, just like we were supposed to talk about the origins of the concept of "Latin America" when we discussed García Márquez. Too bad we wound up arguing about whether it was possible to defend the West without a passing knowledge of ancient Greek!

"It's a kind of poem where the writer pretends to be someone else," Olivares went on. "That's what the word *persona* means in Latin—I mean Latin as in Virgil, not, I don't know, Junot Díaz. Not *person* but *mask*. What an actor wears onstage. Very few things in that poem happened to me. Like the hospitalization. Or the abortion. Or the cigarettes for that matter—can't stand the stench! And I know most readers are going to think that it's all about me. That's the point: I get a kick thinking that thousands of people—well, more like hundreds: it's not like I sell that many books—are going to think I had this insane Parisian youth, when the truth is I spent most of my time in the library, trying and failing to make sense of Badiou's bonkers math."

"I love that," Zoraya said. "I'm taking my first workshop this term, and I've been struggling with how to write about myself without giving myself away. I've never felt the freedom to just make stuff up the way you're saying. Wow! I really love it."

Olivares threw her hands in the air. "See, this is what happens when you let the personal essay become the primary form for people who are starting to write! I have no idea who's been teaching you literature, Zoraya, but it looks like they've done you a disservice. To think that an English major could make it to their sophomore year without being told that they're allowed to lie in their writing? And that such pedagogical dereliction could happen at a university that hosts a nonfiction school where the central axiom is that facts have such a short lifespan that we might as well call it the lyric essay? Shameful! So, let's remedy this, shall we, Zoraya? By the power vested in me by the Free Play of Signifiers, I hereby grant you permission to go forth and make shit up. There're no rules in literature, Zoraya. Well, actually, there're tons of rules, so many and so complicated that the only people who understand them are literary theorists. But you should never become a theorist, okay? Some kid approaches you at a rave and offers you a little Paul de Man? Just. Say. No."

Zoraya burst out laughing, then handed the mic to the moody intern and sat down.

"All right," Olivares said. "I think there was another question? After that, though, we're done, folks. You have no idea how draining this sort of exercise can be for a shy little introvert like poor me. We're all introverts now, aren't we? That's what I've read online. And it's a magical password for getting out of doing things? What a relief! I am so grateful to Gen Z for blazing the trail for us introverts. Thank you, Gen Z."

I was relieved—the questions I'd prepared were now moot. But then, to my alarm, the moody intern started walking toward me, and before I knew it she'd handed me the mic, and I had stood up, and everyone was looking at me. "Do you—do you—" I said, staring at my notebook, suddenly incapable of understanding my handwriting. "Do you think wri—writers should—should be up—upfront about—their—their class position?"

This time Olivares's smile was less a gesture of reassurance than a baring of fangs. "Do I hear a Contadero fry? Where did you go to school?"

"I—I—"

"It can't have been the American School, seeing you're struggling to put together simple sentences in English."

"Tomás Moro. Colegio Tomás Moro."

"Of course. Is that why you're asking me that?"

El que traduce, traiciona

At the midpoint of my time in the Middle West I found myself on a dark highway in the Texas desert. Charlie and a couple other poetry students had decided to drive to Austin for no reason and invited me to join, and since I was trying desperately to fight off the depression that seized me after I'd withdrawn my application for permanent residency, I agreed. Our plan was to reach Paris before sunset, but our pit stop in Kansas City lasted longer than anticipated, and night fell on us not far from Texarkana. We were low on gas and exhausted. To keep ourselves awake, we decided to play Twenty Questions. I went first.

"Human?" asked a poet.

"Yes," I replied.

"Fictional?"

"No."

"Living?"

"No."

"A man?"

"Yes."

"A writer?"

"Yes."

"A European writer?"

"No."

"A South American writer?"

"No."

"A North American writer?"

"Yes."

"Is it James Baldwin?"

"No."

"George Oppen?"

"No."

"Henry Adams!"

"No."

Soon the Americans ran out of questions.

"Well, who is it?" said Charlie.

"Juán Rulfo."

"Oh, come on!"

"What?"

"Isn't he Mexican?"

"Yeah . . ."

"But you said he was North American . . ."

"Well," I said, "Mexico is part of North America."

There was an awkward silence. I turned to face the back seat and looked at Charlie. "I mean, it's part of the North American Free Trade Agreement, so . . ."

She rolled her eyes. "Okay, sure. But does it really make sense to think of Rulfo as a North American writer? Like, would you teach him in a class on North American literature?"

I looked down the road. For a while no one said anything. Then Charlie spoke again. "I'm sorry, Sebas. Did I offend you?"

"Not at all."

Later, after we stumbled into our motel in a drunken daze, I had one of those French moments when the perfect reply arrives several hours late. What I should have said was that in that very moment we were driving through land that used to be Mexico and where half the population was Mexican in one sense or another, and that, if this was North America, so was Mexico City. But the next morning, as we drove on south, I realized there was no use in arguing. The problem at hand was not one of facts but of translation. América del Norte did not mean the same thing as North America.

Para Solmaz Sharif

"Like, I get it," the Decanonizer said during workshop. "We're pissed. Worried. Scared. But does it make sense to call these places concentration camps?"

I looked around the room, wondering if anyone else thought it was insane we were having this discussion, then turned to Mayeli, who was scribbling furiously in her notebook, as if she were trying to deal with the rule that prohibited writers whose work was up for discussion from speaking in their own defense.

"The language we're using feels hyperbolic in an unproductive way," the Decanonizer went on. "This is America. Not Nazi Germany. The government isn't actively trying to kill migrants. And don't get me wrong. What they're doing is awful. But it's not Auschwitz. Comparing your adversary to Hitler is the kind of move you'd expect from right-wing idiots like Ben Shapiro or Brent—"

"Yeah, no," I interrupted. "That's totally wrong."

The Decanonizer scowled with disgust. "Oh-kay, Mr. Yale. Please, go ahead. Explain to me how my stupid little lady brain can't handle logical thought."

"The term is perfectly accurate. We're talking about temporary settlements, which is to say *camps*, where the government is detaining, which is to say *concentrating*, members of a persecuted minority. And, like, a concentration camp isn't the same as a death camp, so the absence of gas chambers doesn't mean we're talking about all-inclusive resorts."

"Whatever. Call them concentration camps if it makes you feel better."

"It doesn't make me feel better. It makes me feel worse. But we should all feel worse. We should all feel really fucking bad all the fucking time."

"I just think it's alarmist vocabulary."

"The most powerful government on earth is imprisoning children and we are arguing semantics?"

"I don't know if you got the memo, Sebástian, but this is a writing workshop. Semantics are fair game."

"What would you call them instead?"

"Detention centers. Temporary housing. Immigration jails. Concentration *camps* calls to mind a situation where you have the secret police hunting down people. And that's just not happening."

"Have you opened a newspaper in the last two years? What do you think ICE is, if not the gestapo?"

"Are you suggesting I'm a collaborator?"

"You're something worse. A useful idiot."

"That's enough!" Irina said. "Let's move on. What did people think of the prose? Are there places where things are working especially well, or where they could work better?"

The discussion shifted to adverbs and commas. Then workshop ended and everyone began packing up their things. Mayeli, on the other hand, made no move to leave. Soon we were the only two people left in the room.

"No tienen idea," I said.

She turned and looked me in the eye for the first time in a long time. "Are you coming tonight?"

"Where?"

"To the Pentacrest. Folks organized a protest."

"No sabía. I'd love to come. But I should probably write."

"Right," she said. Then she got up and left.

For a while I sat alone in the classroom. Maybe the Decanonizer had a point. Maybe it wasn't as bad as it felt. By then night had fallen. I grabbed my messenger bag and walked out of the English-Philosophy Building. As I climbed the hill away from the river and toward the center of town, I realized that going through the quad would add only a couple of minutes to my route.

I turned left and climbed the steps leading to the Old Capitol and its preposterous golden dome, then stepped onto the Pentacrest, pitch-black save for the lamps illuminating the neoclassical buildings. In the center of the quad, at the darkest point, farthest from the road, I could make out the trembling glow of small flames. I headed in that direction, lighting the footpath with my phone, and as I got closer I saw some two dozen people huddling in a half circle, holding candles and hand-painted signs. Mayeli was standing at the edge of the group, so I went around the circle to stand beside her. She bent down and grabbed a candle and lit it with hers and handed it to me, then reached into a bag and pulled out a sign for me to hold. I lifted it, wondering who was supposed to see it in the dark, and looked up to read the slogan. To my dismay, it said: HERE TO STAY.

El arte de perder

It's crucial to remember that Sigüenza's text is a work of theater. Is Moctezuma the Card Player a historical person, as real as the broken bones that lay buried beneath the cathedral? Or is he an allegorical persona, a mask that allows someone else to speak freely, under the pretext that his voice is not his own? Such questions never admit definitive answers, but in this case I believe the solution is obvious: Moctezuma is Sigüenza in disguise. The emperor of Anáhuac is an emblem of the Unhappy Consciousness of the creoles: a king taken prisoner in his own palace, a sovereign born in the Indies who proves to be as Western as the best of the Romans, a misunderstood genius who so despises his masters that he refuses to dignify them with his efforts. In short: a Lord-in-Bondage.

For Sigüenza, this Lord-in-Bondage's decision to lose on purpose is a refusal to recognize the sovereignty of the conqueror and a transmutation of defeat into victory. But what kind of triumph is Moctezuma's? Unfree human beings often convince themselves that aligning their will with the course of events makes those events the product of their will, but freely choosing an inevitable defeat does not make it any less inevitable, or any less of a defeat. In the end my motivations for returning to Sigüenza amount to narcissistic self-regard. He wrote in the seventeenth century, but I have yet to read a clearer description of my relationship to the United States.

Todavía eres la obra maestra

The day after the end of spring break Lee called me. She'd had a blast in Colombia—seen good friends, heard great music. Then I told her that my lawyer had recommended I withdraw my application for permanent residency.

"Oh, Sebas, I'm so sorry."

"Thanks. It sucks. I don't know if I can muster the energy to figure out a way to get another visa. I'm tired of jumping through hoops. Of living like I'm some overachieving high school senior applying to college. So I've just been feeling depressed. Like, having-a-hard-time-getting-out-of-bed kind of depressed."

There was a pause in the conversation. I stared at the brick wall of my studio, surprised to discover I was holding back tears.

"There's a way out of this," Lee said after a while. "One we could take together."

"Which is?"

"We could get married."

Part VI

New Haven/
New York

May–June 2018

In which Your Correspondent travels to New England to spend time with his future wife, receives an unexpected phone call, makes an unseemly disclosure, drinks more than he should, considers the life and work of the creole ideologue of the Mexican Revolution, meets old friends in New York, has several epiphanies, and confronts the limits of his love.

El mito de Orfeo

Early in May I flew to New England to meet up with Lee. The idea was to stay in New Haven for the first half of the recess, travel to Mexico to see my family and California to see hers, and then return to Connecticut for the remainder of the break. I packed a small library and an absurd stock of blank notebooks, hoping to continue working on the essay on creole identity. I was looking forward to having plenty of time to write, but what most excited me was the prospect of seeing Lee. The thought of living with her for three months, longer than we'd ever been together, gave me hope I'd soon climb out of my Iowan depression. This is a test run, I thought, a trial balloon for what a life together might look like. If it goes well, we might as well get married at the end of the summer—for the green card, sure, but also secretly for love.

El niño es el padre del hombre

On a burning plain, a stone's throw north of the muddy banks of the river, behind the whitewashed walls of the schoolhouse with its American flag and its Protestant prayers, a boy of ten narrows his eyes in the glare of the sun, the weight of a switchblade in his hand. Before him, mere feet away, a taller boy raises his palms in surrender.

"No, Joe," says the second boy. "Not like this."

The year is 1890 or 1895, barely two generations after the Mexican-American War. The plain, like all the plains around it, used to be Mexico. Such history is personal for the boy. Yesterday the Americans beat him again, and again for the same reason. "They would constantly bring up the Alamo," the boy wrote many years later:

*That great Aztec massacre that Santa Anna perpetrated on his
prisoners of war. I never felt compelled to make excuses for my
country, for the Mexican fatherland must also condemn the military treachery of our generals, those assassins who lay ambushes
and wreak havoc on the vanquished. But when my classmates
affirmed that one hundred Yankees would be enough to rout a
thousand Mexicans, I had no choice but to stand and declare:
"That is not true!" The worst, however, was when they would
compare the customs of Mexicans with those of "Eskimos" and
say: "Mexicans are a semicivilized people." This struck me as
nonsensical, because in my hometown the common opinion was
that the Yankees had only recently discovered culture. I would
therefore get up again and say: "We had the printing press before
you did!" Then the teacher would intervene and say: "But look
at Joe, he is a Mexican, isn't he civilized? Isn't he a gentleman?"*

It would be simpler if he didn't enjoy school so much. Then he
wouldn't have to cross the brand-new bridge every morning and
speak all day in that barbarian language and endure the mockery
and the beatings. But he is a child in love with books, and the
ramshackle school on the Mexican side of the river simply will
not do. And so the boy crossed the border today ready to fight
and lose. That's how it goes: He always fights back but he never
wins. He goes home covered in bruises, which he explains away
with unlikely tales about falls into ravines.

But earlier today, during the Pledge of Allegiance, another
Mexican kid approached and handed him the blade. "Take it. For
the afternoon. The gringos are terrified of steel."

And now here he is, feet away from the American, a knife in
his hand. The sun is so bright it's hard to see anything.

"No, Joe," the American boy repeats. "Like yesterday if you
want. Just not like this."

The Mexican boy can hear his heartbeat in his skull. These are new passions he is feeling: novel tonalities of anger and fear, the vertiginous rush of risk, the ecstasy of escalation, of power reclaimed, of recognition demanded on the grounds of sheer force.

"No, not like yesterday," the young José Vasconcelos responds. "Like today."

Los dioses abandonan a Antonio

On my third day in Connecticut Lee and I decided to rescue a pair of rusty lawn chairs that languished in her basement and set them up in the one corner of her backyard that wasn't completely overgrown. We brought out beer and chips and books, made jokes about disease-bearing ticks, and sat down to read in the sun. The summer light fell golden over the brick chimneys and the sweating trees, and for a moment the name of the city of New Haven seemed as self-evident as those of Water and Church Streets.

Then my phone rang. My heart stopped. I was not expecting a call from that number.

"I should take this," I said as I got up.

"Watch out for Lyme!" Lee replied, eyes still on her book.

I walked through the house and out to the street before I picked up. It was Charlie. She wanted to let me know she'd tested positive for chlamydia.

I stood motionless for what felt like a long time, listening to the birds in the trees and feeling cold sweat pool behind my neck. A group of young men in wifebeaters and basketball shorts walked past me with a keg and a boom box. They ran into a handful of young women in croptops and started chatting with them. Every few seconds the girls would break into crystalline laughter.

I reached into my jacket for my pack of cigarettes but then

remembered I quit when I left the Middle West. Maybe I didn't have to tell her unless I tested positive? Nonsense—I had to tell her right away. Besides, what was the problem? We'd agreed it was okay to sleep with other people, and that implied assuming some risks. But then why did I feel so guilty?

The young men and women across the street finished their mating ritual and parted ways in opposite directions. I decided I would go to the gas station and not buy cigarettes but maybe get gum or mints or a gun or something else to put in my mouth. I got up and headed down Chapel Street toward the highway. Yes, I thought, we had agreed to it. In fact, she had been the one to bring it up. I stopped at the corner to let a truck pass. A breeze brought me the smell of saltwater, gasoline, and rotten kelp. I wiped the sweat off my face. It was hot, too hot, and she had been the one to bring it up.

There was a line at the gas station. I joined it for a moment but soon lost patience and wandered the aisles in the off chance that the establishment might stock some kind of at-home STD testing kit. Soon afterward the line was gone, so I walked up to the teller and asked for a pack of American Spirits.

"Can I see your ID?"

I handed him my Mexican driver's license. The cashier took the card and raised it against the light, flipped it, tried to bend it, and handed it back to me. "Sorry. Can't accept this."

I felt a surge of rage boiling in my stomach, an anger so deep and total that even as I felt it, I was aware it was ridiculously out of proportion, that I was taking offense almost on purpose. "And why might that be?"

"It doesn't have your date of birth."

"Is it because I'm Mexican?"

"Look, kid, I don't make the rules. Do you have your passport on you?"

"Oh, so now you want to see my papers?"

The cashier rolled his eyes. "No, sir. But state law says we can't sell cigarettes or liquor to anyone who doesn't show a passport or an in-state driver's license."

I stormed out of the gas station and looked at my license. The cashier was right: my date of birth was nowhere on it. I headed back to Lee's house, defeated. Then again, I thought as I unlocked the front door, perhaps I didn't have to worry. Maybe she would just laugh. In the worst-case scenario, we'd have to pop some antibiotics and lay off from each other for a few days.

"What took you so long?" Lee asked when I stepped into the backyard.

"The guy at the gas station wouldn't sell me cigarettes."

"Ah, damn. Well, better that way, I guess? Though you've been so cranky since you quit, I almost wish you—"

"Lee?"

"Yes?"

"There's something I need to tell you."

Para Rafael Lemus

The scene at the schoolyard appears near the beginning of the first volume of José Vasconcelos's autobiographical tetralogy, *A Creole Ulysses*—an unreadable masterpiece that manages to be, all at once, a novel of ideas, a romance of adventure, a political manifesto, an impressionistic history of Mexico, an account of a sentimental education, and a meditation on the power and limits of the will. That the knife fight probably never took place—it's too perfect for nonfiction—matters less than the fact that Vasconcelos chose it as one of his opening images: the anecdote invites the reader to approach the book as the tale of a Mexican intellectual's struggle with North America.

A tragic struggle, condemned to failure from the start. The American kid may have refused to fight, but the Mexican boy must still cross the border every day to get an education. Is it any wonder, the scene seems to ask, that Vasconcelos dedicated his life to ensuring that every single Mexican child had access to a good school and a good library? That this framing is artificial does not make it less effective: Vasconcelos's literary genius resides in his ability to cast the events of his life on a scale so mythical that heavy-handed foreshadowings appear not as sleights of hand but as manifestations of fate.

Then again, he had good material: Vasconcelos's life was nothing short of epic. In the years when he served as the revolutionary government's inaugural minister of education, he supervised the training of thousands of teachers, administered the construction of hundreds of schools, convinced the government to print and distribute hundreds of thousands of copies of Plato, Dante, and Tolstoy, founded the National University, commissioned the murals of Diego Rivera, and in general presided over such a renaissance in Mexican and Latin American culture that the university students of Perú bestowed upon him a honorific title: el Maestro de América.

And who was this Master of America? A man of the world, a Catholic who sinned boldly, a lover of horses, fortified wines, and the Upanishads. "We used to forgive him everything," Alfonso Reyes wrote about Vasconcelos years after the end of their friendship, "because he was such a force of nature." I suspect the Master wouldn't have been displeased by that description: he classified books in two categories, those he read sitting down and those he read on his feet, and he made it clear which ones he considered worth his while. Vasconcelos's philosophical discussions with Reyes often ended with the latter cowering behind the couch after the former threw a glass or an inkwell at him. When the

Revolution broke out, he rode out to join the struggle in the company of his mistress. His life was punctuated by long periods of exile in Europe, where he attended the infamous premiere of Stravinsky's *The Rite of Spring*, and in the United States, where he spent years plotting uprisings while eking out a living as an adjunct lecturer.

In fact, and despite all the ways in which Vasconcelos is the most Mexican of writers, it's impossible to grasp his thought without understanding his experiences north of the border. In America Vasconcelos discovered that the main thesis of liberalism—that all men are created equal—is false. As he writes:

> *There is no such thing as 'race,' we think, until one day we cross the border with the United States and find that we have been classified long before we had the chance to define ourselves . . . After a short time in North America, the poor, naive Latin American, who believed that in his land race had been abolished, discovers that a strict, unwritten ethnic hierarchy determines each individual's place in society.*

Like many writer-men before and after him, Vasconcelos thought of himself as a philosopher who at times condescended to write memoir. Almost no one reads him today, and those who do favor the autobiography over the treatises, but at the peak of his fame, in the late 1920s, Vasconcelos was known as the author of a bewildering collection of essays entitled *The Cosmic Race*. The argument goes something like this:

1. Humanity is divided into several biological races.
2. These races have distinct cultures and differing strengths and weaknesses, which means their interests are often at odds.

3. As such, history is best understood as the product of the struggle between these races.
4. At different points in time one or another group has managed to become dominant over the others.
5. The modern age has been the era of white people, but signs all around us announce the time of white supremacy is coming to an end.
6. The race that will arise to take the place of white people, however, will not be one or another of the ones that already exist, but an entirely new form of humanity—one destined to usher in an era of unprecedented flourishing.
7. In this coming "aesthetic epoch," the political and economic problems that plague our societies will be resolved to such a degree that mankind will finally be able to live according to its nature: allowing the will and desire to guide us to beauty and therefore to happiness.

So far Vasconcelos seems like a cross between a utopian socialist and a social Darwinist. What sets him apart from both Thomas More and Joseph-Arthur, Comte de Gobineau, is that the new master race he foretells won't arise in an imaginary island or in the upper echelons of the French nobility, but in the postcolonial world. The people of Latin America, as the synthesis of the European, Amerindian, and African races, are the vanguard of humanity's collective journey toward self-realization: the race through which the Spirit will speak the cosmic Absolute. It's not hard to see why Vasconcelos became an inspiration to thinking people from California to Patagonia, among them Gloria Anzaldúa. Here was a homegrown answer to American exceptionalism, a philosophy of history that recast the trauma of colonization as a source of power and unity rather than division and misery.

Though *La raza cósmica* appeared after Vasconcelos resigned from the revolutionary government, the book's ideas informed his tenure at the Ministry of Education. The mass alphabetization of Mexican children was meant to accelerate the process of Hegelian sublimation that would give rise to the new humanity. Mexican children had to learn about the glories of both pre-Hispanic civilizations and the Spanish Empire, for the first step toward realizing their cosmic potential was to make them conscious of their own hybridity.

Hence the emphasis that the era's official culture placed on the heroic version of national history on display in Rivera's murals. To this day, public school students around the country gather for weekly assemblies where they perform brief allegorical plays about the deeds of such heroic Mexicans as Benito Juárez and Hernán Cortés.

El cometa reaparece

At first it seemed all would be well. The test came back negative. Lee said it was fine. Underneath her nonchalance, however, I sensed she was trying to keep herself together. Each time she looked at me I saw disappointment in her eyes. I began spending more and more time at an overpriced bar downtown, where I drank round after round of a ridiculous drink made with mezcal and beet juice. As the weeks passed and the temperature increased, dark red stains began appearing in my notebooks. My handwriting declined.

I'd come home in the late afternoon, half-drunk and dehydrated, and find Lee in her studio, practicing Schönberg's *Klavierstücke* on the upright piano she'd gotten from Craigslist. I'd greet her with a perfunctory kiss and retreat to the living room—empty save for a stained green fainting couch, a standing lamp held together with duct tape, a coffee table covered in xeroxed sheet music, and piles of library books leaning precariously against the walls. I'd put on noise-canceling headphones and spend a few hours trying to stop feeling guilty for long enough to read ten pages of the unwieldy anthology of Alfonso Reyes's essay I'd brought from Iowa. Eventually Lee would come out and we'd have dinner in silence and go to bed and not have sex and fall asleep facing away from each other.

"How about we watch a movie?" I said one night.

"Sure. What do you have in mind?"

"What's available?"

"I have access to the Criterion Collection through Yale. Which is great, because it's really fucking expensive."

"How about *8 1/2*?"

"Not super in the mood for Great Men."

"Right. Let's watch something else."

"Never mind. Fellini's fine."

She got up to get her laptop. I headed to the kitchen, opened the fridge, and rummaged around her vacuum-sealed bags of light-roasted Ethiopian coffee—the one luxury she allowed herself. Earlier in the summer she'd tried to convince me to set up a cost-splitting app to keep track of our expenses, a perfectly reasonable request that had nonetheless annoyed me immensely.

"Do you want a beer?" I yelled while I grabbed my fifth tallboy of the day.

"No, thanks. Don't feel like drinking these days."

I came back to the living room and sat down next to her on the couch, leaving space between us so she wouldn't feel crowded. For the next hour or so we watched a motley crew of Pan-European bourgeois make surrealist fools of themselves in black and white.

Then, when Marcelo was in the midst of whipping his harem into order, Lee paused the movie.

"See, that's it. I don't want to become one of those women."

"So I'm *that* guy? Am I that bad?"

"No—that's not what I meant. It's just—it's really dumb—but I keep wondering—did you make her breakfast?"

"Do you really want to know?"

"Forget it. It's stupid."

"I didn't make her breakfast, Lee."

"I just feel like the dumb girl at the party. Humiliated."

And then, one afternoon, as I lay on the couch recovering from my perpetual hangover, I heard Lee walk in and shut the door louder than usual. When she appeared at the top of the stairs, she was unsmiling and tense.

"Hi!" I said, trying to muster some cheerfulness. "How are you?"

"Fine," she said. "Or actually, really not fine."

She sat down on the couch and let her bag fall to the ground. I contained a sigh of exasperation. How many more times did we have to talk it through?

"You have every right to be upset," I said, though even as I spoke I felt like a hypocrite. "But I don't know what else I can say or do at this point."

"It's just—hard. For me. You know?"

"I know. Or rather I don't know. But I imagine. And I'm sorry. I regret it. I wish I could take it all back. We tried it, it didn't work, we'll never try it again. Can we move on?"

"It's just—triggering."

"What is?"

"The combination. You know? Of multiple partners and STDs and Latin American men putting their fucking dicks . . ."

"What the fuck, Lee?"

It's five in the morning a few days before Easter in 1933, and the federal troops move quietly through the dense neotropical forest around the village of Dzulá, in the eastern end of the Yucatán Peninsula, hoping to ambush the rebels in their beds.

But Lieutenant Evaristo Sulub—the octogenarian batab of the masewaal Maya of Xcacal-Guardia—sleeps with one eye open. As the Mexicans advance, his men ready their rifles: antique carbines bought decades ago from Her Majesty's traders in British Honduras.

The sky begins to turn rose-gray. The birds of sunrise stir. The dawning mist condenses into dew and drips down broad leaves to the porous limestone below, filtering underground until it reaches church-like caverns flooded with freshwater, guarded by stalactite-gargoyles and inhabited by bats, centipedes, and the spirits of the land.

The Mexicans come closer.

The Maya take aim.

The seconds grow long.

Time stands still.

Then Sulub raises his right fist and the gunfire begins.

The siege of Dzulá will come to be known as the "last battle" of the Caste War, a brutal conflict that pitted the Maya of the Yucatán against the dzul'ob—*foreigners* or *white people*—who had settled on their peninsula, and that claimed nearly a quarter million lives. In the 1840s, angered by ever-higher taxes and tithes and by the debt-slavery they endured at the dzul'ob's plantations, the Indigenous people of the territory that would later come to be known as Quintana Roo rose in arms against their creole masters. Led by the Talking Cross, a miraculous relic that conveyed divine messages in terms that mixed Catholic liturgy with Maya beliefs, the rebels expelled the dzul'ob from the eastern Yucatán, establishing an independent state that was recognized by the British Empire and defied the Mexican government for half a century.

But the gunfight of April 1933 also had more immediate causes: Sulub and his followers distrusted Vasconcelos's teachers. They'd chased them out of town several times, angering the federal government, which eventually sent troops to Dzulá to guarantee the opening of the new public school. The nationalist educational program that Vasconcelos had envisioned a decade earlier was now compulsory for all the children of the republic, regardless of whether they thought of themselves as Nahua, Ajuuyk, or Maya. The nation needed them to forget their languages in favor of Spanish, abandon their traditional superstitions and embrace modernity, cease to be Indigenous and instead become Mexican—or, more accurately, mestizo.

The discourse that justified this "educational crusade" borrowed directly from the rhetoric of the early colonial missionaries. The teacher—lettered, idealistic, abnegated, and benevolent—was the inheritor of the friar: *The Cosmic Race* was his gospel; Rivera's murals, his church paintings. Across Mexico, sometimes actively, others passively, at times through violence, always forcefully, Indigenous people resisted the demand that they become part of the West, which suggests that Vasconcelos's crusade was the culmination of the conquest begun by Cortés.

El laberinto neurótico

I went down the stairs and closed the door behind me, making a conscious effort not to slam it, stepped onto the street, and headed nowhere. Here it was, again, that familiar anger. I began going through our relationship, reviewing every memory in the light of what I knew, or thought I knew, and to my horror I found more and more evidence for what my wounded-animal mind had already decided was the only logical conclusion. It's a fetish, I thought, recoiling at the word. Her interest in Colombia, in Mexico, in her ex, in me, how she puts on an accent when she speaks Spanish—it's all a *fetish*, a mixture of fear and fascination, desire and disgust. I made it to the Old Campus and sat on a bench. No, I told myself. You are being unfair. Seizing a chance to claim the high ground. Drowning in a teacup. She was upset and said something she didn't mean. Let it go, damn it!

I spent the rest of the afternoon pacing around the Green, trying to slow my thoughts. At sunset I returned to the house and found her on the couch, clasping her knees to her chest.

"Sebas, I'm sorry."

"It's fine."

Now it was my turn to move on. I wasn't going to let such a small thing damage our relationship—not as we considered marriage. But in the following days I found that I, too, couldn't stop thinking about it. Sometimes I'd grow convinced that what she'd said was unforgivable, that she'd revealed her true colors, that she didn't see me as a concrete person but as an instance of an abstraction. Other times I'd begin to wonder whether she wasn't right. Hadn't I behaved like a stereotypical Latin American man? In fact, what I'd done was even worse, because it combined Mexican machismo with self-serving American pseudo-sex positivity: I hadn't just cheated on her but also cajoled her into agreeing to it beforehand.

I began heading to the bar at ever-earlier hours and staying the whole day, trying and failing to write about Vasconcelos. I was still trying to limit the time I spent with her—but now instead of hiding from her anger I hoped to spare her mine. I had enough sense left to realize I was becoming cruel. And she didn't deserve it. Because I wasn't angry with Lee. I was angry with America. With Trump and his voters. And she had nothing to do with it. Except that in my mind now she did.

"I feel terrible, Sebas," she said over dinner during one of countless similar conversations. "It's just—I was worried about falling into a pattern. Like, you date a bunch of jazz musicians, one after the other, and they all mess up in the same way, and after a while you start wondering about the type and . . ."

"Sorry to interrupt, but how's the analogy supposed to work? Is Latin America a musical genre that everyone born anywhere on the continent intuitively knows how to play? How to *dance*?"

She poured herself a glass of water and drank it in one go. She looked at the ceiling. She closed her eyes. "If I'm being honest," she went on, "I was trying to hurt you. I was mad at you and I wanted to make you feel bad."

"Well, it worked. Because that's precisely what *they* say about us, isn't it? It's a fucking cliché. I get you were upset, and I recognize all of this happened because I fucked up. And I'm sorry. Really. But why didn't you just tell me it was triggering to have a man—any man, from any part of the world—put you in that position?"

She covered her eyes with her hands. Stop it, I said to myself. Stop torturing her. "I mean," I went on, "if Latin American men are so awful, then maybe you should stop dating us."

. . . y aunque no me guste la acción, soy un hombre de acción

One day in early June I woke up with a terrible hangover and convinced myself to go to the Long Wharf and at least try to read something. I sat on a bench by the water and took out the Reyes anthology I carried everywhere but never opened. The essay in question was titled "Notes on the American Intelligence," but its subject had nothing to do with the United States. The adjective in the title referred to the part of the continent that extends from the Río Bravo to Tierra del Fuego. The writers of this turbulent region, Reyes wrote, contended with unique advantages and disadvantages:

The disadvantages arise because intelligence, called to the political sphere, confronts the fact that the realm of action is identical to the realm of transaction. Beset by constant urgencies, intellectual production grows sporadic and the mind distracted. The advantages, for their part, result from the very conditions of the contemporary world. In times of crises such as ours, which call for the effort of all—and in particular of writers, the alternative being to cede the role of cartographers of humanity to ignorance and despair— the American intelligence, wiser in the ways of the streets, proves adept to the task at hand. For among us there have never been, nor can there ever be, ivory towers. From this dialectic there emerges an equilibrium of advantage and disadvantage which resolves into a peculiar understanding of intellectual work as a public service and a civilizational duty. Naturally, such an understanding does not annul the possibility of pure literature, that fountain in which one must bathe with some frequency to remain healthy. In Europe, on the other hand, the parenthesis is the norm. The European writer is born on the highest point of the Eiffel Tower: after a few meters' climb, he reaches the summit of the Spirit. By contrast the American writer is born near the center of the earth. After a colossal effort, in which he at times displays an exacerbated vitality that often resembles genius, he barely manages to emerge from the ground. Oh, European colleagues! If only you knew how many mediocre

Americans conceal storehouses of virtue that deserve your
sympathy and respect, and which you would do well to study
and to emulate!

I lifted my eyes from the book. The essay was rough going, and not just because my head hurt and I'd grown unaccustomed to the syntax of literary Spanish. Reyes had become a problem for me. There was something disturbingly familiar about his concerns, his style, even his biography. As a young man Reyes was one of the founders of the Athenaeum of the Youth, the literary and philosophical club that produced a whole generation of Mexican geniuses, among them Vasconcelos, with whom Reyes formed a strong bond. But the outbreak of the Revolution put the two friends at odds: Vasconcelos joined the uprising; Reyes couldn't follow. His father, a conservative politician, supported General Díaz and participated in the counterrevolutionary coup against Francisco I. Madero, only to die in the Zócalo in the first moments of fighting. The younger Reyes fled for Europe, where he stayed twenty-five years and wrote his most famous essay, "Visión de Anáhuac," a lyrical meditation on the history, poetics, flora, hydrology, and mythology of Mexico City.

That Reyes produced some of the best prose written on Mexico from a café table in Madrid always struck me as rather poignant, but that day in Connecticut I was less impressed by the birthplace of the piece than by its birthday. Reyes wrote "Visión" when he was a year younger than I was that summer, and yet his sentences were already so lucid Borges felt compelled to call him the greatest stylist in the history of the Spanish language. Meanwhile there I was, sitting amid the rust of postindustrial New England, chewing Adderall on an empty stomach, trying and failing to make sense of the spiders on the page.

I forced myself to keep reading. Later in the essay Reyes

posited that the synthesis of the *vita activa* and the *vita contemplativa* was the source of the cosmopolitanism of Latin American literature:

> *Our worldview, so rooted in our native land, is at the same time internationalist by nature. The causes of this apparent contradiction exceed the fact that our America offers the perfect conditions for the intermixture that will one day, perhaps, bring about that "Cosmic Race" of which Vasconcelos dreams. They include, for example, the undeniable reality that we have been forced to search for our cultural instruments in the European metropole and have, in the process, become accustomed to taking foreign notions as if they were our own. While the European feels no need to consider America as he constructs his idea of the world, the American studies Europe from elementary school. This imbalance has a rather curious consequence, which I point out without vanity or resentment. It is a professional secret among American writers that American books about Europe fare better than European books about America. Our metropolitan colleagues frequently misquote our classics, misspell our names, misplace our geography, etc.*

I got up from the bench. I needed water and coffee and something to eat. I walked back up Chapel Street, past the Protestant churches, my eyeballs swelling in their sockets. Once again Reyes had said it earlier and better. It was simply a question of replacing *American* with *Mexican* and *European* with *American*. I knew so much about them; they knew so little about me. What they saw as the quirks of my personality were in fact the characteristics of my culture, of the style of intelligence I inherited from my forebears.

As I passed the Sterling Library, I realized I'd misunderstood my grandfather. He'd entered public life not because he felt that being a mere poet was somehow undignified but because the demands of history left him no choice. The notion of literature as a profession—a "craft" one learned over the course of a long apprenticeship in the Middle West—presupposed a stability found only in the metropole. White American writers lived private lives not because they were more dedicated to their art than their Latin American counterparts, but because few of them were ever forced to face down a revolution or consider the possibility of exile.

The exception, of course, were the communists. Like Reyes and Baldwin, George Oppen—whose political commitments forced him and his wife to move to Mexico for nine years in hopes of escaping McCarthyism, during which time the poet did not write a single line and instead worked as a carpenter—had to relinquish his homeland before he could understand what it meant to be American.

Papeles falsos

"I just don't understand," Lee said one night. "If going back to Mexico would be so horrible, why not move to, I don't know, Spain?"

Less than an hour earlier, I had demanded we leave a dinner party after one of her friends from the musicology program laughed at me when she learned I now carried my passport everywhere. "Why do you think, Lee?" I said, slurring with condescension and whiskey.

After a minute or two she shrugged. "Are you going to tell me or not?"

I got up from the bed and walked into the kitchen. I discovered we were out of liquor. I marched back into the bedroom to grab my shoes and coat.

"Look," Lee said. "I'm sorry that Susan said something stupid. I'm sorry that *I* said something stupid—and that I continue to say stupid things. Like just now. Please, can you tell me what was so upsetting about what I said?"

I listened to her as I put on my boots. Then I took a deep breath and looked up at her. "Because I would need a visa, Lee," I said.

"Right," she said. "Of course. I'm sorry. It's just we talked about it, remember? How we'd move to Madrid if Trump got reelected?"

"It was a joke, Lee!"

"But how am I supposed to tell when something's a joke and when it isn't!"

I walked out the door and down to the gas station to get more whiskey—only to have my Mexican license turned down again. I'd left behind my passport.

Estrella distante

The scene takes place at the University of Chicago, where Vasconcelos's contract is about to expire. The Master is strolling around the faux-Gothic campus, arm in arm with an American colleague. "We'd make you a full professor," the American says. "And help you become a citizen."

Like Christ in the desert and Odysseus in the Enchanted Isle, Vasconcelos considers for a moment. The offer is tempting, but there are other voices calling him—though whether they belong to the Fates or the Sirens remains obscure. In any case the hero must make a choice: remain in America and fade into peaceful obscurity or return to Mexico and conjure destiny.

In truth the outcome is clear from the start. A man of Vasconcelos's ambition cannot rest. It wasn't enough to teach millions how to read—and besides, General Obregón had betrayed his revolutionary ideals when he signed away the nation's oil in exchange for American support for his regime. Plato had written about philosopher kings. What Mexico needed, Vasconcelos decided, was a philosopher president.

As it turned out, many agreed. Vasconcelos enjoyed the fanatical support of students, who idolized him, and women, who were mobilized by his promise of universal suffrage. The details of his platform were less than clear—depending on the audience he praised Lenin or the Catholic Church—but few seemed to mind. Vasconcelos's project transcended the realm of electoral politics: he wanted to unleash a "regeneration" of the Mexican race, a spiritual awakening that would render moot the banalities of policy.

The postrevolutionary regime was caught flatfooted. Though Mexico had been a republic almost continuously since independence, the country had little experience with democracy. The rise of a viable opposition candidate was terrifying to the heirs of President Obregón. Perhaps this is why Vasconcelos suffered five assassination attempts in the course of the campaign.

No te enamores si no sabes inglés

"Did you like him because he was brown?"

"Why are you asking me that?"

"I've just been wondering."

"I liked him because he was a great dancer. And because he could be very kind when he wanted to. And because he was beautiful and good in bed. And because he could show me all kinds of new things about a culture and a place that fascinated me."

"But not because he was brown."

"What are you getting at, Sebastián?"

"It's just—we're so different. Him and I. We look nothing like each other. We speak such different dialects of Spanish we might as well speak different languages. I've never been to Colombia. He's never been to Mexico. So I'm trying to figure out why you put us in the same basket."

"Do you really need to have this conversation?"

"I don't even want to have it. But my brain is stuck in this loop. And I want to step out of it—I just don't know how. So maybe if I could understand . . ."

"You and Daniel have nothing in common. He's an asshole and a cheater. You're neither of those things. It was fucked up for me to suggest otherwise. Can we talk about something else?"

"Is it a sex thing?"

"Sebas . . ."

"Is it that we know how to fuck? Because we're Latin American?"

"This isn't productive."

"I just need to know if that's it."

"You're being hurtful, Sebastián."

"It is, isn't it?"

"I love you because you are you. Not because you are Mexican. Just like I loved Daniel because he was Daniel and not because he was Colombian."

"But you've also dated American guys, right?"

"Yes. Plenty of them. They suck. What does that have to do with anything?"

"So it's not like you only date Latin Americans."

"I was living in Colombia. Who else was I supposed to date?"

"But now you're living in America and yet you're dating me . . ."

"Can we please stop? Or do you want me to ask about how you've only dated American girls? Is it that we know how to fuck?

That we didn't get brainwashed into frigidity by Catholicism and machismo?"

"Lee . . ."

"It doesn't feel good, does it?"

"I'm sorry. I'm not trying to make you feel bad."

"Well, you are."

"I guess I still feel bad."

"So do I! Which is why I don't understand why you're asking me if the reason I'm with you is that I want to fuck Latin American men, rather than that I want to fuck you, specifically. Because, honestly? That's what's so painful. That you didn't want to fuck just me. That you also wanted to fuck other white girls."

"The woman I slept with isn't white."

"I really didn't need to know that."

Para Joshua Simon

From a failed essay on the identity of the Mexican creoles:

> *A tentative definition of* creole: *That colonial subject who benefits more than he suffers from the colonial situation. The creoles are to imperialism as the professional and the manager are to late capitalism; their function, like those of the overseer and the comprador, is to mediate between the ruling class and its subalterns—or, what is the same, to administer the colony for the benefit of the metropolitan ruling class. This is why the so-called "revolutions of independence" of the various North and South American colonies were not conflicts between imperialists and anti-imperialists, but between imperialists and aspirants to imperialism. Agustín de Iturbide and Thomas Jefferson had this in common: neither of them objected to the subjugation of Indigenous and African people, but only to*

the submission of creoles to their metropolitan peers. This is why the United States could claim to have been founded on the self-evidence of universal freedom while practicing slavery, but also why the first independent government of Mexico was not a republic but an empire. A corollary: George Washington was born a creole but didn't die one. Creoles become "white" the moment they manage to transform the colony that birthed him into an imperial metropole.

La maldición de Malinche

"Hey!" I said, trying to dissimulate my disappointment at the fact that my precious hours with the house to myself had been cut short. "You're back early! I'm sorry—dinner isn't ready."

"I can't eat right now."

"All good? You seem flustered."

"It's just ... I feel ... this country ..."

"Slow down. What's going on?"

"This—this country. This country is so big. And I'm so small."

"Let's sit. Are you okay?"

"Yeah—sorry—it's just ... it's really happening. You know? Fuck. Sorry. Of course you know. What I mean to say is—it really is that bad. And it could get so much worse. And I feel so fucking useless."

"Don't talk about my girlfriend that way!"

"It's true, though. I feel responsible. I *am* responsible. For the things America does. And I hate myself for not doing anything to stop it."

"Lee ..."

"I tried. I really did."

"Tried what?"

"I don't have many real-world skills. Right? But I can speak

Spanish pretty damn well. As well as any white person I've met. And it's taken me years . . . It's taken me years of sitting down with books and movies and conversations that were way over my head. And, like, I don't know, it's weird to say it this way—but it also took going through a fucking awful relationship. And it took me a long time to even admit to myself it was awful. Because, like, Daniel was this dark-skinned Colombian guy, and I was this blond American girl, so obviously it had to be my fault, right? But yeah. That's how I got so good at Spanish. By getting my heart broken. So I guess I wanted to put it to good use. Because I feel so guilty. Especially after everything that happened with us. And I figured maybe I'd be less miserable if I didn't just sit at the piano playing atonal music and thinking about the concentration camps and Daniel and our fight. And, like, this free clinic in Fair Haven needed translators who could interpret for Central American refugees, so I signed up for a shift this afternoon and showed up—but—but—"

"One second. I'm going to get you a glass of water."

"Thanks."

"That's better, no?"

"Sí. Perdón. I don't mean to make a scene."

"You're not making a scene."

"Fuck, I don't want to cry . . ."

"We don't have to talk about this right now."

She buried her head on my shoulder and burst into sobs. "The people I was supposed to help only spoke Kaqchikel."

Timón de Atenas

It is spring in 1929 and Mexico City is restless with hope and fear. After months of preaching his gospel of "national regeneration" from the desolate hamlets of Sonora to the bustling ports of

Yucatán, the Master of America is finally coming to the capital. Rumors circulate that there will be blood, that the government will try again to kill him, that the army will shoot into the crowd. Nevertheless one-quarter of the city's inhabitants come to hear him speak. The crowd is too large for the Plaza de Santo Domingo, the venue chosen for the rally, and so it overspills into the surrounding streets, bringing traffic to a standstill. People jostle in the cold air of the cloudless day, their children on their shoulders, hoping to catch a glimpse of the man who taught Mexico how to read.

Vasconcelos has made sure every aspect of the event is pregnant with symbolism. Early in the morning of Palm Sunday, inviting comparisons to Christ, he sets out for the capital on horseback, echoing the triumphal entrance of Francisco I. Madero. He leads a procession of young men who aspire to become writers and young women who call themselves feminists. The journey should take two hours, but the road is overwhelmed with people who bring flowers to the Master. Advancing is difficult yet Vasconcelos doesn't hurry. He has to let them see him in the flesh, let them reach out and touch his riding boots, because the time has come to kill the man and become a symbol. And so he gives himself to the crowd, accepting their gifts of garlands with the humility of a prophet who heeds a calling that exceeds the boundaries of the ego.

After long hours he arrives at Santo Domingo. Behind him stands the old Palace of the Inquisition, with its ominous walls of bloodred tezontle. The stage, in the center of the square, rises where heretics once burned at the stake. Vasconcelos, too, will speak dangerous words that challenge the order of terror with which the powerful cling to power—and he, too, is willing to suffer martyrdom. The message is clear: The Master is more than a mere politician. He is a messiah, chosen by history to bring redemption to a long-suffering race.

At high noon Vasconcelos climbs the dais and walks to the podium. For a moment he listens to the crowd chanting his name. He looks to the heavens, takes a deep breath. The crowd falls silent. Then he begins: "Today," he says, his words echoing on the walls of colonial palaces built with the stones of Tenochtitlan. "I feel that the millenarian voice of Quetzalcoatl seeks expression in my throat and gives me strength, so that I, who lack armies, may cry out against those who hide behind their armies!"

But what does it mean to speak with the White God's voice? Who is Vasconcelos, so conscious of historical echoes, imitating here? I ask because I can think of another novelist who assumed the guise of the Feathered Serpent and rode in triumph into Mexico City—the man who Vasconcelos called "the Father of the Fatherland": Hernán Cortés. Such resonances cast the rest of Vasconcelos's speech in an uncanny light:

> *The creation of a universally accepted human value that can unite our wills and synthesize our national aspirations is probably the most urgent need of our race. In these momentous times we should see politics not as an electoral contest to reclaim positions in the government from a morally bankrupt cabal, but as an integral action: an attempt to organize the destiny of the totality of a threatened race. It is with this momentous task in view that we have devoted ourselves to the creation of a large and generous party—a total party.*

Integral action? The destiny of a threatened race? A total party? Such phrases sounded different before Hitler, but this should make us more rather than less suspicious of Vasconcelos. In 1929 totalitarianism was not yet a synonym for evil but the name of a political current gaining strength in Europe. The Master was aware of it, but instead of recognizing its terrible danger he found in it a source of inspiration. Consider one of the few passages where he deigns to describe what would actually need to happen for the cosmic race to be born:

> In just a few generations monstrosities will no longer exist; what is now considered normal will strike us as an abomination. The lower breeds will be subsumed by their betters. In this way, for instance, the Negro could be redeemed: gradually, through a voluntary extinction, the uglier bloodlines will give way to more beautiful ones. The inferior races, upon receiving an education, will have fewer offspring; and the stronger specimens will climb through a scale of ethnic improvement whose final summit isn't precisely the White, but that new race to which even the White will have to aspire if he wishes to conquer the synthesis. By being grafted onto a receptive stock, the Indian would take the leap of thousands of years between Atlantis and our own time; and after a few decades of aesthetic eugenics, the Negro would disappear entirely, along with the other types which the liberated instinct for beauty designates as fundamentally recessive and therefore unworthy of perpetuation.

The ideologue of the Mexican Revolution—the founder of the National University, the patron of Diego Rivera, the renewer of Latin American literature—was a fascist. During the first six months of 1940, the Master served as editor in chief of *Timón*, a magazine that alternated recipes and sports articles with essays about the heroism of Hitler, the perfidy of the international Jewry, and the urgent need for Mexico to join the Axis against the United States.

A week later I got on the southbound Metro-North Railroad by myself. Lee and I figured it would be good for both of us to have some time apart. Since we were flying out of New York to head to Mexico City in a few days, it seemed easy enough for me to head there early and stay with friends and for her to join me the night before our flight.

Carlos and Alanna lived in a railroad apartment near the border of Bushwick and Bed-Stuy. When I knocked on their door and he answered with open arms and his mouth agape in mock-shock, I felt a jolt of unadulterated joy.

"¡Sebas!" he said. "¡Hermano! It's so great to see you!"

We went for dinner at a pizza place and ordered a bottle of wine and a pie with clams and hot peppers. All the while I grinned. Seeing them reminded me that the life I'd left in New York hadn't disappeared, at least not completely. My friends were still my friends, and perhaps this meant I was still the person I used to be—a person I liked far better than the one I'd become.

"How have you guys been?" I said.

"Can't complain," Carlos said. "Magazine's kind of a mess. Trying to save money to go to the Dominican Republic and see my dad's folks."

"I'm quitting my job," Alanna said. "We're a feminist press, but the politics of the books we publish apparently don't apply to our working conditions."

"How about you? How's Iowa? And your girl?"

I told them I was in bad shape, mostly because of my dwindling immigration prospects, but also because Lee and I had tried to open our relationship and the experiment had backfired catastrophically.

"Oh man," Alanna said. "That sucks. For what it's worth, it's not just you guys. Almost all the straight couples I know who've tried to be nonmonogamous have ended up either breaking up or at least going through some shit. But also—and I say this with love, Sebas—nine times out of ten it's the men who want to fuck other people. And that says something, doesn't it?"

Then I told them what Lee had said. The table felt silent.

"Damn, dude," Carlos said after a while. "White girls! No offense, Alanna."

"None taken," Alanna said. "But is it really that bad?"

"I mean, it's not a good look," Carlos went on. "Tying where you come from to the contents of your urethra? Kinda fucked up."

"But it was a slip of the tongue!" I said, suddenly defensive of Lee.

"So why are you so upset by it?" Alanna said.

"I don't know. I wish I weren't."

"Don't get me wrong," Alanna said. "It's the kind of thing you say when you want to twist the blade. But also? Sounds like she was hurt and didn't know what to do. So she reached for white womanhood. Which is bad! But it's not like she's in a position of power over you, right? First, she's a woman. Second—is she wealthy?"

"Not really. Kind of the opposite."

"So she wasn't exactly punching down, was she?"

"No, she wasn't. The worst part is that I can tell I'm doing it to her too. I mean hurting her. Intentionally. Even though I don't mean to. I've been getting mad a lot lately. Even before all of this. When I was still at school."

"You're getting an MFA at Iowa!" Carlos said. "That's, like, white people central. Would get on anyone's nerves."

"But I'm basically a white person . . ."

"Sebas, hate to break it to you, but those motherfuckers don't see you as one of their own. And it kinda sounds like your girl doesn't see you that way, either."

We kept talking and drank a third bottle of wine. Then Carlos proposed we go to Mehanata, the gloriously tacky Bulgarian nightclub in the Lower East Side we frequented when we were twenty-three. We got on the train and stood in line for a while and stepped onto the dance floor, where a crowd of young Americans of all genders and forty-something Bulgarian men moved to the beat of techno remixes of ballads from the Balkans. I drank shot after shot of cheap vodka. Soon I had trouble standing straight.

"I love you, guys!" I yelled as I threw my arms around Carlos and Alanna. "I love you, I love you!"

When the club closed, we took a cab back to Brooklyn. Carlos gave me a wet kiss on the cheek and headed to his bedroom with Alanna. I went to the kitchen for a glass of water. Don't throw up, I said to myself. I rushed to the bathroom, tripping on my own feet, but didn't make it. I vomited all over myself and the hallway. I tried to clean with toilet paper but soon gave up. Then I leaned on the wall and slid to the floor and burst into tears.

The next morning, I woke up tucked under the sheets on the pull-out couch, wearing a clean T-shirt that wasn't mine. I lifted myself with difficulty and saw Carlos and Alanna cleaning the mess I'd made. I collapsed back on the couch and fell asleep. When I woke up again a few hours later, the hallway was good as new, and the house smelled of bacon. I got up and headed to the kitchen.

Carlos handed me a cup of coffee. "He's risen!" he yelled. "Resurrected!"

"Dude, I'm so sorry. This is embarrassing. You shouldn't have cleaned—I made the mess and I . . ."

"Don't worry about it. You're going through some shit."

We sat down for breakfast. Carlos and Alanna chatted about

a novel they were both reading, but I barely said a word. A new question had popped into my head: Didn't *I* fetishize *her*?

La catástrofe

It is February in Paris and the morning sky is overcast. Antonieta Rivas Mercado rises from the hotel bed she shares with Vasconcelos and begins getting ready to go out.

"Where are you going?" Vasconcelos says.

She stands before the mirror, applying dark circles around her eyes, in the fashion of the previous decade, when she was young and felt beautiful and squandered her inheritance bankrolling literary magazines.

"Nowhere."

He's married to someone else but they've been together for years. He's a difficult man to love: impatient, irascible, consumed by destiny. Still, she followed him on the long, nomadic months of the campaign, leaving behind her adored son. By then most of her money was gone, but she spent what remained on his bid for the presidency. She stayed by his side even after defeat turned him bitter. Each time the election comes up, he flies into a rage, yelling that they stole his victory—which they did. According to the official results, the Master's opponent received 95 percent of the vote. The lie was so shameless that in the months after the election the regime found it necessary to assassinate an untold number of Vasconcelos's supporters, even as it appropriated his ideas.

Hence the exile. Antonieta came along even though she wasn't sure Vasconcelos still wanted her. He treats her badly but never goes as far as asking her to leave. And so she stays. At first she hoped they could make peace. Perhaps he'd leave his wife? Yet as the months turned into years—the date is 1939, the sky over Europe darkens—she came to see her cause was lost. Vasconcelos is a sinner but remains a Catholic. Divorce is out of the question.

Vasconcelos gets up from the bed and walks to the desk where he spends his days and nights working on his memoirs. Antonieta stands by the mirror, putting on lipstick and looking at the reflection of his back. He barely touches her anymore. He lives only for the past, needs to account for it, prove he was fated for glory and robbed of it. But this means the present is but an epilogue. And Antonieta is part of that present. And she knows it and it wrecks her—the certainty that nothing she does will bring him back to the world of the living.

She walks behind him and bends to kiss his cheek. "I'm heading out," she says. "I love you."

He doesn't reply. Antonieta closes her eyes. She turns around and grabs her purse and heads into the closet. She opens her suitcase and reaches under the dresses until she finds the revolver. She slips it into her purse. She walks out of the hotel room and down the hallway and into the elevator. She tips the bellboy lavishly. She traverses the lobby and steps into the street and heads toward the river, past the stately white buildings of Haussmann's city, through the gray light of the winter morning, breathing cold, humid air. She crosses the bridge and involuntarily recites in her head:

Sous le pont Mirabeau coule la Seine
    Et nos amours
Faut-il qu'il m'en souvienne
    La joie venait toujours après la peine

She steps onto the Île de la Cité and heads for Notre Dame. A part of her worries it might be too grand a gesture. Still, she walks into the church, sits on a pew before the rose window, and shoots herself in the heart.

Corazón en fuga, herido de dudas

The day Lee met me in New York to catch our flight to Mexico, she and I went on a walk around Fort Greene.

"You've been very mean to me, you know?" she said.

"I know. And I hate it. The last thing I wanted was to hurt you."

"I hurt you too, and I hate myself for it."

"Don't hate yourself."

"I could ask the same of you."

We fell silent and went west on Myrtle Avenue, past the trees and the brownstones, until we reached the park. We climbed to the column commemorating the fallen of the Mexican-American War and sat down on the steps. Before us was New York, the afternoon sun refracting on the glass of the skyscrapers and the water of the East River. This could have been our city, I thought. She and I could have lived here together, in a small apartment in Prospect or Washington Heights, and proofread one another's books, and perhaps raised a daughter.

"I wish I hadn't said what I said. You know that, but I needed to say it again."

"And I wish I'd listened better and hadn't tried to convince you."

"I should have said I didn't want it. I guess I wanted to want it, because it was what you wanted, and I wanted you. Now I can't stop second-guessing myself."

"It was a slip of the tongue. It could happen to anyone."

"It could only happen to a white person."

I thought about telling her that I, too, was a white person, but I decided it wouldn't help.

"Do you still want to be with me?"

"Of course. Do you?"

"Yes. But I'm not sure I can get married now. Maybe later."

"I feel the same way. What if I have to leave, though? I don't want this to end, but I don't know how we'd manage if we lived in different countries."

"What if you tried to get another visa, and then, if that didn't work out, we moved to Mexico together? I should be done with coursework and could write my dissertation anywhere. Chloe never had papers when she dated the Bear and nobody gave her trouble."

Part VII

Mexico City/ San Francisco

July 2018

In which Your Correspondent travels home just in time for an election, revisits the last thirty years of Mexican political history, runs into trouble at the airport, spends time with his ailing mother, recalls an interview with a stronger spirit, ponders his American education, reflects on the nature of history, and begins to realize that he must make a choice.

Para Robert Musil

And then I returned to find the capital overwhelmed by baro-
metric pressure. It was late June, the season of storms, but the
date alone could not explain the heaviness of the atmosphere.
The days were long stretches of unease, endless permutations of
a single anxious question, the same one that my mother muttered
whenever she stepped out on her balcony with arms outstretched
and palms open skyward: When will it rain? That was the refrain
of the summer, repeated at elegant dinner parties from Las Lomas
to Polanco, often in jest but at times in hushed tones that betrayed
ill-concealed panic. The joke was it rained every afternoon, always
at the same time, far more punctually than any of us kept our
appointments. At five o'clock the valley grew dark with portents;
at five-thirty there was thunder; at five thirty-five the water came;
and by six the parks had reverted to marshes and the streets to
canals. Sometimes the storm took the form of raindrops as huge
and viscous as toads; others it appeared as bullets of hail; others
still as an impenetrable mist like the blindfold of a condemned
man. On my way home from the airport, as I watched the almost-
green sky alight with bolts of electricity through bulletproof glass,
I realized something had cracked—though whether it was the
climate, the cosmos, or my nerves, I couldn't say.

Frente a la ley

"What's your parents' address again?"
  "Forty-nine Industrial Avenue, Berkeley, California."
  "I thought they lived in Oakland?"
  "It's technically its own city, but same difference."

Lee and I had just flown back to the United States from Mexico. On the right, moving quickly and astir with animated chitchat, was the line for American citizens; on the left, all but paralyzed and tense with anxious silence, the one for everyone else.

"Why?"

"They ask where you're staying."

"Right."

We stood in silence for a moment. Lee glanced at the impossibly cool teenagers who glared at the crowd from the billboard advertising the latest vapor alternative for adult smokers. I fumbled with the folder that contained the small library of documents I'd accumulated over ten years of temporary visas. After a while the silence grew heavy.

"I guess I should just go ahead?"

"Sure," I answered without looking up. I was certain I'd gotten an updated Certificate of Eligibility for Nonimmigrant Student Status before leaving school for the summer.

"Okay. See you in baggage claim?"

"If they let me through."

"They probably will, though?"

There it was: a brand-new I-20, rubber-stamped with the signature of the appropriate university official.

"You never know."

She leaned in to kiss me and walked away. I turned around and got in line, reciting her parents' address in my head.

After what felt like an eternity the customs officer beckoned me forward with a distracted wave of her gloved hand. I stepped into the inspection booth and greeted her with the smile of a traveling salesman.

"Afternoon, ma'am," I said. "Glad to visit again."

The officer held out her hand and I placed my passport

between her fingers, shivering at the surgical touch of her latex gloves. I hoped she'd notice how I'd made things easier for her by bookmarking the page that held my visa with my certificate, but she began entering my details into her computer without so much as looking at me. Minutes passed. I grew nervous. She still hadn't said anything. No, I was overinterpreting. Her gestures, unlike mine, were not the product of careful consideration. She seemed angry, sure, but the logical conclusion wasn't that she'd decided to punish me for some inadvertent violation. It was far more likely that she had a headache or credit card bills or a pending divorce.

"Is everything all right?"

She looked up from her computer and into my eyes and I realized that my question contained its answer.

"I'm confused. You go to school in Iowa, right?"

"That's correct."

"So why did you fly to San Francisco?"

"To visit my girlfriend's parents."

"And where do they live?"

"In Oakland."

"What's the address?"

"Forty-nine Industrial Avenue."

"That's not Oakland."

"Pardon?"

"That's Berkeley."

"Oh, right! It's just that since they're right on the—"

"But you're flying to Burbank tonight?"

"Yes, we—"

"You said you were staying in Oakland."

"Yes, but we—"

"Who's we?"

"My girlfriend and I."

"Where is she?"

"She's an American citizen, so . . ."

"So you are visiting her family?"

"Yes."

"Have you met them before?"

"No."

"What do her parents do in Oakland?"

"They're artists."

"Really?"

"Yeah, she's a metalworker and he's a—"

"And why are you going to Burbank?"

"For a wedding."

"Who's getting married?"

"My old editor."

"And how long are you staying in Oakland?"

"Ten days, I think?"

"You think?"

"Well, I—"

"And when do you start school again at Iowa?"

"August fifteenth."

"And when are you getting there?"

"August thirteenth."

"You said you were staying in Berkeley for ten days."

"We're going to New Haven for a few weeks after that."

"What are you doing in Connecticut?"

"Spending time with my girlfriend."

"Doesn't she live in the Bay?"

"No, that's her parents. She—"

"How long have you known her?"

"About a year."

"About a year? Don't you know your anniversary?"

"Well, it's complicated, we—"

"Where did you meet?"

"We crossed paths in college but didn't really know each other until grad school."

"At Iowa?"

"Yes."

"But she lives in Connecticut?"

"She's going to school there. We met when she was deci—"

"So you've never lived in the same city?"

"We spent last summer in Mexico and are think—"

"And now you are going to Berkeley to meet her parents?"

"Yes."

"But you have a ticket to Burbank."

"Yes, but—"

"And then you are going to Connecticut."

"Yes."

"When was the last time you entered the US on your current visa?"

"I'm not sure."

"You're not sure?"

"January. Probably January."

"Of this year?"

"Yes."

The officer flipped through my passport, then picked up the phone on her desk. "Hi there. I've got an F-one with an I-twenty from the University of Iowa. Says school starts in August but wants to spend time in Connecticut with a long-distance girl-friend. Has a boarding pass for a flight to Burbank and says he's staying in Oakland but gave a Berkeley address. Says he was last admitted in January but has no current-year stamps. Yeah, that's what I thought. Thanks."

She hung up, opened a drawer beneath her desk, took out a bright red folder, and put my documents in it. She looked at me and let out a sigh and I felt the odd calm that arrives when the worst-case scenario comes to pass.

The officer exited her booth and gestured for me to follow her down a corridor that reeked of disinfectant while looking like it'd never been cleaned. She walked slowly, like a nurse taking a terminal patient on a walk around the oncology floor. I wondered whether she was trying to maximize her time away from the inspection booth or was so alienated from her work that every step she took in the performance of her duties struck her as a small affront.

Then I thought of the flight I had to catch and of Lee waiting for me. I took out my cell phone to let her know what had happened—but the immigration officer turned to face me and stopped dead in her tracks. I looked up and saw her expression had changed from a mixture of boredom and irritation to genuine anger, as if she'd discovered her terminal patient sneaking a cigarette in the bathroom.

"Didn't you see the signs?"

"I'm sorry—I just wanted to—"

"Cell phone use is prohibited in this area!"

I put the phone away, wondering whether I should apologize, beg her to call Lee's name on the loudspeaker, demand to see a consular official, or just keep my mouth shut. Before I could make up my mind, she shook her head and turned around and kept walking, slower than ever.

After some time, we arrived at a white waiting room that made me think of a bus station in the desert or a hospital at the end of the world. There were no windows, but the space was bright with the blue glow of overhead fluorescent tubes.

"Take a seat," the officer said, pointing to the rows of plastic chairs. "They'll call you when they're ready."

She walked to the far end of the room, where several other

officers sat behind a long desk, typing on aging computers. She hung my documents on a rack filled with identical red folders and left without saying a word. I closed my eyes. The calm I'd felt earlier turned to nausea. Of course I had no stamps from that year. I'd flown back for New Year's Eve—the last night of December.

I looked around. I counted five Homeland Security officers and twenty-seven foreigners. Among the latter I saw:

A young man with platinum hair, wearing the jersey of Mexico's national soccer team.

A man and woman with five small children and seven large suitcases.

A pale teenager listening to house music on oversize headphones.

A hijabi in her twenties.

A young woman from East Asia dozing on the shoulder of a young man, also from East Asia.

An elderly African man in a three-piece suit.

A Central American mother with an infant child.

Some chewed gum, tapped their feet, gnawed at their nails, caressed rosaries. Others stared at the map that covered one of the walls. Or at the turned-off television that hung on another. Or at the scowling portrait of the American president. Or at the sign that prohibited eating, drinking, smoking, and using cell phones and other electronic devices. Others still held their heads in their hands. Nobody spoke. The only sounds were the hum of the air-conditioning, the patter of keystrokes, and the crackle of a flickering light.

Con peras y manzanas

There was an election going on, that much was clear. There were three major candidates: a right-wing technocrat, a centrist bureaucrat, and a charismatic man of the people. All that sounded normal enough—so why did everyone seem convinced that the stakes were nothing short of apocalyptic?

The problem, as far as I could tell, was the same as everywhere: growing material disparity. The difference was that in Mexico the discontent of inequality hadn't coalesced into anger against capitalist interests or ethnic minorities, but against the political class. The statistical surveys and the man-on-the-street interviews pointed to the same conclusion: the citizens of Mexico hated the rich, but they reserved the worst of their hatred for those among the rich who pretended to govern.

From my perch in the Middle West, this rancor seemed justified. In the eighteen years that had elapsed since the end of one-party rule, the Mexican political class had accomplished less than nothing, squandering whatever legitimacy it earned by pretending to embrace democracy. The country sure looked like a republic if you squinted—the legislature was pluralistic, the three main parties jockeyed for state governments, the neoliberal factions passed the presidency back and forth like a football—but underneath such superficial indicators of progress the body politic was in critical condition.

A governor of Veracruz proved so voracious in his embezzlement that pediatric patients in his state's public hospitals were given saline solution in place of chemotherapy. President Enrique Peña Nieto thought it advisable to purchase an implausibly affordable mansion from a construction firm that also competed for government contracts. Even those oligarchs who amassed their money through less objectionable means made themselves easy to hate. They bred Lipizzaner stallions and Tibetan mastiffs, dug artificial lakes deep enough for Jet Skis, hired American pop stars to celebrate the graduations of their children, and never left the house without a retinue of bodyguards who threatened anyone who stood in their way. The antagonism between the elite and the masses had grown so bitter that, barring some drastic change, class conflict would soon devolve into class warfare.

And so in a sense there was no mystery: the charismatic man of the people, Andrés Manuel López Obrador, was all but certain to win the election. The problem, or at least my problem, was that nobody could tell me what to expect after the flood. Since there was a good chance I'd have to return to the capital, I wanted reassurance that the new government would limit its revenge on the figureheads of the old regime—such as my father—to humiliation rather than persecution.

To complicate matters, the politics I'd acquired in America meant that my instinct was to sympathize with López Obrador. That doing so would not only alienate my family but also cast my lot with people who wished them ill was a stark reminder that, in the city of my birth, I would always be my father's son.

Deja una evaluación para tus huéspedes

One morning a few days before the election, Lee went off to meet a friend and I walked to a coffeeshop in La Condesa to get breakfast. A young and attractive white couple sat down at the next table. They ordered food in good-enough Spanish, but there was no mistaking their nationality: she carried a *New Yorker* tote bag; he wore his blond locks in a man bun. They were arguing, in English, about the relative merits of two long-term Airbnb rentals in a beach town in Oaxaca.

I stared at them from my table, pretending to read the newspaper's daily tally of atrocities, seething with hatred. I began to daydream a backstory for them. She was from Portland; he was from the Upper West Side. They'd met at Brown and then moved to Brooklyn, where she tried her hand at freelance journalism and he made minimalist sculptures. They subsisted on her barista's salary and his trust fund.

At first they lived in Williamsburg (south of Grand Street, mind you—he insisted on referring to the neighborhood by its old Boricua name, Los Sures) but then their landlord sold the building and the new guy hiked the rent; besides, the Burg had been overrun by junior analysts at Goldman and Morgan Stanley, so who would have wanted to live there anyway? They found a spot in Bushwick—okay, Ridgewood—but the bankers eventually found their favorite bar, and she wasn't getting any bylines, and he hadn't sold a sculpture in months, and they were getting tired of going to magazine parties and gallery galas where they disliked most people. And then one day he stumbled on his old copy of *The Savage Detectives* and found himself thinking: *Why don't we just move to Mexico City?*

And so they moved to La Roma like they'd moved to Los Sures and Ridgewick. Mexico City was for them the last urban frontier, Brooklyn's ultima Thule, a new New York waiting to be discovered. Or perhaps it was a Third World version of the old New York, the one they'd missed by being born too late and too comfortable: the half-deserted city of edgy bars and spacious lofts, of cruising spots and black-box theaters. Or perhaps it was their century's version of Paris, the foreign metropolis where Americans could finally overcome their provincialism and become modernists.

Whatever they imagined it was, it wasn't. The water made them sick. The landlord scammed them. The rich kids who ran galleries grew tired of them after two months; the poor kids who made art hated Americans on principle. The magazine editors in Manhattan were too busy panicking about the rise of fascism in their own country to bother with the destruction of a mangrove forest near Acapulco. He started drinking too much; she started eating too little. They began to fight. In a desperate attempt to salvage their relationship, they tried moving once more—this time to Oaxaca. If they couldn't be hip urban expats, at least they could be beach bums, right? The sun and the sea would do them good, plus they would surely meet other Americans, and it would be so nice to be with people who *understood*.

The manbunned gringo summoned the waiter and asked for the check. By then my coffee was cold. I worried they might have noticed me staring. I paid in cash and walked away. What was wrong with me? Even if everything I'd imagined about them were true, they'd be the kind of people I'd sought out for the past ten years. Wasn't I their negative image? Hadn't I gone to New York looking for the same things they sought in Mexico City?

Then again, I thought as I turned a corner, there was a difference. They didn't have to worry about not being allowed in, or not being able to stay, or being forced to go back. My peers in the ruling classes of the First World crossed borders without friction, gliding from one country to another like free bloody birds. I, on the other hand, remained a colonial subject. Un maldito criollo.

La reacción subterránea

It is 1976 in Tabasco, on the southern end of the Gulf of Mexico, and the jungle's bestial vegetation exhales in the summer heat. The air is half water and carries the hum of a million insects and the cries of a hundred different birds. The octogenarian poet is dressed in the raw cotton worn by the region's Indigenous people. The moist fabric clings to his bent back as he advances through the forest with tentative steps. Following him are a half dozen young men who admire his poetry, which is lucid and luminous, and his politics, which at this point in his life combine leftist convictions and Catholic sensibilities.

After some time, the poet and his followers arrive at a village. The elders have come out to meet them and are waiting near the edge of town. The poet removes his hat and says a few words in Chontal.

"What is he saying?" says one of the young men.

"That he's honored to meet them. That his name is Carlos Pellicer. That he's come to ask for permission to represent them in the Senate."

Pellicer isn't Indigenous and speaks only a few words of the language, but he's made his defense of his state's Chontal communities a centerpiece of his campaign. The truth, however, is that the exercise is ceremonial at best. In those days democracy in Mexico is a ritual to mark the renovation of the government ranks, not to select who should fill them. Pellicer has the support of the omnipotent Party of the Institutional Revolution—the corporatist leviathan that in those days still pretends to be the inheritor of the heroes of 1910, better known for its Spanish acronym: PRI—which guarantees he'll be seated regardless of the vote.

Still, the poet takes his role as a candidate seriously. Many years earlier, when he was a beardless vanguardist rather than a venerable patriarch, he befriended the much older José Vasconcelos. At once student, secretary, and confident, Pellicer was at the Master's side for seven long years that culminated in the disaster of 1929. After Vasconcelos left for exile, Pellicer was arrested by the regime—the same that decades later nominated him to the Senate—and brought before a firing squad armed with unloaded rifles: a warning to stick to poetry.

Pellicer's beliefs have drifted away from his teacher's—the Master began singing Hitler's praises; the poet declared his support for the Spanish Republic—but the core of his politics remains pure Vasconcelismo. He believes politicians should aspire to become heroes, symbols that inspire the people to make history. Crucially, Pellicer has also retained Vasconcelos's notion of the political campaign as a pedagogical project. Hence the posse of young students following him in the jungle. Most will disappear into local government or provincial literature departments. One, however, will prove too ambitious for such an unheroic fate. His name is Andrés Manuel López Obrador.

La vida, la libertad, y la búsqueda de la felicidad

I sat in silence in the secondary screening room at the airport for what felt like hours, trying to decide whether the feeling that I was about to have a heart attack was evidence of my fragility or an appropriate response to the times. I no longer wore a watch, so I looked at the clock on the wall—but it was broken. I glanced at the sign prohibiting cell phones, then at the officer, then at the sign again. I'd lost track of time, and this simple fact, the not-knowing, filled me with indignation. I wasn't a citizen, or even a resident alien, but I was a graduate student in the English Department of a public university in Middle America, and while the immigration status that came with that appointment didn't allow me to assist in the teaching of literature without first taking a language proficiency test, it did in fact grant me the right to spend the summer vacation wherever I damn pleased.

And so I took out my cell phone, making no effort to hide it, ready to be sent back to my country for defending my right to text my girlfriend and know the time. And then I saw the digital clock on the home screen and realized I'd been in the detention room for less than an hour. Suddenly I felt ashamed. Perhaps it wasn't altogether unreasonable to double-check a foreigner's papers.

I waited. Eventually, I needed to piss. Ignorant of the protocol,

I reverted to Catholic school and raised my hand. One of the officers jerked his head in the direction of a hallway toward the back
of the room. I nodded in thanks and headed down the corridor,
trying not to think about what took place behind the unmarked
doors I passed. When I reached a single-stall bathroom and
discovered with relief that the lock worked, I urinated leisurely,
relishing every second of privacy. I washed my hands and replied
to Lee's messages of concern, telling her that she shouldn't worry
but also that she should start looking for alternate flights. Then,
as I opened the door to leave, my eyes lingered on the childcare
station next to the sink. On the edge of the changing surface,
frozen in time like some artifact from Pompeii, I saw a package
of disposable wet wipes.

El héroe lepisosteiforme

It is 1996 in Tabasco and black smoke rises over rust-bitten tanks,
above the tops of ceibas, into the bright February sky. Andrés
Manuel López Obrador stands before the burning oil wells with
a somber expression. He's come a long way from his years leading
the Tabasco branch of the PRI: half a decade ago he joined a
new coalition of social democrats, the Party of the Democratic
Revolution, or PRD, and reinvented himself as a champion of
the poor. It's for them he set fire to the wells—to protest the cal-
lousness with which the elite in the capital extracts wealth from
Mexico's impoverished south.

The truth, however, is that there was no fire that day: López
Obrador merely occupied the wells. I'm unsure whether the
legend is the work of his allies or detractors, but it's become a
central part of his mythos: López Obrador would rather watch
the country burn than allow its corrupt leaders to profit at the
expense of the people.

I headed back to the waiting room, hurrying past the unmarked doors. At the end of the hallway I noticed a poster I hadn't registered earlier. The photograph that covered the top half depicted a person of uncertain gender and age. They sat on a bare concrete floor with their back against a bare concrete wall, holding their knees against their chest and projecting a long shadow at an oblique angle, as if someone were shining a searchlight on them. Overlaid on the image, in large white letters, was written:

KEEP DETENTION SAFE

CBP HAS ZERO TOLERANCE FOR SEXUAL ABUSE &
ASSAULT

BREAK THE SILENCE

REPORT CONFIDENTIALLY

BE SAFE AND GET HELP

I almost laughed. The link between the wall in the poster and the one in all the president's speeches was too obvious to be coincidental. In place of Lady Liberty and her nursery rhyme, the waiting rooms of America were now presided over by a symbol of the violent emotions that animate imperialism: the sadistic need to conquer, to claim, to break and bend, to GRAB the huddled masses BY THE PUSSY and send them THE HELL back, ANIMALS that they were, to the SHITHOLE COUNTRIES from whence they came.

But then I felt a wave of dark green vertigo. The poster, I realized, was not a caution but a threat. One was supposed to see it and tremble with the knowledge that that sort of thing happened in this sort of place, that the bureaucracy of the homeland reserved the right to bring all foreigners to a disinfected purgatory where the clocks didn't work and terrible things happened, that by crossing the border, one tacitly accepted the risk of witnessing or suffering SEXUAL ABUSE & ASSAULT.

I walked back to the waiting room and found myself reconstructing their story from memory—what they'd told me, what they'd left unsaid. They were brother and sister, sixteen at the time. I was not yet twenty-four. I'd met them because my editors at the website wanted a story about education. There was no photographer available, so I took the portraits myself. All but two came out blurry. In one he stares into the distance, arms resting on the handlebars of his diminutive bicycle, his mouth tense in a disarming attempt at a tough-guy smirk. In the other she sits on a plastic chair in a parking lot, arms crossed, her lips half-parted in a skeptical smile.

I sat down on my plastic chair and tried to remember how long it had been since I saw the brother and sister. Two years? No, I realized, surprised to discover I was no longer young enough for half a decade to feel like an eternity: it was almost five years ago, the year of the massacre of Ayotzinapa and the second death of Nazario Moreno—and also, though I didn't know it yet, the happiest time of my life.

By then I'd been in close proximity to various foci of American power for long enough that I'd almost forgotten I was merely a guest in the country. I went through life as a near-perfect facsimile of a white American of my gender and class, with the carelessness that comes from knowing that Fitzgerald was lying: the privilege of American whiteness consists of being granted a life with infinite second acts. I was wasting the kindest years that history was likely to offer me wondering whether I was squandering my talents in the content mines of digital journalism.

In my defense, I wasn't alone. Most members of the bourgeoisie experience history as they do their heartbeat: they only become aware of it when something goes wrong. Good fortune feels a lot like boredom, and one of the essential characteristics of boredom is that, when under its spell, we cannot imagine the end of it. All it takes to make us complacent, to dull our sense of contingency, of danger, is a decade or two in which things largely go our way. The theory of the End of History is a consequence of this complacency rather than its cause. It wasn't that liberal-capitalist democracy triumphed once and for all and therefore the bourgeois of the West grew bored; it was that they were bored and thus convinced themselves that liberal-capitalist democracy would last forever.

Such delusions aren't new: imperial Rome, too, believed itself eternal. We've known since Herodotus that nothing human lasts, that those who are great will soon be meek and those who are meek will soon be great. Since we first felt the need to keep a record of our affairs, periods of stability and prosperity have always been followed by convulsions. What arrogance makes us think it won't happen to us? The thought is terrifying, which is why so many of us prefer not to entertain it. Between boredom and fear, who wouldn't reach for boredom? Still, war, plague, and famine await.

This is why privilege is best understood as a measure of vulnerability to history: the lower your rank, the higher your risk of getting caught in the current. But history, like metaphysics, has a way of intruding into the most lighthearted life. No one is immune—not even those favored by the draw. Neither I nor my peers in the "creative class" of that faux-meritocratic America understood that the Obama years were precisely that: years, an era among others, a period with a beginning and an end. The time I spent as one of New York's half-million aspiring writers was the product of a wild confluence of improbabilities—the financial crisis was over, Facebook's algorithms began favoring news stories, a vacancy opened in a rent-stabilized building in South Slope, the United States government approved three hundred thousand work visas, I happened to be carrying a copy of *Eros the Bittersweet* when I met an actress for coffee—and yet I rode the subway twice a day believing those coincidences were as unremarkable as the coming of spring after winter.

As it happened, even the seasons were changing, but an observer in possession of so much as a half-developed sense of historical irony wouldn't have had to turn to the science section of the newspaper to find omens of disaster. In the span of a few months, more than fifty thousand Central American children had crossed the southern border of the United States without parents or documents, and while the policies of the Obama administration meant most of them were soon released to family members, the detention centers the government built to hold them in the meantime laid the groundwork for the even greater crimes to come. At the time, however, the press corps did not understand the question of the immigrant children as a test of what America stood for but as a matter of logistics and policy. The "unaccompanied alien minors," as the bureaucracy insisted on calling them, were numerous enough to fill a small city. Now the government, which the more naive among us still imagined to be capable of benignity, was going to have to feed, clothe, and house them, not to mention provide them with health care and schooling.

Hence the story about education my editors wanted me to write. The public school districts of the United States were already overcrowded, underfunded, and in general ill-equipped to serve students with complex needs. How, exactly, were they planning to deal with children who'd just crossed a desert and a militarized border? The question was newsworthy, but I resented the assignment. I was supposed to be covering the cops; I didn't know anything about education. My editors replied that most of the children didn't speak English and that I, unlike most of my colleagues, spoke Spanish.

And so I called the only contact of mine who seemed halfway relevant, a source from my days working for a local paper in college: the Catholic priest who led the Latino parish in New Haven. He pointed me to a small solidarity organization—either communists or anarchists, he couldn't remember—and for the next few weeks I commuted on the Metro-North to attend the group's meetings. Eventually, the organizers put me in touch with a man from Guatemala who'd recently taken in two relatives, a pair of younger half-siblings who called him tío.

I met him one bright Sunday morning in August, on the sidewalk outside the priest's church, where the faithful gathered after mass to buy paletas and joke and gossip in Spanish and Mayan languages. He was short and broad-shouldered like Chicago; he wore a cachucha and a spotless white shirt with a clip-on collar just starting to fray. He seemed suspicious, looking me up and down, as if trying to decide whether I was a cop, so I tried to reassure him I'd minimize any risk to the kids. After some time, he cut me off with a wave of the hand.

"All right. But only if they want to."

He gestured to someone behind me, and I turned to see two teenagers running toward us. They were a boy and a girl, both with dark skin, and they wore clothes that struck me as cartoonishly American, like the wardrobe of a television drama set in a suburban high school: Target-brand T-shirts and jeans. The boy shook my hand with enthusiasm; the girl kept her distance. The man pointed at me and said something in Kaqchikel. The boy nodded. The girl shook her head.

"She doesn't want to," the man said.

"That's totally okay," I said, then turned to the boy. "You like pizza?"

He nodded.

"Awesome. They have great pizza in this town."

Es un honor estar con Obrador

It's 2005 in Mexico City and the vestibule of the Chamber of Deputies is packed with besuited politicians, journalists in utility vests, activists in Indigenous dress, common people in their common clothes.

"¡No estás solo!" they chant. "You're not alone!"

Blinded by the flash of the cameras, Andrés Manuel López Obrador, now the popular mayor of Mexico City, advances with difficulty through the crowd. Congress has summoned him to answer impeachment charges. The allegations are frivolous but could have momentous consequences: if he's found guilty, he'll be barred from running in next year's presidential election.

After making his way to the chamber, López Obrador takes the stage to deliver his defense. "I have little to say in legal terms about the falsity of the charges brought against me," he begins, his voice steady with cold anger and conviction, in a style that reminds me of Nazario. "For I am certain I am not on trial for breaking the law, but for my way of thinking and acting, and for what I, along with many others, represent for the future of our country. Those who defame me with foul calumnies believe they are the owners of Mexico. They are afraid the people will choose a true change, and this cowardly fear drives them to try and crush anyone who works to build a fatherland for the humble."

López Obrador will win his trial and accept the PRD's nomination for president, but he'll never forget the affront. His ideology, which when he ran Mexico City amounted to a pragmatic democratic socialism, will harden into a personal hatred of the elite, and especially of a small cadre of conservative politicians—a group that happens to include my father—whom López Obrador believes participated in a secret conspiracy to derail his candidacy by leaking videos where one of his subordinates could be seen stuffing wads of bribe dollars into his pockets. He'll begin to think of his task as moral rather than political, not so much the construction of a welfare state as the resection of a tumor or the exorcism of a demon. A cleanse. A purge. A regeneration.

El imparcial

I called a taxi and the Guatemalan boy and I headed to the brick-oven joint on the corner of Elm and Howe, down the block from a building where I lived in college. I ordered a large pie with sausage and peppers, brought it to one of the tables near the window, and sat across from the boy. I'd known him for less than an hour, but I'd already scribbled down the handful of details I would later use to characterize him at the top of my article: he laughed loud and often, spoke an elegant Spanish that mixed slang with archaic constructions and biblical inflections, and wore his thick black hair in the vaguely punk style popular among Latin American soccer players—short spikes fixed in place with an ungodly amount of gel. I liked him already, and not just because he was almost certainly going to prove a great subject for a profile.

"So, you're starting high school soon, huh?" I said. "Have you met the teachers? Do any of them speak Spanish?"

He'd just bitten into a slice of pizza, so he shook his head for an answer. "But I did meet this chapín who's gonna go to the same school," he said in Spanish after he swallowed. "He lives next door to my tío. He's cabal, a real cool dude. He demonstrated to me this band who call themselves Sepultura. They're from Brazil and they're bien chileros. Have you heard them?"

"Yeah, man, Sepultura. Total classic. But tell me, have they made you take tests to see what classes you should take?"

"He demonstrated to me many things, el chapín aquel. Like the parkour. Do you know about the parkour? It's when you run around the city but instead of running on the street you run on the azoteas, pues, like a caco running from the chontas or a superhero chasing a supervillain."

"Right. But are you nervous about studying in English? And what's it like, hanging with American kids?"

"No, pues, they're real good people. There's many guate-maltecos and hondureños and salvadoreños, pues, and those are real cabalitos. Plus a bunch of mexicanos, gente chilera. And then there's also boricuas and dominicanos. Sometimes it's hard with them, 'cause some of them don't know Castilian. But they are still chidos, gente de calidá. You know what I mean?"

"Yeah, I think I do," I said, realizing that for him *American* meant *US-born Latino* rather than *white person*. "But they get along all right? Even though they're from different places?"

The boy laughed. "¿Qué si se llevan bien? No, pues, ta buena la preguntita, ¿eh? Yeah, they get along. I mean, sure, some of them are in gangas. But mostly it's real quiet, you know? Like, we all hang out and do stuff together."

"Like soccer?" I asked.

"More like BMX," he said, pronouncing the initialism in English. "You know about BMX?"

"That's with the tiny bikes, right?"

He burst out laughing again. I smiled and nodded and dutifully wrote down the quote. I reminded myself that I had no right to be frustrated; that he was giving me a gift; that my job was to listen carefully to everything he said, even if none of it made it into the story, because the only thing I could offer him in return for his willingness to speak with me was an occasion to feel that the fact that his neighbor had introduced him to Sepultura and parkour was a small but crucial part of history.

"Esas meras," he said. "Las bicis chiquitas. My uncle got me one when I got here, you know? As a bienvenida, pues."

I looked up from my notepad. He was still smiling but his expression now had a certain solemnity. I held my breath. This was the opening. All I had to do was give him a gentle push and I would have my story. But a second passed, then another. I hesitated. The boy was sitting with me because one of the few people he trusted had told him he could trust me, but I knew better.

I'd told him and his guardian I intended to write an article based on our conversations, but my disclosure, though accurate in a strict sense, obscured my intentions. What I should have said was that I intended to repackage the boy's trauma into a digestible narrative I hoped would capture the attention of some hundred thousand internet users, who would surrender valuable information about themselves to one or another technology baron, who would then reward the website for which I worked with a better starting position in the algorithmic rat race, which would allow the website's owners to convince a handful of investors to keep funding the company, which in turn would allow my editors to pay me a salary, earn me accolades, and, eventually, if all went well, convince the US government I deserved to live in the country. The boy was for me not an end but a means, and lately thoughts of that nature bothered me often enough I wondered whether I shouldn't do something else with my life.

I was about to tell him that there was no need to relive difficult things, that maybe I could come back next week with a videographer and shoot some footage of him and his friends doing their best BMX tricks on the wide concrete sidewalk down by the harbor, edit it so they looked like real badasses, set the whole thing to a death metal soundtrack, and try to convince my editors to put *that* on the website, because *that*, right there, would be a story about education—but the boy went on before I could say anything.

"It was real nice of him. Regalarme una bici después de tanto caminar."

La pantomima de la legitimidad

Perhaps that's why the 2006 election proved so ugly. Temperamental by nature and incensed by the state apparatus's obvious support for the ruling party's nominee, López Obrador declared that Mexico's brand-new democratic institutions ought to "go to the devil." The elite, worried the man they'd transformed into a sworn enemy was about to become president, embarked on a campaign to portray him as a dictator in the making. Their efforts gave fruit: López Obrador's once-comfortable lead over the conservative Felipe Calderón shrank in the final weeks of the campaign. By election night the race was too close to call. Two tense days later the Federal Electoral Institute announced that Calderón had won the presidency by half a percentage point.

The defeat was narrow enough to be plausible, but López Obrador's supporters distrusted the institutions their candidate had praised so effusively. Few were surprised when he refused to recognize the result. He and his followers occupied Reforma Boulevard, erecting a tent city over some of the Federal District's most important intersections. At first the occupiers enjoyed widespread support, but soon the citizens of the capital tired of spending hours in traffic to make way for a ghost town of empty tents and unemptied porta-potties. For many the turning point came on the anniversary of the Revolution, when López Obrador declared himself the "legitimate president of Mexico" in a make-believe inauguration that came across less like defiant resistance than like a temper tantrum.

López Obrador's reputation didn't recover for years. In 2012, when he again ran for president, he lost to the PRI's Enrique Peña Nieto by three million votes. Later that year, when he resigned from the PRD, many intelligent people declared him finished. Two years later, when he registered his own political party, the Movement for National Regeneration, or MORENA, the same people wondered whether he'd lost his mind. But MORENA's organizers proved disciplined and effective: time and again they won races in regions the traditional parties considered strongholds. In 2018, when López Obrador announced his third run for president, his victory was all but assured. Faced with such an impasse, the Austro-Hungarians drank, lost themselves in frivolity, made plans to move to Madrid or McAllen, hid their fortunes in offshore tax havens, told dark jokes about the guillotine, mocked the poor, flattered themselves, and when all else failed, simply pretended they didn't live in Mexico.

El que habita al abrigo del Altísimo

The boy with spiked hair said he came from the highlands, from a place where the clouds flew close to the ground, the people spoke Kaqchikel, and each family had its own little milpa—a few rows of maize, some beans, a handful of chiles, a lime tree. His father was gone and his mother was sick, so he worked instead of studying, first shining shoes in restaurants, later at a clothing factory. Going north was his mother's idea, he said. She was worried, and it was easy to imagine her reasons. The older kids. The ones with the guns and the tattoos. The ones who had started following him. They'd see him on his way home from the factory, on the dirt road that led up the hill, and they'd walk up to him, until they were real close behind, and then they'd start saying things. That they had work for him. That they could help him out. That they were like a family. Like that—real friendly. But then when he didn't say anything back, they would start with the questions. Was he for real? Did he like the factory that much? How much were they paying him? Was he kidding? Was he fucking with them? What, was he a joto? Was he bien puto? Marica? Güicoy? Chupavergas?

They wanted to know, they said, because she was looking tasty. Bien rica. Buenota. Calientahuevos. Casqueadora. Why'd she dress like that if not? Yeah, they'd say, that's why they wanted to know. Because if it turned out he wasn't just a shumo de mierda, but also a puto; if it turned out he wasn't a real man, un pinche varoncito hecho y derecho, the kind of hidesumadre who has his revolver always ready to defend his viejas and stand up for his kin—then God knows what might happen to such a tasty morrita as his sister.

And so they left, the boy and the girl. They said goodbye to their mother and headed north.

At first they rode a burra, then a troca, then La Bestia. They sat on the roof of the train, holding on to the containers with bare hands. The metal got hot in the sun, the boy said. Real hot. Like red coals held to the face.

The train was slow, so there was no breeze.

They fought off gnats, mosquitoes, borrachos, and ladrones.

The heat made them drowsy but they couldn't sleep because of the babies.

They cried all the time, the babies.

There were dozens of them, tossing in the rebozos of their mothers.

Sometimes the mothers cried too.

The days were long, the boy said, and only got longer after he and his sister got off the train. They kept inching north, one ghastly town at a time, on trocas and burras and sometimes on foot, eating when they could, almost never sleeping. Along the way they paid off a lot of people. The drivers. The soldiers. The municipal cops. The federal cops. The narcos. The other narcos. The cops who pretended to be narcos. The narcos who pretended to be cops. Everyone offered them protection but also warned them about everyone else, and since the children didn't know who to watch out for, they started watching out for everyone.

Their lives became a whirlwind of safe houses where they didn't feel safe: crowded motel rooms when they were lucky, warehouses with dirt floors when they were not. After some weeks, the boy said, the nights became longer than the days.

At last they made it to the border. They met their guide: a boy with vacant eyes, only a few years older than them, who spoke in monosyllables and clutched a rag soaked in paint thinner, which he held over his nose and mouth like a handkerchief. He made them wait several days, dizque because the weather, and then shook them awake in the middle of the night, telling them to get up and leave everything and follow him. The boy with the rag brought the children to a parking lot, where a troca loaded to the brim with grown men waited. The boy and the girl climbed into the pickup truck, trying to make themselves small enough to fit between the men.

And then they drove into the night.

It was very dark and very quiet, said the boy, like those nights when there's mass because it's a feast day and everyone gets out of bed, even though it's real cold, and then the whole town stands outside the church, holding candles, and every time they breathe you can see their souls.

"How do you mean?" I asked.

"Like when smoke comes out of the mouth," the boy said. "Like a cloud. Like mist. Like fog."

"Oh," I said. "You mean steam. Water vapor."

"Yes," the boy said. "That. Vapor."

I nodded and wrote down the quote, though I didn't understand its significance at the time. Later I would realize that, in my obstinate attempts to write a story about the challenges of providing an American education to children who spoke Indigenous languages better than Spanish, I'd mistaken poetry for lack of vocabulary.

Para Paul North

A few months before the election, when I was still at Iowa, an American magazine editor asked me to write about López Obrador. I replied I didn't know enough to say anything intelligent, but I still made a few notes:

Panorama colonial—*A decade ago a right-wing intellectual bestowed a memorable moniker on the perennial candidate of the Mexican Left: "The Tropical Messiah." The epithet, a childish attempt at critique via name-calling, combined an accusation of megalomania (he thinks he's Jesus) with metropolitan snobbery (he's from Tabasco). But the insult, like most mockery, was motivated by fear just as much as by spite. Andrés Manuel López Obrador, the oligarchs insisted, was "a danger for Mexico." His election would spell catastrophe— a death sentence for economic policies that were just about to give fruit.*

In the years since, López Obrador has lost not one but two elections, though in both cases his defeat had less to do with the political skill or rhetorical talent of his opponents than with their willingness to bend the rules and break the law. Still, the moniker and the reactionary alarmism that animated its

*coinage have stuck. Today, as Mexico nears its fourth demo-
cratic election, the notion that the Left candidate is "messianic"
and therefore dangerous has become a central part of the elite's
narrative about the state of the country. In the opinion pages
of the capital's newspapers and in the Facebook posts of my
private school classmates, López Obrador appears as a men-
acing specter, a reincarnation of Hugo Chávez who must be
stopped at any cost, lest the supermarkets of Mexico run out
of champagne and then, inevitably, toilet paper.*

*That the elite's assessment of López Obrador is inaccurate is
obvious. Less obvious is that his supporters, at least those in the
bourgeoisie, also miss the mark. They defend their candidate
by pointing out that the Right's alarmist hysteria is naked
intellectual dishonesty and self-serving bad faith. They argue
that López Obrador is in fact a viable option; that underneath
his grandiloquent rhetoric there is a pragmatic program, an
alternative answer to the ills of the country. They insist, in
short, that López Obrador is emphatically not messianic, even
if there's something undeniably tropical about his fondness for
marigold garlands.*

*López Obrador's supporters are right about their candidate,
and it is precisely for that reason that they are in the wrong.
True messianism is unexpected, unforeseeable, such that only
those who have been touched by the divine can prophesize its
coming, and then only in language so oblique it defies interpretation. The coming of a messiah is the irruption into the
world of something so new that existing words—including,
of course, messiah—cannot name it. If it were ever to occur,
it would be as mysterious and terrifying as comets and solar
eclipses were for the ancients. Nobody would know what was
happening, perhaps not even that something was happening.
It would be a flash of lightning in a clear sky or a word*

*whispered in an empty room; it would happen in the blink of
an eye or over the course of a century—but it would bring us
redemption.*

*That, nothing else, is what Mexico needs. The alternative
is not a cataclysm but something more pernicious: the continuation of the slow-motion catastrophe that has been unfolding
here since 1521. López Obrador isn't dangerous because he is
a messiah but because he isn't one. Beneath his pompous evoca-
tions of Juárez, he is by turns a moralizing conservative and
a corporatist reactionary, a throwback to the nationalist PRI
that ruled the country for decades before the arrival of neoliberalism. He has even promised never to raise taxes, a pledge
that puts him closer to Ronald Reagan than Salvador Allende.*

*This incongruous promise reveals López Obrador's limita-
tions most clearly. Whenever he is asked how he plans to pay
for vast increases in social spending without raising taxation,
the candidate replies that he plans to recapture the 10 percent
of the Mexican domestic product that experts estimate is lost to
corruption each year. When pressed with the obvious follow-up
question, he replies that, since he will be an honest president,
his subordinates will no longer feel entitled to steal public
money, which the government will then be free to spend.*

*The notion is so stupid that one wonders whether López
Obrador is a cynic or a naïf. In any case, and contrary to what
he believes or claims to believe, the real scandal has nothing
to do with moral fiber—his own or anyone else's—but with
the fact that the redistributive program of the contemporary
Mexican Left boils down to the single idea more laughable
than trickle-down economics: trickle-down morality.*

Gradually, the jottings turned away from the election and
toward a broad consideration of the figure of the messiah. Wasn't

that what Maximiliano, Vasconcelos, Nazario, and López Obrador all had in common? The belief that each was the chosen one to redeem Mexico? Mine was a nation of Don Quixotes convinced they were knights errant set upon this earth to right torts. And perhaps they had a point. Perhaps the Mexican catastrophe was so old, so deep and overdetermined, that the only exit from our labyrinth was an apocalypse. Perhaps we'd do well to hasten the destruction of the old world so the new one could be born. I was prepared to say we should. But even as we put our shoulder to the wheel, the essay would conclude, we ought to keep in mind that the future was a mystery, that we were shooting blind.

I plunged into the project. I revisited the relevant texts by Marx, Kafka, and Benjamin, checked out a number of histories of Mexico from the library, and began sketching an essay about the ways in which my country's politics, with their alternation between radical hope and fatalistic cynicism, were at once the product and the cause of a paradoxical experience of temporality—polychrony, Esteban called it—in which time appeared to spin in ever-faster circles and yet stand perfectly still. I grew enthusiastic. Maybe I was onto something. I put aside the essay about creole identity and instead began copying long passages from my growing bibliographical pile, hoping the mere act of setting different thinkers in physical proximity would unleash a phlogistic current that would bring about some kind of revelation. Of these passages, none excited me more than a few sentences from Benjamin's *One Way Street*:

> *Among the trove of sayings through which the way of life of the German bourgeois, welded together out of stupidity and cowardice, reveals itself everyday, the one about impending catastrophe—"things can't go on like this"—is particularly worthy of consideration. The past decades' helpless fixation*

on ideas of security and property prevents the average person from perceiving the new and noteworthy stabilities that underlie the present situation . . . The notion that things can't go on like this will one day discover that, for individuals as well as for communities, there is only one limit beyond which suffering can't go: annihilation.

I tore the page from my notebook and taped it to the wall above the desk where I worked on the essay, which to my frustration became an expanding collection of false starts and wrong turns. For nights on end I sat in the soft blue glow of my computer screen, feeling a gravitational force draw my eyes to the last word of the passage: annihilation.

I was only able to free myself from the essay months later, when I left the Middle West for the summer. Esteban wrote to ask if I had work to show him before we saw each other in Mexico. I was too embarrassed to admit I hadn't produced anything coherent in months—the piece on Vasconcelos, Sigüenza, and my grandfather was still too raw to share—so I put together the more polished fragments from the essay on the messiah and sent them to him. He replied a few days later, asking whether I was okay, because what I sent him wasn't the product of a sound mind. The criticism came as a relief—it gave me license to abandon the project and focus on the creoles—but one of Esteban's comments left me uneasy. It concerned one of the last sections of the essay, the anecdote about oil reporting that followed the allegorical fable about the traveling magician:

El ángel exterminador—*For a time after graduating from college I worked as a reporter at a financial news agency. My supervisor was an irascible Englishman who, when he wasn't busy yelling at his subordinates, dispensed pearls of wisdom disguised as truisms. One of these aphorisms remained in my memory:* never *predict the price of oil.*

The maxim applies to futures contracts both financial and social. Knowingly or not, the Mexican elite has gambled its fortune on its ability to sustain an indefinite crisis—and on the poor's capacity to withstand it. Like all bullish stances, the investment is necessarily hubristic: every *long position is in the last instance a statement of confidence not in the market but in one's own soothsaying capacities. The question, then, is not whether the Austro-Hungarians have a sense of the likely positive or negative outcomes of the present situation, but whether they understand the severity of the worst-case scenario. Entranced by the lifestyle of their confreres in Moscow and Dubai, the Mexican oligarchs are aware of what they stand to win. What they seem to have forgotten is how much they stand to lose.*

"Las cosas no pueden seguir así," they repeat in tones of concern at the elegant restaurants on Avenida Álvaro Obregón, "pero nada tiene que cambiar." The resulting sentence is paradoxical but not necessarily false. Its continued truth, however, is not guaranteed. Mexico may remain where it is: at a breaking point where nothing breaks. But, as anyone who watches the market or the stars in search of signs from the gods knows well, every second is the strait gate through which the messiah may enter. When she does, I hope my family and friends will have a suitcase packed.

"Setting aside for a moment that you apparently thought it'd be interesting to put this Cassandra-in-the-newsroom routine next to the weird (and TBH quite sentimental) stuff about the mystical saltimbanqui," Esteban wrote, "I've got to ask whether you realize what you are saying. The politics of the essay are confusing, but insofar as it's possible to discern something like a stance viz. the fate of the Austro-Hungarians (i.e., what you think could/should/will happen to them after this messiah of yours deigns to show up) you seem to be suggesting they deserve (and here I'm going to quote one of the most overused words of the piece) 'annihilation.' Which I guess is fine (if perhaps a little melodramatic) if you don't mean what you say (though in that case I wonder why you're saying it, given it isn't that funny), but if you mean it (which seems to be the case: the essay is as ponderous as it is self-serious), then, my boy, you are wading into dangerous waters. Because these people, as you point out, are your family and friends. Do you really want them to live in fear? Watch them be forced to flee their country? You come close (very close) to calling for their deaths. Is that what you want?"

Todas las flores

My mother made a point of buying the flowers herself. She left the house when it was still dark and came back before anyone else woke up, bearing tulips and sunflowers that she displayed in vases scattered around unexpected corners of the house. It helped to keep things in perspective, a practice that of late had become more difficult and more necessary.

For months she'd had a stubborn cough: a rasp deep in the chest, an itch in the back of the throat. A month before I arrived in Mexico City that summer, her doctors confirmed what she already knew: her cancer, that widowed cousin who didn't wait for invitations and overstayed her welcome, had yet again returned. This time she'd settled on her pleura, a word that sounded like a combination of *aura* and the French verb to *weep* but described the veil of the lungs.

And so my mother sought occasions to get out of the house,

following Pascal's advice to start by kneeling. She spent hours each week at an orphanage, holding one infant after another to provide them with human contact; she enrolled in a course on cultural administration, hoping to formalize with a credential the years of unpaid labor she'd performed as an ambassador's wife; and twice a month, often enough to ensure the flowers never wilted, she went to the Mercado de Jamaica.

"Oh, do not mind!" she said to Lee after she cut a sunflower too short. "What is that old proverb that you have? Practicing makes perfection."

I watched them work in the courtyard from the second-floor balcony. Her doctors said there was still hope, but over the course of my visit I had come to understand that this time she was unlikely to recover. Perhaps I should move back while there was still time.

Sobre el león y el áspid pisarás

The migrants rode the troca for a long time, the boy said, first on the highway and then on a dirt road. The kid with the rag turned off the headlights, so the children could see the stars, different from the ones in Guatemala—and also, lower on the horizon, the soft red glow of the city. After a while, when they were far from the road, the kid parked the truck by a big tree. Everyone got out and started walking single file, deeper into the desert, until they got to the river, where another kid was waiting with an inflatable raft. The migrants climbed on, trying not to trip in the dark, and then the second kid pushed the raft away from the bank. Everyone be quiet, said the kid with the rag, and everyone listen carefully. When we get to the other side, you run. Fast as you can. Don't stop until I say stop. Understand?

The boy with spiked hair nodded and squeezed his sister's

hand. He took a deep breath. He closed his eyes, opened them, and that was it. They'd done it. They were on the other side.

And then they ran.

They ran for a long time, hours and hours, tripping on jagged rocks, feeling thorns pierce the soles of their shoes and the flesh of their feet, too scared to worry about snakes or consider the pain in their thighs, until the sky went from pitch-black to light gray and they reached a hill with a few low trees, where at last they stopped. The kid with the rag said they should lie down and rest, but the boy with spiked hair didn't close his eyes. He was so exhausted that he wasn't sure if everything he was seeing was real, but he couldn't let himself sleep. His sister was the only girl in the group.

After that point the story became blurry. The boy wasn't sure how many days he and his sister spent in the desert. He figured it was somewhere between three and five, hard to say—his memory played tricks on him whenever he tried to revisit the last part of the journey. He was pretty sure he'd stayed awake the whole time, but his sister remembered events he didn't, and these unnerving gaps made him wonder what else was missing.

In between the gaps there was the incident with the airplane. It was small, no larger than a zopilote, too small to carry a person, and it made a noise like a wasp, and it flew real close to the ground, and when the migrants saw it they panicked and ran away in every direction, and the girl and her brother didn't know what to do, so they followed the men closest to them, and after running for a while they couldn't see or hear the zopilote, so they stopped to rest—and then realized they didn't know where they were or where the rest of the group had gone.

This part the boy remembered well. They tried calling the kid with the rag and at first they couldn't find a signal, but the man with the phone kept trying until the call went through. The kid with the rag said he knew where they were; he was coming to find them; he'd be there soon—but hours passed, then a day, and he didn't show up. By the time the migrants gave up on their guide they'd almost run out of food and water. One of the men suggested they take their chances walking to the city. Even if they didn't make it, he said, they might find a ranch or a shed with a faucet, and besides, if they stayed where they were, they wouldn't last much longer. And so they walked for another day, trying to orient themselves by the desert sun, and as night began to fall they saw a lake and ran toward it, but when they got closer they realized the lake was no lake but the river.

It was at that point the men started talking among themselves. Real quiet. Real suspect. Away from his sister and him. Then one of the men came over and said to the children that he was real sorry, that he wished things were different, that he hoped God would forgive him, but that he and the other men had decided to leave them behind. They were slowing the group down, he said, and the men had children of their own, and wives and mothers, and fathers too. And they had to stay alive for them. They owed it to them. They could not afford to die.

By the time the man was done talking, the other men were nowhere to be seen. The man who'd come to talk to the children said sorry one last time. Then he ran away. For a while the boy went after him, yelling, begging him to stop, turn around, wait a minute—but he was tired and thirsty and couldn't reach him. The boy turned around and walked back to his sister and sat next to her, and then the children held each other and shivered and waited for the desert night to be over, listening for coyotes and drones, watching the stars above them turn again.

América, te lo he dado todo y ahora no soy nada

"So you got NAFTA'd."

"What the fuck does that mean?"

"It's what happens when you trust the gringos. They promise you everything, but in the end, after you've given them all, you're left with nothing."

"You can be such an asshole sometimes."

"I hate to say it. But I told you so."

"It would have happened even if I weren't Mexican. Maybe it would have taken a different shape, but conflict is a normal part of . . ."

"It would have never happened if you weren't Mexican. For the simple reason that you wouldn't be together if you weren't Mexican. More to the point, you wouldn't be who you are if you weren't Mexican—just like she wouldn't be who she is if she weren't American."

"Did you measure our skulls?"

"Admit it. You like her because she's American. And not just American but blond, tall, pale . . ."

"You mean white."

"You have a thing for white girls."

"I've dated all kinds of people."

"All kinds except Mexicans."

"I'm white, Esteban. And so are you."

"In Mexico? Sure. Here we're white. In the States it's more complicated. But more to the point, she's whiter than you. And I suspect that's why you're twisting yourself into knots to find reasons to stay with her even after she reproached you for being Latin American. Which is to say for not being as white as her."

"She reproached me because I could have given her chlamydia. The Latin America thing is secondary."

"Is it? Anyone who's spent time with you two can tell you she wants you to be just the right amount of different. Almost-but-not-quite white."

"I don't think that's true."

"You don't? Or you choose not to?"

"What's the difference?"

"You're trying to convince yourself of something you know to be false."

"I'm trying to save our relationship. Because what we have is fucking rare."

"It's actually quite common. The American abroad and her foreign lover. By the time Godard made *Breathless* it was already a cliché."

"It's rare because we understand the two sides of each other. The North American side and the Latin American side. I'd never been with anyone who . . ."

"But what's her Latin American side? Did she become Latin American like you've become North American?"

"Well . . ."

"Tricky, right?"

"She's the first American I've met who's half as interested in my culture as I am in theirs. And among other things that means she gets it. What it's like to not be American. She offered to marry me just so I could stay in the States!"

"But do you really want to stay? After all they've put you through?"

"If Trump gets voted out . . ."

"Forget Trump. Why do you want to stay?"

"Because in America I can be my own person."

"I think you want to stay in America for the same reason you want to stay with Lee. You want to stop being a creole. You want to become white."

El dinamo y la virgen

From a failed essay on the messiah and the history of North America:

At the individual level, ideology manifests as education. López Obrador studied political science, but each time I listen to his speeches I discover intellectual mannerisms that remind me of the species of reader which a North American retiree who enjoys accounts of the Battle of Midway might call "a student of history." Where the scholar of history seeks to complicate our understanding of the past, the student of the subject has no patience for the splitting of hairs. He wants to understand the world, not obscure it further—hence his willingness to smooth over contradictions in service of an overarching interpretation.

Like Vasconcelos, López Obrador is a practitioner of what Nietzsche called "monumental history." His worldview is not the product of the unglamorous accounting of production, with its charts plotting caloric intake against fluency in Mayan languages; nor the ruthless criticism of ideology, with its demystification of the stories we tell ourselves in order to live; nor the mournful contemplation of the great human catastrophe, with its attendant hope that the debacles of the future might be avoided or at least lessened. Rather, López Obrador's history is an epic of struggle between good and evil, and like all epics, it is defined by transparency. Here everything is legible: the stakes of the contest (power and its trappings), the motivations of the characters (greed on one side, thirst for justice on the other), the realm of battle (the hearts of people), and even the prize of the victor (immortality as a wax figure in Sigüenza's theater of political virtues).

The corollary of this view of history is that doing harm unintentionally or with the best intentions becomes inconceivable. Which is why López Obrador seems incapable of thinking of public affairs as anything other than an extension of individual morality. Politics are for him not a matter of parties or ideologies—never mind classes, genders, sexualities, or castes—but a question of heroes and villains. These figures embody larger dynamics, but their embodiment is literal rather than allegorical. The logic is eucharistic: the hero is the transubstantiation of the people. Hence López Obrador's rather un-Marxist belief that his election, by itself, will transform the country. At the core of his epic there's a prophecy: when the good take power, the people will thrive.

The problem is that, on the morning of his election, Mexico will remain the country it was the night before.

Recordar la dicha en mala hora

The next day the migrant children set off walking in what they thought was the direction of the city. After some time, they saw a gallon of water beneath a thorn tree—but when they got there they saw that someone had slashed the jug. By the following morning the boy decided he'd had enough. He told his sister they should find the highway and surrender to the migra.

But what if they send us back? the girl said.

Then we try again, the boy said.

But we've come so far.

But we won't get much farther.

We can't give up.

The boy didn't reply. Suddenly he was angry. Of course she wanted to keep going. No wonder she was full of energy. Tan pinche talisthe. La pinche shuma cochina. She'd gotten to sleep. She didn't know what he'd gone through. Ishoka mimada. Malagradecida. Chance si no hubiera andado de coqueta. Chance si se hubiera dado a respetar.

Pos como quieras, said the boy. Allá tu.

He walked away. He didn't know where he was going. It didn't matter. As long as it was away from her. That was all he wanted. Never to see her again. Beyond that he didn't care. He'd always known but now he saw it real clear: La vida valía verga. That was la puta verdad. Pa' que decir que no si sí. But he didn't want to just sit and wait. Especially because that way maybe she'd find him. And then she'd cry his ear off. Y ni madres que le iba aguantar sus berrinches. Not now. He wanted silence. Besides, that way it'd be faster. All he had to do was keep walking. Straight into la pucha mugrienta de la chingada madre del mundo. But after a while the boy's anger subsided, and all at once he was sad. He found himself hoping it would come soon and happen quick. Because his feet hurt real bad and his head hurt real bad and his eyes and his guts and his eyes and his guts and his eyes and his eyes and his eyes hurt and they hurt bad real bad they hurt . . .

The boy heard footsteps. He turned around and saw his sister running toward him. Suddenly he didn't want to keep going. He sat down and waited for her. When the girl got closer, the boy realized she was crying. He stood up and went to meet her. She threw her arms around his neck and clung to him and whispered in his ear over and over that she was sorry. The boy stroked her hair and tried not to cry and said soothing words until she stopped sobbing. Then they got up and kept walking.

Para Henry Adams

From a failed essay on messiah and the history of North America:

At the collective level, education is nothing but ideology.
My view of history is less the product of my readings than

of the fact that I grew up around people who believed they had a duty to change the world. That they failed is no secret; that all but one or two had good intentions might be. And so a question arises for those who know from experience that it is possible to destroy the world in an attempt to improve it: Are these people heroes or villains? Or is the dichotomy too simple?

The question pertains not just to my father's generation of Mexican statesmen, but to all historical actors. Though political praxis is a cynic's game, most of its players believe, however misguidedly, that their goals are lofty. Nobody, not even the fascist, thinks they are on the wrong side of history. We all look good from our perspective, which proves difficult to escape except in retrospect. We know not what we do but only what we have done.

Perhaps this is why people of action are often unwilling or unable to develop a genuine historical consciousness: for the protagonists of the drama, the lessons of history are like those Oedipus learns at the end of the play—so devastating that the only possible reaction is to blind oneself to their horror. Perhaps this is also why children of historical actors are often paralyzed by ironic lucidity. When we look at the world, we see nothing but the ruins of our parents' good intentions.

History is not epic but tragic. It is, at best, the systematic organization of regrets.

El caballero de la fé

The children found the highway that same night. It'd been there all along, just behind the hills. They sat by the side of the road and waited until la migra showed up in a troca. The officers gave them water and peanut butter sandwiches and then they took them to las hieleras.

"And what was that like?" I said. "By the way, do you want dessert?"

"No, thank you," the boy said in English, then continued in Spanish: "But I should get home soon."

"Of course. We don't want to get you in trouble. But quickly, before we go, can you tell me about las hieleras?"

"Pa' que te miento. I don't really know. It was real cold, for sure. Every bit as cold as people say they are."

That was all he had to say about his time in detention. He and his sister managed to get in touch with their uncle right away, so Homeland Security let them go after only a few weeks. Besides, the boy slept through most of it. La migra had separated him from his sister—they had a hielera for boys and another for girls—but he wasn't scared, because la migra were awful, real awful, bien canijos los desgraciados, but at least they weren't like the cops back home or the cops in Mexico, the ones who'd say things about his sister, things that weren't altogether different from the things the boys with the guns and the tattoos used to say.

And so the boy slept, at last, for hours and hours, waking up only to eat and use the bathroom, and even though the hieleras were as cold as everyone said they were, and even though la migra kept the lights on the whole time, and even though he didn't know whether the Americans would let them go or send them back to their deaths, he felt that he didn't have to worry about his sister. At least not there. At least not for a few nights.

Para José

I got a text from Arnaut. He was in town for a minute and heard I was too, and he wanted to see me. I considered making up some excuse but decided against it. I thought of suggesting breakfast, reasoning that way he was more likely to be sober, but then I realized that if I wanted to see my friend, as opposed to a hungover shadow, I had to go drinking with him. And so I told him to meet me later that afternoon at El Centenario.

When I arrived he was already there, clean shaven and tanned, giving off an air of health I hadn't expected. He got up to greet me and gave me a bear hug. We sat down across from each other and didn't speak for a while.

"You look good," I finally said.

"Thanks. It's the air of the outback. You can actually breathe."

"So how's it been?"

"Great. I live in a three-hundred-person town. Work as a barkeep at the only pub for many miles. Spend all day talking to cowboys and country lasses, then go home to my little bungalow and smoke a bowl and sleep like a baby. Every so often I help my landlady herd her cattle. It'd been years since I'd gotten on a horse, but turns out you never forget."

"That sounds perfect for you."

"It helps that I met someone."

"Amazing! What's his name?"

"She's a girl, actually. Sarah. She's from Melbourne but came to the outback to take over an organic ranch. Wants me to move there permanently. Says we could run the joint together. Make cheese."

The head waiter came to the table and asked what I wanted to drink.

"Mezcal, please, Cuatrocientos Conejos—no, wait." I turned to Arnaut. "Wanna do some shots of Jameson? For old time's sake?"

"I'm fine with Topo Chico."

"Really?"

"Yup."

"In that case mezcal is fine."

The waiter nodded and walked away.

"That's the other piece of news," Arnaut said. "I quit."

"Don't you work at a bar?"

"I do. But a year or so ago I just stopped. It wasn't planned. I didn't go to AA or anything, and I didn't think it was going to last. But a week went by, then a month, and I felt so much better. So I decided to go along with it. I'm not sure if it's forever. But I'm in no rush to start again."

The waiter came back with our drinks. Arnaut squeezed a lime into his seltzer and took a long sip through the straw.

"The other day I was thinking about the games we used to play when we first became friends," he said. "Last year of preschool. When recess lasted forever. Know what I'm talking about?"

"Vaguely?"

"We used to pretend we were on the Oregon Trail. We'd sneak past the teachers and go all the way to the high school cafeteria, then make our way back on wagons, shooting at bison, rescuing one another from ravines, making friends with the Indians and helping them fight against the evil Mexicans. In retrospect it's kinda sinister. Why the hell were we pretending to be gringos? All the same, I've never been happier."

I drank my mezcal in one go. "Me neither."

"¿Y tú?"

"Not great. My girl and I got into a fight that brought out the worst in me. And it looks like I won't be able to stay in the States."

"I meant with booze. How's that going for you?"

"Oh, that? Fine, I guess? I drink plenty at Iowa. Not much else to do. Same when I'm here—people drink so much here, don't you think? And this summer in New Haven I've been drinking a lot, too, with all that has been going down with Lee, so I suppose you could maybe say that I—"

"Te entiendo. A veces hace falta. But can I speak from pioneer to pioneer?"

"Always."

"Some time ago a good friend told me I had a problem. Least I can do is return the favor."

I glared at him and hoped the stare reminded him of each and every time I'd had to rush him to the ER or bail him out of jail or turn him on his side so he wouldn't choke on his own tongue. He'd never once had to do such things for me—and yet there he was, with the gall to suggest that I was no better than him, that I hadn't escaped predestination, that I'd wound up becoming exactly what the childhood we'd shared augured for us both, a type so common and predictable that it was less cliché than pleonasm: a Wealthy Mexican Drunk.

"You mean I should quit?"

I waited for him to reply, the seconds growing slower the longer our silence lasted, but he just held my stare with an expression that wasn't so much a smile as the ghost of a smile, an almost-saintly quietude that I at first mistook for the unseemly self-righteousness of recovery, but which I gradually realized was the product of the kind of suspension of judgment known only to those who understand that they, too, are in need of forgiveness.

"I don't know," he finally said. "And even if I did, I'd never tell you what to do." He looked at his watch and got up from the table. "I'm sorry. I've got an appointment at the Australian embassy. You know how that goes."

I walked with him to the door and onto the street. He put his hands on my shoulders. "It was great to see you, Sebas. Take care of my friend, will you? The Oregon Trail is treacherous."

For a moment his ghost-smile came back to life, in a way that reminded me of the ironic compassion of the cantina's minor deities. Then he planted a kiss on my cheek, turned the corner, and disappeared.

The afternoon before the election we went to a party. The aesthetics of the event were pure neoliberal baroque: a terrace overlooking Polanco, a long table under a white canvas tent, burgers from a place called Butcher & Sons, a soundtrack of incongruous hip-hop, vape pens filled with organic cannabis smuggled in direct flights from Colorado, and all the alcohol in the world. The guests fell into two categories: Mexican professionals who looked like they'd come straight from Sunday Mass and American expatriates who favored patched leather and facial piercings. I knew virtually no one and felt no desire to change that, so I sat alone at the empty end of the table, sucking on lime wedges and building castles out of cocktail straws.

The afternoon dragged on. Everyone got drunk. I got anxious. Eventually the Bear got up from the end of the table where the guests had congregated and headed to the bathroom. "Hey, Velázquez," I said, grabbing his arm. "Any chance we're leaving soon?"

"To go where?"

"El Centenario?"

The Bear shook his head. "The city's dry today, man. And tomorrow too. Because of the election. You can't buy booze anywhere." He pried my fingers from his arm, patted me on the back, and went on his way.

I picked up another lime wedge, dredged it through the canyon of salt I'd poured on my plate, bit into it, and felt the burn on the ulcers that had formed on the parts of my cheeks I couldn't stop chewing. No wonder the lunch had run so late. No wonder there was so much liquor. No wonder the party was on a terrace several stories above the ground. We were latter-day Antonies and Cleopatras, celebrating one last bacchanal before the firing squads and the cyanide pills. I felt a wave of hatred for the Mexican guests. They were the lords and ladies of the Very Noble and Loyal City of Mexico, the inheritors of a tradition in which even cruelty had been subject to refinement, baroque monsters who'd been given free rein to plumb the heights and depths of human possibility—and yet they were banal. In that moment I would have forgiven them all if just one had shown a spark of intelligence or sensibility.

I looked at the clock on my phone. In less than twenty-four hours our fate would be sealed. I'd decided to take a break from drinking after my meeting with Arnaut, but in that moment I couldn't stand to be sober. I got up and headed to the bar but the daily storm began before I could make it out of the tent. I laughed at the god in the machine's lack of imagination and returned to my seat. For some time the party went on as if nothing was happening, but as the afternoon faded into evening the rain grew more intense. Soon all semblance of festivity was gone. The roar of the storm drowned out the music. The gutters overflowed. The waiters struggled to take apart the portable kitchen and bring the liquor indoors. A stream of rainwater fell down the sides of the tent and rushed across the tiled floor beneath our feet. The canvas walls began to flap in the wind like the sails of a ship in a hurricane.

I smiled and reached for another lime wedge, but I had sucked them all dry, so instead I took a straw from my ill-fated castle and chewed on it as if on a wisp of wheat. I sank into my chair, feeling my shoes soak, determined to enjoy the spectacle of destruction— but then one of the Americans sat next to me.

"Crazy, huh?" he said.

"Truly," I said, making a point of not looking at him.

The American and I had gone to college together but weren't friends. In fact I found him intolerable. He'd lived some of his formative years in Spain, but nothing about him was Iberian. On the contrary, he was as American as they got, and in all the worst ways, not least of which was his insistence that, since he'd been born in Mexico when his missionary parents were evangelizing the natives, he was qualified to pontificate on all subjects related to the country, particularly the theory and praxis of Zapatismo, which he claimed to have learned on a service trip to Chiapas during spring break his freshman year, and about which he was capable of speaking for hours on end, in the halting, inarticulate cadence of full-time stoners who also happen to be pedants.

I looked forward to never seeing him again after graduation, but the white Zapatista was bent on haunting me. Finding himself without passion or ambition, he moved to Mexico City, where to my distress he now ran a successful business that offered SAT tutoring to the children of the Austro-Hungarians. The racket was suspiciously profitable, in good part because it was actually a racket. Liberated from the ideological yoke of the bourgeoisie by teachings of Subcomandante Marcos, the revo-missionary saw no need to abide by the illegitimate laws of a neoliberal state, which in practice meant he declined to pay taxes. This indiscretion was grating for a number of reasons, not least of which was that he quoted his fees in dollars but paid his Mexican employees in pesos.

"Guess we'll be stuck here for a second," said the anarchocommunist entrepreneur as he lit a cigarette.

"Just like in *The Exterminating Angel*."

"The what?" he yelled.

"It's a movie. They end up killing the lambs."

There was a lull in the wind. The rain slackened enough that conversations again became audible. One of the Mexican guests peered out of the tent.

"Looks like it's over!" she said.

"About time," I said, getting up from my chair.

"Leaving so early?" the American said.

"What can I tell you."

The American looked around to make sure there was no one in earshot and then leaned closer to me. "Are you going somewhere else?" he whispered. "It's not like there're a ton of options, but if you know of anything better, you gotta tell me, hermano, because these fresas are way too bougie for me."

I turned to face the American and was about to tell him, in the most polite tone I could muster, that he was not my brother, that I didn't know of any parties anywhere in the Valley of Anáhuac, and that nothing would make me happier than if he threw himself off the balcony—but the rain returned. The ceiling of the tent bulged with the weight of water. It looked like it was about to collapse.

"Hoy shit!" the American said. "The world's ending out there!"

I got up without a word and walked to the entrance of the tent and pushed the flap door open. The terrace was buried in hail. The trees bent close to their breaking point. The sky was green with electricity. Surely some revelation was at hand.

Para Luis Miguel

I paid the bill and called a cab and the boy with spiked hair and I walked out of the restaurant. On the way to his uncle's house, he told me about his god. He'd joined an Evangelical church a few months before he left Guatemala, he said, because he liked the singing and they let him play the drum kit after the service was over. On the Sunday before he set out for North America, the pastor gave him a Bible to take on the journey. The boy kept it with him against all odds, even after the kid with the rag soaked in paint thinner told them to leave everything behind.

"I've been trying to learn it," he said as the car pulled over in front of a large Victorian house that once belonged to a bourgeois marriage, but which now housed several families of Indigenous

Guatemalans, all of whom woke up before dawn and went to bed after midnight and spent the hours in between doing thankless work for significantly less money than the US government considered necessary to live with a semblance of dignity.

"Learn it? By heart?"

He closed the door and leaned to look at me through the window. "Yeah. I want to have it with me always. Even if they take it away."

"Do you have a favorite verse?" I knew that whatever he said would be a good kicker for my article.

"A huevo. Psalm ninety-one."

"Remind me how it goes?"

He laughed and shook his head and lowered his gaze and looked up and fixed his eyes on mine. And then he said, with more conviction than I've ever said anything:

YOU WILL NOT FEAR THE TERROR OF THE NIGHT
NOR THE ARROW THAT FLIES BY DAY
NOR THE PESTILENCE THAT STALKS IN THE DARKNESS
NOR THE PLAGUE THAT DESTROYS AT MIDDAY.

And as he recited, his face took an expression that stayed in my memory. It was peaceful but not at peace, as far from contentment as from reconciliation, and it bore no resemblance to happiness. Its central component was a great weariness in the eyes, a slight drooping of the lids that I later decided was the exhaustion of telling—an echo of the exhaustion of living. But there was something else too: a faint smile, all but imperceptible, which seemed to brush against the edges of hope, and a certain softness in the brow, an unexpected lack of tension that gestured toward an optimism deeper, and therefore quieter, than those of the intellect and the will.

It was a paradoxical face: the expression of someone who remained enough of a child to retain a capacity for earnestness but had nevertheless lived years dense with experience. At sixteen the boy with spiked hair knew sorrows deeper and more varied than most people could fathom. Along the way he'd acquired a visceral understanding of one of the central truths of the human condition: that the gap between the eighth and the ninth circles of hell is wider than the distance between the sixth and the seventh heaven; that the difference between hell and purgatory is infinite; or, to put it in terms so simple that they risk reducing mysticism to banality, that suffering is relative.

This knowledge, I realized even then, was of the most difficult sort. In theory anyone could understand it, but to grasp it fully, as embodied idea rather than abstract axiom, required the harshest and most exacting education. And yet in that moment the face of that teenager suggested that with the difficulty of the knowledge there also came a great consolation: the ability to find something like peace in circumstances that would break other spirits. As the boy with spiked hair turned around and ran across the yard of his uncle's house, I thought that, while there was no home in this world for migrants, there were nevertheless waystations where time slowed down to allow for a moment of respite.

La noche de los cometas

When the hail stopped, we headed back to my parents' house. My sister had friends over, but they were on the roof garden, so we sat in the living room unbothered. Esteban and the Bear found a bottle of bourbon my father refused to drink and poured themselves large drams over ice they'd foraged from the patio.

"The mezcal craze? Nonsense!" Esteban said as he stirred a slurry of brown sugar and half-frozen acid rain. "The rich kids running around, ranting about espadín and tobalá and whatnot are lying to themselves. That stuff is moonshine, village firewater, the drink of toothless old men from the south. Tequila is slightly less objectionable, I suppose, but it's still a provincial concoction, the elixir of barbaric landowners—hard men of horse and rifle, the sort who have killed for love and don't hesitate before whipping the peons. No, as it happens with every colonial elite around the world, the national drink of the creoles is whiskey. Scotch for the older generation, bourbon for the young." He turned to Lee. "Do you know what Faulkner said about bourbon, Lee?"

Lee rolled her eyes. "No, Esteban, I don't know what Faulkner said about bourbon. Would you please tell me what Faulkner said about bourbon?"

"What Faulkner said about bourbon is that the only surefire way to tell a true Southern gentleman from a Yankee impostor is that the latter will drink his whiskey raw, with neither sugar nor water."

"You know you are a parody of yourself, right?"

"Maybe. But I've read Faulkner in English. And Fitzgerald, too, all of it, except a few letters. So I guess I'm a parody of globalism. And between grief and Bannon, I'll take—"

"Are they dancing upstairs?" the Bear interrupted.

"I think so?"

"Over the hail?"

"Maybe they swept it?"

"I'm going to investigate."

He got up from his chair with only the slightest of difficulties, walked to the stairs in an almost straight line, and climbed them without falling once.

Esteban turned to me. "Did Fitzgerald drink bourbon?"

"I'm not sure. Probably?"

"I've always thought of him as a gin man. Slick, silvery, maybe a bit too floral for his own good."

"They made it in bathtubs," Lee said. "During prohibition."

"We've got to get in that racket!" Esteban said. "Before it's too late. If he wins, there's no telling what he'll do, and if they steal it from him, I wouldn't be surprised if they kept the town dry indefinitely to control the people. Either way, it's a sound investment."

I closed my eyes and exhaled. I enjoyed the company of my friends, except when they were mean to my girlfriend—not to mention that they were increasingly plastered and I was stone-cold sober. Besides, Esteban was right. There was no telling what would happen if the Austro-Hungarians stole the election. At best there would be weeks of violent chaos; at worst, the country's simmering conflicts would explode into a full-blown civil war. Both scenarios were so catastrophic only an idiot would mess with the results, but the Mexican elite had many idiots.

"Where did the Bear go?" Esteban asked after a while.

"He's upstairs," Lee said.

"Still? It's been, like, hours." He turned to face me. "Can you call him?"

I took out my phone and dialed the Bear's number. His archaic Nokia buzzed on the coffee table.

"Guess he's out there without a net," Esteban said. "Brave man, that Bear."

"Someone should go find him," I said. "He was pretty drunk."

"I'll go," Esteban said. He got up and finished his glass. "If I don't come back, tell my mother I loved her."

He walked up the stairs and disappeared.

Lee sat down at the piano and played a few Bach preludes. An hour passed. I grew worried.

"Something's up."

"Like what?"

"I don't know. Something."

Then we heard a noise in the foyer, as if someone were shaking the gate.

Lee laughed. "Well! How's that for apropos?"

We heard the noise again. I got up from the couch and motioned her to follow me. I walked to the kitchen, grabbed two knives, and offered one to Lee.

"You're joking," she said as she put the knife in the sink.

I raised a finger to my lips and realized my hands were shaking. I took off my shoes to minimize the noise and walked to the foyer to find one of my sister's friends was trying to open the door.

"¡No mames!" she said when she saw me. "¡Casi me matas!"

I looked down at the knife in my hand, a giant Chinese-style cleaver that had struck me as the most weapon-like in the drawer—and felt ridiculous.

"Everything all right?" I said.

"Yeah. I just can't open the door."

"There's a switch." I walked past her and pressed the button, but nothing happened. I pressed again—it still didn't work. I knelt in front of the door and saw the cables connecting the lock to the mechanism had been torn.

"This is bad," I said.

"What's wrong?" Lee said.

"There's someone in here."

"Sebas . . ."

"Someone cut the cables."

"I know but . . ."

I grabbed the knife, ran upstairs, and knocked on my parents' door. "What is it?" my father said, still half-asleep.

"Someone disabled the lock on the front door!"

I heard my mother jerk awake in the darkened bedroom. "What did you say?"

"Calm down," my father said as he put on a robe. "Let me take a look."

"I'm going to check upstairs."

"A knife? Those motherfuckers carry Kalashnikovs!"

I climbed the stairs to the roof garden and found a small group of people dancing cumbia. I walked up to the Bear, took him by the arm, and motioned to Esteban to follow me downstairs.

"Watch the machete, wey!" the Bear said. "¡Me vas a rebanar, chingao!"

I pushed him against the wall and shook him by the shoulder, precariously holding the cleaver against his chest. "There're intruders in the house!"

Esteban laughed. "Zombies or aliens, what's your guess?"

I looked at him with venomous eyes and headed downstairs. By the time I got to the foyer a small crowd had assembled in front of the gate. My father was kneeling before the lock, holding a roll of electrical tape. "Should hold up until Tuesday."

As it turned out it held a little over a year. A few months after the end of the world, an opinion columnist at a widely read Mexico City newspaper published a piece that cited anonymous sources to report that the governments of both the United States and the United Kingdom had flagged a series of suspicious international transfers between my father's bank accounts. The story was false—neither country had flagged anything, perhaps because the sums the columnist had deceivingly quoted in dollars and pounds were in fact denominated in pesos and therefore worth substantially less than he'd suggested—but López Obrador's anticorruption watchdog opened an investigation nonetheless. That the case had no merit—it was obvious that the administration had planted the story—was immaterial: a charge would have been enough to jail my father for the duration of his trial, which by Mexican standards could stretch for several years.

After a few horrible weeks when the L'Affair Arteaga y Salazar consumed the attention of the entirety of the Mexican press corps, the president sent an emissary: If my father resigned from the court, the government would close the investigation; if he didn't, the ruling party's legislators would begin the process to remove him from office and imprison him. At first my father resisted, but as the days passed, he came to see that, even if he survived his impeachment trial, he wouldn't be able to remain on the court. The judiciary's legitimacy depended on the reputation of its officers, and by that point almost everyone in the country was convinced he was corrupt.

And so, on October 8, 2019, eleven months after I moved back to Mexico, my father resigned in disgrace. Two years later, having amassed thousands of pages of files but no evidence of wrongdoing, the attorney general closed the investigation and declared him exonerated. It didn't matter: nobody believed in his innocence. His role in the drug war had earned him the hatred of most Mexicans long before the scandal. Many were inclined to believe he was not only wrong but also evil.

My father's resignation afforded López Obrador the chance to nominate his replacement—a yes-sayer who was later found to have plagiarized both her JD and PhD theses. The rest of the justices, terrified that they might suffer the same fate as my father, fell into line. This soft constitutional coup allowed the president to control all three branches of government. López Obrador made good use of that power by building a brand-new oil refinery, detaining thousands of Central American refugees before they could claim asylum in the United States, and doubling down on my father's generation's worst mistake: empowering the army to fight the drug cartels.

Ni olvido ni perdón

Such was the face I saw as I stared at the broken clock on the wall of the secondary screening room, waiting to be told whether I'd be allowed back into the country where I'd built my life. Suddenly my predicament felt small, so small that I felt ashamed of ever having felt scared or hurt or angry. But then a disquieting thought broke forth from the back of my mind. That face, the emotion it expressed, the ethics it represented, could only exist because the boy with spiked hair knew or believed or hoped that nothing had happened to his sister during the nights they'd spent in the custody of the Department of Homeland Security.

I sank into the thought as into a pool of oil-slicked seawater. All of a sudden in place of the boy with spiked hair I saw hundreds of faces, some of which I recognized from the photographs that accompanied the earliest press reports on the concentration camps: children, multitudes of them, some too young to walk, others old enough to understand what was happening, torn from their parents, kept in cages, confined for months to makeshift cities where every room was windowless like the room where I sat, neglected, treated like cattle, injected with antipsychotics, expected to follow orders and sign papers in a language they didn't understand, lied to, misfed, kept away from fresh air, from joy, from beauty, from the petty miseries that are the daily bread of lives that have not been destroyed by imperialism—the ordinary unhappiness, the vague dissatisfaction, the boring, benign, intolerable anxiety that is the privilege of white people.

Told to BREAK THE SILENCE.

Told to REPORT CONFIDENTIALLY.

Told to GET HELP.

Told to KEEP DETENTION SAFE.

I saw their faces and the faces of their parents, their uncles and aunts, their siblings, their cousins, their friends, the lovers some of them would have, the children some of them would have, the multitudes who had been touched and would be touched by the horror of that crime; and the sight made me furious, because along with the faces, I saw with perfect clarity that none of it was preordained, that none of it was necessary, that the destruction of all those lives had been the product of a choice, a conscious one, made by a handful of hateful people empowered by a hateful nation and carried out by an army of uniformed nobodies who had credit card bills to pay.

The knowledge that those responsible knew not what they did offered no consolation. If anything, it made the crime more painful to contemplate, because it made it absurd. The world teetered on a narrow perch between redeemable and irredeemable tragedy. The stakes were nothing less than life's worth; every new horror risked plunging humanity into a desert with no waystations at all.

La jaula de la melancolía

My thesis committee wanted to see a draft before I returned to school, so the morning of the election I sat at my father's desk and tried to cobble together a coherent whole out of the failed essays I'd written over the past two years, imitating the logic of Esteban's documentary about time. After a few hours I realized it was in vain. And so I wrote to my teacher:

> *Dear Irina,*
>
> *I write to you in dire straits. My project is a failure. The questions about capital, the baroque, and the relationship between politics and literature; the meditations on the identity of the creoles; the phenomenology of the cantina; the correspondence*

from the drug war; the stories of my father and mother; and now this whole other thing about messianism and the presidential election in Mexico and the tragic nature of history—I'm convinced that all these threads are related; that if I took out any of them, the meaning I want to convey would vanish. The problem is this relation is apparent only to me. I worry I'm going to fail my thesis defense.

But I'd be dishonest if I didn't also say this feels like a fitting end. How could a book about Mexico be anything other than a failure? Our heroes are all losers: Cuauhtémoc, the last ruler of a condemned empire; Hidalgo, the leader of an unsuccessful insurrection; Zapata, the revolutionary murdered by his allies. And don't get me started on the immediate past! NAFTA was a failure. The drug war was a failure. The transition to democracy was a failure, as was my mother's cancer treatment. And if the Left wins the election, it will probably fail as well—though part of me wants to hope otherwise, even if my family must pay.

I don't know, Irina. I guess I'm discovering more and more that I'm in fact Mexican, that my attempts at assimilation were failures too. I come from a place that has always lost, and that therefore has cultivated the art of losing, of finding beauty in failure. America, by contrast, is a country of winners, or, more accurately, of optimists. Let me put it this way: had I written an American book, the protagonist would become a US citizen in the end.

Yours,
Sebastián

Para Carol Jacobs

From a failed essay on the messiah and the history of North America:

The story is told of a traveling magician who, through no ill-doing, incurred the wrath of a cruel and powerful sovereign. Exiled from the land of his birth, he wandered the capitals of the continent, performing on the street corners of the commercial districts and in the hashish dens of the harbors. He acquired a small but devoted group of admirers who were entranced by his manifold tricks: the old toys that came alive, the chess-playing golem that could defeat the greatest master, the ball that danced along as he played the flute.

But even the most enthusiastic members of the magician's audience were puzzled by his closing number. He would produce a small golden ring and hang it from a rafter or a streetlamp, then take a handful of pearls from one of his ragged coat's many pockets and juggle them as if they were marbles. After the beauty of the floating jewels left the spectators breathless, he would let all but one of the pearls fall into his pocket and catch the last one with his left hand. Then, with a single graceful motion, he'd throw the pearl toward the ring, hoping it would go through the narrow center of the band. The pearl, however, always missed the mark. The rest of the show was so dazzling the audience forgave the failure of the last act. But even as they clapped and cheered, the magician hung his head in melancholy.

One night, when the magician seemed particularly dejected, a young theologian who'd seen him perform several times sat next to him and asked why he insisted on attempting the trick, since it was clear that it was impossible.

"It's not impossible," the magician said. "It's merely unlikely."

"Still, if it makes you so miserable, why keep trying?"

The magician raised his head and looked the theologian in the eye. "Because the happiness of throwing the pearl *through the ring just once would be greater than the sorrow of failing a thousand times."*

In the years that followed, the magician and the theologian became friends. They struck up a correspondence, writing to each other about the esoteric problems that were the common ground of their professions. Then a great war broke out and the armies of the cruel sovereign marched into the city where the magician had made his home. He prepared to escape, but not before mailing one last letter to his friend.

"The times are sorrowful," he wrote, "but I am filled with joy. I have discovered the secret of the pearl and the ring. I must leave soon, so there's no time to explain, but I have set it all down on a small sheet of paper, which I have tucked in the pages of the Talmud that I always carry in my briefcase. If anything were to happen to me, you must make every effort to find it. The message is written in code, but I trust you will be able to decipher it. When you do, you must convey it to the world. For the secret that has been revealed to me is no mere magic trick."

The magician made it to the border of a neighboring country but by then all gates were closed. He chose to take his own life rather than surrender his dignity, but before taking the morphine he hid his briefcase in the desert near the border river. Nobody knows whether the theologian was able to find it, let alone decipher the message.

Viaticum

Many months later, after the end of the world, I lay down next to my mother and told her I was heartbroken she would never read my novel.

"Part of it is about you," I said. "How marriage constrained your life. I'm not sure I did you justice."

"That sounds like nonfiction. It's true. I was angry for a long time. But some years ago, I realized it was my choice. All of it. I would have loved to do more, of course—professionally, academically. But when I look at you and your siblings, I feel satisfied. If you were books, you'd be an extraordinary trilogy."

She had resolved to bring her time to a proper close, according to the customs of her people: at home, with the help of a priest, and only after taking her leave. Day after day she received a procession of friends, classmates, colleagues, cousins, neighbors, nemeses, ex-boyfriends. They came in the late morning or the early afternoon—the brief window when her transdermal fentanyl patches had released enough of the drug to make conversation bearable but not enough to make her drowsy—and sat by her bed to take tea and laugh and make amends. Each visit took a toll: she mustered all her energy to play her old role of impeccable hostess, only to collapse in exhaustion the moment her guests left.

She saved her brothers and sister for the end, in part because after her children and husband they were the most important people in her life, but also because she was deteriorating rapidly, and her vanity or her dignity demanded that only close family see her in that state. They came one by one and stayed for longer than the others—all save one, her youngest brother, who made several appointments to see her and then cancelled at the last minute. She was hurt but not for long. The handbook for a good death she'd inherited from her mother taught that forgiveness is the greatest gift the dying can bequeath the living.

Then my father walked into the room. He'd been at her side ever since her doctors concluded her case was hopeless, and she'd accepted his care. "I spoke to Fernando," he said. "He can come tonight."

"That would be perfect," my mother replied.

Later that evening I opened the front door to a balding man

dressed like a folk singer and carrying a doctor's briefcase. "Good evening, Father," I said, bowing my head.

I took his hand to kiss it but instead he gave me a warm handshake. "You must be Sebastián. I'm Fernando."

I resisted the impulse to roll my eyes. I'd always been suspicious of priests who tried to seem modern and accessible. "This way," I said, wondering if he had an Instagram account.

The priest stepped into the house and paused before the crucifix on the wall. He closed his eyes and stood in silence for a moment.

"Can I offer you coffee, Father?"

"Water would be great. But stop calling me Father. Fernando is fine."

I went to fetch his water, then took him upstairs to my mother's bedroom.

"Would you like the sacrament of reconciliation, Laura?" the priest said. My mother nodded. He turned to me and went on: "Give us a minute?"

I stepped out of the room, sat down on the couch, and tried to remember the last time I'd gone to confession. My mother's doctors had discussed with her the possibility of sedating her when her suffering became unbearable, and I worried the priest would try to convince her to refuse care that sounded a little like euthanasia.

"Is he here already?" my father said as he appeared at the top of the stairs with my brother and sister in tow.

"He's taking her confession."

"Good."

"Are you sure this is a good idea? He gives me the wrong vibe. Too friendly. Those are the sneaky ones."

"What do you mean?"

"He insists I shouldn't call him Father."

"That's because he's a Dominican friar. A brother."

"Oh, great, just what we needed, the Hounds of the Lord!"

Then Fernando opened the door. "Ready when you are. I just need to change."

My father, my siblings, and I followed him into the bedroom. My mother was sitting up in bed, looking beatific: at once in pain and at peace.

"How was it?" my sister asked.

"Wonderful."

The friar opened his briefcase and took out a book, a bottle of oil, and a silver box, then stepped into the bathroom. I walked to my mother's side and knelt to be at her height. She brushed the hair from my face. "Mamá," I said. "I know your faith has been a source of strength, but I'm worried Father—sorry, *Brother* Fernando might try to convince you not to accept palliative . . ."

She dismissed the thought with a wave of her hand and was about to speak when I heard the bathroom door close. Brother Fernando had returned transfigured, wearing the black habit of his order, a lit candle in his hand. "Would you turn off the lights, please?"

My sister did as he said—and all of a sudden we were in another century. The flickering light, the bleeding crucifix, the kind man in coarse black wool: it was all so Mexican, so creole.

"Laura, sister," the friar began. "You called me here tonight. Why?"

My mother took a deep breath and replied: "Because I know the day is near."

The friar nodded and invited us to gather and lay our hands on her and pray for the intercession of the Virgen de Guadalupe, and as I recited the familiar words, I realized I was participating in a ritual that belonged to me as a birthright, which is another way of saying that I belonged to it even if I refused it. But I didn't want to refuse it—not then. I reached out and touched my mother's shrinking body and prayed to the dark-skinned Virgin as if she were real; because in that moment, on that night, I wanted to help my mother reconcile with death, which is another way of saying I wanted to help her reconcile with life, with the life she'd led, the life she'd chosen retrospectively, in a gesture of such existential courage that I began to wonder whether that was the meaning of faith.

After we finished the Ave María, the friar anointed my mother with the oil of the blessed. He then took a wafer from the sacrarium and held it before her and said: "For the journey."

Part VIII

Mexico City/
San Francisco

July 2018

In which Your Correspondent considers the comets.

Canta y no llores

In the Year of the Comets—so called because during its antic course certain inexplicable events exposed the fraudulent astrology of the methods for the anticipation of the future, on which I, and many of my generation, had been encouraged to rely, while we assessed the advantages and risks of the various paths that opened before us, as the measurable result of the interplay between the spirit of the times and the cards we had been dealt (by which we, or perhaps just I, meant our gender and our race, our class and caste, our family's past, the letters of our name, our place and date of birth, the relative location of the stars at such and such time, and all the ruling signs that set the course of mortal life), which cards, in my case, amounted to the best and most auspicious hand dealt to any child born in Mexico at the dawn of the end of the last century, in a different world and twenty-seven years before that moment, on that night, the first of July, which month, in the Valley of Anáhuac, is always the season of storms, but also, from time to time, the season of portents and elections—when I, having been tasked, in my capacity as Your Imperial Mercy's Most Foreign Correspondent, with producing a true and veridical account of some of the curious events which in those days were transpiring in my country, walked out of my father's house, where there was sorrow in the air, and headed to the center of the city, in the course of which advance I was surprised to find the streets so empty and quiet that I began to worry something was amiss, which impression only grew after I reached an intersection and waited for the light and looked up and saw the Virgin on a billboard, and next to her, in bold, illuminated letters designed to be seen from afar, the legend *Pray for the Motherland*, but as I kept advancing I came to see that, on the night of an election when the left-wing opposition has defeated a regime of melancholic oligarchs, silence was no omen of disaster but the sound of power changing hands without a single shot, the spacious echo of the clash between the future and the past in which the present is destroyed, and as I left La Roma and stepped onto La Juárez I began to see people in increasing numbers, and by the time I marched onto Reforma I was surrounded by a crowd carrying drums and vuvuzelas, chanting soccer cheers and slanted rhymes, and joking and laughing as if they were going to the fair or as if the lottery tickets that they bought year after year on the birthdays of their mothers had all been drawn at once and made them eligible for a sum not large enough to change their lives but good enough to brighten this moment on this night, and as these thoughts coursed through my head I saw a group of middle-aged queer folk—some dressed in drag, others very formally, many trying their best to pass unnoticed—walking leisurely downtown, and I decided to join them as they marched under the palms, past grand hotels and statues of missionaries and revolutionaries, some of which still bore traces of the bloodred paint with which someone had tagged them with the number *forty-three* during the protests that followed the Night of Iguala (I happened to be in town for one of them, and since my friends were going I went as well, and I remember marching under the brown fog of a winter dawn amid contingents of students in tight jeans and thick-rimmed glasses who carried Mexican flags on which the green of hope and the red of blood had been replaced with mourning black, and militant campesinos, men and women of all ages with dark skin made darker by high noon, their faces tense with a cold and silent rage, their right hands raised in a fist, and in each fist the terrifying incandescence of a machete in the sun, and I remember the line of Federal Police in riot gear, which in the

Mexico of those years meant tear-gas cannons, helmets with mirrored visors, body armor, billy clubs, and tall and narrow shields that made me think of Roman legionaries as they are sometimes depicted in the crucifixion scenes that penitent house painters probably still paint on the walls of certain churches in certain corners of the city, and all at once I was again in Baltimore, on the uprising's second night, wearing a press pass and a gas mask and clutching a notebook and chewing old gum next to the ruins that still smoldered under the blue and red lights of the state, and again I was surrounded by a crowd of young Black folk who raised their palms as if to pray and called *Hands up!* and answered *Don't shoot!* while an older white man stood on a crate nearby, preaching the end of the world—*Some of you will die tonight!*—in a hoarse and bitter voice, and again I felt the breeze of the helicopters flying low and tracing methodical orbits with their searchlights as a ranking officer of the Baltimore Police stood on an armored truck like a draft-dodging president stands on a tank, behind a phalanx of riot cops who carried those same legionaries' shields, yelling orders through a loudspeaker—*The curfew begins in ten minutes! Everyone has to leave!*—and again the hour struck, and again everyone was quiet, and again the cops began to beat their shields with their batons, keeping a slow and steady rhythm, and again someone threw a plastic bottle, still half-filled with Coke, which landed on a shield with an underwhelming thud and bounced and rolled back to the center of the street, where it came to rest halfway between the people and the state, and again I saw the first bomb burst like a portent in the air, or like the rocket's red glare over the darkened rampant of the fort that stood five miles away and a million years in the past, and again there was smoke and coughing and the sound of rushing footsteps and the thud of rubber bullets and a stinging in the eyes that lasted until morning, which felt like a long time but which nonetheless felt shorter than the minute when I stood before the people who had guarded me as a child and I felt the chill of terror in the bottom of my spine, because who was to say they wouldn't open fire on the men and women with machetes, or on the black-clad college students holding Coke bottles, which in Mexico are made of glass, filled with a liquid that looked a lot like gasoline, but instead the city fell so silent that in the distance I could hear the mournful dissonances of the street organs, and it was then, all of a sudden, all at once, that thousands of people began to count—*¡UNO! ¡DOS! ¡TRES!*—slowly, very slowly—*¡CUATRO! ¡CINCO! ¡SEIS!*—and then kept counting and counting, for a very long time, until they reached the number of the dead, and when the crowd had finished counting, a new chant began—*¡JUSTICIA! ¡Y CASTIGO A LOS CULPABLES!*—and once again I shivered, because I understood too well that when they said the culpable, they meant the state, which is to say the elite, which is to say my father, which is to say me) but then we reached the Alameda and waited for history to start, until at last the screens that the victorious campaign had set up in the park cut to a panoramic shot of a lectern in a ballroom, and then the leader stepped on stage, and then the crowd went hoarse, and then López Obrador waved and waited, like a father waits, until the cheers died out, and then the microphone captured the sound of the last breath before the plunge, and then he began to speak—*Today is a historic day! Today we begin the Fourth Transformation!*—and as I listened with attention I had the distinct impression I heard the voice of Vasconcelos, but as I turned to leave a group of young musicians passed me—two violins and a trumpet and a tuba and an accordion and a guitar and a drum—and in that very instant, as if the universe had folded on itself, according to a symmetry that I, at least, associate only with geometry and with dreams, began to play a simple waltz, and before long the crowd became a chorus hoarse from cheering, composed of fatalistic people who had put aside their fatalism in that moment,

on that night, to sing, without irony, a song about singing without
irony:

From the Sierra

M.O.R.E.N.A.

My little darling

They come

Descending

Two little

Night-

black eyes

My little darling

A smuggled present

¡AY!

¡AY!

¡AY!

¡AY!

¡SING AND DON'T CRY!

For bitter hearts

Grow less bitter

My little darling

When they go singing

and then I looked up and saw the cathedral and the palace and
the empty space above the still-smoldering ruins of the temples
of war, and when I looked down I realized that I had lost the
chorus and that I was instead surrounded by a sea of people and
that I could hear the murmur of a thousand conversations and the
distant beating of a drum and the sound of my own heart, and
I exhaled, and I laughed, and I felt very much alive, because in

that moment, on that night, the present was sufficient unto itself, and this sufficiency redeemed the past, and this redemption was not perfect or complete, because history knows not perfection nor completion, and it was not eternal or long-lasting, because a moment lasts a moment and nights last but a night, but it was redemption nonetheless, a cause for astonishment and gratitude at the capricious movement of the stars, which is another name for fate, which is another name for chance, which had granted me the grace of witnessing a great event that, while rare, is known to take place at particular places and at particular times, according to particular patterns, the regularity of which is proved by history and the recurrence of dreams and thus cannot be denied, and this event was the end of the world, or at least of *my* world, the world that formed me and gave me shape and wounded me like everyone is wounded by their world, and for which, in that moment, on that night, I grieved in silence, because mine was a world that was a culture that was a style of life, of dress and worship, rites of coming of age and courtship, a way of marking the passage of time: days of feast and fast and the long hours of waiting—for a letter, for instructions, for permission—that are the lot of colonials, a habit of reading that valued breadth over depth and allowed for the construction of capacious palaces of memory from which they recited long passages by heart; a habit of writing that conceived of composition as a branch of mathematics—as if to write were to play a pipe organ in the dark or to design an impossible machine that would allow us to take flight, if only it could be built—an art of losing themselves in labyrinths of carved limestone, woven silk, embossed silver, and porcelain that was not porcelain but earthenware painted white and blue; a hyperbolic metaphysics where each thing was itself and also something else, where dreams were as real as matter was unreal, and where the mind was full of a tangible energy which, having nowhere to go, folded on itself, forming self-contained caverns that glistened with crystals that were fractals, numbers, symmetries, and signs that held the key to the cipher of the book of the world; a metaphysics which these people—*my* people—possessing a great deal of self-awareness, christened BARROCO, a noun of Portuguese extraction that designates "an irregular pearl," and which is, perhaps, the most perfect and most secret name for that most noble and most loyal and most maddening of cities: Mexico City—*my* city—that *idea made space,* that *tangible number,* that City of Palaces and well-traced streets lined with libraries and convents, many of which still stand on the foundations that the creoles *laid at the crossroads of the wind, to keep their doors wide open to invisible things, to heaven and hell* . . . Which brings me to the wound, because the capital is first of all a graveyard of shallow graves, which people whose language I speak and whose name I carry and whose blood I bleed dug and filled with the bodies of the millions that they killed or allowed to die or worked to death to build their perfect city with the broken bones of that other city, that *white city, city of song,* that *moon plunged into lake,* where *in sunlight the houses were silver—For verily, Your Mercy*—wrote Bernal Diaz, soldier by profession, cronista by choice, of the first moment he saw Tenochtitlan—*the sight was sorcery, something out of* Amadis of Gaul—the real-life book that in the porous world of that other book, so much larger than real life, drove Alonso Quijano, that small-time hidalgo, that petit bourgeois, to a madness so complete that he could no longer tell fact from fiction, stress from strife, poetry from history, literature from life, and it troubles my sleep to think this madness was at play in that moment, on that morning in 1521, when five hundred Don Quixotes stumbled into a city larger and more beautiful than any of them had ever seen and that they proceeded to destroy, in a manner so brutal that many lost their minds—*Will I die here, in this sad war, at the hands of these Indian dogs?*—wrote Blas Botello, astrologer by training, conquistador by choice, in the book of *ciphers, lines and annotations* that his comrade Bernal found among the ruins of Moctezuma's palace in the uncanny days that followed the Sorrowful Night—*After which question*—writes Bernal—*Botello drew more ciphers*, and the words: *You shall not die*, after which he wrote: *But you shall die*, after which he wrote: *And shall they kill my horse?* after which he wrote: *Yes they shall*—all of which felt too familiar, and so I left for North America, where I tried to forget, because the labyrinth is haunted, and the cavern of the mind is full of skulls, and the old excuse—*it happened long ago*—is simply false: it's been five hundred years and yet there still are nights when I feel compelled to play the futile game of trying to make sense of what my grandfather wrote on the front page of a book that satirizes the class structures of imperial Spain, and so I came to see that the world that had ended was better laid to rest and that the world that was being born remained a mystery and that mysteries, like comets, are not omens of disaster, because they are not answers but questions so immense that they cannot be posed but merely felt, and as I stood there I felt it, and it felt like a great calm, in that moment, on that night, when I, being of the sort of temperament which cannot help searching in the course of human affairs for something like sense, by which I understand the clarity of logic, which is true in all places and times and can hence survive translation even into English, or, if there is no sense to be found or made, then something like meaning, by which I understand what others *experience when they avert a tragedy, but barely, and all of their lives are refocused in that moment,* such that the past appears to them like a line on the map of time, drawn to bring them to this point, where the future is less like a riddle than a ship they thought had sailed, but which for some reason is delayed just enough that, if they run and stop for nothing and manage not to fall, they might still be able to board and sail north and change names and become no one, or, if meaning fails as well, because the tragedy is not averted or there is no tragedy to avert, then at least I hope to find something like beauty, by which I understand the sensation of the fullness of an instant when there is no future and no past, and which is, I suppose, an adequate description of what I felt, in that moment, on that night, at the Zócalo, where I—armed with no weapons save the training of the intelligence that the ruling classes of your North American lands, so rich in the wealth of science and learning, call "an education," by which they mean a preparation for life, but which, for those of us afflicted with an unhappy consciousness, is nothing but the cultivation of irony—stood at the center of the plaza, silent while others sang, contemplating history.

Levántate y anda

And then the law called me by my name: "Salazar? Arteaga y Salazar?"

Blood ran through my arteries. My ears rang. My rage evaporated and in its place arose an ugly combination of hope and fear. My body lifted itself from the chair. The world sharpened, as if I had new glasses. I took a step, then another, taking care to avoid the eyes of the other foreigners. What would I be willing to do for a green card? For citizenship? In that moment, I realized, I was willing to do a great deal of betraying. I was surprised by how brittle I'd proven. After an hour in a windowless room, I was all but ready to sell my neighbors.

Air coursed through my trachea. The diaphragm rose and fell. The story now seemed simple: I had remade myself in the image of the rulers of the empire, hoping that if I came to resemble them closely enough, they would welcome me as one of their own.

With the years I came to believe my own charade and convinced myself I had more in common with white Americans than with most Mexicans. As it turned out I'd fooled only myself—not the Mexicans, not the white Americans, and certainly not the US government. There was no denying it anymore: I loved America more than myself, but America didn't love me back. And yet there I was, walking up to the inspection desk in the secondary screening room at the San Francisco International Airport, hoping that America would change its mind.

"I apologize for the wait," the officer said.

"That is quite all right," I mumbled, feeling my accent grow thick and my diction clumsy.

She smiled but didn't look up from her computer. She had light brown skin and Mexican features; she kept her long black hair in an intricate braid; she wore a dark red lipstick that contrasted with the navy blue of her uniform; she must have been around my age; she was very beautiful.

"Is this your first time seeking admission to the United States on your student visa?"

"No. I've had it for two years. I did consular processing at the embassy in Mexico City."

She took my passport from the red folder and flipped through the pages. The desk was unusually high, reaching almost to my chin, and she sat on a tall stool, such that I saw her from below. She didn't seem angry or impatient but instead emanated a calm confidence in her own authority, a sense that she was as comfortable in her skin as she was in her uniform. I wondered whether she'd risen through the ranks quickly, whether her austere but dignified politeness originated in the knowledge that her supervisors saw her as a rising star.

I pictured her a few years younger, recently graduated from college, living with her parents in one of the vanishing Mexican neighborhoods of San Francisco, trying to choose between taking out a loan to go to law school or applying to the Federal Law Enforcement Training Centers. What had she told herself when she made her choice? What had she told her parents? And her grandparents? How many generations did a Mexican family need to live in America before a daughter's decision to become an immigration officer no longer raised eyebrows? Or had her family been in California before the annexation? Before independence? Before the conquest? Did she lack other options? Did she hope to change things from the inside? Or did she truly believe she was working to secure her homeland?

"So, the last time you were admitted was late last year, right?"

"Yes. What happened was—I got confused. Earlier. With your colleague. She asked me and I tried to remember but I didn't remember . . . the date but I remembered that . . . I'd come . . . for a—a New Year's Eve party. And that—that's—that's—"

"That makes sense." She took a stamp from the desk, pressed it on my passport, and handed my documents to me. Then she looked me in the eye and smiled. "Welcome to the United States."

I muttered something grateful and walked away, faster than necessary, sensing the eyes of my fellow foreigners on the back of my head, too elated to feel guilty for my good fortune. It was over. All was well. I was fine. It was all fine. It had always been fine, and it would only get better. Permanent residency was out of the question, but I still had a shot at a temporary visa. Besides, who knew? Maybe they would impeach him.

But as I went down the disinfected hallway, my relief turned into disgust. What was this desire I felt to run back into the detention room and kiss the officer's hands? She had declined to subject me to petty humiliations, true, but if that was my definition of kindness then I had lost most of my self-respect.

No, I thought, this was not gratitude; it was Stockholm

syndrome. I should have never been detained, not even for an hour. In fact, nobody should ever be detained, not at the San Francisco International Airport—built as it was on land stolen several times over—nor anywhere else. I stepped out of the disinfected corridor and into passport control and thought that, of all the fictions of politics, none were falser or more dangerous than borders. I lived on a continent shaped by genocide, slavery, and the forced displacement of millions. In light of that history no nation could claim the moral authority to prevent people from crossing an arbitrary line on the ground. Countries that did so nonetheless were acting on no justification beyond brute force, the basest sort of power, born from the jawbone of a donkey or the barrel of a gun. And so a question arose: Having been born elsewhere and in comfortable circumstances, why had I gone through so much trouble to convince such a brutish country of my worth as a human being?

As I walked past the booth where the officer who sent me to secondary screening was still inspecting passports, I decided I was done with the United States. I would leave of my own accord, before they wrestled the decision from me. I would finish my degree, sell all but the most precious books I'd accumulated over ten years, and buy a one-way ticket to Mexico City. That I did not know what I'd do with myself did not matter. The uncertainty was terrifying but also exhilarating. I would return to a different country from the one I left at eighteen, and perhaps this new Mexico would offer me what I always wanted, what I'd sought in America: a chance to cast off the weight of the past, both the private story and the public history, and begin anew, enjoying at once the freedom of the blank slate and the benefit of hindsight.

Besides, leaving did not mean returning. Anáhuac was vast, but the world was vaster—and most countries did not imprison people for overstaying their visas. Perhaps I should travel, I thought, first across Latin America, making my way by bus or on foot from Guatemala to Patagonia, stopping in each city for days or years as I saw fit, giving myself to the South with the same intensity with which I'd surrendered to the North, getting to know the writers of Guayaquil, Matanzas, Arequipa, Medellín, Montevideo, Bahía, Palacagüina, Santa Cruz de la Sierra, and then, if that wasn't enough, I could find work on a cargo ship and set sail from Veracruz, advancing from West to East, against the entropy of empire, to visit Salah in Argel, Jazmin in Haifa, Haider in Lahore, Ashish in Delhi, and Kirie in Beijing, continuing to the ports of Kamchatka and Japan, down to Malaysia and across the south seas all the way to Dar es Salaam, and from there to teach Spanish in Kinshasa, translate in Cairo, and interpret in Kyiv, and then, only then—having exhausted the body and the world, having known many cities and minds, having spent myself in the pursuit of a truly universal education—come home, once again, one last time, to die in the capital, in the City of Palaces, the Most Noble and Loyal, the navel of the universe, the place between the waters, where the air is clear—and where perhaps I would run into the boy with spiked hair and the girl who didn't speak, freed by some miracle from the bonds of borders, having embarked on a journey not of desperate escape but of passionate discovery.

Yes, I thought as I handed my customs form to the officer in the final Homeland Security checkpoint, I'd come to America to get an education. Now I had it. The time had come, at last, to live. All that was left to do was to break free from the spell that had ensnared me for ten years. The operation would be simple if not easy: I had to purge from my brain the idea that life in America was somehow more real than life elsewhere. The notion was absurd on its face yet proved resistant to reason. It was not so much an axiom as a superstition, an old and dangerous one, the seed of prideful self-hatred I inherited from my creole fore-fathers. The belief that the colonies were but a pale shadow of the metropole was the primary site of the cancer, and, like all tumors, the imaginary that germinated from it was mutable. For my ancestors the poison was a perverse version of the Catholic faith; for me, the emotional correlative of American exceptionalism. At any rate the heart of the delusion remained unchanged across the centuries: the powerful, unsatisfied with power, convinced themselves that they were good, and then, still unsatisfied, convinced the powerful among the powerless that they, too, could become powerful among the powerful, but only if they became half as good as the most powerful of all.

By the time I got to baggage claim I was ready to head to the nearest Greyhound station and get on the first southward bus. But as I searched for her face in the crowd, my courage faltered. Losing on purpose—leaving by choice—would preserve the illusion of agency, but not ameliorate the loss.

I thought of my profession, the unglamorous business of honest-to-god journalism, the tally of works and days, not so much the first draft of history as its opposite: a record that did not offer prophecies.

I thought of my American friends, the intensity with which they approached the business of living, their sincere desire to be good, their earnest embrace of irony, the seriousness of their studies, the shamelessness of their ignorance, their metropolitan world-weariness, their provincial innocence, the way they carried their citizenship with a combination of pride and shame—at once a bloodstain, a carte blanche, a debt to pay, a call to arms, and a question mark.

I thought of the English language, that unruly federation of Romanesque and Norse, its pliable grammar, its infinite lexicon, the rarity of its rhymes, the pleasure of its iambs, the love I'd felt for it since childhood, the years I'd given to its study, the joy I took in writing it—like fencing with the left hand.

But most of all I thought of Lee. We had agreed to meet at baggage claim yet she was nowhere to be seen. The obvious explanation was that she'd gone to the bathroom or was also looking for me, and yet I couldn't shake the suspicion she had left. I would know: moments earlier I'd fantasized about taking a Greyhound without her. That she could offer to follow me to my country as a gesture of generosity now struck me as a stark reminder that we didn't stand on equal footing. For her, Mexico promised a sojourn in a country with a strong literature and a weak currency, an interlude between the infinite acts of an American life; for me, it augured a confrontation with demons. Her passport granted her the power to make mistakes and correct them: she could always go back, with or without me. I, on the other hand, might not have a second chance.

When I finally found her, she was on the phone with the airline, trying to book a new flight. She hung up the moment she saw me and came running to meet me. She threw her arms around me.

"Oh my God," she said. "I'm so glad you're okay."

We walked to the airline desk and got tickets for a flight to a different airport. Then we went through security, got sandwiches from a deli, and sat across from each other at the food court. All the while Lee said all the right things and asked all the right questions, and all the while I refused to answer. Everything she said or did, especially her gestures of kindness, struck me as profoundly American. That I understood what was happening did not make it easier to escape the loop of my resentment. If anything, it made it worse, because now on top of everything I felt guilty for my incapacity to reciprocate her love.

"Do you want to tell me about it?" she asked, reaching across the table.

I brushed my fingers against hers. Then I pulled back my hand and got up from the table.

"I'm going for a walk."

"Okay. Is there anything I can do?"

I didn't reply. Instead, I turned around and walked away, past the corporate newsstands and the coffeeshop franchises, past the bookstore full of American literature, past thousands of people carrying American passports and thousands more carrying American currency, until I reached a tall wide window that overlooked the airport's labyrinth of runways. Night had fallen but only the sky was dark. Countless blinking signals delimited each road and each lane, shining blue or red in synchronized patterns, and a burning halogen reflector drowned the panorama in a light so white that it was nothing but light. It illuminated all things, even the particles of dust that rose in whirlwinds whenever a truck drove over the patches of grass between the service roads, but it shone brightest on the airliners as they ascended, weightless like albatrosses, into the dark.

Epilogue
Emirate of Harar
July 1875

In which nothing is revealed.

Para Roberto Bolaño

But what, the Idle Reader asks, became of the translator—or rather of the traitor? What befell the man who in 1847 sold his nation to save his class, and in so doing condemned Your Correspondent to the misfortunes recounted in this book?

Generations of Mexican scholars have trawled the Archivo General de la Nación (the vast, unindexed collection of water-logged and fire-scorched relations, reports, requests, remands and reprimands, repeals, appeals, addenda, assessments and amendments, minutes, manifests, maps and memoranda, pleadings, proceedings, photographs, telegrams, transcripts, depositions, inquisitions, inventories, inquests, and indictments that is at once the tangible form of Mexico's memory and a monument to the impossibility of knowing the past) in search of clues as to the fate of Sebastián's infamous ancestor—but to no avail. After the end of the Mexican-American War, Luciano Fernando Arteaga y Salazar all but vanishes from the historical record.

New discoveries, however, have shed light on the matter. Some years ago, in the course of researching a vegetarian commune that briefly flourished in rural Massachussets, L. F. Cremer of the University of Chicago unearthed a writ of divorce, dated 1855, that registers the dissolution of the marriage between Amanda Adams, heiress to the gambling debts of a good-for-nothing second son of the storied clan, and one Luciano Arteaga, who is identified only as "a Mexican gentleman of some means." More recently, H. S. Shabaz of the University of California stumbled upon the death certificate of a certain Fernando Arteaga while combing through the records of the ancient city of Harar-Gey, in modern-day Ethiopia. The document, dated 1875, states that this Arteaga was ከአሜሪካ የመጣ በትውልድ ስፔናዊ ሽጉጥ ነጋዴ, and that ከሃዲውን መሐመድ ራፍ ፓሻን በሚቃጠሙ አመጸኞች አጅ ነው የሞተው.

A note on facts

América del Norte is not a memoir or a work of journalism or scholarship but a fiction in the strong sense of the term: it does not purport to represent reality. The characters who populate it are not depictions of real people but allegorical figures who embody abstract concepts. Had I lived in an age more suited to my temperament, I would have named them after the fashion of baroque morality plays: the Creole, the American, Irony, Folly, Fate, and Faith. Any attempt to identify nonfictional equivalents that they do not have is a gross misreading that runs contrary to my authorial intentions. By the same token, though this novel contends with history and current events, it treats them as material for the imagination, not as an object of study. It is full of inaccuracies, most of them intentional. Readers interested in factual accounts of the historical and political issues discussed in this book are encouraged to consult the following bibliography.

FOR A BROAD OVERVIEW OF MEXICAN HISTORY:

- Joseph, Gilbert & Henderson, Timothy. *The Mexico Reader: History, Culture, Politics.*

FOR THE ORIGINS OF THE NEOBAROQUE NOVEL:

- González Echevarría, Roberto. *Myth and Archive: A theory of Latin American Literature.*
- Adorno, Rolena. *The Polemics of Possession in Spanish American Narrative.*

FOR THE BAROQUE:

- Lezama Lima, José. "La curiosidad barroca." In: *La expresión Americana.*
- Deleuze, Gilles. *The Fold: Leibniz and the Baroque.*

FOR THE CONQUEST OF MEXICO:

- Restall, Matthew. *When Montezuma Met Cortés.*
- León-Portilla, Miguel. *The Broken Spears.*

FOR THE VIRGEN DE GUADALUPE:

- Lafaye, Jacques. *Quetzalcoatl and Guadalupe: The Formation of Mexican National Consciousness.*

FOR THE MEXICAN CREOLES:

- Paz, Octavio. *Sor Juana o las trampas de la fé.*
- Simon, Joshua. *The Ideology of the Creole Revolutions: Imperialism and Independence in American and Latin American Political Thought.*
- Villoro, Luis. *La revolución de independencia.*

FOR CARLOS DE SIGÜENZA Y GÓNGORA:

- Leonard, Irving. *Don Carlos Sigüenza y Góngora: A Mexican Savant of the Seventeenth Century.*

FOR JEAN-PHILIPE RAMEAU:

- Girdlestone, Cuthbert. *Rameau: His Life and Work.*

FOR GEORG WILHELM FRIEDRICH HEGEL:

- Buck-Morss, Susan. *Hegel and Haiti.*
- Kojevè, Alexandre. *Introduction to the Reading of Hegel.*

FOR THE MEXICAN-AMERICAN WAR:

- Guardino, Peter. *The Dead March: A History of the Mexican-American War.*

FOR MAXIMILIAN VON HABSBURG:

- Corti, Egon Caesar. *Maximilian and Charlotte of Mexico.*

FOR JOSÉ VASCONCELOS:

- Blanco, José Joaquín. *Se llamaba Vasconcelos.*
- Medina Mora, Nicolás. "Vasconcelos y los secretos de la regeneración nacional." In: *nexos.*

FOR ALFONSO REYES:

- Medina Mora, Nicolás. "El secreto de la *Cartilla Moral.*" In: *nexos.*

FOR MEXICAN NEOLIBERALISM:

- Babb, Sarah. *Managing Mexico: Economists from Nationalism to Neoliberalism.*
- Lemus, Rafael. *Breve historia del neoliberalismo.*

FOR THE MEXICAN DRUG WAR AND NAZARIO MORENO:

- Grillo, Ioan. *Gangster Warlords: Drug Dollars, Killing Fields, and the New Politics of Latin America.*
- Smith, Benjamin. *The Dope: The Real History of the Mexican Drug Trade.*

FOR AMERICAN IMMIGRATION POLICY:

- Dickerson, Caitlin. "We Need to Take Away Children." In: the *Atlantic.*
- Martínez, Óscar. *The Beast: Riding the Rails and Dodging Narcos on the Migrant Trail.*

FOR ANDRÉS MANUEL LÓPEZ OBRADOR:

- Tracey, Caroline. "Austere Moral Economy." In: *n+1.*
- Ackerman, Edwin. "The AMLO Project." In: *New Left Review.*
- Aguilar Camín, Héctor. "El otoño del presidente." In: *nexos.*
- Medina Mora, Nicolás. "El secreto de Carlos Pellicer." In: *nexos.*

FOR THE NATURE OF HISTORY:

- Althusser, Louis. "Reply to John Lewis." In: *Ideology and the State.*
- Derrida, Jacques. *Specters of Marx.*
- Benjamin, Walter. *Notebooks from the Lost Briefcase.*

FOR THE NATURE OF PROPHECY:

- Sullivan, Paul. *Unfinished Conversations: Mayas and Foreigners Between Two Wars.*

Credits

The quotations from Alfonso Reyes's essays on pages vii, 25, 332, and 334 appear in my own translation and with permission from the publisher of his *Complete Works*, the Fondo de Cultura Económica.

The poems by José Juan Tablada on pages 109 and 110 appear in my own translation and with permission from the publisher of his *Collected Poems*, the National Autonomous University of Mexico.

The quotation from Denis Diderot's *Rameau's Nephew* on page 112 appears with the kind permission of the translator from the French, Prof. Ian C. Johnston.

The lines from José Gorostiza's "Muerte sin Fin" on page

217 appear in my own translation and with permission from the publisher of his *Collected Poems*, the Fondo de Cultura Económica.

The quotations from José Vasconcelos's works and speeches that appear on pages 318, 323, and 344 appear in my own translation and with the kind permission of his son, Senator Héctor Vasconcelos, who holds the rights to his father's work.

The lines by Guillame Apollinaire on page 350 appear with permission of his publisher in France, Gallimard.

The passage from Walter Benjamin's *One Way Street* that appears on page 385 is in the public domain and appears in Laura Cremer's original translation, which she has kindly given permission to reproduce here.

The line from Dan Chiasson's long poem "Bicentennial" quoted in a slightly modified form on page 432 appears with the poet's kind permission.

Acknowledgments

América del Norte has countless co-authors. In hopes that a list full of unforgivable omissions might be preferable to the unforgivable omission of a list, here are the names of some of them. Mark Doten, my editor at Soho Press, who instead of steering me toward convention encouraged me to make the novel weirder, longer, funnier, and riskier. Elias Altman, my agent, who believed in me enough to muster the patience to convince me, over the course of two years of developmental edits, that maybe it would be a good idea to have something like a plot and a handful of actual characters. Natalia Reyes, Rebecca Zweig, Alea Adigweme, Jennifer Shyue, Andrea Januta, Ana Cecila Álvarez Ortíz, Caroline Tracey, Haider Shahbaz, Lucas Iberico Lozada, Sophia Cornell, and Tessy Schlosser, brilliant writer-comrades who read several drafts of the manuscript and offered suggestions, solutions, and much-needed warnings. Kelsi Vanada, Orlando Hernández, Cassius Marcellus Cornelius Clay, Hannah Sassoon, Kirie Stromberg, Yemile Bucay, Maya Averbuch, Amna Chaudhry, Ashish Mitter, Aminah Zaghab, Cora Lewis, Elias Rodriques, Rachel Ossip, Jo Livingstone, Cosme Del Rosario-Bell, Hannah Goodwin, Stefan Eich, David Kurnick, Mario Arriagada, Ana Sofía Rodríguez Everaert, Ricardo López Cordero, Marcus McGee, Gibrán Ramírez, Hugo Garciamarín, Jacques Coste, Moriana Delgado, Luciano Concheiro, Juan Caloca, Paloma Contreras, José Ahumada, Brittany Means, and many other beloved friends who offered encouragement and support. John D'Agata, Inara Verzemnieks, Kerry Howley, Kiese Laymon, and Robyn Schiff, my teachers at Iowa, who read my work with care and attention. My classmates at Iowa, who were the opposite of philistines. Roberto González Echevarría, Paul North, Carol Jacobs, Rüdiger Campe, Anne Fadiman, Peter Cole, and Rolena Adorno, my teachers at Yale, who introduced me to the texts of which this text is a collage. Mark Schoofs, Tom Namako, Lisa Tozzi, Ben Smith, Alix Freedman, Josh Schneyer, Katherine Miller, Albert Samaha, Ema O'Connor, Mike Hayes, David Noriega, Saeed Jones, and Sandy Allen, my colleagues and editors at Reuters and BuzzFeed, who taught me that talking to people is just as important as reading. Héctor Aguilar Camín, Luis Miguel Aguilar, Kathya Millares, Juan Pablo García Moreno, Álvaro Ruíz Rodilla, Jorge Landa, Melissa Cassab, Valeria Villalobos, Julio González, and María Guillén, my colleagues and editors at Nexos, who taught me everything I know about Mexico. Mark Krotov, Dayna Tortorici, Marco Roth, Sarah Resnick, Lisa Borst, Tess Edmonson, Nicole Lipman, Juliet Kleber, my editors at *n+1*, who published the essays that became the core of this novel, and whose vote of confidence gave me the courage to complete it. Abel Girma and Rayo Cruz, who generously shared their expertise in Amharic and Zapotec, and Nabiha Syed and Sam Cate-Gumpert, who generously shared their legal expertise. My favorite painter, Rodrigo "El Oso" Echeverría, whose unwavering commitment to art I salute. Bonnie Antosh, who filled my life with joy in the years before the comets. Elba Gutiérrez Castillo, who shared her life with me for four of the seven years that I spent writing this novel, and without whose support I would have probably given up. My siblings, Camila and Tomás Medina Mora Pérez, who trusted me with our story. My elective siblings, Laura Cremer and Santiago Mohar, who taught me how to write. My late mother, Laura de Guadalupe Pérez Vázquez, who taught me how to read.